SAWKILL GIRLS

SAWKILL GIRLS

CLAIRE LEGRAND

Katherine Tegen Books is an imprint of HarperCollins Publishers.

Sawkill Girls

www.epicreads.com

Library of Congress Control Number: 2018943193
ISBN 978-0-06-269660-1

Typography by Aurora Parlagreco
18 19 20 21 22 PC/LSCH 10 9 8 7 6 5 4 3 2 1

First Edition

to all the girls who have my back—
the queens and the witches
the poets and the mothers—
to the girls who raise their voices
and
to the girls who light the way

SAWKILL GIRLS

EVERYONE KNOWS ABOUT THE ISLAND of Sawkill Rock:

The silly old legends of its healing waters, which are impossible to altogether dismiss when one considers the people of Sawkill themselves—their hard white teeth and supple limbs. The brazen, easy way they walk and shop and love. Their flagrant indifference toward life beyond the Rock, and their deft handling of even the bleakest tragedy: *Oh, what a shame that was*, they say, and bow their shining heads for a moment before gliding on, untroubled.

The beauty of the Rock's rolling horse farms. Groomed flanks that gleam in the pale Atlantic sun. Grass like a glossy carpet that blows and shimmers, even at night. Especially at night. Black trees, wind-curled and water-bitten.

The houses like palaces, old but solid-hewn, gray and white and shingled. Sprawling and manicured. Careless and dignified. Old money: the taste of it sits on every tongue like a film of stale sugar.

The way the dark, rough sea bites up the shoreline. How the winds on the eastern side groan like old-time beasts turning in their sleep.

Come for a while, reads the sign at Sawkill's ferry dock, *and stay forever.*

The Rock has always hated that sign.

MARION

The Accident

These are the things people said to Marion Althouse after her father died:

> Oh, God. You poor girl.
> Marion, I'm so sorry.
> What a loss.
> What a terrible, terrible thing.
> Your mom. Jesus, I just— I can't imagine.
> How is she doing?
> What about Charlotte? They were always so close, those two.
> If you need anything, you let me know. Okay?
> I'm here for you.
> You're such a rock. You see that, right?

They're depending on you.

They're lucky to have you. Blessed.

Marion, you're so strong. How do you do it?

How did she do it?

It was a good question.

Marion asked herself the same question that first morning: *How do I do this now?* There had been *before* October thirteenth of last year, and, now, there was *after*.

After David Althouse crashed his car coming home from a late night at the office, so tired he probably couldn't see straight, ready to lay down his bones by the light of dawn.

After some drunken scum-of-the-earth asshole took the mountain turn too fast, and her father was too exhausted and distracted, Marion assumed, to react in time.

After his car crashed through the guardrail and over the cliff, careening into rocks and plowing into a tree before coming to a still, smashed stop.

After the previously mentioned asshole drove away in a panic, maybe crying and shaking, too spineless to own up to their crime, leaving her father to die in the remains of his ruined fifteen-year-old Toyota.

After all that, this is what people said more than anything else:

I'm sorry for your loss, Marion.

Her loss. As if she'd misplaced her car keys.

When people said that, a part of Marion wanted to slap them, knock the cards and casseroles out of their hands.

I'll tell you what I've lost, she wanted to say, and then open up her chest so they could see the hollow pit where her heart used to live. It was stuck in a state of collapse, this pit—a tiny, organ-shaped singularity, sucking down the bleeding ravaged bits of who she used to be.

But Marion did none of this.

She accepted their bland sympathy and uncertain smiles, tucked the wrapped food into the packed fridge, sat by her mother to make sure she didn't sneak pills, and held Charlotte when she woke up sobbing.

She was Marion Althouse: devoted daughter and trusted little sister.

She sat alone on the bench outside the restroom on the ferry, arms full of everyone's purses, while her mother vomited in the toilet and her sister flirted with a boy who drove a Lexus.

She was a rock. A blessing. A good, steady girl.

She did not give in to rage or self-pity. Not ever.

Not once.

"There it is!"

Charlotte leaned against the deck railing, the wind whipping her honey-brown hair around her face.

"Don't lean out too far," said Marion. She sat on the polished black bench across from the railing and held her mother's gloved hand tightly in her own, anchoring it in place on her lap.

Charlotte, seventeen-nearly-eighteen, glanced back with a magnificent roll of her eyes.

"*Marion*," she said. "Honestly."

Marion, sixteen-nearly-seventeen, agreed. Since birth, she'd been a bit of a fusser—something she'd prided herself on, if only because it drove Charlotte batty to have Marion always chirping at her shoulder—but since their father died, her ability to nag and worry had skyrocketed to a whole new level.

Really, what did anyone expect?

There were only three Althouses left now, two and a smudge on their mother's bad days. You couldn't know which day would be the last one, and you couldn't trust Charlotte not to lean out too far or run too fast or fall in love too easily, and you couldn't trust their mother with pill bottles or sharp objects.

So Marion didn't. She held their purses and followed doggedly behind their every flighty, stumbling step.

"It looks amazing out here." Charlotte pulled out her phone to snap pictures. "It's like this . . . this *thing*, perched out there on the water. A beetle. A monster. Some magical lost place."

Marion would have preferred to be napping in their car's back seat, not talking to anyone and not looking at the rocking water and, maybe, not waking up.

But her mother wanted fresh air, hoping it would settle her stomach, and Charlotte refused to sit around being boring—God, *perish* the thought of Charlotte Althouse ever being accused of such a thing. So Marion sat without complaint and watched Sawkill Rock approach on a sheet of gray waves.

The island really did look like a *thing.* Black and solid, craggy. A little bit fearsome, a little bit lonely. That part didn't bother Marion, though. She would have lived on a barren dusty rock with no horses or people or yachts tied up at the docks, if she could have. Just her and Charlotte and their mother, a little clean white cottage, a pebbled path down to the water for sunbathing. That's all they needed—quiet, and one another. To be left to themselves for a while. No constant doorbells and phone calls. No more sympathy cards.

The salt-specked wind surged past them. In Marion's grip, her mother shivered.

Marion glanced at her and took stock: Pamela Althouse. Eyes fairly bright, observing the deck, the passengers, the water. Shoulders not so stooped as they could be. A small smile tugging at her lips as she watched Charlotte snap selfies at the railing.

Smiling was a good thing. Their mother, for now, was not in danger. Not of sneaking off, fog-brained, to unearth a knife. Not of rummaging through Marion's luggage for the hidden medicine. Marion could relax.

What a joke.

Marion had never been good at relaxing, and now, *after,* she was even worse at it. Her mother had often teased that Marion was born with ten lives' worth of tension knotted in her shoulders.

My little rock, her mother would say. *My grave little mountain.*

"Having second thoughts?" Marion gently nudged her mother's side.

"Not at all." Her mother breathed in, her eyes falling shut. "The sea air is invigorating, don't you think?"

"It's definitely cold."

"This is just what we need. A change of scenery. New faces, new roads."

A familiar litany. Marion nodded. "You're right, Mom."

"I'm excited to meet the Mortimers, aren't you?" Her mother squeezed her hand once, gently, before releasing her. "Such lovely people, on the phone. They breed award-winning Morgans. I told you that, right?"

"Yep." A hundred times. "They sound great. Real down-to-earth types."

"I thought you'd like them," her mother said with a little nudge. "A family of women who keep their mother's surname, generation after generation? Men that come and go, and never stay in the picture? A matriarchal dynasty." Her mother smiled a little. "Isn't that your thing, darling? Girl power and all that?"

Marion rolled her eyes. "Mom. No one says 'girl power' anymore. That being said, the surname thing is kind of cool. But . . . then there's the fact of their filthy rich–ness."

"Oh, Marion. Don't be a snob." Her mother clucked her tongue, fumbled with her zipper. When her fingers began to shake, Marion took over and zipped up her mother's jacket to the neck. "The Mortimers are good people," said Mrs. Althouse, her voice muffled in her scarf. "I have a sunny feeling about this. Val, their daughter. She's Charlotte's age. Did I tell you that? I'm sure I did."

At the mention of Val Mortimer, Marion looked away, down the ferry deck, to the rows of parked cars. Their faded blue station wagon, rust lining the wheel wells, was a plucky little weed in a garden of Range Rovers.

"Yeah, Mom," she said quietly. "You told me about Val."

Actually, Marion had looked up Val online, because Marion wasn't the type to let things remain uninvestigated. That's how she found out that Val Mortimer was just the kind of bright-smiled, gorgeous, damaged girl to whom Charlotte would easily attach herself. Last year Val had lost a friend—a girl their age whose death had gone unsolved, her body never found.

So Val and Charlotte had both suffered losses. Both had, presumably, endured the endless cloying condolences of friends and neighbors. Both were carelessly, shockingly beautiful—long limbs and perfect noses and poreless pale skin. Lips that curved just right. Their online lives a parade of endless friend lists and beaming, perfectly filtered photographs snapped at parties, bonfires, dances, football games.

Marion was holding out hope that Val Mortimer would be too much of a snob to befriend the housekeeper's daughter. Charlotte was hard enough to keep track of on her own, without someone like Val in the picture.

"Selfie time!" Charlotte sang, flinging herself down on the bench beside them. Before Marion could protest, Charlotte had pulled them all close and touched her phone.

"Lovely," she declared, turning the screen so Marion and Mrs. Althouse could see. "That's us. The Althouse girls."

Marion leaned in to take a look.

Yes, that was them all right:

Charlotte. Pink-cheeked, windblown hair falling in wisps around jewel-blue eyes. Worn parka framing her face in faded red nylon.

Mrs. Althouse. Dark, graying hair. Tiny lines of grief, new and alarming, etched around her eyes and mouth. Her zipped-tight jacket making her look small and squashed.

And Marion. Pale and serious. Dark-haired, gray-eyed. A near-copy of her mother, if not as old and tired. Awkward, though. Not quite smiling. Looking not at the phone but rather out to sea.

"It's all right, he won't bite. You can come say hello, if you want."

Marion had been trying not to stare at the police officer and his gleaming horse but had failed miserably.

She glanced up from her phone. "Oh, that's okay. I'm good."

"His name is Nightingale. He's fast but gentle." The officer smiled at Marion, his dark-brown face wind-bitten and clean-shaven. "I'm Ed Harlow, by the way. Sawkill Rock's police chief."

Ah, yes. Marion recognized him now, from an interview about Val Mortimer's dead friend.

"Marion Althouse." Marion shrugged back at the station wagon, packed full of everything they owned. She did not let herself think of the house they had sold—the house of her father's life. The house of her father's memorial service.

New faces, new roads. A change of scenery.

"Oh, right. The Althouses." *Ah.* There was the awkward, sympathetic smile. "Moving into the Mortimer cottage, right?"

"You know about that?"

"Small island. News spreads fast."

Marion glanced behind her, at the market into which her mother and Charlotte had disappeared to buy groceries for the night. She had claimed seasickness from the ferry ride so they'd let her stay behind by the car. A rare shirking of her duties.

Really she felt fine, stomachwise. It was her head that was the problem, and, weirdly, the soles of her feet. Since leaving the ferry, they smarted awfully, like she'd been running barefoot for ages and had scraped them raw on the concrete.

Besides, she wasn't sure she could bear the cramped lights of a grocery store at the moment, nor the curious eyes of new neighbors upon her.

Marion slipped her phone into her pocket, absently rubbed her throbbing left temple. "He's a really pretty horse."

"He's one of the Mortimer Morgans."

She placed a hand on Nightingale's sleek neck. His coat was the rich brown of a dark roast.

Despite her headache, she had to smile. "He's beautiful. Aren't you, boy?"

At her touch, Nightingale flinched. He twisted his neck around to whuff at her back and then stamped his foot against the parking lot; the impact reverberated up Marion's legs to settle like a swampy knot in her belly.

"Want to ride him?" Chief Harlow's aviator sunglasses mostly hid his eyes. "Just around the parking lot."

Marion touched her right temple. The headache appeared to be shifting back and forth between the lobes of her brain. "What, like a pony ride?"

Chief Harlow laughed, adjusting his tan cowboy hat. "This fellow is no pony."

"Well." Marion played with Nightingale's coarse mane, trimmed short. "I guess so. I mean, I've never ridden a horse before."

"Never? Well, then." Chief Harlow laced his fingers together. "Put one foot in my hands, then push up and swing your leg over the saddle."

"Jesus!" Marion hissed, fumbling to get her leg over Nightingale's back. "It's really high."

Nightingale pawed the parking lot asphalt with one hoof, then another.

"Don't worry, I've got him." Chief Harlow gestured with the reins. "Lean forward a little, pet his neck. Talk to him."

"Hi, Nightingale," Marion muttered, rubbing her hand up and down his neck. "Hi, boy."

Muscles quivered beneath her fingertips. Nightingale snorted, then shifted to the right and sharply flicked his tail.

"He seems nervous." A spike of fresh pain behind Marion's eyes threw her vision out of alignment for a solid two seconds.

She gripped Nightingale's mane, convinced she was about to slide to the bottom of the world. "Is that normal?"

Nightingale tossed his head, giving Marion a good view of the wild whites of his eyes.

A sick, cold feeling dripped down her arms. "He's freaking out. Is he freaking out?"

Chief Harlow frowned. "Hey, boy, hey, what's going on, huh?"

Nightingale backed away, lashed his head from side to side. The reins flew out of Chief Harlow's hands.

Marion tightened her legs around Nightingale's belly. Her headache careened from temple to temple, and then the pain zipped right out of her head and down her spine, got caught somewhere in her lower back, and exploded.

She cried out and lurched away from the pain, but it was everywhere, it was inescapable. Her fingers tingled sharply. "I want to get down, all right?"

"Hey! Hey!" Chief Harlow's whistle pierced the quiet parking lot.

"Get me down!" Marion could barely hear herself over the panicked roar of her blood. "Do something!"

Nightingale reared up, let out a neighing scream. Chief Harlow stumbled back, fell hard on his tailbone.

A whip of something cold smacked across Marion's shoulders, like the wind had suddenly picked up and sharpened. Marion tasted ocean echoes, the grit of wet sand, the earthy tang of close-growing trees. Her feet were on fire, and so was her head, and so were her palms against Nightingale's trembling neck.

He reared up with a savage shudder. Marion grabbed his mane to keep from sliding off.

"Marion!" came Charlotte's panicked shout.

But this horse would wait for no sister. It was out of its head, though Marion couldn't imagine why. Rabies, maybe. Something had spooked it. A snake?

Nightingale bolted.

With each slam of his hooves against the hard ground, Marion imagined her father tumbling over the cliff, his head smashing against the car over and over until there was nothing left.

ZOEY

The Snoop

Thora had disappeared seven months ago, and they'd never found the body.

No one had any answers other than the usual litany: you kids shouldn't run around on the cliffs, they're too dangerous, haven't we told you that a million times?

Zoey had had just about enough of pretending she was okay with this.

She didn't think, generally speaking, people were allowed to wander in off the street and go snooping around the police station like they owned the place. But Police Chief Harlow was in charge of things, so Zoey Harlow could do what she wanted to do.

It was the one paltry joy of living on Sawkill Rock alongside its army of gleaming people, with their smooth, untroubled faces and their sweat-stained riding jodhpurs and their cars that cost more than Zoey's house.

Rosalind, sitting at the front desk, offered Zoey an oatmeal-raisin cookie and nodded at Zoey's notebook. "What're you writing today?"

"Haven't decided yet!" Zoey replied. Which was true. She *hadn't decided yet* since Thora died. Her half-filled notebook remained half-filled. The only thing to come out of Zoey's pen over the past few months besides schoolwork were doodles of farting unicorns.

She rounded the corner, parked herself in the staff lounge, showed an old scrap of a poem to her father's nosy deputy, and doodled flatulent mythological creatures for a half hour. When the place had emptied out for lunch, Zoey retrieved her dad's office key in her pocket, crept through the quiet hallways, unlocked his door, and slipped inside.

Her heart raced. She'd been in this office hundreds of times since moving to Sawkill two years ago. But she had never entered it without her father's permission—and *definitely* never with the intent to snoop.

Zoey crept around the desk, opened the six desk drawers, leafed through papers. The office was immaculate—no surprise there—but that meant she had to go slowly, make sure she put everything back exactly where she'd found it. Ed Harlow was the kind of guy who'd flip out—mostly good-naturedly—if someone misplaced a single book.

He'd told her once, *The world is a crazy place, Zo. I like to keep my part of it as neat as I can.*

Which was all well and good, albeit painfully dorky. Still, this wasn't the first time Zoey had wished her dad was a slob.

Nothing in the desk. Nothing *on* the desk.

Zoey turned around, eyed the row of file cabinets lining the back wall—*eight* altogether—and blew out a sharp breath.

"Wow, Dad," she muttered. "Got enough file cabinets?"

She opened the first one, thumbed through the hanging files. A bunch of administrative crap. Forms and forms and more forms. Useless.

Next: Three-ring binders packed with training manuals.

Next: Employee files. Performance reviews. A handwritten letter of complaint from Sergeant George Montgomery III about the hazardous levels of perfume Rosalind insisted upon wearing. *Really, Chief,* Sergeant Montgomery had written, *I fear for my health.*

Smirking, Zoey closed the third file cabinet, stretched her arms over her head, yawned.

Then she saw it. A new addition to her father's office: a small, square picture in a silver frame, sitting in a lineup of other framed photographs on a narrow corner table. Zoey's own brown face—skin a bit lighter than her dad's rich brown, dusted with a few of her mother's freckles—smiled up at herself. Her chin-length black curls framed her face like a cloud, and she had her arms thrown wide, as if to declare that the person grinning beside her was a revelation to be flaunted.

Zoey touched Thora's image—white skin, mousy brown hair, cheeky grin, shining eyes. Zoey's tears came so quickly that their arrival made her choke a little.

Thora.

Presumed dead at seventeen, and no one knew why, or when, or *how.*

Zoey closed her eyes, turned away from the frame and Thora's giddy image. She remembered the day from the photo: Zoey's seventeenth birthday party. Thora and Grayson were the only attendees, and the only ones Zoey had wanted to see (and the only ones who would have come to a party of Zoey's, but whatever). A movie marathon—*Alien*, *Aliens*, then, at Thora's request, *The Breakfast Club*, then, at Grayson's request, *sleep*, for the love of God. It was 4:30 a.m. Thora's voice, giggling: *Grayson, you are such an old man.* All of them piled on the couch in Thora's basement. Thora snoring against Zoey's shoulder. Grayson's hand touching Zoey's.

They hadn't yet had sex, her and Grayson. And she hadn't yet broken up with him.

And Thora hadn't yet been murdered.

Well, and that was the thing, wasn't it? No one thought Thora had been murdered. Not officially, anyway. There had been no evidence of murder; everyone's alibis had checked out.

"There are wild animals on our island," Zoey's father had said in an interview with the mainland paper, "not to mention very dangerous areas on the cliffs where the ground can give way without warning. Please, to all our young people, and to any visitors: do not go wandering in the woods after dark."

Wild animals. Collapsing cliffs.

Sure. Zoey *guessed* so.

But those were the same bullshit reasons people had been giving for Sawkill's disappearing girls for years. Decades, even. Zoey had never bought it.

And now, with Thora gone?

Thora, who'd always understood when Zoey wanted to stay in instead of go out. Thora, who'd obsessed over fandoms even more obscure than Zoey's. Thora, who'd always whispered the old island monster tales before bed when Zoey and Grayson slept over, even when scaredy-cat Grayson had begged her not to:

Beware of the woods and the dark, dank deep.
He'll follow you home and won't let you sleep.

Zoey slammed open the door of her father's fourth file cabinet, blinking back her tears.

With Thora gone, Zoey was no longer satisfied with the non-answers of the local law enforcement. Not even when their boss was her dad.

But just as she started flipping through a new drawer of hanging files, a scream cut through the silence—a horse scream. The most terrible sound in the world.

Zoey felt like she'd stepped through a veil into winter. She kicked the cabinet door shut, then hurried to the window and squinted into the sunlight, just in time to see Nightingale, her father's horse, rear up in the parking lot of the market next door, his front legs clawing the air. Her father fell back, hit the ground hard, but Zoey wasn't worried. Ed Harlow was made of granite.

The reins went flying. Someone was on Nightingale's back.

Zoey didn't recognize her—some white girl with long dark hair.

"Marion!" Another white girl, wearing a faded red parka, rushed across the parking lot, grocery bags swinging from her hands.

But it was too late.

Nightingale surged through the rows of parked cars. His coat glistened with sweat.

The girl on his back held on for dear life, hair streaming behind her. It was painfully obvious that she wasn't a Sawkill girl.

One, her clothes looked secondhand, like Zoey's—except they lacked what Zoey liked to refer to as her middle-finger flair. Artful rips, plain fabric dyed in shocking colors, wild fringe where there had previously only been a plain, uninteresting hem.

And two, the girl couldn't ride for shit.

Zoey sympathized. Her first and only riding experience had ended with a full-blown panic attack on the back of a sedate whiskered police horse with woebegone eyes.

"Jesus," Zoey spat.

She sprinted down the hall and outside, grabbed her mud-splattered mountain bike from where she'd left it hidden behind the hedge, and took off pedaling.

Nightingale was taking the Runaround Road, pebbled and dusty white. It circled the outskirts of town, along the Black Cliffs that capped the hilly shoreline of the island's western face, and eventually sloped down into the Spinney.

It was a road meant for pleasant seaside strolls, not for panicked horses on a tear. Nightingale would fall, break his leg, throw the girl. If she was lucky, she'd hit a bush beside the trail.

If she wasn't lucky, she'd land on the black sea rocks below the cliffs.

Zoey pumped her legs as hard as she could. From behind her came the wail of her father's patrol car, the pounding of feet as people ran after them down the road.

"Come on, come on," she muttered, glaring through the wind at Nightingale's racing dark form. "Calm down, you stupid horse."

At Runaround Road's highest point, Nightingale let out another one of those awful, bloodcurdling screams and disappeared over the other side.

Shit, shit, shit.

Zoey's muscles burned as she pedaled up the slope, and then she was cresting the hill and flying down the other side. Runaround Road ended in a tiny tree-ringed overlook that Val Mortimer had long ago claimed as her favorite hookup spot.

There, in the center of what Zoey had coined the Viper's Den, the girl lay unmoving in the dirt.

Nightingale tore off into the trees, reins trailing.

"Damn it," Zoey muttered, braking hard. She sprinted to

where the girl lay with her eyes closed, checked for blood.

No blood.

Breathing?

She checked her pulse.

Yes, breathing.

Zoey smoothed back the damp hair clinging to the girl's forehead.

"Hey," she murmured, cupping the girl's right cheek with her right hand. "Can you hear me?"

Over the years, Zoey had remade herself from the kind of girl who cried when she saw roadkill to the kind of girl who shoved down her tears so deeply it sometimes felt she'd forgotten how to cry at all. Things were easier that way.

But now, kneeling in the chalky white dirt beside this girl, Zoey felt her eyes well up for the second time in ten minutes.

"Look, you've got to open your eyes," she said, "because I could use another secondhand girl around here. You know what I'm saying?"

"Zoey? She all right?" Her father was running down the hill, shouting into his phone. "Yeah, we're at the White Rock Overlook. No, I can't tell yet."

"Marion?" More footsteps racing down the hill, lighter ones. "Marion! I'm coming!"

"Is that your name?" Zoey leaned closer. "Hey. Marion? I'm Zoey. You're gonna be okay."

The girl from the parking lot, wearing the red parka, knelt beside Marion with tears in her eyes.

Zoey, afraid to move Marion, kept the girl's face in her hands. If she woke up, she'd feel the comfort of warm skin on her face and know she wasn't dead.

"Hush now," came another voice, light and feminine. "I've got you."

Zoey froze at the sound of that voice. She knew it well, and she was sorry she did.

At the edge of Zoey's vision stretched a pale hand with shining manicured nails, trimmed short.

Parka Girl took the hand and rose.

"She's not moving," said Parka Girl, voice thick with tears.

"She'll be all right," answered Val Mortimer, in that voice that wasn't fooling anyone, and yet it did in fact seem to fool everyone. It had even fooled Thora.

It did not fool Zoey.

Zoey concentrated on Marion's unconscious face so she didn't have to listen too closely to Val and Parka Girl talking. But she did catch some things: The girl's name was Charlotte. She was Marion's sister.

Their father had recently died.

"Don't worry," Val reassured Charlotte. "Chief Harlow *always* knows just what to do."

Zoey couldn't help it. She glared back at Val. Bitch bitch *bitch.*

Val had her arms around Marion's sister. Her smile was made of diamonds and beestings, and she flashed it at Zoey as if to say, *Go ahead. I dare you.*

And to think that after Thora died, Zoey had actually considered reaching out to Val:

She was my friend, too.

At least, she used to be.

It was at that moment that Marion's bloodshot eyes snapped open.

And she began screaming.

VAL

The Viper

Val ignored Nightingale and the girl clinging to his back.

Instead, she watched the girl running after them.

This second girl wore a red parka, and though she ran alongside the crowd of gaping, shouting shoppers, she somehow existed apart from them. There was a sharp shine to her pink cheeks. The fragility of her fearsome, fearful girl-body made Val's chest ache, and electrified the fine hairs on the back of Val's neck, and awoke Val's deep-gut appetite that belonged to herself, a little, but mostly belonged to him.

A force pulled at Val's flat belly. She took a step against her will.

He had noticed. He'd sensed the girl, and Val didn't want to follow her, but *he* wanted her to, and that was that.

Or was it?

Was it really?

Val, feeling bold, decided to test him. Her grandmother had warned her against defying him too often, but she had also warned Val against *never* defying him.

Don't lose yourself to him, my darling one, Sylvia Mortimer had said. *Not all of you.*

Keep a morsel for yourself.

Val closed her eyes, remembering her grandmother's words: *That's what the first of us said—your great-great-great-grandmother Deirdre. She told her daughter, and so on, until my mother told me, and I told Lucy, and now I'm telling you, because your mother . . . Well. She's harder than the rest of us. She's had to become that way, because it's hurt her more than anyone else.* He's *hurt her more than anyone else, and now there's nothing left of my daughter but a brittle shell.*

So just listen to me, Valerie: keep a morsel for yourself. Whatever happens, hold that scrap tight.

A bramble took root in Val's stubborn feet. Maybe if she stood there long enough, briar tangles would wrap her up within an enchanted wall, and the wall would stand guard around the sleeping girl until the prince came and burned everything down.

That's how the story went, right?

Go.

Val's spine snapped to attention, all hungry teeth and whetted knives and manacled rows of bones. Her mouth dropped open and tears sprang to her eyes. He hardly ever spoke to her directly. Not in parking lots. Not under the open sky.

She'd pay for her hesitation, later, in the stones.

Val ran, sprinting ahead of the crowd, and she looked good doing it, in her second-skin yoga pants, her blond hair piled on top of her head. Of course she looked good, everyone knew it—her most of all. She'd spent a lifetime maneuvering all manner of things to make it so.

Plus, good genes. She'd been blessed with stellar DNA.

"Make it stop!"

The girl on the ground—Marion was her name—screamed the words over and over, thrashing against the rocks. She gripped her hair, her head, she wept and wailed.

Zoey Harlow swore, jumped to her feet, and backed away.

For once in her life, Val agreed with the little shit.

"Marion?" Parka Girl, the girl *he* wanted, rushed to Marion, her pale face gone ghostly. Her name was Charlotte Althouse, and she was the daughter of the new housekeeper, and Val wanted to throw back her head and laugh because this situation was unfolding so perfectly it almost couldn't be believed.

"What's happening?" Charlotte cried. She reached for Marion, but Marion slapped her hand away.

A siren's wail. Chief Harlow to the rescue, straddling Marion and pinning her arms to the dirt in a way that made Val's mouth fill with bile and her limbs go hot-cold. She didn't like seeing people trapped. Not strangers, not friends, not even the hateful boys she slept with.

Valerie Mortimer's nightmares were of being pressed into a shrinking space that compressed all her disjointed parts into an invisible cage. She endured them every night.

"Marion?" said Chief Harlow, in that booming voice like a deep canyon. "You're all right. You're all right, help is coming. Okay?" His eyes flicked up to Zoey. "Did you see what happened?"

"No." Zoey crossed her arms over her chest and chewed on her thumbnail. Her Afro of soft black curls, recently peppered with bright orange streaks, bobbed slightly in the sea wind. "Came over the hill, Nightingale was gone. She was just *lying* here."

People were crowding around, finally having caught up with them. Their sweat sickened Val. All these dirty flesh-bags, acting like they were something, with their horse farms and their tricked-out sedans, their portfolios and their trust funds, when it was her, it was *her* who had the power here, who knew more than they could ever fathom. How *dare* they inch up close like they were all in this together?

She whirled around. "Back up," she ordered, in the voice her mother had taught her—one part sweet, two parts you'd-better-damn-well-listen-to-me. "Give them some air. And put away your phones. Have you all forgotten how to be human beings?"

Her latest conquest, Collin Hawthorne, hovered nearby. He watched her in a sort of stupid half-smiling daze.

Val recognized that awestruck look and imagined how it

would transform, were he to stumble upon her in the stones one night. She almost wished he would, even though it would get messy. Just to see him, for that final flash of a second, understand exactly what he'd been sleeping with.

"People!" he called out, mimicking her, which Val found hysterical. "Back up, all right? Let the paramedics work."

Two paramedics hustled past and gave the weeping, stricken-faced Marion some kind of shot. She relaxed immediately, popped-out veins smoothing themselves back into her neck.

Val saw a shell-shocked woman struggling to get through the onlookers. Recognizing that pale skin and dark hair, Val thought, *Ah*, and strode forward.

"Move aside," she commanded. Gently, she took the woman's arm. "Are you Marion's mother?"

"Yes," whispered the woman. No color in her cheeks or lips. Wide eyes trained on her sedated daughter. "I'm . . . I'm Pam."

"She'll be all right," said Val. "We've got wonderful doctors on Sawkill, the very best. They'll help her." Val squeezed the woman's hand. Softly now, Val. Kindly. "Please don't be afraid."

And as Val passed Mrs. Althouse over to Charlotte, Charlotte's eyes met Val's.

Thank you, said Charlotte's grateful smile.

Val returned the smile—gentle, endlessly compassionate—and even with her sister unconscious on the ground and her mother stunned and frightened, Charlotte seemed to relax a little.

Val's black heart rolled over on its back and wriggled, because everything was happening as it should.

God*damn*. She was good at this.

She was good at being queen.

ZOEY

The Pink Paper

Zoey only dreamed in black-and-white.

This dream was no different, except instead of aliens and tornadoes, dinosaurs and flying up, up, just pushing off with her feet and flying to a desert land with no water anywhere in sight, she dreamed about running horses, each of them carrying a girl on its back.

Which one to choose?

Which one to save?

She thought about it, her dreaming mind choked with indecision, and then followed the one on the left, because that dark hair and white skin reminded her of Thora.

Wait, was Zoey on a horse herself?

Or was she running? Flying?

What did it matter? She reached the horse, finally, and

yanked Thora free. When the world stopped spinning, she looked down at the girl in her arms.

Val Mortimer's face stared up at her from a mess of tangled dark hair. Wrong: Val Mortimer's hair was molten gold. But it was indeed Val's face, laughing so hard her face looked ready to crack open.

There—a fissure in her cheek. Zoey plunged her thumb into it.

The fissure widened, and blackness poured out. A thick tar sea.

The other horses ran on, girls clinging to their backs, until the horizon swallowed them.

Zoey woke up with her heart pounding in her ears, safely tucked beneath the quilt her dad had made her two years ago, as a Welcome to Sawkill present.

The quilt had this marvelous quality of absorbing all the best smells of their house—her father's cigars, the cilantro and rosemary and basil of their indoor herb garden, the chemical lavender scent of their laundry detergent, last night's arrabiata pasta.

It was a crooked quilt, and more than a little ugly. When her father had presented it to her, wrapped up in brown paper and tied with twine, she'd opened it and laughed. A honking guffaw. The laugh she'd inherited from him.

Because Zoey was more than a little screwed up, and part of the whole teaching-herself-not-to-cry thing was resorting to the default of inappropriate laughter in moments when she didn't know what to do with her emotions. Laughter was safe, and it scared people a little, that she laughed when lovers died in movies. When she crashed her mountain bike the first day she'd ridden it, she'd lain there in the center of Sawkill's main drag with torn bloody knees, cackling at the sky.

But Zoey knew her father had made this quilt for her because it was the sort of thing her mother would never do—take the time to learn a new thing, simply so she could do something nice for her daughter. So she could make her feel more loved, and maybe a little steadier.

It was why Zoey had moved in with him when he'd asked, instead of moving from Baltimore to San Francisco with her mother.

Zoey hadn't yet decided if she regretted that decision. Moving to Sawkill had brought her Thora, sure. But the loss of Thora had carved out a piece of Zoey's heart, and she didn't think she'd ever be able to replace it, and she was fairly certain she didn't want to.

Zoey grabbed her phone and sent a text:

You awake?

A few seconds. Then:

Barely. What's going on?

Zoey snuggled deeper under her quilt. Grayson Tighe was the only trustworthy male on the island, besides her father.

Can I say, once again, how thankful I am that you actually spell shit out in your texts?

And use proper punctuation?

It's pretty hot, ngl.

Looks like you forgot some vowels there.

That's how the youths talk, yo.

So I've heard.

Zoey felt the tension drain from her body. God bless Grayson. She headed downstairs for a glass of water. Her throat felt like she'd been the one screaming.

So did you hear about the new girl?

Marion Althouse.

Yeah.

I heard she had some kind of fit.

It was fucked up.

Use your words, Word Girl.

Fucked. Up. Sorry, love. Sometimes you've just gotta say it.

She could practically hear Grayson's sigh through his text.

So you were there, right?

Right.

Zoey?

She turned on the tap, filled up her favorite cup—a chipped plastic relic that was as bright an orange as her newly dyed curls.

Yeah.

It's 3:00 a.m. You know that, right?

Is it really? Wait, what are these numbers on my phone?

Zoey.

What do they mean??

Zoey.

Is it a code?? WHAT IS THIS? WHERE AM I? WHAT YEAR IS IT?????

ZOEY.

At your service.

So what really happened with Marion?

Zoey gulped down her glass of water. She stood by the sink, watching the lighthouse beacon circle slow and steady.

I couldn't sleep, she replied at last. Maybe Grayson had fallen asleep by now.

Marion freaked me out.

How?

She was screaming like . . . I don't know. It was wrong

Wrong like what?

Wrong like normal people don't scream like that. She was practically convulsing.

Not how people usually act after being thrown from a horse.

Not so much.

Maybe she has health problems. The fall could have triggered something.

Maybe.

Zoey dug the heels of her palms into her eyes, so hard it hurt.

On the counter, her phone exploded:

We can dance if we want to

We can leave your friends behind

She answered before it could wake up her father. "Grayson, what the hell?"

"You weren't answering my texts," came his voice, as untroubled and matter-of-fact as always. A hint of an old New England accent clung to his words. She'd given him shit about it when she first met him; now that she knew he wasn't an unbearable ass, she found it charming. "I didn't want to go to sleep without making sure you're okay."

"You beautiful sap."

Grayson let out a little sigh. A happy one, Zoey thought, and then came the familiar, traitorous litany: *Maybe I could have sex again, for Grayson's sake.*

Maybe it was a mistake to break up with him.

Maybe I would stop dreaming about Thora, if Grayson was mine, just like before.

"Please tell me you don't still have 'Safety Dance' as your ringtone," he said.

"'I'm sorry, Dave,'" Zoey intoned. "'I'm afraid I can't do that.'"

"Are you doing the creepy HAL head tilt?"

"Of course."

"Even though he was a computer console and not an android, and therefore couldn't actually *do* the robot-head-tilt thing?"

"Missed opportunity. Kubrick should have hired me."

"You weren't alive back then."

"Says you." Zoey raised herself up onto her toes, lowered herself into a plié. "I'm a resurrected feline. I'm an old soul. I contain multitudes." She returned to a relevé position, brought up her left arm over her head, stretched her fingers like a dancer. "In my next life I'm going to be a ballerina. Like a hard-core ballerina. Sparkly tutus but also knife-throwing. Daggerina. And I'm gonna have so much money I'll buy Sawkill and kick off all the rich assholes and run wild with the horses and open a drive-in movie theater."

"For who? You and the horses?"

"The concession stand will serve popcorn hay bales."

Grayson chuckled, a warm, rich sound that kept Zoey happily twirling.

Then, he said quietly, "Val has a party next Friday."

Zoey's heels plunked back onto the ground. "Way to kill a girl's buzz."

"Hey, now. You requested I keep you updated with the social calendar."

"I already knew about this one."

"How?" Grayson sounded confused.

Understandable. No one even remotely associated with Val talked to Zoey except for him, so. There was that.

"Got an invite in the mail, a whole eleven days in advance. What do you think? I think she really wants me to come. I think she wanted to give me enough advance notice so I could keep that day open for the party of the season."

Up in her room, the crumpled pink invitation and crisp white envelope smelling of Val's gardenia perfume sat in the trash can.

"Shit." Grayson hardly ever cursed. There was a clean, empty silence. "Zoey, please don't."

"You can't control me, Grayson."

"I'm not trying to control you, and I don't want to control you. I also don't want you to get hurt."

Once, Zoey had decided caution was for pansies and shown up to a Val Mortimer party uninvited. She'd barely made it out of there with her nose unbroken. Only Grayson's interference had saved her from an ass-kicking. Not from Val; Val would risk neither her sparkling reputation nor the integrity of her manicure.

That was what other people were for. Minions. Val had dozens of them.

And wouldn't it be easy, whispered a Thora-shaped voice in Zoey's mind, *to do away with someone, if you had an army of minions at your disposal?*

It was a thought Zoey couldn't shake, even though, really, it made no sense. At first Zoey had assumed Val had stolen Thora away from her just to prove to Zoey that she could. Because Val was Sawkill royalty and Zoey didn't fit the Sawkill mold, didn't care to, and thought Sawkill social politics were bullshit. The nerve of that seemed to stick in Val's craw like a trapped popcorn shell between her teeth.

And what better way for Val to give Zoey the finger than by stealing away her best friend?

But as the months crept by, it became clear to Zoey that Val adored Thora, without pretense or pretend.

So it didn't make sense that Val would have murdered her.

And yet, Zoey's mind buzzed around the idea like an angry bee. Mostly because it was a nice fantasy, to imagine your nemesis doing something so heinous. *All the more reason to hate your guts, my dear.*

But also . . . there were the other girls.

"Val was all up in Charlotte Althouse's personal space yesterday," said Zoey, pacing.

"Wait, who?"

"Marion Althouse's sister. Pretty girl."

"Okay . . ."

"You wouldn't kick her out of bed, is what I'm saying. If you were into having people in your bed."

"I don't see what this has to do with—"

"She seemed nice, and I don't want Val getting her claws in her, okay? Like . . ."

Zoey, the noncrier, was not immune to throat lumps. She swallowed hard, fighting to reclaim her words as she made her way back upstairs.

Grayson's voice was gentle. "Like Thora?"

Once in her room, Zoey lifted up her mattress, withdrew the bulletin board hidden on top of the box spring. She propped it up against the wall, sat cross-legged in front of it, stared at the canvas of newspaper clippings, computer printouts, and the smiling gazes of twenty-three girls.

Evelyn Sinclair. Fiona Rochester. Avani Mishra. Grace Kang. Natalie Breckenridge.

Thora Keller.

Decades of dead girls. Poor girls and rich girls. Black and brown and white girls.

All of them Sawkill girls.

Not all of them had been close friends of the Mortimer family—but enough had, making Zoey wonder, and theorize, and drive Grayson nearly out of his mind with her rants.

"Yeah," Zoey replied. "Like Thora. Plus, she sent me a freaking *Barbie-pink invitation*. So. Challenge accepted."

A beat of silence. "Tell me again," said Grayson, "what is it you think Val's family did?"

Zoey bristled at the reasonableness of his voice. "Don't patronize me."

"Zo, really, I'm just trying to understand—"

"I don't know what they did!" Zoey threw up her hands. "And I don't know why they did it, but they did . . . *something*."

Grayson sighed softly. "I see."

"How many girls have disappeared from Sawkill over the years, Grayson?"

"A lot."

"And all of them were . . . ?"

"Zoey, *everyone* on Sawkill is friends with the Mortimers. That doesn't mean—"

"I'm not. You're not."

"Well, my mother actually did have tea with Val's mother last week—"

"Shut up, Grayson," Zoey said, but there was no heat behind it. She slumped onto her bed, flung her arm across her forehead.

"All right," he said agreeably. A beat of silence, followed by another, and a third.

"Thora was *my* friend." Zoey's eyes burned with exhausted tears she refused to let fall. "She was *our* friend, Grayson. Then, out of the blue, Val decided to take her from us, and three months later, she was dead."

Grayson said nothing. He'd heard it all before.

Zoey pushed herself off the bed and stabbed a thumbtack into place on her bulletin board—not the hidden one, but the one that hung in plain view over her desk. Val's invitation now fluttered beside magazine clippings of actors and actresses so beautiful it pained Zoey to look at them. Poetry scribbled on notebook paper. Polaroid photos—of her father, of herself and Grayson and Thora exploring the beach below the Black Cliffs, of a smiling white woman with a five-year-old Zoey in her arms.

"Don't worry, Grayson," Zoey said. "I'll forget about Thora, and all the other girls, too. Just like everyone else on this shithole rock."

Then she hung up.

MARION

The Doctor

"Marion? I need you to open your eyes for me."

But Marion couldn't open her eyes. Part of her skull felt caved in, and if she opened her eyes, she'd have to face the horror of it.

Instead, she forced her fingers to creep up the pillow until they found first her hair, which someone had combed neat and straight, and then her scalp.

She whimpered.

She was going to find a whole gaping section of her skull missing, she just knew it. She was going to smooth the pads of her fingers along the side-part in her hair and feel a whole jagged hot wet section gone, carved out.

"Marion?" A patient voice kept repeating her name. "Marion, please open your eyes."

It took her a good two minutes to make the full inspection.

Rubbing her head again and again. Preparing for the absolute worst, for brain bits and blood-soaked hair.

But somehow everything was intact. How was that possible? She distinctly remembered something hard slamming into her head. A sensation of flying, then falling, then the slamming, and then a soft nothingness. Except it hadn't entirely been nothingness, because there had also been this fear so visceral it sounded like an angry wasp nest breaking open in her head, and there had been a cry—

A cry. Yes, there had been that, too. A cry, a shriek. A shrill grinding noise, like her bones rubbing against one another. The scream of bones, both quiet and unbearably loud.

"Mom?" She forced out the word between cracked lips, struggling to order her brain. "Hello?"

Then, urging her eyelids open, Marion blinked at a dim, soft world.

"Can you follow this light for me?" asked the patient voice.

The world brightened. Marion followed the light source—back and forth, back and forth.

"Excellent." A soft rustling movement. "Can you tell me your name?"

"Marion Althouse."

"Wonderful. What day is it? Will you tell me the date, please?"

"June nineteenth. Thursday. I think?"

"Outstanding. You're going to be all right, Marion. The worst of it has passed."

"Worst of what?"

"You had an accident. A concussion. Do you remember?"

An image of a slender gray bird flitted through Marion's mind. What did it mean?

"Nightingale." She said the word, and suddenly things became clearer, like she was sliding up out of water into clean, sweet air.

She sat up. She was in a bed, pillows piled at her back. Across the room, fluttering white curtains flanked a wide window. And beside her bed sat a white man in a button-down shirt and tie underneath a sweater pale as sand.

He stared at Marion, unblinking, a small smile frozen on his lips.

"Nightingale threw me." Marion coughed. Her limbs were stiff, her mouth sour with sleep. "He took off from the market and we went down this road. There were cliffs on one side. There were trees, and he threw me. I don't know what happened then."

The memories ran at her face like a movie on fast-forward, and she couldn't look away from them.

"Is he okay?" she croaked. "The horse, I mean."

"Nightingale's fine," the man reassured her. "Something spooked him, but he's back home now. Sometimes animals are unpredictable." He tilted his head to the side. "Can you tell me what happened before Nightingale started running? Did anything strange happen?"

"Strange?" Marion breathed in and out. Each time, she felt more like herself. She faced the man with clear eyes.

"Yes. I'd like to know if something frightened him." The man folded his hands on top of her leg. A thick cotton blanket with satin trim covered her waist-to-toe, but still she jumped. She wanted, suddenly, to kick him away. "Did you see anything out of the ordinary?"

A faint grinding noise started spiraling up the back of Marion's skull, like the bow of a violin moving slow across one discordant string. She dug her finger in her ear. Something was stuck in there that needed to be dislodged.

Something was trying to wake up.

What a strange thought to have.

"I didn't . . ." She shook her head, trying to clear it. "Do you hear that?"

The man was very still, watching her. Had he blinked even once? "Hear what?"

It occurred to Marion that this man was sitting at her bedside with his hands resting on her leg, and she had not a clue who he was. She scooted away from him. He didn't follow her. His hands sat limp on the mattress edge like a pair of fleshy crabs.

"Who are you," she asked, "and where am I?"

The man did blink then, once, though his eyelids didn't touch. A half blink. "These direct questions are wonderful. A positive sign. I'm Dr. Wayland. I'm the Mortimers' family physician, and they asked that I check up on you."

A doctor. Marion's shoulders relaxed. All right, that made sense.

"What did you hear, Marion?" Dr. Wayland's thumb stroked the edge of the mattress. "You mentioned hearing something. I wonder if you might describe it for me?"

"How is she, Doctor—? Oh! Marion, sweetheart, you're awake!" Pamela Althouse, kerchief tied around her head, looked smaller than usual as she hurried over to Marion, like a child hurrying to their mother after a bad dream. She crowded onto Marion's bed.

"Mom, I'm all right."

"I was so frightened, sweetheart. I thought—"

Marion held her mother tightly. "I know what you thought."

Mrs. Althouse sagged gently against Marion's side, with Marion bearing all the weight. Minutes passed, and then eons.

"Mrs. Althouse," came Dr. Wayland's mild voice. "May I speak with you for a moment?"

"Of course." Mrs. Althouse kissed Marion's head. "I'll be right back."

"Okay."

"I'm not going anywhere. I promise."

All of a sudden Marion's skin felt hot enough to sear anything she touched. "No, you wouldn't, would you? You wouldn't go anywhere, not for long."

Because without me, Mother, what would you do?

Without me, where would your sadness go?

Marion curled her fingers around the edge of her blanket.

"What?" Her mother's brow furrowed. Dr. Wayland paused at the door—a still, watching, gray-and-cream bird.

"Nothing." Marion shook herself, disguised it with a yawn and a tight smile. "I'm just tired."

The adults escaped to the hallway, but before Marion could take two breaths, Charlotte appeared around the corner, with a girl Marion at first didn't recognize at her side. Something about the girl's penetrating blue gaze made Marion want to cover herself, even though she was wearing an utterly inoffensive T-shirt and half-covered in blankets.

"There you are," murmured Charlotte, a warm smile brightening her face. "You're awake, my little starfish."

Charlotte crawled onto the bed next to Marion, and a knot constricting Marion's heart loosened. *Charlotte.* This was good, this was wonderful. Because Marion remembered now that only minutes ago she'd been dreaming up a world in which Charlotte no longer existed.

She turned her face into Charlotte's neck, into the soft hollow of her throat, where the silver starfish charm lived. Charlotte had a wonderful smell, like clean laundry and clean skin, and the rose-scented perfume she sprayed on her wrists and throat every morning.

Marion touched the silver starfish sitting on its chain around her own neck. "Remember when we got these?"

Charlotte laughed softly. "God, how old were we?"

"Thirteen and twelve. Come on. Don't you remember?"

"Four years is a long time."

Marion fell silent. Yes, four years was a long time. Four years ago, their father had still been alive. Four years ago, they had lived in a suburb of Boston, found two matching starfish necklaces at a cheesy jewelry kiosk in the mall, and exchanged them on Charlotte's bed by the light of three candles, while reciting a "spell" they'd written after watching *Practical Magic* for the eighteenth time.

"*Not even death can part our souls,*" twelve-year-old Marion had intoned, throwing rose petals into a yellow ceramic bowl they'd snuck up from the kitchen.

Charlotte, giggling, had sprinkled sugar and salt and dirt from the rose garden over the petals. "*Even when we're rotting and full of holes.*"

"Don't laugh!" Marion had scolded, stifling her own smile. She'd clasped the necklace around Charlotte's neck. "*Sisters two and sisters true.*"

"*You love me,*" Charlotte had concluded, fastening Marion's necklace, "*and I love you.*"

The memory made Marion's throat close up, and suddenly that's exactly what she wanted—to dig out their copy of *Practical Magic* and watch it from within the safe nest of Charlotte's arms.

But there was a girl sitting on the edge of her bed—a beautiful girl, pouty-lipped like a French model, clear-skinned like a starlet—and at the sight of her, Marion's belly warmed, despite everything. Marion wanted her to go away, she wasn't in a state fit for such beauty, but she couldn't find the voice for it. That was a common affliction of hers—not being able to find the voice for things. Mountains couldn't talk, anyway, could they?

No, voices were for birds and wolves and the wild, wild wind. Mountains watched, taciturn and solemn and bearing the weight of the ancients, while the world careened and howled on by.

"Who's this?" Marion asked.

The girl gave a small smile and extended her hand. "Val Mortimer. I was there, yesterday. You probably didn't know."

Oh. *Oh.*

A ferocious blush crept up Marion's cheeks. Suddenly, her eyes filled with tears. She remembered people hovering around her, shouting her name. She remembered the pain cutting her head in two.

She remembered the scream of her bones.

Charlotte squeezed her hand. "Marion?"

"I'm sorry. I didn't mean . . ." Val crossed her arms over her chest. "Are you okay?"

"I'm fine." They were Marion's most frequently used words. She wiped a shaking hand across her eyes. "I, uh . . . Sorry. I recognize you now."

Val raised her eyebrows.

Marion's blush intensified. "You look a little different in person. Smaller. Not that you look fat in your photos or anything," she added quickly. "Not that I looked at, like, a ton of photos, I just . . ."

"We had to internet stalk you before we moved," Charlotte told Val cheerfully. "Just a little bit."

Marion kept her arms board-stiff at her sides, resisting the urge to curl up into a sweaty ball of mortification.

"Can't really judge you," Val replied, her mouth sliding into a smile so lovely that the word seemed inane to Marion. "Internet stalking is practically my avocation."

Charlotte laughed, touched Val's leg with her toe.

Marion leaned back against the pillows, watching them, listening to them chatter about Val's boyfriend, about Charlotte's clothes, about Val's summer reading project, about Charlotte's collection of classic children's hardcovers.

Their words slithered across the folds of Marion's brain. Each slip and spill sent a shock of pain butting against her temples. She tilted her head left, then right. Maybe the buzz in her ears would roll right out of her ear and down her neck—a warm, wet phantom thing waking up and then promptly exiting her body.

"So what did you find out about me?" asked Val, toying with the white bedspread. She smiled up at Charlotte, glanced at Marion. Her eyes lingered on Marion's face in a way that made Marion want to squirm. "When you were stalking me."

"Valerie Elise Mortimer," recited Charlotte, in a faux English accent, which was good, because it made everyone laugh a little. "Eldest daughter of the richest family on Sawkill. Champion equestrian. Accepted to Yale, Harvard, Sarah Lawrence, Princeton, Brown. Ruler of the great manor house of Kingshead. Boss bitch. Et cetera."

Marion turned away from them—their laughter, their softness, their floral-scented nearness. Val had scooted closer, leaning into Charlotte like they were old friends, long used to huddling on beds and whispering secrets.

Marion barely resisted the urge to grab Charlotte, pull her under the bedspread, and smother all her air away, so Val could have none of it for her own.

Why couldn't we have gone to a desert island instead? Marion wondered hopelessly, already aching with loneliness. She could see the future clearly: Valerie Mortimer, Charlotte's new best friend. Far more interesting and appealing than Marion, with her nagging and her worrying and their dead father's crooked smile, could ever be.

Rolling over on her side, Marion closed her eyes. Quiet waves of agony pulsed through her head and down her spine. She dimly noticed the voices of her mother and Dr. Wayland murmuring in the hallway outside her room, along with a third voice that, via eavesdropping, Marion realized was Ms. Mortimer, Val's mother.

Silence, utter stillness, and then a shift against the mattress.

"Are you all right?" Val's quiet voice, closer now. "Charlotte's getting you some more water. Is something hurting?"

Honestly, Marion didn't know what was wrong with her, but she knew she was tired and needed a shower. Her scalp itched; a greasy film coated her skin. She'd never been drunk, or high, because the idea of so grievously defying rules made her break out in hives. But the room was spinning and rocking, and Marion wondered if this was what it felt like, to be under the influence. If so, why would anyone do this to themselves?

She pressed down on her temples. Hot swells of pain pulsed under her fingers. This beautiful girl was looking at her, was sitting warm and near, and Marion probably absolutely reeked.

"After Dad died, Charlotte started sleeping in my bed," she found herself saying, starting to panic a little, because the pain in her head was unlike anything she'd felt before, and because she was mortifyingly conscious of her oily hair. "I did that when we were little, slept in her bed. I was afraid of lightning, back then. Every time I saw lightning flash, I'd be afraid it would strike our house," she kept saying, or maybe not-saying, who could really know? "Totally fry us. Did you ever wonder that? What do you think it feels like to be electrocuted?"

"Well," Val began, with a tone of *Why oh why did I come into the crazy girl's room?*

Marion cut her off, blushing madly. "Doesn't matter. Anyway, I'd go into her room and she'd never get mad at me for waking her up. She'd let me wrap myself around her so tight, she'd call me her starfish, and I'd breathe her in until I calmed down. We traded starfish necklaces, made a spell for it. A sister spell. We're not allowed to take the necklaces off, not ever. That's what Charlotte decided. So no matter what, we'll always be with each other. Cheesy, right? I love her for it."

A solid heat was building behind Marion's eyelids, filling up her throat. "She'd comb my hair with her fingers, on those nights," she whispered, because if she spoke any louder than that either she'd completely lose it and start sobbing, or the insect buzzing around in her head would know right where to find her and dive down for the sting. "Really smooth, over and over, until I fell asleep. Even if it took an hour for the storm to roll past and for me to calm down, she'd keep going. She never complained. Not once."

"That's nice," said Val, after a silence so long Marion wondered if she'd left the room without Marion noticing.

"Yeah. And after Dad died, I wanted to do it again. But I couldn't. Because Charlotte came to me instead. She cried on me, she needed me, every night. And then I had to be the one to comfort her. I never felt like it was okay for me to ask for help. Because she'd done it for me, when we were little. And now it was my turn, right? And somebody had to hold it together. Hold *us* together."

Marion closed her eyes. When they'd come over on the ferry the day before, she'd stared at the vastness of the choppy black sea beyond Sawkill. It had overwhelmed her. Always churning, never satisfied. There was something inherently malevolent about the sight of the ocean.

That blackness was in her head now—moving, gnawing, unknowable. Shifting back and forth, crashing against the hard curve of her skull, carrying within it all manner of creatures not yet recorded by scientists. If she drilled down deep enough, right to the cold, dark floor, maybe she'd be the one to discover them.

She pressed her fingers hard against her temples. Harder. She ground down in tight rapid circles. Brilliant electric supernovas spun behind her eyelids.

"Hey," said Val's distant, dim voice. Gentle hands circled her wrists, tucked them down into the blankets. Soft fingers combed through Marion's hair, cautious and slow.

"Like this?" Val's voice was hardly a whisper. "Is this what she would do? Is this all right?"

With some astonishment, Marion realized she was crying. Her hair stuck to her neck in damp black sheets, but Val didn't seem to mind. She turned over to face Val, but the waves in her head muddied everything. Val was a pulsing gold blur beside her on the pillows, lined in shuddering jagged black lines.

Marion wished she were a painter, so that later she could re-create Val, and the strange golden-dark moment surrounding them.

"Yes, thank you," she said to Val, her eyes fluttering shut. Right before she fell asleep, Val's fingers brushed against her cheek—careful and tender, like the slick-soft stretch of a bird's wing. Marion leaned into her touch. "Just like that."

THE ROCK REGRETTED NOTHING.

There was no room for regret when battling an invasion.

Yet when the girl's feet stepped off the boat and hit the shore, when the Rock felt her solid weight and knew at once that hers was a resilient spirit, one that could wake up others like her and bear the agony to come—there was a moment, a pang, of hesitation.

As much as a rock could experience a pang, this one did.

It did not relish tying an innocent to the burden of its ancient might.

But the Rock required an infantry.

VAL

The Child in the Woods

It was the magic hour, everything soft and purple-limned, which was not a time during which Val preferred to venture into the woods. Something about the quiet clarity of twilight, how it transformed the colors around her into otherworldly shades—green to silver sage, blue to fairy moss, brown to underbelly black—twisted together her gut and heart, left her toes and fingers cold.

But she was running late, so she reminded herself how unfairly gorgeous she looked in this lighting and plunged into the trees.

Better to be uncomfortable than to keep him waiting any longer than she already had.

They had made a deal, long ago: Val would meet him at the appointed time, three times a week, with no delays. And in return, he would not interfere with her daily schedule too terribly much.

Her sandaled toes wedged under a tree root, and she stumbled. Bark scraped a slender stripe of skin off the top of her foot.

"Shit," she whispered, bending down to inspect it.

"There you are!" A towheaded boy, his bright pink cheeks smudged with dirt, his khaki knees grass-stained, bounded out from between two bowed sycamores. He extended one pudgy hand. "I missed you!"

Oh, God, she hated when he took this form.

And he knew it. That cherubic smile beaming up at her, those twinkling eyes. Oh yes, he knew, and delighted in it, and he was better at assuming shapes now than he had ever been. He was more solid, more believable. Once, details had been off, details that would have given him away—unblinking eyes, malformed words, arms held straight at his sides when he walked. In those days, years and years ago, he had hardly ventured out of the woods, much less the stones. So Val's grandmother had told her.

But he was growing more powerful. He was learning.

The world had the Mortimer women to thank for that, for allowing him to exist outside the realm that had birthed him and to live in theirs instead.

You're welcome, world.

Val hesitated, then took his hand. The boy wrapped his sticky fingers around hers, bone rubbing hard against bone, and led her deeper into the trees. Val bore the pain in silence.

Her mother had done worse, many times.

You must be strong, Valerie, her mother had said, her hands around Val's young throat, her perfectly shadowed eyes daring Val to scream. *He doesn't take kindly to weaklings.*

"Sing to me?" the boy asked, plaintive.

Val swallowed. "I don't know if—"

"Sing." The boy turned hard blue eyes upon her. "I like it when you sing."

A sharp pain tugged Val's stomach into a knot, and she complied at once, singing a song her grandmother had composed as a girl. Val had made the mistake of sharing it with him one day, when she was young and still thought this whole thing a fine game, a delightful secret between her and her mother: A beast from a hidden land who favored their family above all others. A beast who feared nothing except a Far Place where all life went to die, and of which they must never speak, if they wanted to keep him happy and calm.

Ever since that day, when he'd first heard the song, he often requested it of her.

It curdled Val's insides to perform it for him.

She knew her grandmother had kept it private all those years—private from *him*. Sylvia Mortimer's own private morsel of self. So here she was, Val the traitor, singing her grandmother's secret song. But there was no going back now.

"I love this song," he sighed, swinging their joined hands between them. "Your voice is lovely, Val."

There was a game Val and Natalie Breckenridge had played

when they were young. One girl closed her eyes, and the other pretended to crack an egg over her head—a soft thump of the fist against the skull. Then, the yolk sliding down, down—fingers spider-trailing down the neck and arms and back. It had been a shivery thrill, raising all the blond hair on Val's legs. Once, she had kissed Natalie after, and then it had become a different game—let the other girl crack an egg somewhere on your body, and if you didn't shiver, didn't flinch, didn't make a single sound, you'd get a kiss anywhere of your choosing.

But now Natalie was gone, and Val dated fine, handsome young Sawkill men. The Breckenridge estate had been sold. The grieving Breckenridges themselves had moved back to the mainland, fleeing ghosts, and Val was, as ever, alone.

Val felt the same shivery sensation now, trailing down her body like invisible fingers, as his tiny child's hand crept up to circle her wrist. He sang along with her, her grandmother's words:

Little fairy girl, skipping down the sea
Little fairy girl, pretty as can be
Who is the fellow with the bright clean grin?
Do you want, fairy girl, to weave a spell for him?

As they sang, trekking through the woods like sister and brother, cousin and cousin, Val's mind wandered back to the clean white room in which Marion now lived.

Marion, Marion. It was a pretty name, really. Marian the

Librarian. Maid Marian the noblewoman.

Marion Althouse, with slick black hair, soft pale skin, a low voice like the slide of honey.

Val stumbled again—these awful trees, their roots were everywhere, she wanted to mow them all down—and the boy shoved her. She fell, knocked her knees against the cool ground, packed hard with mud. They had reached the circle of stones. Val would recognize that mud anywhere. She'd grown up with it wedged under her fingernails.

Once, he wouldn't have dared push her quite so hard.

Once, he'd needed her more than he did now.

"You're distracted," came the little boy's voice. His smile was small and cold. He stood over her as she twisted around to sit properly, inspecting her scraped palms.

She didn't look up, but felt his eyes on her all the same. He examined her, head to toe, like her mother looking after one of the horses. And he would like what he saw—her long, lean lines; her shining golden hair; her trim waist. She made sure he would like what he saw, and so did her mother, and so had her grandmother, before cancer got her.

Or so Val had been told.

She couldn't imagine her mother thought she actually believed that bullshit. But Val was good at pretending. Her mother had made sure of it.

"I'm sorry," said Val, looking up, but the boy was no longer there. Instead, shadows writhed around the edge of the stones. They were only stones from the beach—small, pale, innocuous—but even so, Val saw them whenever she shut her eyes at night. They encircled her every shrinking dream. He didn't want her ever to forget who she was and what she had been born to do.

"What are you thinking about tonight?" came his voice from the shadows. The shadows shifted and curdled, sometimes tree-shaped, sometimes wing-shaped, sometimes arm-and-leg-and-shoulder-shaped.

"I was . . . I don't know," Val said, shaking out her stinging palms. "Do you have instructions for me?"

"Are you thinking about the Althouse girl? Is that what's distracted you?"

Marion.

God, surely he wasn't interested in Marion? She had a plain face, a soft body. Thick thighs and a round face and wide, limpid eyes like a trapped puppy. She was dull where other girls shone; you'd walk by her at a party and mistake her for the pattern on the wall. Marion didn't make Val hungry like Natalie had, like Thora had. Marion didn't stir his appetite, which lived like an alien egg inside Val's womb, waiting to be passed on.

"Charlotte is lovely," he said, a dark triangular shape, now perched beside her. She blinked, and he jolted across the edge of her vision. She could feel him curled around the back of her neck. "She's hungry. She's lonely. She aches, and she fears." He licked his little-boy lips. "What's the word? She is *pliable.* Don't you think?"

The relief that rushed through Val was like diving into the

surf in high summer. She nearly choked on her own breath.

Charlotte. Of course. Not Marion. *Charlotte.*

She pressed her bleeding palms flat against the mud. Her grandmother had taught her that it never hurt to offer some of herself to the stones, so Val did whenever she could. It kept the trees serene. It reminded Val that, no matter how tightly he wound her chains around his wrists, she was still a girl, still a human, still an independent being who decided when she breathed and when she ran and when she stood her ground.

Well. Mostly.

"She's exquisite," Val agreed. Her voice rang out strong and clear in the glen. "You've chosen wisely, as you always do."

He squirmed in delight against her back before leaving her alone in the dirt. His nails crab-claw clattered across the stones. Then he was up in the trees, jerking from branch to branch like the stabs of an angry painter's brush.

"Bring her to me," his voice crackled back to her across the woods. "Tonight."

Val blinked. "I need more time than that."

A thick silence made Val's stomach tighten and sink.

"More time?" He was horribly calm about it.

"I've already befriended her, but it takes time to really gain trust," Val explained, battling the instinct to cover her chest with her palm and hide her beating heart. "If she suspects anything, if the hunt doesn't go smoothly, that could ruin everything. You taught me as much yourself."

Another fraught silence. Then the clearing seemed to exhale.

So did Val, faintly dizzy.

"I have taught you well," he agreed.

"I wouldn't be the girl I am without you."

"You won't be a girl for much longer," came his low voice.

No, and he would soon no longer need any of them, Val knew—not her, not her mother, not Val's someday-daughters. Soon, he would be grown and free, able to kill whomever and whenever he pleased. Her mother's estimate: weeks, maybe, until that day. Two months. Three, at the most, depending on how quickly Val helped him feed.

And then what would she and her mother do? What would they be? Would he turn on them?

Would he set them free, too?

Unlikely, thought Val.

That was an absolution her kind did not deserve.

She gathered herself and stood tall. She had long ago taught herself to look only peripherally at the truth of what she was, what she did. Any closer, and she would lose her mind. "I will not fail you."

"You never have, child."

There—a note of affection in his voice. Val swayed where she stood, her eyes falling shut. A fierce warmth expanded in her chest and slid down her belly, her thighs, her legs. Her traitorous body—groomed to serve him, birthed to anchor him—responded gleefully to his approval.

When she opened her eyes once more, a supple smile curled across her face. She had one goal, one purpose. It was the thing for which she had been conceived: she would make him proud.

But first, back to Kingshead. Her party was in a week, and there were arrangements to be made. Booze to select. Most important, an outfit to be crafted.

Val Mortimer never showed up to a party looking anything short of to die for.

ZOEY

The Find

A week after the Althouses arrived, Zoey lay in bed, stricken with insomnia. It had been a problem since Marion's fall. That day had kicked off a series of agitated nights and black-and-white dreams that never quite left her.

After two hours, Zoey crept through the house, stopping at each window and staring outside like somewhere out there lay her wandering sleep. She drank two glasses of water and stretched on the floor in the living room until she lay limp and worn-out on the braided orange-and-blue rug.

She looked right: Her father's leather chair, his pilled pink blanket draped over the back. A lopsided stack of mail that needed sorting.

She looked left: The faded brown couch—stained and sagging but outrageously comfortable. Underneath it, a field of dust bunnies and lost coins, a pen, a book.

A book. An unfamiliar one.

Zoey reached under the couch and dragged it out. It was a small thing, bound in faded black fabric with mismatched pages stuffed within, the first few of which were blank.

Then Zoey reached a page of text. Written not in English but in Latin, the cramped, inked lines went on for paragraph after paragraph, so messily scrawled that even if they'd been written in English, Zoey would have struggled to read them. She didn't recognize the penmanship. Not hers, not her father's. She ran her fingers across the paper. A thin creeping sharpness scraped its way up her arm.

She flipped through a few pages and then landed on one that made her stop and stare:

A collection of figures stared back at her, sketched in black ink, every one of them scratchy and misshapen. Some sported scales and matted tufts of fur. Others wore top hats and sleek coats with tails. Some looked human; others not human at all, or at least some sort of unholy hybrid.

All had perfectly round, perfectly colorless white eyes.

All wore wide grins packed to the brim with teeth.

They were vaguely familiar to her, these monster-men. Had she seen these images before?

Under one such image, three scrawled words proclaimed: *ILLE QUI COMEDIT.*

"Couldn't sleep, either?"

Zoey yelped and flung the book across the floor. Skid, slide, thump, it hit the opposite wall. She jumped to her feet and wiped her hands on her pajama pants and hit the floor lamp with her elbow.

A jolt of static discharge shocked her, a real violent son of a bitch that made her rub her skin and look at her fingers, expecting to see blood.

"What?" Her voice cracked open, high and shaky. "Dad?"

Ed Harlow stood in shadow at the bottom of the stairs, robe and slippers and glasses on. He walked to where the book had fallen, picked it up without even glancing at it, and tucked it into the pocket of his robe.

Then he smiled. "How about some hot cocoa?"

Normally Zoey would have said yes, because they'd enjoyed hot cocoa in the middle of the night since Zoey was small, whenever she'd visited her dad in the summers—first in Baltimore, then in Newton, New Jersey, and finally in Sawkill. From the beginning, Zoey hadn't liked the place. Even that first summer, when she'd kept mostly to herself, she'd walked down the blandly clean streets of Sawkill Rock and seen people eye her Afro and eccentric thrift-store outfits with mild dismay. The next summer, she'd gotten a job at the public library, which had introduced her to a level of snotty rich-person entitlement she'd never dreamed could exist in a place as well-meaning as a library.

Then, the next summer, she'd met Grayson. And suddenly an army of Sawkill mothers who'd been circling the Tighe boy for their daughters shot Zoey dagger-eyed glares whenever she approached.

But when her mom had gotten the job in San Francisco,

Zoey had decided that, as miserable as it would most likely be to live on Sawkill, it would be better than moving to the West Coast. At least from Sawkill she could take the ferry to the mainland, then hop on a train down to Maryland and visit friends.

Not that she'd done that very often, since moving to the island.

Ed Harlow was an excellent guilt tripper, maybe even more excellent than he was an organizer of file cabinets, and whenever Zoey talked of leaving Sawkill for even a short weekend trip, he'd act like she was proclaiming her intentions to abandon Earth for the moon.

But Zoey didn't agree to the hot cocoa this time. She frowned at her father's pocket and stayed solidly put.

"What is that book?" she asked.

"Nothing for you to worry about," he replied, in this voice of manufactured calm that set off alarm bells in the back of Zoey's skull.

"I'm not worried," she lied. "I'm asking what it is."

"It's personal."

"It's *weird.*" Zoey crossed her arms over her faded Wonder Woman T-shirt. What she wouldn't give for a Lasso of Truth right about now. "Some random book full of Latin in our living room?"

Her father turned away, toward the kitchen. "You want your orange mug?"

"Dad. What the hell?" Zoey followed him. "There were *monsters* in that book."

"Zoey, I don't go poking through your possessions, do I?"

Zoey tried to look him in the eye, but as he pulled out mugs, cocoa mix, marshmallows, he kept his face turned slightly away from her.

"I don't know," she answered shortly. "*Do* you?"

"No. So kindly return the favor, please."

"I wasn't trying to poke around. There was a book right there on the floor, I didn't know whose it was—"

"Can you hand me a spoon, please?"

"*Dad*. Look at me." She was undoubtedly going to butcher the pronunciation. "*Ille qui comedit*. What does that mean?"

For an answer, he slammed his mug onto the countertop, a little too hard. A crack slapped the air; ceramic shards scattered, spinning out across the Formica.

Zoey froze.

Her father stood at the sink, facing away from her, gripping the edge of the countertop, saying nothing, saying nothing, saying nothing.

Outside, the lighthouse circled. A bright beam looped through the kitchen and disappeared. Her first summer on the island, Zoey, recently introduced to Tolkien, had named the lighthouse the Eye of Sawkill.

"Do you remember when I found your and Thora's notebook of fake fiction?" her father said at last.

Even freaked out as she was, Zoey bristled. "*Fan* fiction, Dad."

"All right. Fan fiction. Do you remember that?"

Oh, yes. Zoey remembered. She wasn't sure a girl could

ever forget her father stumbling upon the sexually explicit, extremely plotless *Star Trek* fan fiction she'd cowritten with her best friend, no matter how diligently said girl might have tried to scrub the memory from her brain.

"You were mortified, as I recall," he continued.

Zoey wondered if she could will herself to melt into the floor. "*Mortified* is a kind word for it."

"Well, then." He turned to look at her. His wide, deep-brown eyes were the same ones Zoey had seen her whole life, the same ones she saw whenever she looked in a mirror, and yet suddenly they looked different to her—alien, and opaque.

Was she dreaming? Was the book, and the broken mug, and this entire conversation, all some kind of weird-ass dream?

"Imagine me feeling something like that right now," her father continued, "and try to grant me a little bit of mercy."

Zoey tried valiantly to wrap her mind around what was happening. "You mean this book is, like . . . your fan fiction?"

He shrugged. "It's as important to me as your fan fiction was, and is, to you."

"It's weird, then," Zoey said slowly, "that you would leave it on the floor, under the couch."

"Even dads can be careless," he replied with a wry smile. "Listen, I don't fault you for looking at it, but I also hope we never talk about it again." He withdrew a pack of cards from the junk drawer. Another hot cocoa ritual: Go Fish. "Deal?"

Zoey took the offered cards. When her fingers brushed her dad's, she barely resisted the urge to flinch away from him. But instead she shrugged the careless shrug she had perfected in the months following Thora's death.

So, Zoey thought, *my best friend disappeared.*

So no one can figure out why.

So Dad can't solve the case, so Dad has a freaky secret book, so it feels like he's lying to my face.

So what? Could be worse. I could be dead, like Thora probably is.

Zoey forced a smile. "Deal."

MARION

The Heart-Hole

Marion was about to give up, return to her room, and go to bed when she heard the door to the back porch creak open.

She scooted across Charlotte's bed, peeked out the bedroom curtains, and saw Val gliding back toward the mansion. Val paused where the lawn ended and the terraced landscaping leading up to Kingshead began. She stretched, shook out her starlit tresses. The tree-shadowed lines of her body in that tight violet shell of a dress: supple and smooth.

Then Val looked back over her shoulder—and up.

A static shock bit Marion's fingers, like she'd touched a car door in winter. She jumped back and snapped the curtains shut.

"*Oof.*" A muffled curse from the direction of the stairs. The door opened, and Charlotte stumbled over the threshold.

"Where have you been?" Marion had stayed up until two

o'clock waiting for Charlotte to come home, pacing around, looking at her unanswered texts and squinting out the window at the drive and worrying about the dangerous cliffs that might have killed Thora Keller, and who had asked Marion to do that, anyway? To wait up and worry?

Absolutely no one.

It was like she couldn't help herself. She was a masochist of the highest order.

And her head wouldn't stop *throbbing*. She glared at Charlotte, rubbing her right temple with the heel of her palm.

"I was out," said Charlotte with a glutted sigh. She barely managed to kick off her shoes before she tottered into her bed and wriggled under the covers.

"Out *where*?" Marion insisted.

Charlotte blinked sleepily up at her. "With Val," she said, as if there could have been any other answer.

"Doing what?"

"Just . . . around. Exploring. You know." Charlotte snuggled Marion's arm.

"I know you reek of beer."

Charlotte frowned. "Are you mad at me or something?"

"Mom and I cleaned the third floor of Kingshead by ourselves. It took us six hours." Marion hated the petulant, petty note in her voice. She switched her massaging fingers to the other temple. She needed to call Dr. Wayland. Her head shouldn't still hurt this severely, eight days later. Should it?

"That place is like twenty thousand square feet." Marion

glared through the sheer curtains, at the dark shape of Kingshead. "My knees are killing me. My head *still* hurts from my fall."

"I'm sorry," said Charlotte, not actually sounding very sorry. "I just needed a night off. You know?"

"You had a night off last night."

Charlotte sat up with an annoyed sigh. "If you have something to say to me, why don't you just say it? I'm tired."

"I'll bet." Marion twisted the edge of Charlotte's downy white comforter in her hands. Charlotte had gotten rid of her old quilt before the move. This new fabric, rich and unfamiliar, scraped Marion's fingertips like a prickly hide. She wondered darkly if that was a metaphor, there in Charlotte's bedding. Out with the old and dingy sister, in with the new, rich blonde.

"Marion, what the hell?" Charlotte snapped. "What do you care if I hang out with Val?"

"Nothing." Marion swung her legs free of the bed. "Never mind."

"Whatever." Charlotte turned away, toward the window.

Marion had her hand on the doorknob, her eyes stinging with a rush of tears, when Charlotte said quietly, "It's all right for me to have fun, you know."

"I never said it wasn't." Marion swayed a little; nausea, her constant companion since the accident, collected in hot pools behind her eyebrows.

"You can come with us next time, if you want."

"Right." Marion gestured expansively at herself—her baggy

gray T-shirt and unkempt hair, legs that needed shaving. "I'd fit in great with that crowd."

"You'd like her." Charlotte sat up, brought her knees to her chest, suddenly beaming. "She listens to me talk about Dad and doesn't say a word. Just listens in this way that makes me feel like, *Jesus*. She *gets* it."

"Yeah? Is her father dead, too?"

Charlotte's eyes narrowed. "You're being a dick."

"I listen to you, too, you know."

Marion stared at the floor, wishing she hadn't said anything, wishing she'd stayed in her room and let Charlotte run off into the woods to live forever with Val. Maybe then she could nurse her evil overlord headache in peace.

"Oh, Marion." There was the familiar Charlotte voice, no longer so nettled. "Is that what—? Of course you do. You listen, starfish, you get it more than anyone. But . . . it's just nice, you know? To talk to someone who isn't you or Mom. It makes losing Dad feel smaller. Beatable."

Charlotte patted the bed, and Marion considered storming off in a huff, but the thought of storming anywhere made her skull feel collapsible. Instead, she allowed Charlotte to pull her close, smooth back her hair. She tried not to gag at Charlotte's beer breath, considered suggesting they brush their teeth, decided to stay put.

As Charlotte sank into sleep beside her, Marion wondered if Charlotte's new friendship blossomed, maybe Charlotte wouldn't need Marion as desperately as she had over the past few months. Would that mean Marion might actually feel some relief? To exist merely as herself, and not as an anchor for her mother and sister—what would that be like?

She might have to then take the time to stitch up the gaping heart-hole her father's death had left behind.

Might have to take a hard look at the cobwebs her life had gathered over the past murky few months.

Might not like what she saw.

She held Charlotte and squeezed her tired eyes good and shut—a small girl once more, terrified of lightning. Praying someone would keep it from striking.

ZOEY

The Underbelly

Well, this was unbearable.

Zoey had been wandering around Val's party for all of two minutes and couldn't stop thinking about that stupid book.

She sipped water from her red plastic cup, fiddled with the hem of her deliberately shabby *WILD ALASKA!* T-shirt with the howling, rhinestone-framed wolves, and wiped her palm on her faded pink skinny jeans.

A couple of years ago, Zoey had arrived on Sawkill and realized almost immediately that, by moving to the island, she'd made a terrible mistake. Sawkill crawled with the untroubled, clear-skinned, immaculately groomed offspring of oil tycoons, old-money socialites, hedge fund managers, world-renowned plastic surgeons. They existed within the confines of an intricate and esoteric sociopolitical structure Zoey didn't understand, and didn't care to. They never said the wrong thing. They played nice. They didn't make unsightly scenes. And though they acknowledged that there was a world beyond Sawkill—beyond the insulated bubble of their money and their easy lives and their veneered smiles—they were content to watch that world pass them by, tragedies and injustices and all. Ugliness couldn't touch them, so why pay it any mind?

Except ugliness *had* touched them, over and over.

Zoey silently recited the names, mentally pushing past the din of Val's party to remind herself why she was there: to sniff around, to observe Val in her natural habitat, to keep an eye on Charlotte Althouse.

Evelyn Sinclair, Zoey recited. *Fiona Rochester. Avani Mishra. Grace Kang. Natalie Breckenridge.*

Thora Keller.

Tragedy had touched Sawkill, again and again and again, but after each girl's disappearance, once a respectable amount of time had passed, everyone seemed to stop caring.

The world's a nasty place. But what can you do? We don't like to think about such things. Not here. Not on these blessed shores.

Living on the Rock was enough to make Zoey physically ill. She existed with a permanent knot of unease wedged in her intestines. But where else could she go? Cali-freaking-fornia? No, thanks. Besides, leaving her father would wound him so deeply Zoey figured she would feel his paternal agony from the other side of the continent.

So she stayed put and counted down the days until graduation. One more year. When she left then—and she *would* leave, and never look back—her father wouldn't be able to blame her for it. College, the future, et cetera.

A nondescript, endless, Thora-less future.

Zoey took another long gulp of water, blinking her burning eyes. Maybe she didn't so much care that leaving would hurt her father. Maybe she didn't care about a father who kept a secret, freaky book full of scrawled monsters and encoded words in the house and wouldn't tell her what it meant.

Why did I come here again? she texted to Grayson. Her fingers shook a little as they hovered over her phone.

A few seconds later:

Because you're determined to give me a nervous breakdown.

I'm being careful.

I trust you. I don't trust Val, or her minions.

SHE invited ME.

Last time you came to a Val party, what happened?

I got drunk.

And?

I accused Val of killing Thora. In front of everyone. And then threw up.

Right, and then?

Zoey's lips thinned.

Val broke down crying, and her shit-faced friends threw firecrackers at me.

Can we please go home? We'll go to my house. We'll binge *30 Rock*. Where are you?

By the Droop.

The Droop was a practically prehistoric oak tree with long, misshapen branches that crawled across the ground like tentacles. If you disappeared into the branches of the Droop at Val's parties, you were trying to hide—to make out with someone, to try something more hard-core than alcohol.

Or to simply not be found.

This was Zoey: Wandering through the branches, ducking under them, stepping over them. Tossing her empty cup over her shoulder. Going back to find it, cursing under her breath because she was a helpless tree-hugging hippie. Mad at herself, too, because why bother coming to show Val she wasn't scared of her if she was going to spend the whole time hiding?

She found the cup, crushed it, and shoved it in her back pocket.

"So what do you think about the new girl?"

"Which one?"

People were talking nearby—a girl and a boy. Zoey ducked behind a branch, tried to mold her body into a branch shape. Out in the clearing, the party's light shifted—bonfire, torches, candles to ward off the bugs.

But in the Droop it was dark as death.

"The freak one," said the girl. Jane Fitzgerald. Zoey recognized the voice, the smooth brown skin, the expensive-as-hell, board-straight weave that fell to the dip of Jane's back. "Not

Charlotte. The one who had a seizure or whatever last week."

"Oh, right." Harry Windemeier, wearer of doofy frat-boy expressions and Top-Siders and too much cologne. "God, I hate coming under here. Couldn't we have just gone to your car?"

"Why? Are you *scared*?"

"No."

Jane wiggled her fingers. Val's party outlined her silhouette in fire. "Scared of the Collector? You are such a pussy. *Beware of the woods and the dark, dank deep—*"

"Yeah. That's exactly it. I'm scared of a kid's bedtime story. Fuck off."

"*He'll follow you home and won't let you sleep.*" Jane made a cheesy ghost sound, her voice full of laughter.

Zoey didn't laugh. Grayson thought the old island tales about the Collector were silly, like any ghost story about boogeymen and dark creatures lurking in the trees, hungry for a meal of children. Grayson had family in New Jersey, and he often reminded Zoey that every place around the world had its urban legends, its kiddie-nightmare fuel. In New Jersey, it was the Jersey Devil. On Sawkill Rock, it was the Collector.

But even before Thora died, even before Thora had left her for Val, Zoey had decided it was unwise to completely dismiss such stories, no matter how often Grayson rolled his eyes. Maybe it was the writer in her, who believed even the tallest tales were rooted in truth.

Or maybe, Zoey thought darkly, *legends about monsters weren't so funny when girls were actually dying.*

"If you don't cut it out with that Collector bullshit," Harry was scolding Jane, "I'm gonna leave you high and dry, Fitzgerald."

Jane sighed. "You are no fun whatsoever."

"And yet here you are," Harry teased.

The slight crunch of damp leaves marked Jane and Harry's approach. Zoey was still, still, still. She hugged her hiding branch with one arm.

"Nightingale's okay, right?" asked Harry. "After the accident?"

Typical. Of course a horse's life was worth more than a human's to someone like him—if the human didn't shit diamonds, that is. Poor Marion. She probably didn't even realize yet just how insignificant a flea she would seem to these humorless rich wankers.

Zoey felt her chest constrict, remembering how many nights she and Thora had stayed up late talking crap about the Sawkill elite. *Humorless rich wankers* had been Thora's phrase, uttered in the most obnoxious English accent she could manage.

Zoey leaned harder against the Droop, stroked its rough bark. *Nice tree. You don't care about money, do you?*

"Yeah, Nightingale's fine." Jane sighed, stretching in an obvious fashion. Her sweater rode up her torso, leaving a large stretch of stomach bare. "Just a little spooked."

"I can't believe Chief Harlow let some random stranger ride his horse," said Harry. "I mean, really? Come on. Asking for trouble."

Harry sat on one of the branches, not ten feet from Zoey's,

and tugged Jane onto his lap. She giggled, shook back her hair.

"What do you expect?" Jane gasped. Harry had his hands up her shirt. "Harlow's useless. He never found Natalie, and he'll never find Thora. The incompetence is staggering. Mayor Harding should fire his ass. Oh, Harry." Jane performed an obscene, breathy groan. "That feels so good."

Zoey didn't move from her hiding spot, but nevertheless she felt all the pieces of herself shift into formation. Gears grinding, claws sharpening. The hissing branches of the Droop touched their leaves to her shoulders.

"I still can't believe Zoey and Grayson dated." Jane was *still* talking, between kisses and half-hearted porn sounds. Harry sighed, annoyed. Zoey could relate.

"Look, what's the big mystery?" Harry snapped. "Grayson wanted to screw her, and he did. He got what he wanted, then he left. Now, stop talking. All right? You're wasting my time."

Jane murmured something and sank slowly to her knees.

The cool, damp world under the Droop wasn't so cool anymore. The bonfire's heat pressed against Zoey's skin, pooled under her feet, pulled tears from her eyes that left her breathless.

It wasn't that she believed what they were saying.

It's that she almost wished it were true.

It would be strangely easier that way: Grayson wanted to get laid, and then he cut and run.

But the truth of why she and Grayson had broken up was almost too embarrassing for Zoey to think about without wanting to puke.

After they'd finally had sex, Zoey had decided she never

wanted to do that again. Not with him, not with anyone. She would never forget the sight of Grayson sitting forlorn and defeated on his bed, tears trailing down his pale cheeks, as she told him, hollow-voiced, that it just wasn't going to work.

Zoey wiped her eyes, her fingers carving hot trails across her skin, and stepped out of her hiding spot. Jane gasped, jumped up from the ground. Harry hopped around, zipping up his pants.

"Neither of you know what the fuck you're talking about," Zoey declared, then turned on her heel, ignoring the sound of their half-embarrassed, half-gleeful laughter, and stalked away. A prickly glove of shame wrapped itself around her throat. She imagined each slap of her checkered high-tops against the ground would help split it open. The earth would swallow Jane and Harry whole. Just for a little while. Just to scare them.

She only made it three strides before she heard Jane scream, and whirled back around.

Harry cursed, slapping at his skin, his clothes.

Jane shrieked, spat, and staggered away from him.

A dozen dark coins dropped from the trees, gathering on Jane's and Harry's arms, scalps, sleeves.

Zoey squinted, then cursed and jumped away.

Black spiders, fat and thin-legged, scuttled up Jane's cheeks and into her hair. They crawled down Jane's collar beneath her top, and they skittered across Harry's lips. They gathered there in clumps, seeking entrance.

Jane, gagging, fell to her knees.

Zoey ran.

ZOEY

The Wolf Pup

Zoey headed for the bonfire, her body pumping bright red electricity.

Then she slammed into Grayson, and clung to him to keep from falling over.

"Zoey, what—? Shit, what's wrong? What happened?"

"I've gotta get out of here." Zoey glanced back over her shoulder. Jane and Harry weren't emerging from the Droop. She'd prefer them to come charging out with accusations, howling for Val. But the Droop stood still, black, silent.

Grayson wasn't budging. "Did someone hurt you?" He pulled out his phone. "I'll call your father."

"Stop it." Zoey shoved him away, stumbling. He looked wounded, dark brows crinkling over those gentle blue eyes, and Zoey did not give a single fuck. "Just . . . something weird's going on, okay?"

"What do you mean?"

"I don't know, we just need to leave."

The music blasting from Harry Windemeier's silver Mercedes changed from one song to the next. A crowd of girls by the bonfire cheered, undulating. Zoey caught a flash of golden hair—Val.

Val's voice was a bell: "Charlotte, come dance with me!"

Suddenly, it was eight months ago. Junior year had just started, and Zoey was waiting by Thora's car in the Sawkill Day School parking lot, when behind her Val called out, "Oh, hey, Thora! Your story for Mr. Everett's class was *awesome*. Holy shit, girl. You can *write*."

Zoey had squinted through the sun to find them, just in time to see Val, with that beaming Hollywood-starlet smile, pull a dazed, blushing Thora in for a hug. (To be hugged by Valerie Mortimer! And, lo, the clouds did part on that day!)

Then Val had looked over Thora's shoulder, right at Zoey, and her smile had widened, just a little, and she'd wiggled four fingers at Zoey. A wave hello? Or some kind of taunt?

Thinking back, Zoey figured she knew exactly what that wave had meant: *Farewell, mortal. She's my Thora now.*

And Zoey had been too jealous of their new, inexplicable friendship, too shell-shocked, too *proud* to step in and stop it.

And now Thora was dead.

But Zoey wouldn't stand idly by this time.

She pushed past Grayson and into the knot of Val's dancing wolves, turned around and around in the pumping bass and the snapping fire until she found Charlotte. Charlotte, dancing beside Collin Hawthorne, arms thrown up over her head, radiant smile on her face. Charlotte's light-brown hair was piled on top of her head. She wore dark skinny jeans and a sheer plunging top that tied behind her neck—a top Zoey recognized instantly as Val's.

Jesus. Less than two weeks after Charlotte had arrived, and they were already sharing clothes. Thora and Val had done that, too. They'd shared clothes; lip gloss; a quiet, genteel indifference toward all things Zoey.

A tiny silver shape on a chain glinted between Charlotte's collarbones.

"Charlotte, we've gotta go," said Zoey, shoving her way in. She realized the silver thing was a starfish charm and remembered where she'd seen that same charm before. "Marion needs you."

"What?" Charlotte brushed a sweaty strand of hair off her cheek. "Is she okay?"

"She's fine, she just . . . she had a nightmare. Something about . . . you know, about her accident." Zoey swallowed hard, shifting from one leg to another. Since Thora vanished, a tiny pocket-Thora had lived inside Zoey's brain. Sometimes she showed up at the most annoying times, flashing smiles at Zoey, whispering old inside jokes to Zoey. She was a hard ghost to shake.

Maybe if Zoey could get Charlotte home, the ghost would leave her alone for at least an hour or two.

"My dad and I went to check on her," Zoey lied. "She was asking for you."

Collin Hawthorne, cheeks flushed a splotchy red, said, "Harlow, what's up with your arms?"

Zoey realized she'd been standing there scratching her wrists so hard she'd nearly broken the skin. But she had to scratch, or the spiders could find their way inside her.

"Come on, Charlotte," Zoey managed, her stomach rolling. "Grayson and I will walk you home."

Collin looked over Zoey's shoulder, saw Grayson standing there, and gave him a bro nod. "Tighe, what's up with your girl?"

"Her name is Zoey, Collin," Grayson answered with a tight smile. "I'm not sure why that's so hard for you to remember."

"What's going on?"

Zoey's stomach dropped.

Val.

Charlotte and Collin made way for her like an ocean for its goddess. She wore a slinky sequined dress that clung to her lean curves and shimmered silver and would have looked ridiculous on anyone else.

What sane person wears a sequined cocktail dress to a forest party?

But Val's hair hung long and windblown to the small of her back, and she was barefoot, one of her feet marked with a thin red cut, her crimson toenails like beads of blood. It was a look. It worked.

Val's smile was brittle, wounded. Trying to make Zoey feel bad for the last party? For the ill-conceived murder accusation?

Fat chance of that.

"You came after all," said Val, "even after what happened last time. I didn't think you would." Her gaze flicked up and down Zoey's body, then to Grayson. "Hasn't poor Grayson suffered enough? Let him go, Zoey." Val's voice slid low like a deep-sleep dream. "Have you come here looking for another heart to break? One wasn't enough for you?"

Zoey nearly choked.

"That's uncalled for, Val," Grayson said.

Collin smirked and reached for the small of Val's back. She batted him away like she would an irritating child.

Zoey couldn't look at Val anymore, otherwise she'd erupt or cry. Either would be a fatal last move.

She waved at Charlotte. "Come on, Charlotte, let's go."

"I'm not going anywhere." Charlotte moved away, teetering slightly. "Mom's there if Marion needs anything. I just want to have some fun for once." She grabbed a cup from an overturned crate and gulped down its contents. A leaf dropped down from the trees, coming to rest on Charlotte's shoulder.

Zoey flinched, expecting spindly legs to sprout from the leaf and go crawling up Charlotte's throat. She glanced back at the Droop. Nothing. No Jane, no Harry.

Zoey's fingers tingled, like at the science museum in the static electricity room. Put your hand on the thrumming metal ball and watch your hair stand on end!

Charlotte wiped her lips with the back of her hand and laughed. "Do you know how long it's been since I've had fun?"

"Yeah, yeah, your life is a tragedy, I get it, but come on." Zoey didn't look back at the Droop, but she could feel its unseen eyes watching her. "It's time to go."

Val hooked her arm through Charlotte's. "Charlotte, babe, listen to me. Marion's fine. She wouldn't want you to leave a party for her. I mean, that wouldn't be fair. You deserve to have a good time."

Charlotte dropped her cheek against Val's shoulder. "God, I really do. But if Marion needs me—"

"She doesn't," Val said, not so gently anymore. "She's fine. Stay here, come on. The night is young."

Red flags flapped in Zoey's deepest gut like taut sheaths of skin. Val sounded a little too desperate, a little too prickly. And although Zoey hadn't swallowed a sip of alcohol, as she stood there, sweating in the firelight, her head spinning, the soles of her feet buzzing in her sneakers, Charlotte became Thora, and Thora became Charlotte again, and Val stayed Val, sharp-eyed and clinging.

Suddenly, Zoey couldn't help herself. She curled her hands into fists. "Evelyn Sinclair," she began quietly, ignoring Grayson's quiet plea to stop. "Fiona Rochester. Avani Mishra. Grace Kang. Natalie Breckenridge." The blood in Zoey's veins crackled. "Thora. Keller." She glanced at Charlotte, eyes full and hot. "Those names ring a bell, Charlotte?"

Uncertain, Charlotte looked back and forth between Zoey

and Val. "Aren't those the girls who—"

"They used to be friends of Val and her mom and her grandma and her great-grandma. They used to be Sawkill girls. And now they're gone, vanished without a trace. You want to be next?"

Collin Hawthorne flung his drink into the fire. He clenched his meaty fists. "You've crossed a line, Harlow. Do you really want to do this again?"

"Hey, listen," Grayson began, holding up his hands between them, "she's just a little bit tipsy, okay? She doesn't mean it."

"Oh yes, I do," Zoey spat.

Val ignored everyone but Zoey, her eyes bright with unshed tears. "You piece of shit," she said evenly. The wind off the water whipped her hair around her face. "I loved Thora."

Zoey felt capable of breathing fire.

Instead, she snapped, "Yeah? Well, I loved her, too—"

And then, before Zoey could finish her sentence, before Val could respond, Charlotte strode forward, her eyes bright and hard, the air all of a sudden crackling like someone had infused it with venom, and struck Zoey across her chin. It was a sloppy hit, and Charlotte yelped with pain right after, but it was enough to light Zoey's face on fire.

Grayson caught her before she could fall. "Jesus, Zo," he whispered, pressing his handkerchief to her cheek. Sawkill boys and their handkerchiefs. What a world Zoey lived in.

Grayson snapped over his shoulder, "What the hell, Charlotte?"

Encircled by Val's wolves, all of whom hooted and raised their cups in her honor, Charlotte stepped back, wide-eyed. She shook her head, cradled her punching hand against her chest.

"Zoey," she whispered, her eyes filling with tears, her words slightly slurred, "I'm so sorry, I don't know what came over me, I didn't mean to—"

Val pulled Charlotte gently away, back into the pack. "Leave her," Val suggested. "Let her walk it off."

Jaw throbbing, Zoey turned away from them, stumbled toward the dirt road that led back out of the woods.

Harry and Jane emerged from the trees hand in hand. Spider-free and beaming, though Zoey saw them glance at each other once, shifty. Then it was like they came to an unspoken arrangement—who would believe them? *Go easy on the booze, you two!*—and moved on with their lives.

"What did we miss?" asked Jane brightly, only a tiny bit shaky. Harry ran his fingers nervously through his hair. Looking for stray arachnids?

"Zoey, stop, please," Grayson said, hurrying after her.

"She changes them." Zoey stormed through the trees. "I don't know how, but she changes them. Thora, and now Charlotte."

"What do you mean, she changes them?"

"Did Charlotte Althouse even for a second strike you as the type of girl to go off and punch someone she barely knows?"

"Well, no, but she had been drinking—"

"Grayson? Honestly?" Zoey whirled around to face him

and had to glare way, way up to meet his eyes. For a second she remembered how sweetly her five-foot-nothing frame had fit against his five-foot-ten, how she'd felt protected in his arms but never diminished.

"If you're not gonna believe me," she said, tears shimmering at her lashes, "even after what you just saw, even after everything we've been through, then leave me the *fuck* alone for a while, okay?"

Then she turned and left him standing alone in the dark.

THE ROCK WAS A PIECE of the larger whole, indistinct from the tectonic plates and the shrinking forests and the bubbling magma deeps of the world.

The Rock was also its own small, lonely self, surrounded by heartless waves jealous of its own unmoving solidity.

The waves gnawed and lapped at the Rock's edges. They groaned and longed and shattered and shifted. They sprayed and they wept.

But the Rock ignored the resentful cries of the sea and reached up into the trees that furred its hide, shaking loose a world of shadows.

Go, it instructed. *Find them.*

MARION

The Bone Cry

The noise was faint and shrill and out of tune.

Since her fall, the noise had infected Marion's dreams; it had teased the edges of her waking thoughts. It had come and gone, elusive enough for her to rationalize it away.

Now it ripped her out of sleep, properly formed at last.

It crept into her quiet white room with the fluttering curtains, the window cracked open to let in the cool night air, the ceiling fan turning lazily around like the circling wings of a hovering jungle insect, mammoth-size.

Marion lay splayed and stiff on her mattress, pinned for inspection. She recited facts, to make sure she existed, in this bed, in this house, on this island:

It was Friday. Nine days since the Althouse family had arrived on Sawkill Rock. Five hours ago, she'd polished the floor of the Kingshead ballroom with her mother.

Her name was Marion.

She was sixteen.

She had hit her head.

She had liked horses once, but not so much anymore.

The noise remained.

It wasn't in her ears as much as it was in her bones, working its way out from the inside. It vibrated in her marrow as though her entire self teemed with tiny burrowing bugs. Like summer cicadas buzzing in the trees at dusk, the cry droned. Escalated. One cicada. Four. Fourteen. Four hundred. Fourteen thousand.

Marion jumped up from her bed, dug her fingers in her ears. Root out the noise, right? Unplug those dirty canals.

Her head throbbed.

Her jaw ached like she'd been grinding her teeth as she slept.

She needed medicine.

She stood in the center of her room, eyes closed, breathing in and out. What had that therapist suggested, after her father died with his skull split open, alone in the dark with his car smoking around him?

Breathe in one nostril, then out the other.

Concentrate on the air passing in and out of your built-in breathing tubes.

Concentrate on the sensation of your two feet planted solidly on the ground.

You are here, in this world. You exist. The sensation of being alive and human—isn't it a marvelous thing?

But standing still made her body itch to move, and when she did—pacing around the room, shaking out her arms and legs, stretching her fingers to the ceiling—this only made her body want to move faster.

That's where the answer lay: Racing across the ground, chasms cracking open where her footprints used to be. If she did that, she'd understand. Everything would become clear.

Marion stumbled to the full-length mirror in the corner of her room, an old-fashioned ornament with a polished cherry-wood frame and clawed feet holding it down.

She peered at her face, her sweaty nose nearly touching the glass.

She muttered to herself, "What's wrong with you?

"Are you sick or something?

"What's happening, why do you have to be this way?"

She gathered her damp black hair into a merciless ponytail, pulled shining and tight against her skull.

Still, the cry remained—a rattling in her bones, a vibration of wings and crawling tiny feet, a resonance of crunching teeth and a distant relentless turning, like the black water surrounding Sawkill.

And something else, something amid the cicadas and the rattling and the grinding that she couldn't put her finger on.

A pull, she thought. In all the noise, there was a pull.

Something telling her: *Follow me.*

She stumbled to the bathroom down the hall, splashed icy water on her face.

The cry of her bones would not cease and desist, no matter

how kindly she asked it to. She left her eyes closed too long; the ground tilted and lurched. She was on the back of a behemoth, knotted muscles rolling as it trudged its way endlessly along the sea floor.

She stood hunched over the sink, shoulders heaving as she forced deep breaths inside herself. Maybe that would drown out the screaming of her bones, right? That made sense. Flushing out poison with fresh air.

But wait.

Her head snapped up. She saw her reflection in the bathroom mirror—wide-eyed, gray-eyed, fuzzy shadows playing hide-and-seek across the soft pale planes of her face.

This wasn't fresh air.

No, this was house air. Downstairs, her mother slept; down the hall, so did Charlotte.

There were chemicals in this cottage—bleach and hand soap and burning liquid to unclog your drain.

She gagged, thinking of dark, knotted hair.

Coughing, she threw up into the sink, but nothing much came out except for spit.

Something was stuck in her throat, that was it. Remove it, and everything would be fine. She'd enjoy silence once more, and she could sleep again.

She reached into her throat with two fingers, nearly scraped her tongue raw, searching.

Ah. There.

The end of a lock of hair—but thick and coarse, not as soft and slick as her own.

She tugged.

Something deep inside her moved, too—a dark piece of Marion's gutty insides, jerking like a hooked fish.

Her eyes teared up. She gagged around her questing hand.

What *was* this, lodged at the turn of her throat, where mouth turned to esophagus turned to stomach?

She tugged, and up it came—a long dark clump of hair, sliding up her throat.

She gagged once more. She was pulling out her very essence. She'd reach the end of this dark foreign string and find her own fleshy, pulsing heart.

Finally, she stood, panting, her eyes leaking tears, and stared at it—a clump of tangled hair resting in her palm.

She was no expert, that was true. But she'd never forget how Nightingale's coarse cropped mane felt, clutched between her fingers as he flew down that hill.

This was horse hair.

Marion's fingers fisted around it, and the buzzing cry in her bones—now flapping wetly between her ears like a beetle's damp wings—told her to leave. Get out, or you'll regret it.

Follow me.

So she did, slipping out the cottage's back door and down the gravel path that led through Kingshead's manicured gardens. The rocks cooled her bare feet. Her shorts and sweater were nothing against the nibbling sea wind.

But her bones screamed, *Faster*, and she had to obey.

ZOEY

The Dead Fish

An hour after leaving Val's party, Zoey made the trek through the Kingshead Woods, pushing past tangled weeds and nearly tripping on the clusters of charcoal-colored rocks spilling down her path.

In the near-dark, for the moon that night was a mere sliver.

Hauling a net full of dead fish.

It wasn't her idea of fun, but the aftermath would be.

"Screw Val Mortimer," she grumbled, "and screw Collin Hawthorne. Screw these rocks, screw these trees." For emphasis, Zoey whacked a low-hanging branch out of her path. "Screw this island, screw these fish." The net of fish slapped against her back.

"Screw Charlotte Althouse," she went on cheerily, "and screw Harry Windemeier."

She stopped her little dark song.

Harry Windemeier. Jane Fitzgerald.

She heaved the net to her other shoulder. Spiders could fall from trees. That wasn't a strange thing. Horrifying, obviously, and conveniently timed, but nothing to fret about. Nature being nature.

She made it out of the trees and onto the edge of the Kingshead estate. She set down her fish, wiped her brow, and stared up at the imposing edifice that was the Mortimer family palace.

Every time she saw it, Zoey felt a little like Maria in *The Sound of Music*, the first time she saw Captain von Trapp's mansion. But instead of muttering, "Oh, help," Zoey thrust both her middle fingers at Kingshead and danced around like she'd just scored a touchdown.

She was right in the middle of this when she realized someone was standing in the trees a few feet away, watching her.

Zoey shouted, "*Shit*," and staggered back, almost tripping over the net of fish.

"Sorry," said the someone, and Zoey realized it was Marion Althouse, who looked sketchy as hell standing there in the trees, her skin freaky pale, her hair dark and wild. Just standing there, arms at her sides. "Didn't mean to scare you. What are you doing out here?"

Zoey aimed for wry nonchalance, to cover up how obviously *chalant* she was. Was that a thing?

"I'm about to go dump some fish into the back seat of Val's Lexus," she replied. "Want to come?"

Marion didn't answer. She turned, staring into the trees. "Do you hear that?"

"Hear what?"

"It's like . . ." Marion shook her head, gripped it between her hands. Her eyes glinted, full of tears. "It doesn't make any sense to me, but I've been hearing it on and off for days, and it's the worst it's ever been tonight. I think the accident might have shaken loose something inside of me. Something important."

Zoey shifted awkwardly. "Hey, it's okay."

Marion shook her head. "I can't make it stop! I've tried everything." She laughed—a high, soft burst. "Almost everything."

Zoey grabbed Marion's hands and pried them away from her skull. "What is it? What are you hearing?"

But Marion didn't answer. She went rigid, her neck elongating as she whipped her head around to search through the darkness. A deer that had heard the snap of a twig beneath a hunter's boot.

The funny thing was, in that moment, Zoey felt it, too—a sudden heaviness, as if another person had entered a dark room and now stood waiting beside them.

Like the trees themselves were watching.

A shiver zipped gaily down her back.

"This way," Marion whispered, taking Zoey's hand gently in hers. "Quietly. We don't want to scare it."

Zoey swallowed. "It?"

But Marion didn't answer.

Zoey abandoned her fish and allowed herself to be led along. She kept glancing at Marion, inspecting her face. Marion didn't seem to mind. Her eyes were wide, ringed in darkness.

"I put my hair into a ponytail," Marion explained, staring straight ahead. "I thought that would help, but it didn't. I had to take it down. I had to take it all down. It was going to carve my skull open."

With difficulty, Zoey asked, "What was going to carve your skull open?"

Marion glanced at her. "The sound. It wants me to follow it."

A page from her father's black book flashed before Zoey's eyes: The figures sketched in pen. The top hats and the long coats. The tufts of fur. The eyes white and without pupils, the wide grins.

ILLE QUI COMEDIT.

Zoey had looked up the phrase in an online translator:

HE DOTH EAT.

Now she remembered, with the woods shivering on all sides, where she'd seen those illustrations before. Not those exact renderings, but similar enough to match. When she'd found the book under the couch, something inside her had pinged at the sight of those sketches, but she hadn't been able to place them until this moment.

Her pocket-Thora opened a door in her brain and whispered, slippery and cold like the ghost she was, *Took you long enough, Sherlock.*

Those drawings were of the Collector.

Monster-obsessed Thora had tried her own hand at

illustrating the Collector in various forms, had even submitted Collector stories to online horror magazines—fully illustrated, every time, and always accompanied by images very much like these.

Which meant . . . what? That her father was also a secret Collector fanatic?

"Marion, have you heard the stories about the Collector?" Zoey flushed a little, placed a hand on her abdomen as if that could quell her slight nausea. To be talking about this with someone who wasn't Thora felt like violating an unspoken pact. But in the quiet moonlit woods, with Marion trembling beside her and the air ripe and taut, Zoey felt like if she *didn't* say the words aloud, something terrible would reach up out of the ground and grab her. The words were a defense. The words held power and deflated nightmares. "There are these old island stories, about this boogeyman thing—"

"It's like a cry," Marion whispered, ignoring Zoey. "My bones are crying. Or, not only my bones. My bones, and someone else's, too."

"Crying like . . . weeping?"

"Crying like screaming." Marion stopped and faced Zoey, her eyes clear, alert. "If you think this is bullshit, you can leave. It's fine."

"I don't think that." Zoey clenched her teeth, steeling her bones. "Earlier, at Val's party, these spiders fell out of the trees, onto these kids, right in front of me. Not one or two spiders. Like . . . *dozens*." Zoey blew out a breath. "It feels like a weird night, is what I'm saying."

She didn't mention her father's book to Marion, part of her hoping that if she never spoke about the book, about her father's reaction to her finding it, then it would never have happened. She would be able to once again look him in the eye without feeling like she was staring down an ominous closed door.

Zoey shook her head and wiped the back of her hand across her forehead. "Thora always said, if there's a place in the world where crazy shit could and would happen, it's in the Sawkill woods."

"Thora," said Marion quietly, still as a tree herself. "Your friend who's missing?"

"She's dead. I know it." Zoey cast her eyes toward the ground. "She was such a good writer, you know. Her stuff was raw, and weird as all hell. The kind of writing that makes you ache because you feel like you're getting a peek into a secret place."

"I'm sorry, Zoey. I've seen death, too." Then Marion held out one of her hands; a long tangle of black hair rested in her palm.

"This was inside of me." Marion gazed imploringly at Zoey, tear tracks drying on her cheeks. "I pulled it out."

"Christ." Zoey was reminded, most unpleasantly, of the spiders trying to force their way into Jane Fitzgerald's mouth. Looking at the hair gave her the same upside-down feeling. The feeling of *am I awake, or am I dreaming?*

She swallowed hard. "Why don't we just go ahead and ditch that?"

She turned over Marion's hand. The tangle of hair fell to

the ground. They were on the other side of Kingshead now, past the gardens and the stables, down into the woods on the other side.

Ugh. More woods.

"Can you describe the sound to me, in more detail?" Zoey asked, when she could no longer stand the silence. Up and down her neck, her skin itched. "Maybe if I know what to listen for—"

"Stop."

Zoey obeyed. She stayed put as Marion moved slowly into a cluster of thin, dark trees . . . and disappeared.

All sound vanished. There had been noise, just a moment ago—night birds, night bugs, the rustling of trees and leaves, the hoot of an owl.

Now, there was nothing.

It was dead still in these woods.

And animals, they go quiet when a predator is near.

"Marion?" Zoey's mouth filled with the sharp, sour flavor of adrenaline. She followed Marion's path into the trees. "Where'd you go?"

Past the trees was a well-trod dirt path, and at the end of the path stood a circle of small white stones.

Marion stood in the center of them. Head tilted to the side. Birdlike. Listening.

"Marion," Zoey whispered again. "What is this place?" She took another step forward, tripped over a root, and caught herself on its tree.

Her hand landed in something hot and wet on the bark.

She brought her hand away.

Her fingers glistened black. The tang of blood slithered inside her mouth to curl across her tongue.

A sound came from the stones—a gathering army of winged bugs, a rattlesnake warning away intruders.

Marion whirled. Her wide eyes found Zoey.

She whispered, "Run."

There came a cold shattered crack like a fist through glass, followed by the ear-popping feeling of a quick pressure change. Marion flew out of the stones, a rag doll flung away by a temperamental child.

Zoey lurched forward, grabbed Marion's hand, yanked her to her feet.

This time, when Zoey ran, she wasn't alone.

VAL

The Lullaby

Val figured Zoey would try to get back at her for what had happened at the party.

Even though Zoey was the one to behave so dreadfully, that was the kind of person she was—throw around vile insinuations like she existed alone and righteous on a lofty pedestal of morality, then turn around and paint herself as the victim.

So Val sat at the window seat in her bedroom, rereading Thackeray's *Vanity Fair* for the seventeenth time, waiting, and was unsurprised when she saw Zoey trudge up from the woods toward the housekeeper's cottage.

But she was surprised to see Marion with her.

She closed her book, padded downstairs, and slipped outside. Barefoot, through the hedges, Val followed Zoey and Marion, hidden under the branches beside the long drive.

"We'll go back tomorrow, in broad daylight," Zoey was saying. "We'll bring reinforcements. We'll bring Grayson. We'll record the whole thing." She wiped her left hand on her pants, keeping her right hand firmly around Marion's.

Val's eyes narrowed on the point where their fingers joined. So Zoey and Marion were friends now? Val did not approve of this development.

They walked up the white steps to the cottage's back door. Val hid in the hydrangea bushes, crouched panther-style. She curled her bare toes into the black dirt.

"We can try," Marion replied, her voice thoughtful and measured where Zoey's words practically tripped over themselves in panic. "I don't think we'll find that place ever again."

"I don't even get what that place *was*," Zoey went on. "Part of the Mortimers' gardens or something? Some kind of fairy circle . . . thing?"

Val's blood stopped circulating, screeched to a halt, and reversed course.

A fairy circle.

The stones?

The world dropped away from under her feet, leaving her flailing in midair.

How could they have found the stones? They couldn't *possibly* have found the stones. His power kept the stones veiled from anyone but his hosts: Val, and her mother, and no one else. Not even Val's father had ever seen it—whoever he was, long gone before Val was old enough to remember him, some man Lucy

Mortimer had seduced and then sent on his way. The Mortimer women selected vital, virile men as mates, but never kept them around long enough for them to discover the truth.

Val's crouching knees gave out. She sank clumsily into the cool mud, her skin pulling tight across her bones. If he realized others had happened upon the stones, he would find a way to blame Val for it. Or he would blame her mother, and Val noticed the way he looked at Lucy Mortimer these days—like he was tired of looking at her, like he was itching for fresh meat. And there was, of course, only one fresh meat option left for him, at least until Val let some hapless fool plant a daughter in her belly.

But then, if her mother had estimated correctly, he would free himself before that day came, and Val wouldn't need to bear him a daughter after all. He would free himself, and her body would then, perhaps, be her own, at last, and no one else's.

Unless he killed her, once he was free, and before she could be truly free herself.

She bowed her head, pressed her palms against the mud, and inhaled.

He will try to rule your life, your every breath, your every choice, with fear, Val's grandmother had told her. *And for the most part, he will succeed. Every scrap of dread he senses in your blood is his fuel. He will use your panic to grow his power.*

Close every door to your heart.

Keep your fear close and quiet.

"There was blood on that tree," Marion was saying. She

glanced at Zoey's hand. "You're sure you didn't just scrape your hand?"

Zoey held up her palm, flat and rigid. "Do you see any wounds? Because I sure don't."

Marion inspected Zoey's hand, running her fingers gently up and down every finger, every crevice.

If Val had claws, they would have slid out from underneath her fingernails, carved hateful lines in the mud beside her black-soled feet. She wanted to jump out from her hiding spot and barrel headfirst into Zoey, sending her flying. She wanted to dig through Zoey's skull until she found her answer: *How did you find the stones?*

"I guess not," Marion said, doubtful. "I'm not sure I'll be able to sleep tonight."

"I'm not sure I'll be able to sleep again, *ever*," said Zoey.

Marion sat on the porch's top step. She wore a pale oversize sweater and dark shorts that showed off her soft white legs.

Val's fretful heart mewed inside the cage of her ribs like a hungry kitten.

"What happened to your fish?" Marion asked.

"Damn it. I totally dropped them when we ran." Zoey glared at the woods, hands on her hips. "So much for that. I'll have to think of something else. No way am I going back in there for a bag of dead fish."

"What's up with you and Val anyway? Why don't you like her?"

"I hate her," Zoey corrected. "She stole Thora from me,

turned her against me. I spent the three months before Thora's death being pissed at her because she chose Val over me."

Marion hesitated. Then, quietly, "How exactly did Val turn Thora against you?"

"I don't know," Zoey admitted. "But I'm not kidding, Marion. You should stay away from her. And Charlotte, too, though if tonight's party was any indication, it's too late for that."

"Too late?" Marion frowned, hugging her middle. "You make Val sound . . ."

"Dangerous? Good. Because she is. Her whole family is."

"I don't understand. Her family's dangerous because Val broke up you and Thora?"

Zoey laughed bitterly. "You're starting to sound like Grayson." She threw up her hands. "I don't have proof, all right? You got me. I just have my gut, and my gut's telling me that there's a connection between the Mortimers and the girls who've vanished—"

A car door slammed.

"Zoey? Home. Now."

Zoey straightened and squinted in the darkness. "Dad?"

Chief Harlow stopped at the edge of the yard, arms rigid at his sides. "Come on, let's go."

"What the hell?" Zoey looked as startled as Val felt. "Where'd you come from? How'd you know I—"

"*Now.*" Chief Harlow turned a little to the side, and past him Val spotted his patrol car—lights off, dark and hulking. He must have crept up the drive without headlights, Val too distracted to hear the crunch of his tires on the gravel.

"No explanation for showing up like this, all quiet and sneaky in the dark like a stalker?" Zoey stood at the bottom of the porch steps, arms crossed over her chest. "I told you I was going out tonight."

"You told me you'd be at Grayson's," Chief Harlow replied. "But Grayson called me an hour ago saying you'd left a party all upset, that some girl had hit you, and that he couldn't find you." Chief Harlow's voice sounded ready to splinter. "Yeah, Zoey, sorry to show up out of the blue and ruin your night, but I'm gonna drop everything and find you after a phone call like that."

Zoey glared at him for a long time, neither of them moving.

Marion cleared her throat. "Chief Harlow, I'm sorry, I've been talking to Zoey for a while and distracting her—"

"Don't apologize to him, Marion," Zoey snapped. "You didn't do anything wrong. And neither did I." With that, Zoey started walking toward the patrol car. When Chief Harlow reached out to touch her shoulder, she jerked away from him.

"I'll call you tomorrow," Zoey told Marion. She slammed the car door closed, nearly catching her father's fingers.

For a moment, he stood unmoving, staring away from the car, his shoulders rigid and his mouth in a furious thin line.

Interesting, thought Val. *Trouble in paradise?*

The thought brought her a savage satisfaction. She'd always watched Zoey and Chief Harlow with envy—how open they were with each other, how clearly the chief adored his daughter.

He muttered good night to Marion, slid into the driver's seat, and peeled out onto the driveway, headlights on and wheels squealing, apparently no longer so concerned with stealth.

Alone, Marion sat on the steps for a few quiet moments.

Then the song began.

Little fairy girl, skipping down the sea
Little fairy girl, pretty as can be

The melody floated down from a cracked-open window on the cottage's second floor. White curtains fluttered out into the night.

Marion stood, listening. Then she smiled, slow and easy, like the first spill of sunlight.

Val rose slowly to her feet in the shadows. Suddenly, she wasn't worried about stone circles and someday-daughters. Ice ribboned her body where her veins used to be.

That was Charlotte's voice, singing.

Charlotte, singing the lullaby Val's grandmother had always sung to her before she died.

Val's skin prickled, awakening. A shift in the air alerted her to his nearness; a shift in her gut reflected his appetite.

It was time.

Marion slipped inside the back door, and Val walked slowly to the cottage. For a moment she considered planting her feet in the dirt and saying, *No.*

Not tonight.

I need more time.

But only for a moment. His need pushed her on; if she kept him waiting, he'd throw her to the ground, send her convulsing, whack her head against the mud until she acquiesced. He'd do it all without leaving the woods. He'd do it from the inside out.

Val wasn't new to pain, but she didn't seek it out, either.

Maybe I should, she thought. *Maybe, if I were braver—*

Tears stung her eyes. Frantic, she blinked them away. She stumbled into the shrubbery, and from underneath the open window, she could hear everything the Althouse sisters said and did.

Charlotte: "Where've you been?"

Marion: "Couldn't sleep."

Charlotte: "Again? Where'd you go?"

Marion: "Nowhere." A sigh, a rustling of covers. "Can you sing to me? You were singing something just now. What was it?"

The egg that lived inside Val shifted, awakening. She licked her lips, tasted their cherry gloss.

"You know," Charlotte was saying, "I have no clue. I just made it up, I guess. Do you like it?"

No, you didn't, screamed Val's brain. *It's my grandmother's song. Are you too stupid to realize it? Can you not understand that you're being hunted?*

Of course not.

The girls he chose could never tell, not until the end.

Not until Val led them to it.

Marion: "I didn't know you could write songs."

Charlotte, laughing in delight: "Me neither! Sawkill inspires me, I guess."

Marion: "Sing it to me? Maybe it'll help me sleep."

"My little starfish," mumbled Charlotte, sleepy. Then she resumed her song. The lullaby of Sylvia Mortimer.

Who is the fellow with the bright clean grin?
Do you want, fairy girl, to weave a spell for him?

In the reflection of one of the cottage's first-floor windows, Val saw him moving behind her—a black shape that could have been described as a man, mostly. If she turned around, she knew she would find nothing but the hissing woods. Her reflection, though, it never lied. It showed him moving crookedly, listing to one side. A long coat. A wide smile, frozen in place like that of a doll.

He would, it seemed, play the boogeyman tonight. A favorite form of his.

They would wait, together, until the right moment.

It was almost time.

Almost.

MARION

The Cold Pillow

Whoever was kissing Marion was doing a good job.

God, it felt good to be kissed.

Over the past couple of years, she'd had a not inconsiderable number of wild fantasies involving virtually everyone she'd ever met.

No one seemed interested in kissing Marion in real life, so in her mind, she did it for them. Mr. Romero, her bookish history teacher. Katrina Day, the beautiful black girl who played the piano and used to sit in front of Marion on the bus. Duke O'Hara, the big, burly white boy with the gorgeous red curls.

In her mind, she'd straddle them on her couch, she'd tug them into the stairwell at school, she'd sneak into the quiet stacks at the library and let them press her up against the books and kiss her until her head buzzed.

But those kisses were never soft, like this one. They were urgent and frantic; they'd wake her up and have her slipping her hand between her legs, craving release.

This kiss, though—whoever was kissing her was so gentle it made her chest ache. Soft lips brushed against her own, whispered warm along her cheeks and jawline, traced her eyebrows with a sigh.

Once she thought she felt her dream lover's tongue slip between her lips—cautious, respectful, playful.

She arched up out of bed and awoke, a soft cry on her lips.

Her lips.

A moth sat there, on the curve of her bottom lip. A white moth with black spots like eyes on its wings. One, two, the wings beat slow and sure. Fur and tiny legs and twitching antennae, tickling Marion's mouth.

She screamed and smacked it away, hitting her jaw in the process.

The moth flew off, toward the window.

It wasn't alone.

Hundreds, thousands—the room was full of them. Tiny white moths, silent but frantic, an army of those black wing-eyes staring at her. They swirled around her bed, her legs. She flung off the sheets, scrambled to the center of the room. The moths covered the ceiling fan, the walls, the carpet. Charlotte's room shivered, a four-walled mass of wings and little furry feet.

"Get out of here!" Marion screamed, her skin wriggling and alive. "Get out, get away!"

She grabbed her sweater from the back of Charlotte's desk chair, sending up a flurry of moths. She swung the sweater through the room, smacking everything she could find. She knocked over the desk lamp; she shoved their father's framed art off the walls. She shook out the curtains, sent the moths flying. They were confused, they were a tornado. They settled on her arms and between her fingers and toes. They tugged her toward the window, and she couldn't fight them. They were tiny but they were many.

They whispered words she couldn't understand—high, soft voices, childlike, murmuring over one another.

Beware of the woods and the dark, dank deep.

The moth words fought their way into her mouth and down her throat like a sharp bite of food that hadn't been chewed properly. She hunched over, gasping. Not the hair, not again.

He'll follow you home—

The bedroom door flew open.

The moths rose into the air as one—silent wings flapping madly, black eyes staring.

Freed, Marion crouched on the floor by the window, hands over her head. Duck and cover.

"What do you *want*?" she screamed.

"Marion? Marion!" Hands grabbed her shoulders, shook her. "Stop screaming! What is it, baby?"

Marion's eyes flew open, trembling with terrified tears.

"Marion?" It was her mother, dark hair messy from sleep, discolored circles under her eyes because, Marion was convinced, her father's death had painted them there permanently. "What happened?" her mother asked. "Why were you screaming?" She glanced past Marion. "Where's Charlotte?"

Charlotte. *Charlotte.*

Suddenly, Marion knew what the moths had been whispering. A queasy, hot-cold feeling descended upon her skull like the drop of the final velvet curtain.

The moths hadn't been trying to kill her.

They'd been trying to tell her something.

Marion pulled free of her mother's grip and stumbled to Charlotte's bed. She'd fallen asleep there, early this morning, Charlotte's sleepy voice singing lullabies at her ear.

Marion felt Charlotte's pillow, the mattress where Charlotte had curled up beside her.

Where Marion had slept: warm and worn soft from Marion tossing and turning.

Where Charlotte had been, only a few hours ago: Cold. Cold like the open window. Cold like Marion's legs, shivering last night on the porch while she watched Chief Harlow drive Zoey away.

Marion stared at the pillow in her hands.

"Marion?" Her mother's voice, suddenly nervous. "What is it?"

The wings returned, buzzing at her ear, in her teeth, down her throat—not the moths' wings. The other ones, shiny and fluttering. The ones that belonged to the bones. A high whine threaded through the buzzing sound—one long nail, dragging across a shiny slab of metal. Across and down, down, down.

Marion followed the sound to the open window and looked down, squinting. The dawn light illuminated the grooves trailing through the flower bed. Ten furrows—eight fingers, two thumbs. Charlotte-size. They carved jagged lines through the dirt. Uprooted begonias and small chunks of mud lined their path.

Then, a few feet away, the marks vanished. Undisturbed grass. The soft call of a mourning dove.

"Marion?" Her mother knelt before her. *"Where's Charlotte?"*

Marion stared at her. She wanted to throw up everything she contained, stuff the viscera inside her mother's mouth so she wouldn't have to hear her talk, ever again, and ask horrible questions that required horrible answers.

But instead, she croaked, "Charlotte's gone."

IT HAD HAPPENED AGAIN.

And it would continue to happen, over and over—here on the Rock, and elsewhere throughout the wide-reaching world. The Rock would feel every meaningless death like a stab to the flesh of its great old aching heart.

If the Rock didn't act quickly, more would die, and soon.

But if it was simply a matter of action, the Rock would have long ago flattened every last one of the invaders into the ground, then swallowed them into oblivion.

Slaying the beast was a task the Rock could not complete alone.

The Rock felt its daughters' feet beat angry paths into its ravaged flesh, and sent out its call, and waited for them to wake up.

VAL

The Softie

Would the woman ever stop crying?

Val stood at the entrance to the Althouses' living room, wet tissues crumpled in her fists.

Chief Harlow and his deputy had arrived, and they were asking Mrs. Althouse questions about her missing daughter. It was a valiant effort but ultimately fruitless, because of the aforementioned crying.

Ugly crying, too, it was full-blown sobbing, with snot trails and great heaving breaths and unintelligible wailed words.

Val couldn't stand to look at the woman.

Val's lungs were stones in her chest, being screwed tighter and tighter into place by a relentless machine.

Val's ears rang with the memory of Charlotte's screams, and if she thought about the expression on Charlotte's face for one more second, that look right at the end when she appealed desperately to Val for help, then Val thought she very well might beat her head against the wall until her brains gave out.

But, for Val to do that, to put an end to things, she would have to scrape together a shred or two of courage.

So instead, she swallowed her disgust like downing a mouthful of poison, and watched Pamela Althouse sob.

If *Val* had disappeared, her mother wouldn't think to put on such a display. She would dab her eyes on occasion, answer Chief Harlow's questions succinctly and with a brave little smile that would make even that brainless deputy, brute that he was, gentle his voice and wonder if maybe Lucy Mortimer's soft hand on his shoulder meant he was special.

"I don't know what else to tell you," said Marion. She sat beside her mother, holding her mother's hand. Back straight, eyes clear, voice steady.

Mostly.

Val could hear a tiny trembling thread in that soft voice, which probably no one else noticed because of her mother's fit.

But Val noticed. Val noticed how Marion's other hand clutched the starfish charm around her throat.

Val noticed everything.

"I fell asleep next to Charlotte in her bed," Marion continued. "It was maybe three, three thirty."

Chief Harlow scribbled something in his notebook. "Shortly after I took Zoey home."

"That's right." Marion inhaled, her breath catching on tears, but her shoulders remained square. "She sang me to sleep.

When I woke up this morning, she was gone."

When Val swallowed, she tasted mud. She glanced down at her fingernails—clean, now, spotless and smooth. Cleaning her fingernails was always the first thing she did, after.

She kept her eyes open until they watered.

"Miss Mortimer?"

Val met Chief Harlow's eyes right as a tear slid down her cheek. She wiped her nose. "Yes, sir?"

Chief Harlow looked over his notes. "You had a party last night. Is that correct?"

"Yes, sir."

"And Charlotte attended this party?"

"Yes, sir."

He glanced up at her, his face unreadable. "It was in the usual place, I assume?"

Val bit the inside of her lip. Oh, how it grated on Ed Harlow that he couldn't do a damn thing about Val's parties in the woods, with the dry-brush bonfires and the underage drinking, and God only knows what else those kids got up to in the dark.

Once, he'd tried. One Sunday morning, he'd come marching up to Kingshead at dawn, Val at his elbow.

"Seems your daughter throws parties in the woods on Down Hill," the chief had said, once Lucy Mortimer opened the door. "I found piles of beer cans. The place reeked of alcohol."

"I see." Ms. Mortimer's blue eyes had slid to Val, taking her in from head to toe—clouds of blond hair, wide curls falling loose after a night outside in the damp.

"If you'll come with me, please, Chief," said Val's mother,

and then she and Chief Edward Harlow had disappeared into the Kingshead library, and Val had fled to her room.

A few minutes later, she'd watched the chief drift out to his car, like a fish cast off a line, caught but now discarded, and more than a little shaken.

He'd paused at the driver's side door, looked up at the window where Val stood between the drapes. He'd quickly averted his eyes, then slipped into his car and driven away, wheels spitting up gravel.

He hadn't bothered Val about her parties again.

"Yes, sir," Val said, showing Chief Harlow her sweetest smile. "The usual place."

His jaw clenched.

"Charlotte and I stayed out until, I guess it was two or so," Val continued. "We walked back to Kingshead together. Then she went to the cottage, and I went to my bedroom."

Chief Harlow turned a page in his notebook. "Others can vouch for you?"

Val nearly laughed. Yes, others could vouch for her. She could spin a hundred lies and find a hundred people to back her up without question.

"Yes, sir," she said. "I can send a few people from the party to the police station for questioning, if you'd like. Would that be helpful?"

Chief Harlow ignored her, his mouth thin. "And, Marion, you didn't go to this party?"

Val watched Marion closely. No, Marion hadn't gone to the

party. She'd gone for a stroll in the woods with her new friend.

"No," said Marion. "I was at home, reading, until maybe about one. I went on a walk and found Zoey. We hung out until you found us."

Marion glanced at Val, those big gray eyes of hers red-rimmed and sleepless. Val's throat zipped up to the back of her tongue.

"If that's all, Chief," Val said, turning away, "I've got to be going. My mother and I are bringing lunch to the search parties."

As Val left the cottage, she felt Marion Althouse's gaze resting on the hot tense spot between her shoulder blades like the scorch of a brand.

"You're upset."

Val fell to her knees as soon as she entered the stones, and lowered her head onto her arms. Breathing in the chalky white rocks, the caked black mud, the thick tangy scent that clung to the trees after a kill night, Val almost felt like herself again.

"Look up. Let me see you."

Val obeyed, sitting back on her heels. The hated boy-child stood before her, shimmering dark at the edges, eyes white and alert and unblinking. After eating, while he digested, his form shifted, and it was more difficult for him to believably look like a creature of this earth. Though today, Val noticed, only a few hours after his meal, he was already regaining cohesion. He could stand on his own; he didn't need to lean those pudgy boy hands against a tree to prop himself up.

He was indeed growing stronger. How many more kills would he need before he could break free and end them all?

Three?

Five?

One?

A cold, hard finger curled under Val's chin, forcing her to look up at the swaying branches, the half-baked sunlight fighting its way down.

"Who upset you?" he asked, inspecting her. "Who, Val?"

"No one," she replied. "I'm just tired. We had a long night."

"You're lying to me," came his cold voice, and then he was gone, off in the trees somewhere, shadow-shaped, brooding. "Stop lying to me."

Val lifted her fingers to her nose; she still smelled Charlotte's blood. He'd sprayed her with it. An unfortunate accident.

A loneliness so profound it felt like she'd been battered with it settled hard and cold in Val's belly. Her eyes filled with tears she didn't have to fake.

But she wasn't really alone, was she? Mortimer women never were. They lived at Kingshead, they kept their mothers' name, and they miscarried boys until they birthed a girl. They were vigorous and vital and so lovely they made people cry for wanting them, and they would have been long-lived, if he had allowed them that. They never got sick, and they never broke bones. The blood in their veins wasn't entirely their own, and that gave them power over the unwashed masses, made others sit up and listen, too afraid to interrupt. There was a magnetism to the Mortimer women, and they knew it, and they used it. It was their right, this witchery; they'd given up their souls for it.

So they grew up on the island, these enslaved goddesses, and taught their daughters how to keep him happy. How to serve him and feed him, how to guide his blind and fumbling self to the kill and lure in the catch, because it was that much sweeter to him, when his meals came willingly. A Mortimer woman taught her daughter how to keep him solid and strong in this world, how to never question his orders, how to remain in peak physical condition so he could draw upon her energy when he needed to and fortify himself.

And to never, *ever* speak of the Far Place—never ask what it is, never ask where it can be found, never ask why he fears it—*not unless*, her grandmother had said, wryly, *you crave his wrath.*

But sometimes Val did crave his wrath, if only because feeling it meant feeling *something.*

She closed her eyes. She needed to calm down.

"Tell me you're proud of me." It was barely a whisper.

"I'm proud of you," came his voice, curious and fond from the shadows.

Thank God, he hadn't left her. If he left her, she'd have nothing. If he left her, who would she be?

She'd thought about it, on occasion: Leaving. Rejecting this life she'd been born into and moving across the world and hiding. Talking to no one.

Hurting no one.

But he would find her, wherever she went. Val was sure of that. Or maybe another one would. She'd learned that much, from his sated ramblings after eating: He wasn't the only of his kind. In fact, there were many.

Maybe it was a good thing that she couldn't run and escape him. Maybe, without his presence and his will and his instructions, holding her up from the inside out, she'd collapse.

Maybe, after he fed enough to break free of her family, Val would disintegrate. Purposeless and aimless.

Would that be so terrible? The world would be better off.

But the idea of disintegrating terrified her. Val wanted to live. And if this life she'd been born into was the only one allowed her, then here she would stay, gutless and shackled.

She licked her dry lips. Her head fizzed, chaotic. She couldn't stop thinking of Marion's soft round face, how she'd held it together while her mother and her house and her life fell apart around her.

A quiet ache bloomed in Val's chest. She knew that feeling. She *breathed* that feeling.

"You're shaking," he observed, nearer now.

"I'm tired," she replied, hating the puny quality of her voice. "And Charlotte . . ."

Charlotte.

Natalie.

Thora.

"Charlotte what?" he asked.

Val shook her head. "Charlotte won't stop screaming in my mind."

After a moment, he said, sounding pleased, "You're so weak."

"Yes," she agreed. Her mother never cared about the girls she helped him hunt. Her mother never cracked, but Val was fracturing all over.

"You need a distraction."

Soft lips touched Val's own. She opened her mouth and her eyes, saw the pale-eyed, pale-faced form of Dr. Wayland bending over her. A small thrill shook her: He'd shifted forms so quickly it startled her. Once, it would have taken him long minutes. Once, he would have writhed in the dirt, half-made—part boy-child, part man, part monster—while Val watched in silence, guarding him.

But now—a blink, a shift, and he was changed, and he was kissing her.

The doctor was his favorite form for this kind of thing. Kissing fascinated him; he liked to experiment, and practice made him all the more convincing.

The kiss deepened. Val let it happen, craved it, welcomed it, fought ferociously against the tears rising behind her eyes. With one arm looped around her back, he lifted her to her feet. He would kiss the Althouse girls right out of her brain, then send her home, dazed, with a tender pat on the head.

He was such a softie when he carried buckets of blood in his belly.

ZOEY

The Spinney

There were five distinct woodlands on Sawkill Rock, a dark patchwork of wind-beaten trees hugging dozens of horse pastures:

The Down Woods, on the southern curve of the island, dense and wild, where Val had her parties.

The Stony Woods, which hugged the northern shore, sparse and boulder-strewn, ending in sheer slate cliffs that dropped off to choppy slate water.

The Spinney, inappropriately named because a spinney is a small cluster of trees, a mere thicket, and the Spinney was the largest woodland on Sawkill. Lazy and innocuous, it was on the western side of the island, facing the five tiny uninhabited islands called the Smalls, which lay about a mile out into the water. The western side was the soft side, the people of Sawkill called it, because it faced the mainland.

There were the Heart Woods, at the center of the island, thinner and sweeter than the others. Sheltered by the other woods, the town, the dead spot in the island valley where the winds couldn't reach so well.

And then there were the Kingshead Woods, stately and cold on the eastern shore. Named for Kingshead, the Mortimer family estate and the largest single-family property on the island.

Naturally.

That's where Zoey and Marion had stumbled upon that circle of stones—in the Kingshead Woods, downhill and downwood from Kingshead itself.

Zoey had been hiking through these woods with Search Team A for three hours, flashlights and whistles and walkie-talkies at the ready, before she managed to give her dad the slip and go off on her own.

He'd requested she stay near him. Scared, maybe, that another girl had gone missing and that his girl might be next? He wasn't the only one. Something had shifted in the two days since Charlotte's disappearance. Another girl gone, so soon after Thora? The air snapped quietly, like a bad winter come early. The streets hushed at twilight. You walked into a coffee shop, a restaurant, the grocery store, and jumped at the shadows of familiar shapes and looked at everyone who got too close with dread leaping up your throat.

Would you be next?

Zoey was not immune. *Will I be next?* she wondered, trudging through the woods a few yards from her father.

But if she hovered around him, she wouldn't be able to find

the stones again, and finding the stones was the priority.

She needed to see them for herself, alone, with her own two eyes, in the clear afternoon light. Was there really a tree wet with blood? Was there really some force that could throw girls off their feet?

As Zoey slipped away from the search party, her traitorous brain whispered: *Thora would have loved this.*

Not the fact of a missing girl, but the mystery of it, the potentially supernatural intrigue. First of all, Thora would have been able to say *potentially supernatural intrigue* with a straight face and a blazing conviction. She was a Believer. She saw the extraordinary in the ordinary, the magic in the mundane. It was, Zoey thought, why Thora's writing thrummed the way it did.

She could almost hear Thora's voice, rumpled from staying up too late reading aloud under Zoey's quilt: *Someday, we'll write real books together, Zo. You and me. We'll travel the world. We'll write stories that matter. Stories that save people.*

That word was awful: *Someday.* Once, Zoey had loved it. An authorial future, writing stories with Thora? Bashing about the world and turning over stones to find the secrets they sheltered? And then *writing* about them? It had been her greatest, most fervent dream. But now . . .

Now, Zoey couldn't imagine writing again. Not for a long time. Maybe not ever. Not when even looking at books made her feel sick to her stomach.

She certainly wouldn't write again until she found some actual goddamn answers.

Was her gut onto something, or was her gut full of shit?

The stones will know, thought Zoey, stepping into the Thora-owned part of her heart that she hadn't dared touch for months.

She could almost hear Thora's voice say it: *The stones will know*.

But when Zoey found the right spot—she would never forget that piece of land, how the earth turned down along that well-worn path that led to the stones, how the trees surrounded the circle like people come down from the mountain to pray—she found no path at all. Some thin grasses, some black Sawkill boulders. A small thicket of bone-dry trees gray as gulls.

Zoey ran her finger down the nearest tree. The bark scraped her skin. She pressed her finger harder, and the bark scraped harder, and when she finally pulled her hand away, it was brown and clean.

No blood this time.

Maybe no blood ever?

Zoey stood there, in the center of where the stones should have been, breathing hard. She looked around without moving her feet, checking the trees, the afternoon sky, her place on the island in relation to Kingshead itself.

If she looked back up the hill, through the whispering woods, she could see the top of Kingshead's peaked black roofs. Yes, this was the spot. This was it.

So what did it mean, then?

Zoey asked herself the question over and over as she scoured the woods, looking for her lost fairy circle.

What did this mean?

Thora, she thought, into the ether. *What does it mean?*

There were three possible answers:

One. She was in the wrong spot. But she knew she wasn't. She *wasn't.*

Two. She'd been hallucinating the stones. But she hadn't. Marion had been *thrown* from the stones. Zoey had touched a bloodstained tree.

Three. Someone—or something—was hiding them from her.

Thora's ghost whispered: *Because you weren't supposed to be there.*

Because that place wasn't yours to find.

When Zoey stopped walking at last, she had reached the edge of the Kingshead Woods. She watched as Val and her mother drove toward town in their silver Porsche SUV.

A branch snapped behind her.

"They're going to pass out sandwiches to the search teams, I think."

An electric shock snapped up Zoey's legs. Her fists clenched without her permission, and she dropped her phone. The hair on her arms stood up, and she had the sudden unquenchable desire to punch something.

She whirled, then froze. "Marion?" She exhaled, clapped a hand to her forehead. "*God.* You scared the hell out of me."

Standing a few feet away, Marion smiled. Amber afternoon light flooded the woods; branch-shaped shadows whispered across Marion's pale skin.

"Sorry," she said. "Didn't mean to."

Zoey's heart was pounding way too hard for her to know how to talk to a girl whose sister had gone missing. She glanced down; her arm hairs were seriously standing on end.

"Hey, so . . ." Zoey shook herself, tearing her gaze from her arms. "Are you . . . you know . . . okay?"

I really should not be allowed to speak to people, Zoey thought, wondering how weird it would seem if she thunked her head against the nearest tree a few times.

"I'm a little tired," said Marion quietly, "but that happens from time to time."

"I just . . ." Zoey tried to imagine losing a sister, and her body revolted, her stomach clenching up tight. Such thoughts were too close to Thora, too close to the long fugue of months through which Zoey had been dragging herself. "I'm so sorry, Marion. I don't even know what to . . . We'll find her. I know we will. My dad's got everyone out looking."

The words felt flimsy on Zoey's tongue, like ghosts of the words they should have been.

"It's fine," said Marion, shrugging.

Zoey blinked at her. "It's *fine*?"

"I saw you, and I thought it would be fun to walk with you." Marion moved a step closer, watching Zoey keenly. A tongue of wind snapped through the trees, pulling thin black strands of hair across her cheeks. "What are you looking for?"

"The stones." Zoey, her heart rate picking up speed once more, felt torn. On the one hand, Marion was grieving, and most likely needed the comfort of a friend.

On the other hand, Marion was acting really fucking strangely, and Zoey kind of wanted to not be there anymore.

She took a step back. Her shins burned, like she'd scratched them too hard and irritated her skin. "You're acting weird."

Marion tilted her head to the side. "How?"

"Uh . . . that?" Zoey waved her hand at Marion and took another step back. Marion followed—a step for a step. "Also, you're not blinking."

"You mentioned stones," said Marion, blinking with great emphasis—once, twice, thrice. "What stones are those?"

The back of Zoey's neck prickled. "The ones we saw the other night? The ones that threw you through the trees?"

Marion smiled kindly. "I don't know what you're talking about. Maybe we should go look for them together. Maybe you can show me?"

"You don't . . ." Zoey's mouth went dry. "You don't remember?"

"I'm afraid not." Marion reached for Zoey's hand. "Are you sure you aren't imagining things?"

"How can you not remember?" Had she really imagined the whole thing? But they'd *talked* about it, after. They'd talked on Marion's porch. "Please tell me you're joking."

"Just come here." Marion's gentle voice suddenly had a slight edge to it. "Come here, and we'll go together."

"Zoey?" The voice of her father's deputy, Sergeant Montgomery, came booming through the trees. "Where'd you go?"

Marion whirled, black hair flying. She recoiled, like an animal caught rooting through the trash cans.

"Right here!" Zoey waved, hurrying away from Marion. She saw the sergeant's hat, suddenly ready to burst out crying with gladness. "Over here, Marion and I were—"

A shift in the air behind her made Zoey turn with a yelp.

Marion was gone.

"Zoey?" Sergeant Montgomery sounded not too pleased with her. "Your father's looking for you. You really shouldn't go running off, considering the circumstances." His walkie-talkie crackled to life, and he turned away to answer it.

Zoey thought she saw a dark shape that could have been Marion's swinging, shining hair flitting away through the trees. She retrieved her phone, half crawled up a ridge blanketed with damp leaves—away from the distracted deputy, away from where Marion had been standing.

Or . . . not Marion?

Zoey's vision pitched from side to side; the citizens of Wonderland were rearranging the planes of the world so she could never find her way back home. She clamped her right hand over her left arm, tried to rub away the goose bumps.

Then, thumbs shaking, she texted her father:

Staying at Grayson's tonight. Be home for breakfast.

To Grayson she sent:

Meet me in the woods at the bottom of Kingshead Drive as soon as humanly possible.

Bring your lock picks. Just in case.

MARION

The Mansion

Marion couldn't stay inside the cottage for one more minute.

With Charlotte gone, the whole structure seemed to be shrinking. She'd be crushed in this house of ever diminishing returns.

"Mom?" She slipped into the master bedroom on the first floor, a tray of food in her hands. "You awake?"

Pamela Althouse lay flat on her bed, the heavy drapes drawn shut. At Marion's approach, she turned away, let out a tearful moan.

"Charlotte," she murmured. "Please, Charlotte. *Please*, come home."

Marion set the tray on the nightstand. Dry-eyed, her thoughts thin and gummy, she stroked her mother's shivering back.

"It's okay, Mom." She said it again and again, this mindless lie. "She'll come back. They'll find her. It's gonna be okay."

She lied through her teeth until her mother had fallen asleep. She did this every few hours—soothe her mother back into a fitful sleep with cuddles and falsehoods.

Because she knew—the moths had told her—that Charlotte was gone. She wasn't just missing. She no longer existed. Marion didn't know how, or why, but she knew that much. She knew it like she knew her own name.

With the Mortimers gone to the police station to help the search parties, Marion had Kingshead to herself.

Ms. Mortimer had told the remaining Althouses—*two down, two to go!*—not to worry about the housework just now. They needed time to rest, to work with the police.

But Marion liked the work. It occupied her cells and kept them from endlessly spinning.

And besides that, she wanted to investigate.

Investigate *what*, she wasn't altogether sure, but she couldn't stop thinking about what Zoey had said: *My gut's telling me that there's a connection between the Mortimers and the girls who've vanished.*

Which, honestly, sounded like something of a wild conspiracy theory to Marion, but her sister was gone, her Charlotte, and the heart-hole her father's death had left in her chest had been pushed open so wide she felt like one false move could send her splitting into two irreparable pieces.

So she started off dusting, because Kingshead was flush with ornamental wood carvings, ancient chests and chairs with clawed feet, banisters thick as serpents.

Clean one railing, one leg, one tabletop, and move on.

Scan the books, the art, the furniture, the walls. Suspicious papers left untended? Significant artifacts that could double as murder weapons?

Marion worked her way through the house in her bare feet. She felt along the main hallways, looking for cracks in the dark wood paneling. Secret entryway, leading to some lair that revealed all?

Marion laughed, which was a mistake. It knocked loose a few tears, and she leaned heavily against the railing on the second-floor landing, overlooking the green-and-glass winter garden. She clutched the polished banister so hard she wondered if she'd bruise her palms.

She thought Charlotte's name on repeat until she could think it without wanting to throw up.

She retrieved her dust cloth and kept moving.

Art hung on the walls in dark gold frames—renderings of Sawkill, mostly. The Down Woods, the Spinney, the Black Cliffs on the western shore.

A thin and far-off whine ground against the gears of Marion's brain, dragged its claws along the chalk of her bones.

"Quiet," she told the bone cry, but it didn't listen.

Instead, it pulled at her stomach, like it had the night Charlotte had disappeared, when she'd followed the bone cry into the woods and found Zoey, and the stones.

It was like a resonance, fisting in the soft skin of her belly and tugging her on. She resisted, dug her heels into the carpet.

The resonance remained, waiting. Respectful, though. It didn't pull her against her will.

Marion swallowed, shook her head to dislodge the grinding metallic shriek reverberating up through her skeleton.

The vibrations thrummed to her: *Follow me.*

Marion swallowed, and agreed.

She hurried through the house, following the bone cry's moaning trail. Guest rooms, a study, a small parlor decorated in pastels, a music room with mirrored walls and a grand piano. Another set of stairs, on the house's east side, and another, by the kitchen.

Closed doors, marking the Mortimers' bedrooms. The bone cry grew louder still. Marion put her fingers in her ears; that made it worse.

She paused outside a closed door that stood all alone at the end of a wide hallway. The bone cry jerked to a halt, making her stumble, and then fell silent.

Val's room?

Marion's fingers caressed the door. They hovered over the door handle, considering.

What would she find inside?

She touched the latch, ready for a peek.

Something cold and urgent pinched her fingertips, like the air around them had snapped in two.

"Ow!" She sucked on her fingers. Val's door latch grinned a metal grin.

Downstairs, a door opened—an explosion in the vast, freshly dusted silence.

Marion turned and listened. When she heard voices, she hurried downstairs, remembering with a sudden burst of alarm that she'd forgotten to lock the back door. She came to the bottom of the stairs right as the intruders started up them.

The boy jumped so hard Marion thought he'd fall over. His hand flew to his chest. He blew out a startled, "Good God."

"Marion!" Zoey stared at her, frozen on the bottom step. She looked as though Marion had dropped some cursed relic into her lap. "How long have you been here?"

Marion glanced at the grandfather clock ticking ponderously against the wall. "About an hour, I guess?"

"But I *just* saw you. Like, twenty minutes ago. In the woods."

"I haven't been outside today," Marion said. "Just here and home. It must have been someone else."

"But I talked to you." Zoey's face was crumpling fast. "We had a conversation. I saw you, right there." Zoey waved her hand around. "Right in front of me, just a few feet. We *spoke*."

A slow chill pattered across Marion's arms.

The boy Marion didn't know frowned at Zoey. "Somebody in one of the search teams, maybe?"

"No. *No*." Zoey gripped chunks of hair in her hands. "It was Marion. If it wasn't . . ."

Zoey's distress was contagious. Marion glanced at the boy,

her own panic rising fast. "I'm sorry, who are you?"

"Oh, sorry." The boy stepped forward, extended his hand. "Grayson Tighe. Zoey's best friend."

Zoey blew out a slow breath. "Marion, you swear you've been here for an hour?"

"I swear," Marion replied. "Maybe a little less than that? But not much."

"But this doesn't make *sense*. I was in the Kingshead Woods, I was searching for—"

Zoey stopped talking. She watched Marion carefully.

Marion glanced at Grayson, unsure of how much to say around him. She'd been so preoccupied with Charlotte, with her mother, that she hadn't had a moment to think about it for the past couple of days, but now, with Zoey here, the memory returned to her in shadowed flashes.

"The stones?" Marion said quietly.

"You remember." Zoey's eyes glittered with tears. "You saw them?"

"Of course. I've got a giant bruise on my butt from where I landed."

Grayson's eyebrows knotted. "Wait. You saw these stones, too?"

"See?" Zoey grabbed Grayson's sleeve. "I told you! Oh, Marion. Oh, thank God." Zoey flung her arms around Marion's shoulders and held on tight. "When I saw you in the woods, you didn't remember. You were acting so weird, I thought I was losing my mind, but— Hey."

Marion, without realizing what was happening until it was

too late, had begun to cry. It was as though she'd been wandering through a mist that blocked the sun, and now Zoey's arms around her had ripped away the gray, leaving the world too bright, too sharp, too painful.

Charlotte.

Not even death can part our souls.

Sisters two and sisters true.

She clutched the starfish charm at her neck, let out a choked sob.

"Hey," Zoey said again. Her hand cradled the back of Marion's head. "Hey, it's okay."

"She's gone," Marion whispered against Zoey's soft abundance of dark curls, once she'd found her voice. "She's *gone*."

"We'll find her. My dad's out looking, the whole force, the whole island."

Marion shook her head against Zoey's shoulder. How could she explain the moths?

"I don't think they will," she mumbled.

Zoey pulled away, searched Marion's face. "Why do you say that?"

Marion couldn't meet her eyes. They'd shared the experience of the stones, but as far as Marion knew, Zoey hadn't seen any talking moths, and . . . maybe that was one bridge too far. "Just a feeling," she said simply.

"They never found Thora, either." Zoey crossed her arms miserably over her chest. "Sorry. That isn't helpful. *God.* I need to stop talking. I'm a really awkward person. It's a chronic condition."

"Well, that's painfully true." Grayson, coming in from the next room, held out a glass of water and a handful of tissues. "I found a box in the kitchen."

"Thank you." As Marion wiped her face, she noticed how Zoey looked at Grayson—her eyes shining, her smile tiny and adoring. "You two are dating?"

"Used to," Grayson said, pushing his glasses up his nose in a Clark Kent–ish fashion that made Marion instantly like him. "Now we're friends."

"Best friends," Zoey corrected.

Grayson smiled softly at her. "Best friends."

Marion, aching a little as she watched them, suddenly remembered a strange thing. "Wait. You said, when you saw me in the woods, I didn't remember the stones. What did you mean by that?"

Zoey hesitated. "It's gonna sound nuts."

"Tell her, Zo," said Grayson. "Tell her what you told me."

"I saw you, a little while ago, in the Kingshead Woods." Zoey squared her thin shoulders and looked Marion straight in the eye. "I talked to you. You didn't remember the stones, but you wanted to go with me to find them. You wanted me to show you. You . . ." Zoey shifted uneasily. "You weren't blinking. You were moving in this weird way that didn't seem like you. Then my dad's deputy came over and you ran away."

Marion's heart pounded drums of doom in her ears. "But I didn't. I've been here. I don't . . . I don't remember any of that." She stepped back, a little dizzy. "You saw wrong."

Zoey shook her head. "I didn't."

"Then . . . what? I just don't remember? I've lost the memory?" Marion laughed bitterly. "It would make sense, I guess. I fell, I hit my head, now my memory's shot."

But she didn't believe that. She remembered absolutely everything since waking up two days ago in a world without Charlotte. She could account for every last excruciating second.

"But you don't believe that," said Zoey, watching her.

Marion shook her head. "No."

"So where does that leave us?" Grayson scratched the back of his head, frowning.

"If you saw me, but it wasn't me," said Marion, "then logic suggests—"

"It was someone else," Zoey finished.

Grayson sighed, staring despairingly at the ceiling. "What's that quote?"

"'When you have eliminated the impossible,'" Marion suggested, because she'd been thinking the same thing, "'whatever remains, however improbable, must be the truth.'"

Grayson smiled at her. "I knew I liked you."

"Some of the stories Thora told me about the Collector," Zoey said quietly, glaring at one of the nearby Sawkill paintings, "is that the monster could take different forms, depending on who he was trying to catch."

At Zoey's words, the drafty house air twisted across Marion's skin. "These stories, they're just things everyone knows?"

"Local Sawkill legends. Every place has them, right? People create their own folklore based on where they live and what actual real-life things happened there."

"Like girls who go missing?" Marion suggested, her voice hollow.

Zoey took Marion's hand fiercely in her own, which made Marion feel a little less like she might float away on the tide of her own grief.

"Thora loved the stories," said Zoey. "She adored creepy shit, loved how legends form and change. She was like the resident expert on the Collector. And . . . Oh, what was that one rhyme? *Beware the kind face you see by the gate. He'll sidle up close and it'll be too late.*"

And then Marion could think of nothing but trusting, openhearted Charlotte being called out of her room by a friendly face, someone she thought she could trust, someone she wouldn't think twice about leaning out the window to say hello to . . .

She heard herself make a terrible noise, but didn't realize she had moved away from Zoey until she stubbed her toe on the bottom stair and yelped in pain.

"Zoey," Grayson said gently, "can we maybe not with the creepy rhymes right now?"

Marion ignored him, tears in her eyes. "So you think there's a monster who can disguise itself?" she asked Zoey. "And it's . . . out there, somewhere? You think it got Charlotte?"

Zoey nodded, shoulders hunched. "Yes. Maybe. I don't know."

"And you think Val and her mom are somehow involved?"

"Val was friends with Natalie Breckenridge, who disappeared. And Thora Keller, who disappeared. And now

Charlotte, who's . . . who has disappeared." Zoey's eyes were bright. "You tell me."

Marion nodded slowly, then glanced at Grayson. "And you think this, too?"

Grayson shrugged. "Honestly, it all sounds ludicrous to me, but . . ." He looked at Zoey with such unwavering focus that Marion lost her breath a little. "I trust Zoey."

Zoey marched over and embraced Grayson hard enough to make him stumble. Face buried in his shirt, she said, muffled, "Thank you."

Grayson's arms went around Zoey as automatically as breathing. "So now what?" he asked, his voice a little rough.

"I was searching the house when you came in," Marion said, turning away from them before her heart imploded with jealousy—but she didn't get far.

A set of colossal double doors stared her down from the far wall, across the foyer. As soon as Marion laid eyes on them, the bone cry pitched back into her skull like a crash of glass that wouldn't end.

There.

Marion moved across the polished brick floor. She hadn't been in that room yet, she didn't think. It was hard to keep track of such a labyrinth, especially when her sister had up and vanished.

Eyes blurring, ears ringing from the horrible rattling cry clogging her every vein, Marion reached for the latch on the right door—a grooved metal knob—and then lurched to a stop.

She hunched over like someone had kicked her in the tenderest bend of her gut. She opened her mouth for a scream that never came.

The bone cry vanished. In its place, something mean and soundless and foreign gripped her, rooted her down.

She could go no farther. No, this was the end of the line. A bilious feeling rose up in Marion's insides, following the old track of horse hair:

Trespassers will be taken out back and hanged.

MARION

The Library

Marion forced her eyes open, even though something hard and heavy was pressing them down, trying to keep her blind.

The doors, the double doors a few feet away from where she stood—black and monumental they were, carved shapes covering their every inch. Vines and peaches one minute; then the lamplight shifted, or maybe Marion's brain shifted, and they metamorphosed into tongues and plump hearts.

Marion tried to move away, but the doors held her in their gravity.

Heat skewered her, temple to temple. Her world was static—black, white, and crackling.

This was different than the bone cry. This was a warning, and a punishment. Something was trying to keep her away—but from what?

The double doors slammed against Marion's head. Trying

to flatten her, clamp her like a vise, squeeze out her juice to serve at suppertime.

And then Marion remembered. Lucy Mortimer's instructions floated blithely back to her.

The double doors in the north foyer. This is my private space. My library. Please leave it untouched.

Marion gasped out a shrill bite of laughter. *Oops.*

"Marion. Marion! Look at me."

Marion forced her eyes back open. Squinted through the pain to see Zoey crouched before her, Grayson at her side.

"I can't," Marion gasped, squeezing her eyes shut once more. It hurt too much, to exist in this static-filled world. The noise was digging into her every orifice, clogging her lungs and blocking up all the exits.

"We should call an ambulance," came Grayson's frantic voice.

Zoey snapped, "Chill out, Grayson, she's fine."

"She's not fine! Look at her!"

Marion broke free of Zoey's grip, slammed her head into the library doors. It hurt, but if she cracked her head open, she could never break the rules again.

"What the *hell*?" Grayson cried.

Something small but strong grabbed Marion, yanked her back into a soft surface. Arms came around her, legs hooked over hers.

"Let me go!" Marion shrieked, thrashing in the grip of her captor.

"No," Zoey said firmly, her lips next to Marion's ear. "I'm

not going to let you hurt yourself. Grayson, get her legs."

"Oh my God, oh my God," muttered Grayson, obeying.

Marion began to sob. Her limbs were being pulled in twenty different directions. "Zoey?"

"I'm right here, Marion," said Zoey.

Through chattering teeth, Marion inhaled. "I'm scared."

"It's okay. You can be scared. Just hold on."

Minutes passed. Marion's energy seeped away, water spiraling down a long dark drain. Her body relaxed.

She wilted in Zoey's arms, turned her cheek into the warmth of Zoey's shoulder.

"You okay?" Zoey asked quietly.

"I don't know." Marion's voice was ruined. "I think so?"

"You're lucky you didn't crack your head open," said Grayson, holding his own head, his eyes wide.

Like father, like daughter. One lucky, one not. Marion let out a shaky sound. "I guess I am."

"What happened?" Zoey's expression was grave.

Marion sucked in a breath, hesitating. Surely she couldn't say such a thing aloud? But Zoey's big brown eyes held neither judgment nor skepticism.

"The doors didn't want me to touch them," Marion replied.

Zoey nodded at once. "Like the stones didn't want you inside them, so they threw you out."

The relief of discussing the impossible made another impossible thing—Charlotte's return—seem a fraction more likely. The fantasy of that gave Marion the strength to rise to her feet.

Zoey jumped up to support her.

"Ever since the accident," Marion began, "I've been hearing this sound."

"The crying bones," Zoey said matter-of-factly.

"The bone cry," Marion corrected.

"Semantics."

"Well. Sometimes I hear the cry in my sleep and it wakes me up. Sometimes I hear it randomly in the middle of the day. And when I hear it, I have to follow it. Like you know when you're in danger and you have to run. I don't know what it means, but I think . . . I think it's trying to tell me something." She glanced at the library. "It told me to touch the doors."

"But then the doors . . ." Grayson waved his hand at them. "They tried to hurt you."

"Which means they have something to hide," Marion decided.

Zoey nodded grimly. "I agree."

Grayson looked back and forth between them. "You want to go inside, don't you?"

"I do," said Marion, as Zoey said, "Of course."

Grayson blew out a breath, then slid his hands into his hair. "Why is this happening?"

Zoey looked affronted. "You're not chickening out on me."

"No, I meant *this*," Grayson clarified, gesturing at Marion, at the doors, at the island itself. "Why is all of *this* happening?"

Marion stepped toward the doors, then hesitated. "Maybe someone else should try opening it."

Zoey took her place at once, but Grayson stopped her with a gentle hand on her elbow.

"Please, Zo," he said quietly. "Let me?"

Zoey glared up at him, looking prepared to scold, and then her expression softened. She relented, stepping back and letting Grayson approach the doors. He reached for the right handle, paused, reached again.

Marion tensed, her skin prickling.

His fingers touched the metal, depressed the latch—and nothing happened.

"It's locked," Grayson reported.

Zoey hurried over. "So pick it."

Marion crept closer. With each step, the doors seemed to loom taller, like a cartoon with its proportions gone wrong. "You know how to pick locks?"

"He's a man of many talents, my Grayson," said Zoey, chucking Grayson lightly on the arm. "You look at him and think he's all virtuous, but don't be fooled by those baby blues."

He frowned at the door, scratching the back of his neck. "You know, on second thought, Ms. Mortimer is not a woman I want to piss off. And I'm sure Marion doesn't want to get in trouble—"

"Grayson," said Marion calmly, "if there's something past these doors that could help me find my sister, or prove that Val or anyone in her family have information about what happened, I'm sure you can understand why I'm not concerned about getting in trouble."

Grayson slid his glasses to rest on top of his head, scrubbed a hand over his face, and sighed. "Why do I let myself get dragged into situations like this?"

Zoey beamed at him. "Because you love me."

Grayson stiffened. An instant later, Zoey did, too. The smile faded from her face. She stepped carefully away from him.

"Sorry," she mumbled, fists clenched at her sides. "Grayson, I'm—"

"It's fine," he said quietly. He pulled picks from his pocket and got to work. A few tense minutes later, the lock clicked open.

Marion braced herself as she led the way inside, expecting the furious static to return, or some many-eyed monster to come leaping out with fangs bared.

But it was just a library, like one might find in any old ancient mansion—bay windows, shelves from floor to ceiling, a ladder on wheels for the higher-ups. Cushy red velvet chairs, one with a cozy throw draped over the arm. A quiet hearth.

"We should not be in here," whispered Grayson. "This is trespassing."

Zoey snorted. "You're just now worried about trespassing?"

Marion moved past them, scanning the shelves for some kind of proof, *any* kind of proof—something that would leap at her, itch at her, something she would have to look twice at, something about missing girls, something that would wake up the bone cry again and make that strange fist grope once more at her belly, tugging her toward the answer.

She walked along the bookshelves, ghosting her fingers through the air beside the books' spines, too wary to touch them.

"What percentage of these books do you think Their Royal Highnesses have actually read?" Zoey mused. She picked up a marble horse figurine from an end table. "Eight? Eight point two?"

Something sharp snagged on Marion's drifting hand and yanked her to a halt. A vibration rocketed up her legs, straight to her fingers. A whine began, deep inside her ears, like the rub of a dry bow against an out-of-tune string.

Here.

She inspected her buzzing fingers, the same ones that had touched Val's door. No wounds. She peered more closely at the bookcase before her, touching every shelf and spine.

"What'd you find?" Zoey whispered, coming up behind her.

"Not sure. I had this feeling, though. Something stopped me, right here."

"Oh my God. Look." Zoey shifted, squinting at the row of books at eye level.

Marion followed her gaze, pivoting until she achieved the right angle of lighting—an uninterrupted line of dusty books, except for four.

They were marked by fingerprints.

Marion and Zoey exchanged a glance.

Grayson whispered, "Please don't."

But Marion did. She reached out and slid the closest

fingerprinted book back against the shelf.

It caught on something, clicked, and locked into place.

Grayson swore quietly.

Zoey stared, eyes huge. “Keep going.”

Marion did. One book, two books, three books, four.

The bookcase swung a few inches loose from the wall, revealing a set of narrow stone steps that circled down into the earth. A wood-raftered ceiling dotted with naked light bulbs in black wire casing. Gleaming wood-paneled walls.

As she stood on the top step, looking down, the light bulbs flickered to life. The bone cry grew layers, harmonizing discordantly with itself. The whine of it hurt Marion’s teeth. Like one of her moths, drawn to the amber glow, she took one step forward. Then another, and another. The passageway was cold and dry. She exhaled; her breath fogged the air. She took another step.

Zoey caught her hand, the one the books had pricked. At Zoey’s touch, the throb in Marion’s finger lessened, like dipping overheated skin in cold water.

Marion glanced back at her. “You all right?”

Zoey nodded—wide-eyed, square-jawed, her other hand wrapped firmly around Grayson’s. “We’re all right. We’re with you. Keep going.”

Inside Marion’s frantically beating heart blossomed a tiny cautious warmth. She squeezed Zoey’s hand, then turned and continued down. She counted each step as she walked—three, nine, fifteen, twenty-one.

At the bottom of the stairs, they emerged into a tiny foyer, lit by a single light bulb and a thin moon-white window that looked up out of the earth and past a line of shrubs.

"What the hell?" Zoey murmured, peeking over Marion's shoulder and into the room past the foyer.

The door was slightly ajar. Marion hesitated, then pushed it open. On the other side: nothing but a four-poster bed, piled high with red and plum silk.

The walls were bare. No art, no light switches. Just a single softly glowing lamp, stuck into the wall beside the bed.

"The lamp's on," Grayson observed tightly.

"Do you think it turned on when we opened the door upstairs?" Zoey whispered.

Marion didn't answer. She stared at the other door, across the room—dark wood, heavy-looking and plain. Barely visible in the shadowed wall. Where it led, she couldn't imagine.

But worse—

Zoey must have seen, too, at the same moment; Marion heard her soft gasp.

Grayson, panicked: "What? What is it?"

Claw marks.

Or were they tracks from fingernails?

Marion didn't want to get close enough to investigate further. They crisscrossed the wall above and beside the bed. Tally marks carved by a lunatic, counting the days in this bedtime cell. They cut grooves in the tall dark bedposts. They even—Marion did dare take one step closer, squinting—yes, they even marked up the floor surrounding the ruffled red bed skirt.

She couldn't ignore the fact of the bed.

Were the claw marks because someone had been having the time of their life?

Or because someone had been fighting for it?

Zoey put her hands in her hair, let out a shaky laugh. "What the shit is this?"

From outside and above, a distant car door slammed. Then another.

Marion whirled, looking wildly for the small foyer window. She half expected to see Val's mother crouched beside it to peer through the glass, searching for them.

Grayson led them running back up the stairs, the lights switching off at their heels. Back in the library, they pulled the secret door closed. Marion tugged the four books back out of their grooves to match up with the others. Grayson tugged up the hem of his shirt and frantically wiped them clean.

"Fingerprints!" he hissed.

"You dumbass." Zoey tugged him away. "The books were dusty, now they're not!"

"Go!" Marion shoved them both toward the library doors, still standing ajar. "Out the front door. I'll stall them at the kitchen."

Zoey nodded, mouth in a thin line. She lunged forward and hugged Marion so tight and close that fresh tears sprang to Marion's eyes.

Then Zoey fled, Grayson at her side—two shadows in a dark palace.

VAL

The Fireflies

Val stepped out of her mother's car and stood at the driveway's edge.

She faced away from Kingshead, listening to the precision clicks of her mother's heels against the pavement.

The mansion sat on a crest of land, the highest point on Sawkill, so in front of Val stretched the entirety of the island—first the stables, the training paddocks, the grazing pastures. Miles of black fences in perfect condition, dotted with gray barns full of sleepy Mortimer Morgans. On the horizon shimmered the amber windows of downtown Sawkill, and every now and then a pair of white lights marked a car winding its way across the island from wood to wood, farm to farm.

But that night Val could only watch the bobbing fireflies, moving slow and steady through her family's woods. Flashlights that searched, but would never find.

"Charlotte!" a distant male voice cried.

The search teams had been out all day, and Val had dutifully manned her post at the police station—handing out sandwiches, coffee, water bottles. The teams would keep searching all night, all day, until Charlotte was found.

"Charlotte?" A woman's voice, that time. "It's okay, honey! We're gonna find you!"

Val stared at the fireflies so long she could have sworn she felt wings kissing her eyelashes.

Then she turned and made her way inside, shoulders back and head high. The long day had made her tired; she could hardly keep her eyes open. She would sleep soon, and well.

So she told herself, as the plaintive calls followed her indoors:

"Charlotte!"

"Charlotte?"

"Charlotte, come home!"

Inside, Val found her mother sitting with Marion at the kitchen table.

The sight stopped Val dead in her tracks.

"Oh, good," said Ms. Mortimer, blue eyes flicking up to meet her daughter's. She smoothed back Marion's hair and stood. Her own hair, in a tidy blond knot at the back of her neck, gleamed in the soft kitchen light. "Valerie, could you sit with Marion for a moment? I'd love to get out of these clothes."

"Sure," Val heard herself saying, like an idiot, because being alone with Marion Althouse was the last thing she wanted to do at the moment.

Val had managed to put Charlotte's dying sounds out of her mind all day, but now, staring at Marion, the girl's big gray eyes forlorn and red-rimmed, Val heard them again.

And again.

And again.

Ms. Mortimer squeezed Marion's shoulder, and on the way out the door, her fingers brushed against her daughter's. Every touch of Lucy Mortimer's, every glance, meant something. This meaning was clear: *Get her out of my house, as quickly as possible.*

In the silence, Marion and Val stared at each other. Marion held a cup of steaming tea between her hands; it looked unsipped. She blinked. Two quiet tears raced each other down her cheeks.

Val, once again idiotically, felt inspired to ask: "Are you okay?"

But Marion didn't scorn her for the question; she shook her head, her face crumpling.

"Come on." Suddenly, inexplicably, knowing that this was *not* what her mother had meant, Val held out a hand. "Let's go on a walk."

There was a small overlook on the rocky cliffs behind Kingshead, facing the sea. Val took Marion there, leading her carefully down the switchback trail. Solar lights stuck throughout the rocks lit the way in soft white patches.

Marion's feet were bare, Val realized about halfway down. "Do you want to go back?" Val gestured at her feet. "The rocks can get sharp."

Marion shook her head. Her gaze was fixed on the sea; her windswept hair carved glossy black lines across her face.

"No, it's okay," said Marion softly, and offered a small, crooked smile that pounded Val's murderous heart like hateful fists out for blood.

A bench marked the stretch of gray rock where Val liked to go when she needed to escape from her mother, from Collin Hawthorne, from *him*. It was tiny and weathered, its paint a peeling sage green. It seemed transplanted from another, shabbier world, far from the regal one of Kingshead.

"Well," Val said, gesturing pointlessly at the bench.

Marion sat, hands clasped in her lap. A blast of sea wind raced up the cliffs, and when Val saw Marion shivering, she knew she shouldn't—she *knew* it—but she sat beside Marion anyway, scooted as close as she dared. Thigh to thigh.

"It can get kind of cold out here," she explained. Again, pointlessly.

God help me, Val thought. *I must be losing my mind. Get a grip, Valerie.*

Then, at the idea of any god helping a creature like herself, she stifled a laugh. Stuck in her throat, the sound felt sad, like the start of a sob.

"I like it," said Marion, hugging herself. Her fingers bumped against Val's bare arm. "It's quiet. Well, not quiet. The waves are loud, and the wind, but . . . no people. No one watching you or needing you. You'd be hard to find, if the person looking for you didn't know about this spot. You'd be as good as gone."

Marion inhaled, her breathing ragged. She sat very still for a moment, then brought a shaking hand to her mouth.

Val watched her, an oily weight settling in her stomach. She imagined, for an instant, throwing herself off the cliff to the rocks below. Was hell real, and if it was, would whatever punishment she'd receive there be more bearable than this?

Was hell the Far Place he so dreaded? If Val did throw herself down into the sea, would she end up there, in the scorching company of devils even worse than the one she currently served?

"The night she disappeared," Marion was saying, "I fell asleep wondering what it would be like if she didn't need me anymore. If she . . ." Marion glanced at Val. "Well, if she was your friend, actually. If you got close. Then maybe you could take care of her for a while, and I wouldn't have to. I started wondering what I would be without her crying on me all the time, and then I tried to remember what it felt like to exist before Dad died. When Mom was still herself, not this . . . shadow of who she used to be. When Charlotte wasn't so needy. I tried to remember, and I couldn't." Marion shook her head, gripped her knees hard.

Val's blood ran hot as the hellfire that licked through her dreams. All Mortimer women, since Val's great-great-great-grandmother, enjoyed raging-hot blood—one of the side effects of being linked through the generations to a beast. Val could sleep naked in the dead of winter and awaken painted with sweat. She could plunge to the depths of the icy Atlantic and come up needing a cold drink.

But every time Marion shifted beside her, Val's skin erupted in goose bumps. So enamored was she of the sensation—the slap-you-awake sting of it—that she didn't realize at first that Marion had begun to cry again.

"Actually," Val said, staring at the crashing black water below their feet, "I know what it feels like, to be trapped like that."

She felt Marion look over at her. "You?" she asked, surprise in her voice.

"Long story," Val said darkly, "but . . . yes. My mother has a lot of expectations for me. Ideas about what my future should look like, and the kind of person I should be. My mother is . . ."

After a beat of silence, Marion suggested, "Terrifying?"

Val laughed before she could think better of it. The brittle shell pressed against her skin, like glass ready to shatter, melted into something softer, something that sent a cautious warm glow spilling down her limbs. "You could say that. Everyone thinks I live this charmed life, that I can do anything I want to do, that the future is full of possibility, but the truth is . . ."

Val hesitated. *The truth is, I'm enslaved to a monster, and so is my mother, and so was my grandmother.*

The truth is, I've had chances to end it, to end the line with me, and haven't had the guts to do it.

The truth, sweet Marion, would make you despise me.

Marion placed her hand between Val's shoulder blades and drew small circles so gentle that Val hated her a little—but not enough to make her stop.

"What is it?" asked Marion. "You can tell me."

Val's smile was hard, her vision swimming with unshed tears. "The truth is, I'm an asshole who should suck it up and stop complaining to the girl who's missing her sister."

Marion let out a tired sound and leaned her head against Val's shoulder. "You're not an asshole," she said quietly. "You're being really nice to me. Thank you."

With the soft weight of Marion's cheek against her skin, Val's throat twisted around itself until she could hardly breathe, and a tugging feeling like the fall of gravity got its hook in her gut. As if she were standing on the cliff's edge and seeing how far she could lean out over the water before tipping over.

She stayed silent until the feeling passed, because if she opened her mouth to say anything else, it might very well have been a confession.

ZOEY

The Push

The Tuesday after Charlotte disappeared, Zoey pedaled to the police station at eight in the morning with a bag full of doughnuts hanging from the handlebars. Because screw the haters and their cop jokes; doughnuts were delicious, and her father and his officers had been working around the clock for three days.

She chained her bike to the rack on the side of the building and was about to head for the front door when she heard a girl say, "The Collector? It's just a story."

Zoey froze in place. It was like a hidden electric cord had reached up through the ground and snagged her with its sizzling teeth.

"You tell it to kids to get them to stay out of the woods or whatever," the girl kept saying, her voice floating from around the corner of the building. Zoey knew the spot: Two picnic tables, a small gas grill, a hammock, a small stone wall on the top of a ridge, with a good view of the ocean. A popular lunch break destination for the police department staff.

Zoey crept to the corner, peered around it to see who had gathered. She scratched her itching calves hard enough that they started to hurt, wondered distractedly if she was allergic to something.

"It's because of the girls who've gone missing over the years. One of those urban legend things." The girl, Zoey now saw, was Quinn Tillinghouse, one of Grayson's friends, and only slightly abhorrent. She and three others—John Lin (moderately abhorrent), Peter Von Neumann (a bona fide dick), and Grayson himself—gathered around the picnic tables, dressed for the woods. Ready to join the next shift of search teams, Zoey assumed.

And standing near Grayson, arms crossed over her middle, listening intently to Quinn, was Marion.

"Do you think it's real, though?" Marion asked. "I mean, could it actually be true?"

Peter, a broad-shouldered white boy who looked like he could be an inept security goon on *Star Trek*, took a sip of his coffee and shrugged. "Oh, sure. The world is just full of actual, real-life monsters. Big ones, with scales."

Quinn hooked her arm through John's and giggled.

Grayson glared at Peter. "Look, you need to take this seriously."

"No, I don't think I will, Grayson." Peter tossed his empty coffee cup on the ground. "You know, you've been really annoying since banging Zoey, I have to say."

"So sorry to have disappointed you," Grayson replied.

"*Beware of the woods and the dark, dank deep,*" John started chanting against Quinn's neck.

"*He'll follow you home,*" Marion whispered, "*and won't let you sleep.*" She looked at Grayson. "What do you think that means, though? Are there clues in the rhymes?"

"Let me text Zoey again." Grayson grabbed his phone from his pocket. "I think she has all of Thora's notebooks. Maybe there's something useful in there."

"The Collector *eats girls,*" John whispered next to Quinn's ear, licking his lips. "Get it?"

"You're such a disgrace." Quinn rolled her eyes with a little grin. "Stop being gross."

Grayson, Zoey thought for the millionth time, had way too many friends.

Peter leaned against a picnic table, looking at Marion like she was only a somewhat interesting oddity. "If you're serious about investigating this like it's some kind of paranormal monster hunt, you're both certifiably insane. No offense, Marion, I know your sister's dead and all, but—"

"Shut the fuck up, Peter," said a new voice. Val was coming down the slight hill from the road with a cardboard carrier of fresh coffees in her hands. And taking the words right out of Zoey's mouth, to be perfectly honest.

Peter shrank back at Val's approach, just enough for Zoey to not completely hate her for a few nanoseconds.

But then Zoey saw Marion backing away from the group, her eyes wide. She brought her hands to the sides of her head, the heels of her palms digging into her temples, and Zoey's heart sank.

It was happening again. The bone cry.

"It's happening again," Marion whispered, squeezing her eyes shut.

Grayson followed her. "Marion?"

"Whoa, is she okay?" John asked.

Marion tripped over a crack in the patio and fell, hard, before Grayson could catch her. "It's so loud," she moaned. "Holy shit, it's never been . . ."

She cried out sharply, huddled against the ground like a burrowing animal.

Zoey pulled free of the electric bite shooting sparks up her ankle and marched forward. "Everyone back off. You're freaking her out."

"She's already pretty freaky to me," said John, hopping off the table and moving away as if whatever Marion had was contagious.

Quinn's voice came out shaky. "Is she having a seizure or something?"

Zoey ignored them all and crouched beside Marion. "Is it saying anything this time?"

Marion nodded, rocking back and forth. "It says run." She looked up at Zoey, pleading. "It says *run*."

Zoey's skin thrummed, like her whole body had fallen asleep and was now waking up in an explosion of pins and needles. "Come on, let's get out of here. I'll take you to my house."

Marion shook her head, now emitting a stream of increasingly loud whimpers.

"What's wrong with her?" Peter demanded.

"I'm getting help," said Quinn, hurrying away toward the police station.

Grayson whispered to Zoey, "What do we do?"

"I have no clue." Zoey tugged on Marion's shoulders. What had even *happened*, to trigger this? She had been fine, until—

The world slowed, sharp and clear, as the answer came to her.

Marion had been fine, upright, and healthy—until Val arrived.

"Make it stop." Marion clutched Zoey's hands to her heart, her eyes wide, her neck straining. "Please, Zoey."

Zoey shook her head helplessly. "I don't know how. Come on, I'll take you home—"

"*Please!* It's ripping me apart!"

"Zoey?" Val knelt beside them, her voice surprisingly soft. "How can I help?"

And Zoey felt such a wave of electric rage crest within her that she actually thought for a second: *If I push off the ground, I'll rocket up into the stars.*

Instead, she pivoted around on her heel and pushed Val away from Marion.

Hard.

Harder than she'd meant to.

Harder than she'd thought possible.

The instant her hand came into contact with Val's chest, blazing energy jolted up from the ground through Zoey's skinny legs to her angry-coiled belly to the hot flat of her palm.

And Val flew—*flew*—back from them, like she'd been caught in a shock wave. She skidded twenty feet away, past the picnic tables and into the flower bed, flattening a clump of pale snapdragons.

She slumped there in her leggings and hiking boots, bringing a shaky hand to her head. She met Zoey's gaze with wide, bright eyes.

Peter and John stood in shocked silence.

Grayson touched Zoey's elbow gently, like he was checking to make sure she was real, that this entire impossible moment was real.

"Zoey?" Val whispered, like a hurt child.

Zoey's eyes filled with tears in a hot, blinding second. She tugged Marion to her feet. Grayson helped, then slung Marion's right arm over his shoulder. With a quiet moan, Marion turned her cheek into Grayson's chest.

Meanwhile, Peter hurried to Val and was helping her sit up. He shot an ugly glare at Zoey. "You've got three seconds to get out of here before I come for you, Harlow."

"No," said Val, staring after them with an expression Zoey couldn't decipher. "It's all right. Let them go."

Zoey didn't need to be told twice. She turned, Grayson

following, and helped Marion stumble up the hill to the road. As they climbed, the echo of Val's voice lingered against the nape of Zoey's neck, following them home like a pair of curious eyes.

THE ROCK HAD TO MOVE QUICKLY.

The beast's hunger was climbing once more, and faster than the Rock, even with its veins full of eons, felt equipped to combat.

The Rock allowed itself a moment of despair: Would this world to which they had all been born ever be free of war?

Then the Rock remembered it was no longer alone:

First one girl, and now two.

A pair of daughters, bright and blazing.

Daughters who listened. Daughters with shoulders strong enough, with hearts soft enough, to bear the long weight of battle.

The Rock would need one more.

A beginning, a middle, and an end.

MARION

The Promise

"I think Val has a crush on me," Marion said quietly. She sat on Zoey's bed, sandwiched between Zoey and the wall, a cup of water clutched in her hands.

Zoey faced away from her, holding a wooden baseball bat Grayson had found in his truck, and staring down Marion's bedroom door like she was convinced it would, at any moment, admit their doom.

But at Marion's words, she turned around with eyebrows raised. "Excuse me, what now?"

"I mean . . ." Marion flushed. It *did* sound ludicrous—a goddess crushing on a plain-faced peasant? "I guess I could be wrong, but the other night, we took a walk on the cliffs beside Kingshead, and the way she talked to me and looked at me made me wonder." Marion took a sip of water. "Is Val gay? Do you know?"

"Ever since I've known her she's been dating some empty-headed Sawkill boy," Zoey replied. "So, if she's gay, maybe she doesn't know it yet, or she's in denial. Or maybe she's bi. Or maybe," said Zoey, her voice coming out slightly strained, "instead of pondering Val's sexuality, we could talk about how thirty minutes ago I went Jean Grey on her ass."

They fell silent, listening to the sounds of Grayson clattering around in Zoey's kitchen downstairs. It was his thing, Zoey had explained. When Grayson gets stressed, he bakes. Or cleans. Or both.

"What did it feel like?" Marion asked at last. "When you . . ." She mimed what Zoey had done, thrusting out her hand with her palm flat and rigid.

"Energy shot up from the ground and into my body," Zoey said tightly. "It was like every jolt of adrenaline I've ever felt in my life, all bundled up into one second. My heart's still pounding. Jesus."

Marion glanced at Zoey, noticed her bright eyes, and gently nudged her knee. "It was pretty awesome."

Zoey laughed, wiping a shaky hand across her face. "Yeah, I guess it was."

"When Thora talked about the Collector, did she ever talk about girls who could do . . . that?" Marion asked.

"Or girls who heard voices and weird noises?"

Marion flinched. "Yeah. That, too."

"No. Not that I remember. They were just monster stories. Nothing about superhero girls in them. Just . . . just missing girls."

After a long moment, Marion asked quietly, "How many girls?"

"Twenty-three," Zoey answered at once.

"And none of them were ever found?"

Zoey hesitated. "No. But that doesn't mean—"

Marion waved her silent with one hand and clutched her starfish necklace with the other, her eyes filling up fast. "Over how many years?"

"I've looked back about a hundred and fifty years. It gets harder to find stuff earlier than that."

"I guess twenty-three girls over one hundred and fifty years isn't . . . too bad? That's like, what, one girl every six or seven years?"

"Yeah," Zoey said flatly. "Not too bad." She didn't sound entirely convinced.

Marion didn't *feel* entirely convinced.

She closed her eyes, took another sip of water, and listened to the sounds of Zoey's breathing. Her own breathing felt erratic, thin; it was difficult to sit still beside the furious tension emanating off Zoey's tiny hunched body.

When Marion opened her eyes, she saw one of the tiny moths with the black-eyed wings peel itself off the ceiling and alight on the black-and-orange mass of Zoey's hair. It perched there, wings moving in rhythm with Zoey's breathing.

Its little moth whispers came to Marion like the rustle of meadow grasses. She knew what it was trying to tell her: *Safe.*

"I know," she told it, and squeezed her eyes shut, because it was humiliating and terrifying to be talking to a moth and absolutely believing it could hear her.

"What?"

Marion cracked open her eyes. The moth was gone. Zoey was glancing back at her. "What'd you say?" she repeated.

"Do you remember the . . . not-Marion?"

Zoey shifted, hugging herself. "Yeah."

"I see these moths." Marion ran a hand through her hair. "There were hundreds of them, when I woke up and found Charlotte gone. Maybe thousands. I think . . . I think they're trying to talk to me."

Zoey watched her, wide-eyed. "Like the bone cry?"

Marion nodded slowly. "Maybe they're related, but I have no clue what that means or why, or what to do, or why these things are happening to us and no one else. But . . ." Marion took a deep breath and pressed on before she could talk herself out of it. "I do think I can get us some answers. Maybe about the moths and the not-Marion. Maybe about Charlotte and Thora, too."

"How are you going to do that, exactly?"

Marion looked Zoey straight in the eye. "Val. I'll get close to her, spend time with her. If she doesn't have a crush on me, fine, I'll just insist upon our friendship until it happens. She won't turn me away, she'll feel too sorry for me to do that. Or if she doesn't feel sorry for me, she'll feel like she has to at least act like it. But if she *does* have a crush on me . . ."

Marion hesitated. A cluster of images flashed through her brain: Val's lovely clear skin, her full mouth, her long, lean runner's build, how warm she felt pressed next to Marion on the cliffside bench.

"What," said Zoey, "you'll seduce her or something?"

Cheeks burning, Marion squared her jaw. "If it'll get us answers, then yes."

Zoey blew out a breath. "You could maybe get access to rooms at Kingshead that no one else knows about."

"And maybe find out about that room underneath the library."

"And also get to know her mom, and fish around for information." Zoey shook her head, glanced out the window. "That woman has *got* to have like a hundred sketchy dealings going on at any given moment. You don't get to be that rich by being a good person."

Suddenly, Marion remembered Val's words: *I know how it feels, to be trapped like that.*

"Based on the conversation I had with Val the other night," Marion said slowly, "I wonder if Ms. Mortimer *is* up to something terrible, and Val's maybe involved but doesn't want to be."

Zoey snorted. "Val is seventeen years old. If she's caught up in something terrible, she's old enough to do something about it."

"I'm not sure that's entirely fair—"

"Don't feel sorry for her." Zoey tore her eyes from the window to glare at Marion. "If you're going to do this, you have to promise me that: Don't let her fool you. Don't let her change you."

Marion bristled slightly. "Nobody can change me without my consent."

"That's what Thora always said, too," Zoey replied, her voice thick, "and look what happened to her."

For a long time, neither of them spoke. Marion felt like her thoughts were inching dangerously close to a precipice past which lay an abyss that howled only one word: Charlotte's name.

She sniffled, blinked her eyes, wiped her face—then felt the mattress dip as Zoey scooted close and hooked her arm through Marion's.

"Promise me you'll be careful," Zoey whispered fiercely. "I know you miss your sister, but she wouldn't want you to get hurt, too."

What a delight it was, to have been protected by Zoey twice over, and to now feel buoyed by the warmth of Zoey's strong body next to hers. To feel safe, and worried-after, and even a little bit treasured—not for the comfort she could provide, but for the very fact of her existence. To feel that Marion the grave little mountain had, at least for a time, another mountain to lean against.

Without Zoey, Marion would have bashed her skull open on Lucy Mortimer's doors.

Without Zoey, the world would cave in.

With Zoey, though, maybe—maybe—the world would keep spinning.

Marion whispered, "I promise," crooked her pinkie finger over Zoey's, and squeezed.

ZOEY

The Second

The next morning, Zoey awoke to an empty house and a note pinned to the refrigerator with a magnet:

Zo—

Back for lunch at noon. Do dishes, please, and start a load of towels.

Love,

Dad

Zoey crumpled the note in her hand.

Sure, she'd wash the dishes.

Then she was going to snoop.

If Marion could scheme and seduce, then Zoey could get off her ass and find that damn book.

And, maybe, experiment with whatever new talent for

throwing heavy objects she apparently possessed?

She shook her head. *Focus, Zoey.*

After she started the dishwasher, she brought the trash to the garbage can by the fence, opened the lid, and dropped the bag inside. She stood there, hands on hips, breathing just a little bit hard. She'd slept terribly and hadn't managed to stomach breakfast. Every time she closed her eyes, she felt her palm slam against Val's chest. She saw Val skidding into the flowers, and the horrified stares of John and Peter.

"Whatever." Zoey shook out her body, her fingers and toes. "What*ever*."

It was fine. Everything was fine.

And it would be better once she had that book in her hands.

Her phone beeped. A text from Grayson:

You all right, Zo?

Zoey replied:

Fine.

Another text came almost immediately, but Zoey ignored it.

She stomped through the yard, back to the house. She stewed in the kitchen until the towels were done, then threw them in the dryer, then stewed some more until they were dry, then folded them, then took the stack that belonged to her father into his bathroom and placed them in the proper cabinet.

And then, as she passed back through his bedroom, thinking about where to begin her search, she saw that the stack of books her father kept on his dresser had fallen over—the books he was reading, the books he would soon begin to read. A cascade of books across the top of the dresser, and one spine-up on the floor next to the wall.

That was an odd thing, given her father's irritating tidiness. But then, it was an odd time on Sawkill, and perhaps not even Ed Harlow had wanted to stop and clean up his books on the way to search for a missing girl.

Zoey straightened the books on the dresser, then leaned down to pick up the fallen one. Glanced to the right on her way back up. Froze.

Leaned slowly back down.

In the chasm between the dresser and the wall, there was a door. A door cut into the wall, fastened shut with a tiny silver combination lock.

Zoey set the book on the dresser and stood there for a moment. Maybe it was like the not-Marion. Maybe it was a not-door. She'd look again, and it would be gone.

She held her breath. She looked again.

No, still there—a door, hidden behind a dresser Zoey wasn't sure she could move. She stood there staring at it, wiggling her fingers. She squeezed her eyes shut and tried to summon up the same furious, electric sensation she'd experienced behind the police station.

Come on, come on, she muttered—half-ready for the return of that incredible strength, half-dreading it. *Some dresser-shoving power would come in real handy right about now.*

But her arms, her hands, her skin all remained disappointingly mortal.

She sighed and glared at the ceiling. Whatever strength had surfaced before, it apparently was no longer interested in helping her. Maybe it had been like one of those situations when a mother, in a fit of maternal fury, lifts up a car to save her baby? Was Zoey the mother and Marion the baby?

She shook her head. *Focus.*

She had to move the dresser. She *had* to. She checked her phone: eleven thirty, and a text from Grayson, and another from Marion. Her father would be home at noon.

She ignored the texts, slipping her phone into her pocket.

She considered emptying everything from the drawers; the dresser would be easier to move. But she doubted her ability to put everything back in its place, and her father would notice.

Maybe it didn't matter. Maybe she'd confront his sorry ass the moment he walked in the door.

But . . . just in case.

With the dresser full, it took her a solid five minutes to move it away from the wall. She crouched in front of the door, stared at the combination lock. Four numbers.

She tried his birthday. Her birthday. Her mom's birthday. Her grandparents' birthdays. Every permutation of the numbers she could think of. She tried the code that locked his phone, the code that locked *her* phone. The code for the garage door. His ATM pin code, which she'd learned while spying on him when she was eleven. He'd never changed it.

She glanced at her phone: 11:38.

"Come *on.*" She slapped her hand against the wall.

Then it hit her.

Shaking a little, she entered the numbers on the lock: 9-6-3-9.

Z-O-E-Y.

Surely not?

The lock clicked open.

With a tiny laugh, Zoey pulled on the latch. The door opened to reveal a wooden staircase leading down into darkness.

Shaking a little more now, she called Marion, and didn't move until she heard Marion's voice: "Hey, Zoey—"

"Yeah, hi. Listen." Zoey sat on the edge of the threshold and swung her legs through. Her feet met the stairs. "I found a secret room in my dad's bedroom, and I'm going inside."

Silence. Then Marion said, "What the hell?"

"My thoughts exactly. Will you stay on the phone with me? In case . . . I don't even know." She laughed, feeling her way down the alarmingly steep stairs. No fancy light bulbs in this secret passageway. Dark flat carpet lined the walls. Zoey felt like she was climbing into the throat of a beast.

"I'm right here," came Marion's voice. "Keep talking. Tell me what you see."

"I'm putting you on speaker, FYI. I need the flashlight."

"What do you see?"

"A bunch of stairs." Zoey glanced back over her shoulder, at the dim square of her father's bedroom. "I guess my house has a basement?"

She followed the bobbing light from her phone, then hit

the bottom stair. The floor was dirt, covered with loose wooden planks. The air felt damp, like after a soft rain.

She searched the room—packs of bottled water, boxes of supplies, a first aid kit.

Guns, hanging from racks on the wall.

"Cool, cool," said Zoey, sounding a little shrill. "My dad is a secret survivalist, I guess?"

"What are you seeing?"

"Water, supplies, some automatic rifles, I think? You know. Typical bunker stuff." Zoey crept carefully around the room, her heart pounding in her ears. "Can I just say that I'm really disturbed by the number of secret rooms on this island?"

"And how many of them we've found in the last few days?"

"It's a rare talent we have. Wait, hang on."

Zoey had found a computer. Not a particularly nice one, but then, Ed Harlow was not known for his technological savvy.

Above it, nailed to the carpeted wall, hung an enormous map of the world.

And beside the keyboard sat her father's black book.

She stared at it, a tight, squeamish feeling blocking up her throat.

"Zoey?" Marion asked tensely. "Say something. Are you okay? What is it?" Zoey heard rustling. "I'm coming over there."

"No, wait." Zoey sat down in a swiveling desk chair. She switched on the desk lamp, turned on the computer. It whirred softly to life. Zoey touched her fingers to the black book's soft leather cover. She would deal with that in a second.

First: the map. She snapped a photo of it.

"There's a map of the world in here," Zoey told Marion. "And it's covered by a grid."

"A grid? What do you mean?"

Zoey wasn't sure. Red lines divided the map into sectors, each of them numbered in her father's meticulous hand. Red dots scattered across the map like drops of blood.

"He's divided the whole thing into numbered sections," Zoey whispered. "And there are these red dots all over. Hundreds of them. They're marking . . . cities, I guess? But not all of them are on cities." She squinted, stretched up on her toes. There were too many details to absorb. She was standing in a *secret room* beneath her house. Her eyes glossed over the map like she had fallen into a dream. "Some of the dots are in the middle of nowhere. Some are in the ocean? There's even one in Antarctica."

Marion's quiet question came like an explosion: "Is there one on Sawkill?"

Zoey's eyes flew to the northeastern coast of the United States, to the patch of water that hugged Sawkill Rock.

A red dot stared back at her—bright and round in the island's heart.

"Zoey?"

"Yeah." Zoey shook her head, hand over her mouth. "Yes. There is one. There's one on Sawkill."

Marion exhaled. "But what does that mean?"

Zoey glanced at her phone and saw a notification:

A text from her father.

At Windham and Irongate, it read. *Be ready to leave. We're going to the police station.*

"Shit," Zoey spat. "*Shit.*"

"What is it? Zoey—"

"My dad will be home in two minutes. I've gotta go."

Zoey hung up, turned off the computer and the lamp, ran for the stairs. She remembered that the desk chair had been pushed in, turned back, and shoved it into place.

The black book.

She hesitated, then grabbed it and tucked it into her pants, beneath her shirt. She fled up the stairs, ducked out the door, slammed it shut, and locked it.

The dresser.

If she took too long to move it, if her father came inside looking for her, how would she possibly explain this?

"God*damn* it," she gasped, pushing the stupid ancient thing as hard as she could. The books fell over once more. She stepped back, sucked in a breath, and surged forward, prepared to ram her whole body into the dresser.

But it moved on its own, before she could reach it.

It slid across the carpet a good six inches, with Zoey still a foot away.

Zoey, expecting to hit the dresser, hit nothing instead, and stumbled forward until she caught herself on the dresser's edge. A bookend crashed to the floor, and more books slid off right after it.

Her fingers tingled, hot and ready. Twin cords of energy

thrummed up the back of her legs, joining at the dip of her spine and stretching like a single rushing current all the way up to the crown of her skull. She was on fire, but in a good way. She'd been ignited. She was *sizzling*.

Breathless, laughing a little, tearing up a little, she grinned down at her hands.

Then, from outside, a car door slammed.

Her ribs clamped around her lungs in sudden panic. She grabbed the toppled books, shoved them back into place, straightened them, turned, and ran.

Wait.

She froze at the bedroom door.

The books hadn't been orderly. They'd been in a messy pile, which was the thing that had caught her attention in the first place. One had been on the floor. But which one?

She riffled furiously through her memory until the image of the fallen book returned to her, settling back into place like a key into a lock.

Down the hall and around the corner, the front door opened. "Zo? Did you get my text?"

"Yeah, one sec!" Zoey cried. "Putting away the towels!"

She untidied the books, hoped they looked right, then arranged the one that had fallen on the floor: *A Wrinkle in Time*. One of Zoey's all-time favorites. She had endlessly bugged her father about reading it until, finally, about a month ago, he'd thrown up his hands and said with an aggrieved sigh, "Okay, fine, I'll read it. But, Zo, please don't be mad if I don't like it."

She had thrust the book into his hands. "I can't promise that, my dude."

Zoey wiped her forehead, took three deep breaths to try to calm down, then sauntered out of her father's bedroom and around the corner, dusting off her hands with a flourish.

"Towels clean and folded and returned to their nests," she proclaimed. "Who's the best daughter in the world?"

Then she froze. Her father was standing at the front door, looking stricken. A hot prickly rush flooded her body. "Dad?"

"Another girl's gone missing." Every uttered word seemed to tug harder on the tired lines of his face. "Jane Fitzgerald."

A flash—Jane under the Droop with Harry Windemeier, spiders dropping like dark snowflakes onto her skin.

Zoey stood in shocked silence, adrift, then distantly heard the crisp drum of her heartbeat and followed it back into herself.

"Oh, Dad." She didn't want to do it, not really, not now, but she would have, before discovering her father's lair. It's what he would expect, what he would hope for. Part of her wanted to confront him anyway, throw the book in his face and yell at him until he explained why he had a secret room, what the map meant, and why he was keeping it all from her.

Instead, she hurried forward, flung her arms around him. At least she didn't have to fake the tremor in her voice. "Holy shit. What's going on?"

"I wish I knew, Zo," he whispered, and when his arms came around her, Zoey had to fight the urge to flinch away from his touch.

VAL

The Reckless

After Jane, he recovered in two and a half hours.

His form shifted, in half-second flashes—Dr. Wayland to boy-child to shadow-splatter to their old groundskeeper with the midnight-black skin and cloud of white hair to Val's own grandmother, and back into the gloom of the woods. Then the cycle began again, and again—a horrifying movie on a rapid-fire loop.

And Val realized, with a sinking-stone feeling, that he was *playing.*

He could change forms easily now, like snapping one's fingers and suddenly donning a new outfit in the blink of an eye, and clearly this delighted him. As the towheaded boy, he crawled happily out of the trees, laughing so hard his face turned red. He collapsed in the center of the stones, clutching his stomach and wriggling in delight.

Gritting her teeth, grasping for calm that wouldn't come, Val began cleaning up the evidence of his feeding. It was a process that would take days to complete, but she liked to get started right away.

Besides, she wanted to see how long he would require, this time, to regain control over his body. Once, he would have needed hours, days, *weeks*.

He caught her sneaking glances at him.

"Do you see something you like, Val?" he asked her, as Dr. Wayland now, lying in the mud with glazed eyes, blood-caked lips, a round belly. He picked his teeth with one long white finger. Then he stood up, stretched, flexed his muscles, popped the joints in his neck and shoulders. The air around him seemed to quiver. A ripple of movement passed underneath his pale skin, like his bones were rearranging themselves.

"I was just making sure you've had all you need," Val answered smoothly, gathering the shreds of Jane's torn clothing from the undergrowth, trying not to think about Jane, trying not to think about Zoey throwing her behind the police station, trying not to think about anything but her own two feet on the solid ground, and her own two blood-spattered hands.

"You're worried this will all end soon," he replied. "That I won't need you."

Val did not trust her voice enough to answer him. Her stomach jerked, as though he'd hooked his claws in her innards and given them a tug, just to remind her that he could.

When his hands cupped her shoulders—warm, paternal,

slick—she flinched. A chittering, wet-throated noise crept through the clearing like the flap of shining dark wings.

"You're right to be worried," he said at last, his voice clear and crisp. He'd lost the glutted slur; he had recovered himself, and so quickly that it made Val want to crawl into the trees and never come out. "Soon everything will change."

It took Val ten seconds to find her voice. "How long?" she croaked. "How much longer do we have?"

He did not answer.

She turned to find him and saw only a wicked black crown of branches, nodding mournfully in the wind.

Val didn't usually care about the blood on her hands, but this time it was different. This time she couldn't get it off, no matter how fiercely she scrubbed under the scalding faucet.

"I don't understand it," she whispered, staring at her reddened palms.

"Don't understand what?"

Val's head snapped up. She was sitting on the floor, her back pressed against her white ruffled bedspread, and there was her mother, standing at the threshold to her bedroom, crisp white blouse and crisp navy-blue pencil skirt and crisp coils of blond hair pinned at her nape.

"I can't stop thinking about it this time," Val explained, and realized too late that it was stupid to confess such weakness, but she couldn't seem to shut her mouth. "I can't stop seeing her face." She raised her hands and stared at her mother through shaking red fingers. Was it burned skin, or was it Jane's blood? "I can't get it off. I can't get Jane off of me."

For a long moment, Lucy Mortimer stood at the door and considered her daughter. Then she moved swiftly across the room, heels silent on the thick rug, and slapped Val so hard her head nearly flew off her neck. It wouldn't have been such a bad thing, to lose her head. She'd considered it before—provoking her mother to such anger that she would do to Val what Val couldn't find the guts to do to herself.

Val stared up at her. The slap had knocked tears from her eyes. She couldn't find the will to hide them.

"He told me we don't have long," she whispered. "He said we should be worried."

Her mother's face was a porcelain mask with one too many cracks in it, too haggard for cosmetics to hide. She always looked this way as he digested, while he was at his most vulnerable and drew upon her own life force to steady himself. She held one hand flat against her abdomen, as if to soothe cramps. Val's own stomach twinged in sympathy; she didn't feel the drain on her strength as keenly as her mother did, but she felt enough to dread the future.

"He'll need one more, I think," her mother said, her voice tight and clipped. "Maybe two. Three, if we're lucky."

Val laughed, which hurt her tender cheek. "When have we ever been lucky?"

But Val's mother was not moved. "Pull yourself together, Valerie," she said, her jaw working, and then she straightened her shirt and left the room without a backward glance.

So Val did. She pulled herself together.

She squared her shoulders and lifted her chin and undressed. She took a shower in silence, the scalding water battering her body, which hadn't truly belonged to Val since she'd been born, not even for a second.

He owns your body, her grandmother had told her, *and your mind, but he doesn't own your soul, Val. Not all of it.*

Her grandmother had been a goddamn liar.

Val conditioned her long golden hair, moisturized the sweet turn of her jaw and the high planes of her cheekbones, and then stretched on the rug in her bedroom. She dressed in exercise pants and a sports bra and a loose gray tank top. When she got outside she pulled on her muck boots and went to the stables to work. She hardly noticed how her body ached, tender from the punishing shower. She hardly noticed the whuffing of the horses in their stalls as she shoveled out the old straw and the dung, and shoveled in new, fresh straw that smelled of summertime and horses and fresh growth. The exact opposite of the rot and ruin stewing inside her.

She hardly noticed anything at all.

Which was why she didn't realize anyone had entered the stables until she felt a gentle hand on her arm.

Val whirled, sweaty hair clinging to her flushed cheeks, ready to swing her shovel and take the head off anyone who looked at her funny.

But it was only Marion.

At the sight of her, Val's heart split in two. One half went floating and quietly giddy, like she'd dropped down a roller-coaster hill she hadn't been expecting to ride.

The other half plunged to her toes, drawing sick fault lines down her body.

She resisted the urge to hide her hands behind her back. She wore work gloves, but still, she hadn't scrubbed her fingers well enough, not by far. If Marion took one look at them, she'd see those stubborn clinging bits of gore and know them for what they were:

Jane residue. Lingering Thora.

The echoes of Charlotte.

"Marion," Val said softly, taking a step back. "Hey."

"I wanted to see if you were okay," said Marion, steady gray eyes fixed on Val's face.

"If I was . . . okay? You mean . . ."

"Jane." Marion's pale face was so pinched and tense that it made Val's stomach knot up. "I heard about Jane."

Val leaned heavily against her shovel. Her mouth and nose were full of familiar horse smells that suddenly made her want to gag. Did his own beastly scent linger upon her? Could Marion sense his ravenous appetite?

"Hey." Marion moved closer, took the shovel from Val and set it aside. "I'm sorry, I didn't mean to . . . Why don't you sit down for a second?"

"I don't want to sit down." Val felt unsteady on her legs, out of place and ill-fitting. She had always pulled it together just fine, just as her mother wanted her to, just as she had been taught, and now nothing was working as it should.

Girl-ghosts swarmed Val's brain. She could hear nothing but their wails, calling for her damnation.

Marion hovered close, hands twisting at her waist. "I'm so sorry about Jane. I don't know what to say. Everyone's freaking out, I . . . God, Val, what are we all going to do?"

"I'm trying not to think about it," said Val shortly.

Think about what, exactly, Val?

About what had happened.

About what she had done.

Oh, how terribly Jane had screamed. Twenty-three times she'd called Val's name, begging her for help, for mercy.

Well. Twenty-three and a half. And then . . .

"Val." Marion stepped closer, searching Val's face. "You're crying."

Val turned away, ripping off her gloves. Would Marion see the blood, the flesh scraps and girl-bits? Val didn't care. She couldn't wear those gloves for one more second, couldn't stand the sensation of the stiff fabric imprisoning her fingers. She glanced at her nails—clean and gleaming, long enough to gouge. Maybe if she scratched out her eyes, she would stop seeing Jane's face.

It had hardly looked like a face, at the end.

"I'm not," Val said, her body so rigid it felt ready to snap.

Marion caught Val's fingers in her own. "What can I do?"

"You?" Val's laugh was bitter. "You've lost your sister. I

should be the one helping you."

"Cut the bullshit, Val. I don't buy it."

Val froze. She turned, saw Marion's breath catch a little. Val had practiced crying in her mirror enough times to know that she was one of the fortunate few who looked even lovelier when weeping.

"Jane was your friend. Pain is pain. It's not a contest." Marion shook her head, her gaze bright. "I never feel like I can freak out around my mom because of everything that's happened. She needs me to be strong. I look at her, and I think to myself, *Pull it together, Marion.*"

Val watched Marion, hardly daring to breathe. *Pull yourself together, Valerie.*

"I don't want you to feel that way around me, Val," said Marion, with a shy smile. "You don't have to be strong. You can be what you need to be."

And suddenly Val knew exactly what she needed.

"Say my name again," Val breathed. Warmth uncoiled in her gut; a tingling ache spread from her belly to her spine to her fingers. This was reckless, this was not what she had been instructed to do. She was meant for Collin Hawthorne. He was a solid, respectable match and would serve her well. Someday he would plant a daughter in her, and the line would continue.

Or at least, that had been the plan.

But now? Now, soon enough, *he* would break free of Val and her mother, and they would no longer be needed.

Maybe then he would kill Val, just because he could.

Maybe then he would ignore her, let her do as she pleased.

Let her kiss who she pleased?

When Marion stepped closer, and said once again, "Val," so close that her lips brushed Val's cheek, Val let her eyes fall shut, and hooked her arms around Marion's shoulders, and couldn't bring herself to care about anything but the soft press of Marion's lips, Marion's warm thigh wedged between her own, the solid stretch of the wall against her back.

With Marion's hands cupping her cheeks, Val forgot that her blood ran black and vile.

With Marion whispering her name against her hair, Val felt scrubbed bright and clean as the dawn.

MARION

The Plunge

In retrospect, it probably hadn't been wise to kiss Val.

But sweet heavens, the kissing had felt good.

It shouldn't have felt good; it was supposed to have been a maneuver, a farce. She hadn't planned on kissing Val, but when the moment had arrived, she had thought, all right, this whole getting-close-to-Val thing couldn't have been developing more beautifully, could it?

Then Val had melted under her touch, and let out a tiny ragged sigh of relief against Marion's mouth, and Marion's whole body had morphed at once into something beastly and divine—nerves pulled tight and legs wobbly as sticks, her brain slip-sliding into a slick, shifting heat she'd only ever before experienced in her most private fantasies.

For a while, Marion had forgotten about her unsettling

phone call with Zoey and the fact that Chief Harlow had a secret room of his own. She had forgotten that Charlotte had vanished, that her father was dead, that her mother existed in a half-lit haze of grief. She had forgotten that she was only supposed to be getting close to Val in order to extract information from her.

While kissing Val, Marion had felt, simply and deliciously, like a girl.

Night had fallen on day one of Jane's disappearance. Marion was alone, freshly kissed, a smile haunting her lips and Val's touch lingering against the curve of her back.

She wandered across the Kingshead grounds, hoping the moonlight and sea air would cool her skin and shrink her back into a manageable shape. Otherwise she wasn't sure she would fit back inside the cottage; the stale air in that house wasn't fit to be breathed by a sprite such as herself. She sparkled with a vitality she hadn't known she possessed.

She had kicked off her shoes by the back steps and now wandered barefoot through the wet grass—black and clinging, rimmed silver by the moon. The cool earth seeped up through her soles; she swallowed and tasted the dark loamy tang of the forest.

Then she heard a soft snuffling sound, like that of an animal foraging for worms in the damp. She'd reached one of the grazing pastures—vast and rolling, a glossy shivering imitation of the ocean.

Marion froze.

A beast was watching her.

A horse, soot-dark and tremendous. Marion recognized him as one of the prized Mortimer stallions, a world-class stud. He stood on the other side of the pasture fence, his ears pricked, alert. With his front right hoof, he pawed the wet ground, scraping up strips of mud.

"Hello," she made herself whisper. Calm the beast. Let him know you're a friend. This horse wasn't Nightingale, but he reminded Marion of that horrible day nevertheless.

As if in response to her memories, the bone cry roared to life. She sank to the ground in silent despair, hands rising automatically to cover her ears. The high whine rang on, so piercing it carved grooves into her teeth. In the distance came the sharp flutter of beetles' wings, the cicadas' droning call. The earth seemed to tremble beneath her bare feet.

The cry was building up from inside the ground, Marion thought. It reached up from the mud and grabbed her bones and shook them until they shrieked.

"What are you trying to tell me?" she muttered. "What do you *want*?"

A sudden silence fell across the pasture—no birds, no bugs. Just the bone cry, droning on, and a brimming, soundless weight, like the world holding its breath.

From behind Marion, in the trees, a branch snapped. A weight hit the ground. Something heavy dropping from the trees?

Run.

The horse kicked the pasture fence.

Marion's head snapped up.

He kicked the fence again.

A hot knife plunged into one of Marion's ears and out the other. She staggered away from the fence, back toward the woods. Maybe if she ran, her feet would pound out the pain. And if she ran fast enough, maybe the bone cry wouldn't be able to catch her.

The horse reared up, his eyes wild. With his hind legs first, and then with his front, he kicked at the fence like a prisoner bent on escaping his cell, even if he had to smash all his bones to do it.

"Stop," Marion gasped, blinking hard to rid the fireworks of pain from her eyes. She reached toward the horse, her arm shaking. "Stop, it's okay! It's okay!"

But the horse wouldn't stop, and the fence was splintering. When he let out a shrill cry of fear, Marion saw a light switch on inside Kingshead.

The fence shattered, black wood flying. The horse ran. A jagged piece of destroyed fence scraped up his side as he fled.

And Marion followed.

The bone cry told her to. A physical force accompanied it that night—a searing hand, unseen but unmistakable. It whipped up from the ground like an electrical charge and slapped down between her shoulder blades. It pushed her on, hooked into her bones and tugged, and said, with a slight shake, *Go.*

She couldn't possibly keep up with a horse; she was a mere human, and the farthest thing from a runner. But she pumped her legs hard, ignoring the shocks of pain that jolted her knees as her bare feet slammed against the rocky ground. Wet black branches struck her across the face, dragged red lines across her arms.

The horse was tearing through the Kingshead Woods like it was the end-times. Marion kept running after him, though the horse was by now far away, vanished into the trees. Her side cramped, her lungs were twin hives of fire. Whenever her feet hit the ground, energy snapped up to smack her knees. Her legs couldn't keep up with themselves. Her vision blacked out, tilting. She stumbled over a tree root, out of the woods, and into an out-of-body experience:

She'd reached the northern edge of the island—past Kingshead, past the old Breckenridge farm. She emerged from the trees by Aurora Park, a tiny playground with red swing sets that offered the best view of the northern sea.

It wasn't possible. She had been running for . . . five minutes, maybe?

And these cliffs, they were miles away from the Kingshead pastures.

Ahead, the Mortimer stallion jumped over a hedge, landed wrong. Marion heard a sickening snap, and yet the horse pushed himself on, gait uneven, favoring one of his legs.

"Wait!" Marion's voice cracked. She ran across the playground, shoved past the swings and sent them flying. "Stop, please!"

But the horse, if he heard her, had no intention of stopping. Without another sound, without pause, he jumped over the little fence that kept kids from plunging to their deaths and flung himself over the cliffs, into the ocean.

Marion fell to her hands and knees, wrapped her arms around her head. She was a shaking ball on the ground. The bottoms of her feet were burning, and her body was marked by the fingernails of the woods.

"Help me," she whispered. The bone cry grew louder, rattling her from skull to toes. She tried to shove her thoughts against it, like shutting a door against a battering wind. She shuddered on the cold wet ground as daylight split open the east. The bone cry was thunderous in her ears, and as she braced herself against the ground, she felt a force rise up beneath her like the earth was going to crack in two.

A sharp static force grabbed hold of her. The bone cry's shrill whine exploded into a ringing, white-hot silence.

Marion opened her eyes.

She was no longer in the mud by the cliffs where the horse had jumped.

She was on a beach, but not a Sawkill beach.

This beach was soft and white. The water lapping at its shore was a rippling amber like pools of heated gold. Overhead, feather-thin clouds streaked a lavender sky. On the distant horizon, chunks of land white and craggy as glaciers hung in the air, capped with glittering structures.

Marion shivered. It was cold in this place. She shifted in the sand, dislodging a fine coating of snow, and looked around.

Detritus littered the beach—wreckage, maybe of boats? Planes? A propeller. Garbage, washed up from the water—a Frisbee, a toy truck, a steering wheel, a helmet.

Piles of clothes.

Piles of *bones*, charred and heaped.

A whisper came from her left. Marion whipped her head around.

Fat white trees dotted a field of shimmering blue grass. The trees were rural neighbors with long, quiet space between them, their leafless, bony arms reaching crookedly for the sky.

From her right: a low, soft clicking like the tap of tongue against teeth.

Marion cried out, whirled right. Her limbs gave out. Her cheek slammed into the snow-covered sand. *Home*, screamed her brain, desperate for it. *Safe.*

The world changed. It darkened and stilled. No more beach, no more whispering grass, no more sky-ice.

She was in her bedroom, in the housekeeper's cottage, at Kingshead.

Her clothes were drenched with dew and sweat, and her feet throbbed red-hot. She'd scraped them raw, running after the doomed horse.

A moth perched on the carpet in front of her face, watching her shiver. Its feelers inspected the tip of her nose. *Sssss, sssss*, whispered the quiet flap of its black-eyed wings.

So said the moth: *This is only the beginning.*

ZOEY

The Phone Call

Zoey sat cross-legged on her bed, her father's book open in her lap and her heart pounding a staccato beat against her breastbone.

Grayson's voice came through her phone: "There's a lot of text to translate here, Zo." She heard the clicks of his computer as he scrolled through and magnified the images she had texted him. She'd snapped photos of the first twenty or so pages in the book and sent them to both Grayson and Marion. "This will take me a while."

Zoey gently flipped through the book's brittle pages—passage after passage of Latin text. "Well, good thing you've taken, what, three years of Latin now? Like a big ol' dork."

"A dork whose services you desperately need," Grayson pointed out.

"Don't push it, love. Just get to work."

"Aye, Captain," replied Grayson, in a terrible Scottish brogue. "I'll give it me best shot."

Zoey rolled her eyes, smiling despite herself. "Don't make me laugh. I'm too freaked out right now to laugh."

"What does Marion say about all of this?"

"I don't know yet. She's not answering my texts." Zoey glanced at the clock on her nightstand with a twinge of worry. Ten thirty in the morning already. Marion had said she would come over at nine, for breakfast and book-analyzing.

"Are there more pages than just these?" Grayson asked. "Did you photograph all of them?"

"Not yet," Zoey said, distracted, gazing out the window, "but, yeah, there are a lot more. . . ."

A tiny white moth was fluttering silently down from the pale morning sky, and suddenly Zoey was interested in nothing else. She watched it descend with more trepidation than the sight of a moth would typically warrant.

But she couldn't put Marion's words out of her mind:

I see these moths.

I think they're trying to talk to me.

Nor could she silence her own spinning thoughts:

I can throw girls.

I can move dressers without touching them.

"Zo?" came Grayson's voice. "Did you hear me?"

Zoey ignored him, transfixed by the flickering black eyes on the moth's white wings. It was a small world, now—a world for her and the moth alone.

The moth came to a hovering stop, three inches above the windowsill. When it spoke, its voice was distant and small, like that of a child screaming from miles away:

Run.

Suddenly, Zoey felt eyes on her back.

She spun around to meet the furious dark gaze of her father, who stood at the threshold to her bedroom.

And there was the stolen book, lying on her mattress.

And there was Grayson's voice, on the phone: "Zo? Zoey, you're freaking me out. Are you there?"

The moth fluttered at the back of Zoey's neck. *Run!*

But Zoey hesitated. This was her father, after all. She shrugged a little, offered him a sheepish smile. "You left your book lying around again."

Her father did not return the smile. His hands hung in tight fists.

"That book," he replied evenly, "is not for you, Zoey. You need to stay out of this."

Zoey lifted her chin, chills popping like static up and down her arms. "Stay out of what, Dad? What's going on? Who wrote this?"

She almost asked him about the room downstairs, but it was possible there was more down there to be found.

She held her tongue, asked instead, "What aren't you telling me?"

Her father shook his head, his shoulders tense and square. The quiet air of Zoey's bedroom crackled, ready to ignite.

Grayson's voice broke the silence: "Zoey, I'm coming over—"

Zoey's father lunged for the book.

Zoey scrambled across her bed for the window.

Her mind exploded into a thousand frantic thoughts: She could crawl onto the roof and climb down the deck lattice to the backyard. Her bike was leaning against the fence. She would ride it to . . . where? To safety.

To Grayson?

No. To Marion.

Zoey's instinct screamed this at her, or maybe it was the moth shouting at her in its strange moth voice: *To Marion. To Marion.*

She was halfway out the window when her father grabbed her right ankle and pulled her back toward him. She kicked out blindly with her left leg. Her socked heel slammed into his jaw, and he grunted in pain and released her.

"Zo, what's the matter with you?" he cried.

But Zoey was already out on the roof, shoving her phone into her pocket and the soft leather cover of the book between her teeth. It hung like a heavy dead thing from her mouth while she crouched at the roof's edge. She turned and clung to the gutter with slick hands, searched for footing in the deck lattice. Five seconds later, and she was dropping to the deck, tears of relief in her eyes—*I didn't die, keep running*—and then she kicked open the gate, except she didn't kick it, she simply thought about it. She flung out her leg, and the gate flew open before her toes made contact. It flew open so hard that it crashed back into the fence, swinging wildly. Zoey let out a tiny sob, jumped on her bike, and sped out onto the driveway.

The front door slammed. She looked back over her shoulder, saw her father hurrying down the porch steps. She let out a frantic gasp and realized somewhere in her climb that she'd dropped the book.

It didn't matter.

Grayson had the pictures. So did Marion.

Besides, she hadn't run to keep the book from her father.

She'd run because, for the first time in her life, she'd been afraid of him.

And because the moth had told her to.

Great goddesses of the universe, Zoey thought, a little hysterically, *I'm listening to moths. I can open gates with my mind, and also I'm listening to moths.*

She looked back one more time. In the driveway, her father bent to retrieve the fallen book.

Zoey pedaled on, not stopping until she'd reached the edge of the Heart Woods at the center of Sawkill. She braked hard, left her bike lying on the ground, and walked around in circles through the trees until the world returned to her—blue sky, green grass, black trees that hummed and whispered like they were having a secret conversation with the sea.

Zoey withdrew her phone from her pocket and sat on the ground in a patch of sunlight. She'd hung up on Grayson at some point, and now had seventeen frantic texts from him, but he would have to wait.

A quick search online pulled up the number she was looking

for. Her eyes burned while she dialed, but if she blinked, she might absolutely lose it.

Since Thora's death, she'd heard the mean whispers about her father. First Natalie, they'd said, then Thora, and now? Now Charlotte and Jane.

Incompetence, was the word she'd heard most often. Also *negligence*.

Zoey had always been the first to jump in and defend her father to anyone who so much as rolled their eyes at him, which didn't exactly help her own popularity.

But now there was the matter of the secret room, the red map, the black book.

Now, Zoey didn't know what to think—except that not enough was being done. Three girls gone in a span of eight months? She didn't think she could stand looking her father in the eye long enough to tell him that she, seventeen-year-old failed writer, didn't think he was doing his job the way he should be.

And that she, his daughter, didn't think she could trust him.

That she was even more than a little afraid of him.

The phone stopped ringing. A crisp recorded voice announced, "You have reached the Boston field office of the Federal Bureau of Investigation."

Zoey exhaled, followed the menu options. When she finally reached a human, it was a woman. At the sound of her voice, Zoey blinked at last; her tears spilled over, and she clutched the phone to her cheek like a precious treasure.

"Hi," she said, shaky. "My name's Zoey Harlow. Z-O-E-Y. Harlow with a W. I live on Sawkill Rock. I need to report two missing girls."

There was a long silence. Zoey checked her phone to make sure the call hadn't dropped. "Hello?"

"One moment, please," said the woman, and as Zoey sat there listening to orchestral hold music, she searched the trees for moths.

Then the music stopped.

"Zoey?" came a new voice, male and pleasant. "Zoey, are you there?"

Zoey drew her knees to her chest. "Um, who's this?"

"This is Roy Briggs, Zoey. I'm an agent with the FBI, and I'm an old friend of your father's." The man had a thick Boston accent, and wherever he was, the sea was near. Zoey heard the cry of gulls. "We met when you were little, but I don't imagine you'd remember that."

"Nope. I don't." Zoey frowned at her filthy socks. The name Roy Briggs did sound vaguely familiar, but she couldn't find a face. "What kind of old friend, exactly? Did you work together?"

"Something like that." Briggs sighed. "So, Zoey, you called the Boston office? What's going on, honey? Does your dad know you called us?"

Zoey's frown deepened. "Look, we may have met before, supposedly, but I don't remember you, and I don't want you to call me honey."

Briggs didn't skip a beat. "Fair enough, Zoey. I'm sorry about that." Then he paused, laughing softly, and when he spoke again, there was less performative friendliness in his voice. "You two are so alike, you know. He called me maybe a couple of hours before you did."

That was surprising. "Oh?" Zoey said, keeping her voice casual. "He told you about what's been happening out here?"

"He did." Briggs sounded tired. "Two girls gone, so close to each other. I tell you, it makes me sick. I know people are scared, and that you are, too. I'm going to help you, and your dad. I don't intend to leave until we've gotten some answers, all right?"

"Wait." Zoey straightened. "Leave? You're coming to Sawkill?"

"Actually, Zoey," answered Briggs, his words punctuated by the familiar foghorn blast of the Sawkill ferry, "I'm already here."

The Cover-Up

Val crept through the Kingshead Woods at her mother's side, a bag of dead girl-parts in her arms and her stomach a snarl of knots.

Jane had been a particularly messy meal, and Val had decided she had no choice but to recruit her mother's help.

She was already beginning to regret that decision.

"Walk faster, Valerie," snapped Lucy Mortimer, shoving a stray lock of hair behind her ear.

Val obeyed. The sight of her mother's unkempt hair lodged in her chest like sickness. Normally, Lucy Mortimer would have never set foot outside her bedroom with even one misplaced strand, much less left the house in such a state.

The reason was obvious: her mother was panicking.

Val decided to keep breathing. One step, one inhale. One

step, one exhale. With every footfall, she concentrated on dissecting her newest secret:

During the night, she'd heard a crash and a cry from outside. She'd squinted out her bedroom window to see one of her family's horses break out of his pasture and tear off into the night.

And Marion had run off after him.

But she hadn't just *run*, no. One moment she had been on the ground by the ruined fence. Then she was gone, vanishing into the trees so quickly that Val thought she'd imagined it.

She'd woken her mother, told her one of the horses had gotten loose—and said nothing of seeing Marion.

They'd searched the pastures together, then received a call from the police station. Gregory Hainsworth, out night fishing off the island's northern shore, had called the station in a panic. From his boat he'd seen a horse topple off the cliffs and hit the rocks in the water below.

A quick trip to the cliffs, a police boat searching the water with a spotlight, had revealed the gruesome truth: one of Lucy Mortimer's stallions, American Glory, dead in the water.

Val's mother had burst into quiet, dignified tears that disappeared as soon as Deputy Montgomery returned to the station. Val thought maybe even some of the tears had been real.

But there was no time for mourning. Her mother was now convinced someone was after them. That someone was close to unraveling the truth.

"I assume it's Chief Harlow," she had told Val, matter-of-factly drying her tears in the kitchen. "He's always hated us. Him and that horrible daughter of his."

"Neither of them would hurt a horse like that," Val protested, trying not to think about seeing Marion by the pasture. Marion wouldn't hurt a horse, either. Would she?

Marion couldn't disappear in the blink of an eye.

Could she?

Except Zoey had thrown Val twenty feet through those flower beds like Val was a toy, like Val was nothing.

Her mother had fixed her with a cool stare. "No. I suppose they wouldn't."

Val knew what her mother was thinking: if someone found out what their family had been doing, if the line broke at last and the mansion was closed, the stones destroyed, the red room below the library filled and buried—then it would be Ms. Mortimer's fault, not only that their way of life had been disrupted, but also that his impending freedom had been threatened. And no form of punishment humankind could think up would be worse than what he would do to her mother for that.

So they left Kingshead once more and scoured the woods until dawn, just to be sure.

After an hour of silence, Val dared to speak. "Did you ask him? Did you confirm a number?"

Lucy Mortimer, crouched in the weeds beside a small ridge, didn't even look up from her search. "I did."

Val waited until she couldn't. "Well? And?"

Her mother straightened and stretched. "He requires two

more meals before his growth is complete. Then he'll no longer need us and will be free to roam across the world as he pleases."

"I see." Val worked so diligently to keep her face expressionless that a headache formed behind her eyes. "And what will happen to us then? Did you ask him that, too?"

A light shifted in the trees, casting shadows across Lucy Mortimer's face. "He said that all depends on you, Valerie. How quickly you work. The quality of your hunts. Satisfy him, and we'll be allowed to live our lives as we see fit, as long as we maintain the property and grounds as he wishes, and provide for him in every fashion he desires when he arrives for a visit."

Val swallowed. *When he arrives for a visit.* As if he were an eccentric uncle who tended to drop by unannounced. "And if he isn't satisfied?"

"He wasn't specific on that topic." Val's mother scratched the side of her mouth, her eyes unblinking. "He simply said you would regret it."

You. Not *we.*

Val would regret it.

Another girl might have cried then. Another girl might have worried for her life.

But as Val watched her mother dig through the brush, she could think only of Marion. Marion, pressing her against the barn wall. Marion's warm hands cupping Val's hips. Marion's tongue, clumsy but earnest, opening Val's mouth.

"What will he do to everyone else?" Val asked. "Once he's free, what will he do?"

Her mother looked up at her, frowning as if utterly bewildered.

"Haven't you thought of that?" Val asked, knowing the answer. "Haven't you worried about what will happen to them?" She took three swift steps toward her mother. "Mom, we can end this. I know it's terrible, but we *can*. It can end with us, before he has the chance to finish."

"I will feed," came his voice abruptly. A shapeless shadow jumped from tree to tree over their heads—agile, dizzingly swift. "That's what I will do, once I am free. I will find the others, in all our worlds that you are too stupid to find, and we will make many more. And if you try to die, you will fail. I will make sure of it."

Val silently bent low to search the woods, her eyes stinging, but with the memory of Marion's lips on hers, she was no longer quite so afraid.

Don't lose yourself to him, my darling one, Val's grandmother had told her. *Not all of you. Keep a morsel for yourself.*

Val clung to the memory of Marion's kiss as if it were the last crumb of food in the world and thought, *Mine*.

It was hers, and hers alone.

He would not take it from her.

The island still crawled with search parties, officers, and volunteers calling for Charlotte and Jane. Yet none of them noticed the Mortimers, not even when Val and her mother walked right past them.

He made sure of this. He delighted in his power, in his ability to so thoroughly pull the wool over so many eyes.

Val kept her own eyes on the ground, the back of her neck tingling from the weight of his unblinking gaze overhead. Had he also seen Marion, by American Glory's pasture? And if he had, just how close had he gotten to her? Val's stomach turned at the thought of him watching Marion from the trees.

Together, uninterrupted and unseen, Val and her mother collected a small sackful of body parts.

Val identified them at once: Jane Fitzsimmons's shoe. Charlotte Althouse's unblinking blue eye, marred by burst blood vessels.

Now Val carried a burlap sack rank with forest rot and decomposing flesh. Dutifully she followed her mother out of the Kingshead Woods and into the network of tunnels her great-great-great-grandmother had dug out underneath the mansion—with his help, of course. She had been a doomed woman, Deirdre Mortimer—abused and destitute, she'd assumed a new name and come to Sawkill in its early days. Desperate for work, she'd fallen for the owner of Kingshead at the time, a financier named Richard Carrington. He'd hired pretty young Deirdre as a maid, then seduced her. Then he began to hurt her, with his fists and his words, because that was all he knew how to do. Because he was powerful and she was not. Because he was man and she was not.

Could Val really blame her ancestor for making a deal with a devil, once he found her? Long life, health, power, vitality, safety, and disposing of that awful Richard Carrington, too—all in exchange for helping a monster from another dimension find his meals and use her blood to host his own growth?

Val clenched her fingers around the bag she carried.

Yes, Val blamed her.

And no, Val didn't.

Theirs was not a world that was often kind to women. And if Deirdre had decided to sell her soul for a bit of comfort, an illusion of safety, power she had long been denied?

Well, thought Val mutinously, *maybe that's the world's fault. Maybe these monsters are what they deserve.*

One of the tunnels below Kingshead led up to the red room, where he came when he wanted to play at being human, when he longed for the sensation of silk against his body as he lay with Val's mother in that awful empty room of stone. Sleeping with his human form, Lucy had taught young Val, was a way to strengthen the bond and make it easier to serve him.

It was a room that would someday belong to Val.

Another tunnel led out to the gently lapping waves below the cliffs, where Val had sat with Marion on her favorite bench. Val and her mother emerged here, in a tiny boat, rowed out into the deep of a small cove—a private inlet that only people at Kingshead could access, and that he made sure to keep veiled from prying eyes. They added a few heavy bricks to the bag of girl-parts and dropped it into the mumbling black water.

As Val rowed her mother back to shore, she imagined she could feel the sack sinking to the ocean floor, where it would come to rest in the cold dark, with the bottom-feeders and the luminescent creatures, with the abandoned and the never-to-be-found.

By the time they reached the tunnel and started climbing back up to the mansion, Val had decided she wouldn't confess what she had seen during the night. Not yet. Marion's secret, whatever it was, whatever allowed her to vanish in the blink of an eye—whatever secret enabled Zoey to fling Val away from her like she was some kind of superhero—these were secrets Val would keep, for now. She'd threatened Quinn, John, and Peter so thoroughly that she knew they wouldn't dare mention the incident with Zoey, not to a single soul, not while Val still drew breath.

A girl who can vanish, and a girl with incredible strength.

These impossibilities, Val thought, might be two sides of the same fantastical coin.

And she didn't want to share that notion with anyone just yet.

Not because I want to protect Marion, Val told herself, almost believing it. *It's because I want to watch her, and uncover her secrets on my own, and Zoey's, too.*

It's because one kiss isn't enough.

It's because, Val thought hollowly, the sea wind at her back, *I might die soon.*

Trailing her mother up the darkened stairs of Kingshead, Val looked into the shadows and saw a tiny fluttering piece of white—a moth, with peculiar black eyes on its wings.

Ssss-ssss, hissed the moth's wings, hovering close.

Val extended a hand toward the moth, and when it landed on her index finger, a sly chill ricocheted down her body, nape to navel.

Mine, came a small, faint voice. Val's weary mind ascribed it to the moth. She allowed herself the moment of fancy, cradling the tiny creature against her chest as though guarding a flickering flame.

BUT, OH, THE MOTHER AND daughter had missed one.

Because, the Rock thought, the woman loved few things in the world, but she had loved that stallion, and the loss of him clogged her senses, left her cloudy and distracted.

Because, the Rock knew, the daughter was thinking of a girl she had kissed, and grappling with terrors no child should have to face.

The Rock saw that they had missed it, and cried out for the girl to warn her:

A pale hand, bleached white and bloodless, clutching a starfish charm on a silver chain.

ZOEY

The Tesseract

Forty-five minutes after fleeing her bedroom, Zoey hid in the shrubs down the street from her house, waiting for her father to leave.

She watched his patrol car drive down the street, stop at the corner, and turn west. Maybe heading for the docks, to pick up Agent Briggs?

Zoey peered out of the bushes and scanned her surroundings one more time. Honestly, she would have preferred to remain hidden in the shrubs, possibly forever. But if there was actually an FBI agent on the island, then Zoey needed to do a thorough search of her father's secret room and remove anything incriminating or encoded or just plain weird before Briggs could start poking around and jump to terrible conclusions.

If, Zoey thought, *Dad hasn't removed it all already.*

Zoey's nose started to tingle. She rolled her eyes skyward until the feeling faded.

She did not have time to sit in the bushes and cry about how unfair it was that she had to worry about whether her father was lying and what he could be lying *about*.

She waited five more minutes, then hurried to their backyard, dropped off her bike, and slipped inside the house. She rushed to her father's bedroom, heaved the dresser aside, unlocked the door, and held her breath, desperately hoping that the combination would still work—and it did, thank God, and maybe that meant her father wasn't a terrible person or unforgivably weird or hiding something unforgivable, and that he *did* still love her, even if she had stolen his book, thank God, thank *God*.

Muttering a prayer of gratitude to the universe, Zoey climbed down the stairs. The carpeted walls swallowed away all sound. She switched on the desk lamp, then the computer. Next she opened the voice recorder on her phone, set it on the desk, and started searching the room.

"Hi, Future Zoey, this is Past Zoey," she announced. "I'm looking through Dad's secret room and I'm going to tell you all about it, so I don't forget anything. And also because it's super creepy down here, and I like the sound of my own voice. So." She crouched by a stack of plastic tubs against the wall, tried to move them, couldn't. Way too heavy. She found an old wooden chair, climbed onto the seat, opened the topmost crate.

"Ammunition," Zoey said. "Bullets and shit I know nothing

about. Great. Awesome. Closing that immediately."

On a set of metal shelves: "About a million cans of beans and vegetables and fruit. Also, SPAM. Gross."

Hanging on the wall: "Also, the guns. We can't forget the guns. Five of them. Super. Fantastic."

She returned to the desk and opened each drawer.

"Top drawers are just pens and notepads and tools," Zoey dictated. "A hammer, screwdrivers, wires." She sighed sharply. "I'm gonna be really pissed if he's building a bomb."

She moved to the deeper bottom drawers.

"Hanging file folders," she said, thumbing through the nearest ones. "They're packed with newspaper clippings, and some printed online articles. Each file's labeled with a year. Not every year, there are gaps. And they go back to . . ."

She squinted at the last folder. "1923? 1929, 1935, 1941 . . . Wait. I know these dates."

Then she saw the folder labeled 1975, and the spinning pieces of her mind settled and calmed.

1975. The year Evelyn Sinclair had disappeared.

She glanced through the other folders, scanning quickly.

"1986," she whispered. There it was. "Fiona Rochester." 1994? Yes. "Avani Mishra." And 2002? Grace Kang?

She pulled the folder labeled 2002 from the drawer, laid it on the desk, opened it. A stark newspaper headline stared back at her:

BELOVED TEEN DISAPPEARS FROM IDYLLIC SAW-KILL ROCK.

"Grace," Zoey whispered, running her fingers lightly across the black-and-white photo of a beaming Grace Kang in her Sawkill Day School graduation robes. Zoey had seen the photo a hundred times while researching the missing Sawkill girls. Another copy of it was pinned to the hidden bulletin board under her mattress.

She collected all the folders from the drawer and stacked them on the desk.

"So, Future Zoey," she said after a moment. "It's not weird for my dad to have these files, right? He's the police chief. Of course he would want to research this stuff. Obviously. Naturally. But then . . ." She approached the desk slowly. "There's this map. Not just of Sawkill, but the entire world."

She stared at it for a long time, then felt like kicking something, because staring at the map did nothing to illuminate the reason for it. She stalked around the room, pointedly ignoring the guns hanging on the walls. What could she do with the guns? It wasn't illegal to own them, unfortunately, unless some of these were truly illegal weapons, but how was she supposed to know that? Regardless, it certainly didn't look good, to have a secret underground room filled with guns. Zoey couldn't imagine Agent Briggs would be particularly pleased.

She marched back to the desk, and then she saw the black book, sitting beside the computer.

She really didn't have time to peruse the book. She needed to take it, and the files, and the freaky red map, and whatever else she could carry, and burn them all, and throw the ashes into the sea. Then if Briggs found the room, her father would just look like a plain old survivalist. Nothing strange or encoded to be found.

Zoey glared at the book, fear plugging her throat. "How am I supposed to know what's suspicious and what isn't?" she whispered to her dutifully recording phone. "How am I supposed to know if I can trust him?"

A thought she couldn't bear to voice: *What if he's involved with something terrible?*

Am I daughter, then, or am I citizen?

"Do I tell Briggs about all of this?" she muttered, sitting down at the desk and opening the book. "And what do I even *tell* him?" She started flipping through the pages of Latin text, past the first set of Collector illustrations, then past another dozen or so pages of text, and then landed on another collection of illustrations. These were meticulously rendered human figures: a white girl with pigtails, a black man wearing an old-fashioned tailored suit, a freckled man wearing overalls, an Asian woman in a beautiful flapper-style gown.

The illustrations grew darker and less faded as Zoey kept turning the pages, as though some had been recently added. And they all had one small detail in common:

Their eyes were round and white, like tiny headlights. No pupils. No irises.

Heart pounding, Zoey flipped back to the Collector drawings, just to check.

"Okay," she said, snapping pictures. "Future Zoey, see what

you make of this: both the monsters and the humans in this book all have the same eyes. Thora said the legend is that the Collector can assume different forms. So maybe these illustrations are of the different forms he can take?"

Zoey tried to imagine her father hunched over this book, underground in the dim lamplight, adding a sketch of a not-Marion with white eyes, and felt like she could quite possibly throw up.

She flipped the page, came across a chunk of pages filled top to bottom with cramped lines of Latin. Throughout the text were drawings, diagrams. Sketches of . . .

She peered closely, tilted the book toward the light, and saw a girl in scratchy silhouette. The girl carried a sword, her other arm thrust out with a rigid palm. A phrase scribbled beside her read: *SEMPER TRES.*

Zoey exhaled sharply. She was so sick of all the Latin. The Latin was creepy. It was a language of the dead.

She took a photo of the sword girl, then was about to turn the page when she noticed two things, one right after the other:

Her eye caught on a tiny line of English text sandwiched between the Latin, lettered in ink a little darker and sharper than the rest:

There is such a thing as a tesseract.

Zoey's blood crawled hot-cold just underneath her skin.

"'There is such a thing as a tesseract,'" she whispered. "Holy shit. Holy *shit.*"

It was a line from *A Wrinkle in Time*, the book her father had promised her he'd read, and, judging by the ink, this sentence had possibly been written recently.

A ping sounded from Zoey's phone. She glanced over to see a text notification, from Marion:

i chose Thora because she was fascinated with me

Then, a second text:

i craved her obsession

And a third:

she tasted sublime

The Distraction

Val followed her mother's trim form up the running path from the Kingshead Woods back to the house. It was a tradition of theirs, these mother-daughter runs. Three mornings a week, six miles each, and no amount of missing girls or panicked neighbors would change that.

As they passed the Althouse cottage, running lightly in single file—her mother in the lead, always—Val thought to herself, *Eyes front, Val. Just keep running. Eyes front.*

But she couldn't resist.

Mine.

She glanced right.

A canvas hammock stretched between two oak trees that grew on the cottage's eastern lawn, and Marion and her mother, clinging to each other like two people lost at sea, lay inside it.

Val's heart skipped sweetly along her ribs.

Her eyes flicked to her mother, then back to the hammock. The running path took them near enough for Val to hear that Marion was humming something, a song Val didn't know.

Val's mother waved at the Althouses. "I'll come check on you after I shower!" she called out, gesturing at herself. It made Val cringe, that false bright note in her mother's voice. Lucy Mortimer was not accustomed to being so chummy with the help, and it showed. "We'll have lunch, all right?"

Marion waved at them as they passed. Mrs. Althouse had snuggled up beside her like a child. A book lay facedown on Marion's stomach. She stroked her mother's hair, graying where Marion's was black as a starless night. Val wondered what it would feel like, to be curled up beside Marion's safe, solid body like that, and talk for hours, hiding nothing, pretending nothing.

She wondered if Marion also couldn't stop thinking about the previous night in the barn. If, in Val's arms, Marion had felt as seen and obvious and expansive and fully realized as Val had in hers.

Then Val's stomach lurched.

A cruel inner fist punched her ribs before plummeting down to slam against her pelvis.

Val stumbled over a tree root, and coughed, gasping for breath.

Her mother caught her by the arm.

"Was that him?" she asked, a slight tremor in her voice.

Val nodded. She touched her neck; her throat burned, like she'd recently gotten sick. "Yes," she whispered, "but I don't know why."

A lie. She suspected why: he'd noticed her noticing Marion.

Or, he knew what Marion had done, and he knew Val had seen it, too. And he wondered why she had yet to say anything to him about it.

Her mother, expressionless, shook Val free and ran ahead, as if it were imperative to put distance between them. Val did not look back at Marion, but she felt the pull of her all the way up the hill and into Kingshead, like the call of a warm bed after an endless winter.

MARION

The Other

Marion hadn't slept all night.

Instead, she sat on the floor beside her bed and acclimated herself to the moth.

Since she'd somehow appeared back in her room, sweaty and aching and doubting her own sanity, the moth hadn't left her side. She'd crawled to the bathroom, not wanting to dirty the floor, cleaned off her feet in the bathtub, and applied bandages to every scrape, then put on a pair of clean socks and hobbled back down the hallway.

The moth followed, fluttering unevenly beside her shoulder. When she returned to her spot on the floor next to her bed, the moth alighted on her knee. Its wings sighed open and closed like paper-thin lungs.

At first Marion thought: *I will smack this moth off my leg, like I would any bug. I will crush it under my palm and toss it in the toilet.*

But if she did that, she would be left alone, with no one and nothing else who understood that she had transported herself from the forest to the cliffs to an alien beach and back to her bedroom.

She said it aloud, the words feeling fat and unfamiliar on her tongue:

"Something's happening to me." Instead of smacking away the moth, she extended a finger. "Do you know what it is?"

The moth climbed aboard. Where it stepped, tiny coins of warmth bloomed on Marion's clammy skin. She raised her finger so she could look at the moth's eyes. Rimmed with white fur, they stared black and unblinking at her.

Marion watched them until her frantic heartbeat slowed.

Then she laughed, tears rising fast. "I'm talking to a moth." She lowered her finger. Agreeably, the moth fluttered onto her knee. "I'm losing my mind."

She climbed into bed, desperate for sleep. Sleep would cleanse her brain of the images she couldn't erase—the Mortimers' horse running with its broken leg and then throwing itself over the cliffs. The snowy beach. The smoking piles of bones.

But when Marion closed her eyes, that was all she could see. She tried for hours, but she couldn't quiet her brain, and her bed felt like stones under her sore limbs.

At last she opened her eyes and saw the moth perched across the room on her desk chair. Watching her.

"All right," Marion said. It was late morning, nearly noon. She sat up, returned to the floor. The moth floated down to meet her. Marion waited until it touched her knee, then nodded and took a long, steady breath. Trapped in her throat was a hysterical laugh, which made steady breathing difficult. But whatever. Never mind.

"Doesn't matter," she whispered. She thought of the snow-covered, sand-covered beach. The strange amber water, the lavender sky.

How had she gotten there the first time?

She glanced at the moth. "Do I have to go scare another horse or something?"

For answer, the moth began cleaning its antennae with its furry front legs.

Marion sighed. "Great. Helpful."

She leaned against the footboard of her bed. The thin metal post dug into her back, and with a jolt she remembered the electrical charge that had surged up from the ground and slapped her between her shoulder blades. It had told her to run after the charging horse. It had told her, *Go.*

She looked back at the moth. "Do you know what that was? What it means?"

The moth stared, its wings quivering so fast they became a blur. The slight whisper of wing against wing made words Marion couldn't understand.

She closed her eyes, her heart drumming fast, trying to re-create the previous night—how the air had felt against her skin, what frantic thoughts had blazed through her mind, what emotions had seized her as she watched the horse stagger.

Memory pictures formed behind her eyes—the black forest, the black night, the salt in the air, the crash of nearing waves, the horse's terrified cry.

A buzz tingled Marion's bare legs. The fibers of the rug itched and scratched. Sawkill Rock stretched vast and unmovable beneath her, but Marion was not afraid of it. Its existence was a comfort. It was a seal basking belly-up in the water. It was ancient and tired and it reached up for Marion's legs with tender tendrils, like a song traveling on invisible currents.

How had Charlotte described it, that first day on the ferry?

It's like this . . . this thing, *perched out there on the water.*

The bone cry arose, faintly, like the sound of approaching traffic—power, contained and far away, but coming up fast.

Marion welcomed the sound. She imagined her body opening to receive it. She was not a girl of dense muscle and clumsy bones. She was a network of air-filled tubes, of inflating balloons. She was a symphony warming up before the big night.

The moth fluttered away, leaving Marion's knee cold. She had the sudden, unshakable feeling that the Rock was watching her. Against the glass of her window tapped a branch from the fat oak tree outside.

"Hello?" Marion whispered.

The charge humming along the rug detonated, zipped up her spine, and planted itself at the base of her skull. The world shifted, like a cube squeezing through another cube to emerge whole and immense on the other side. Marion's breath caught in her throat, trapped between realities.

She opened her eyes.

She was no longer in her bedroom, nor was she on a foreign beach with cities in the sky.

She was downstairs, in her kitchen, on the breakfast table, of all places, beside the fruit bowl. In front of her was the window over the sink, which looked out over the twin giant oak trees and the hammock and, beyond, Kingshead.

Marion sat, legs crossed, trying to catch her breath. The hair on her arms stood up; the old static-balloon trick. The bone cry remained, shriller now, discordant. Urgent.

She wasn't sure if she wanted to laugh or cry. "What the *hell*."

A woman's voice called out from outside: "I'll come check on you after I shower! We'll have lunch, all right?"

Then the moth appeared, diving down from the ceiling to thump against the window—again, and again, and again.

At first Marion just stared at it. The moth, the trees, the sea, the horse.

Sawkill Rock.

Disparate pieces? Or one and the same?

The back of Marion's neck still tingled from where the charge had hit her.

She scrambled off the table and hit her knee on a chair. "Stop!" She raised her cupped hands, moved them between the moth and the glass. The moth climbed up her fingers and pressed its antennae against the window.

Marion followed its gaze:

First, Val and her mother, jogging up the running path toward Kingshead.

Oh, Val. Marion tried to remain unmoved by the sight of Val—her hair in a long golden braid, her arm muscles glistening with sweat, her face bright and open. Val was not to be trusted. Val was a mark.

But Marion couldn't help it; heat floated up her body to greet her fingertips. *Everyone thinks I live this charmed life,* Val had said, just before Marion had kissed her, her eyes luminous with tears, *but the truth is . . .*

What, Val? Marion should have said. *Tell me your truth.*

Marion's mother lay beyond Val, sleeping in the hammock. And beside her . . .

The bone cry's crescendo smacked Marion in the chest like a hammer.

Beside her mother was Marion herself. Stroking her mother's hair, holding her close, gazing furiously after Val.

The world slowed. The moth fluttered at Marion's ear.

Zoey's words returned to her: *Not-Marion*.

Marion slammed her hands against the window, screamed, "Mom! Wake up!"

The not-Marion in the hammock sat up, whipped her head around to stare. In the glare of the sun, her eyes flashed round and white.

She jumped out of the hammock, nearly sending Mrs. Althouse toppling to the ground, and ran for the woods.

MARION

The Message

Marion grabbed the car keys from the wall hook and burst out of the house. She flew down the porch steps so fast she fell off the bottom one, skinning her knee on the pavement. She pushed herself up and ran for the hammock. Her tender feet were on fire.

"Mom! Get up!"

Her mother was looking around, dazed, her cheek pink from sleeping with it pressed against not-Marion's shoulder. She squinted at Marion. "Marion? You nearly knocked me over."

"Come on, get up." Marion heaved her mother out of the hammock. "Faster, let's go."

"Marion!" Her mother pulled against Marion's grip. "What's wrong with you? Where are we going?"

"Mom, *move your feet*," Marion cried. Limping, she pushed

her mother down the hill toward the station wagon, and looked back over her shoulder toward the woods—just trees, no doppelgängers.

Mrs. Althouse let out a frightened sob. "You're scaring me, sweetie, slow down!"

Marion opened the passenger-side door and shoved her mother toward it. "Please, get in. Close the door and lock it."

Then Marion limped around to the driver's side, looking up once more at the woods. A movement at the corner of her eye—the front doors of Kingshead opening, revealing a slim golden figure. Val? Or her mother?

Marion jumped into the car, turned the key in the ignition, floored the gas pedal.

"Marion?" Her mom was staring at her, clinging to the door as if prepared to jump out if necessary. "What's going on? What did you see?"

Marion spoke into her phone—"Call Zoey"—and sped down the drive.

She watched the road ahead. She didn't dare look into the trees on either side.

Twenty agonizing minutes later, after dropping off her mother at the police station—which crawled with both staff and volunteers—Marion reached the Harlows' house.

"Zoey?" She jumped out of the car, limped toward the porch. She had called Zoey thirteen times during the drive, but Zoey had never picked up. Marion hadn't been able to stop scratching her skin. Her forearms stung, branded from elbow to wrist with red nail marks.

The house's front door flew open. Zoey marched down the steps to meet Marion in the driveway, and Marion laughed through her tears.

"Oh, thank God," she breathed, reaching out for a hug.

Zoey shoved her away and held out her phone. "What the fuck is this, Marion?"

Marion stared at the screen: her own name, their text conversation. She read the three latest messages once, then twice, and took a step back from the phone as if it had struck her.

i chose Thora because she was fascinated with me

i craved her obsession

she tasted sublime

"I didn't send those," Marion said at once.

Zoey's eyes were bright with tears. "This is sick. You're *sick*. This isn't funny."

"I swear, I didn't send them!" Marion pulled up their text chain on her own phone, ready to show Zoey that those messages were fake, that they'd been sent by someone else—but then Marion saw the letters staring back at her from her own screen, just as they'd looked on Zoey's:

she tasted sublime

"Holy shit," Marion whispered. She felt like she was teetering on the edge of a fatal drop. "They're here. They're in my phone."

"Right," said Zoey. "Because you sent them."

"I didn't! Please, I . . ." Marion scrolled uselessly through her phone, trying to find something, anything, to prove her innocence. "I didn't send them. I *didn't*. I don't know who did, but it wasn't me." She shook her head, burst into breathless tears. "Zoey, please, I . . . I saw her. The not-Marion. She was with my mom. She saw me, and her eyes changed. They were white; they *flashed*. She ran into the woods, and I grabbed my mom and drove away, brought her to the police station."

Marion tried to slip her phone back into her pocket, but her hands were shaking, so she could barely manage it. "I don't know what's happening. The horse. Last night, I . . . Jesus, Zoey, I don't know what to do."

Zoey watched her through narrowed eyes, then pulled up an image on her own phone and held it up.

"Did her eyes look like this?" she asked.

Marion squinted at the photo—a sketched little girl, hair in pigtails, eyes round and solid white.

A chill scraped across her arms. "Yes, like that, exactly! One moment her eyes were normal. They were *mine*. And then . . ." She gestured at the phone. "Where did you get that?"

Zoey hesitated.

"The secret room?" Marion reached for Zoey's hands, but Zoey flinched, her expression closed. Marion backed off, her hands in the air. "Please, will you show it to me? If there's something in there that helps explain any of this . . ." Yes. She was going to say it. She set her jaw, made herself look Zoey in the eye. "Zoey, I *teleported* last night."

Zoey went very still. "You what? Wait, no, hold on." She looked around the quiet neighborhood—freshly painted mailboxes and trimmed hedges, waterfront bungalows topped with lazy spinning weather vanes. "Let's go inside."

"Okay," said Zoey, once they'd climbed down into the secret room. She sat at a desk, in front of a computer that was asking for a password, and stared Marion down. "Continue."

Marion inhaled. The air was too close down here, too still and damp. "Remember, behind the police station, when you threw Val away from me like you were a superhero or something?"

"No, I'd forgotten all about that," said Zoey blandly.

"The same thing happened to me last night," Marion whispered. "I mean, not the exact same thing, but . . . I was walking around because I couldn't sleep"—*because after kissing Val, the world flipped on its axis, and how could I possibly sleep after that?*—"and one of the Mortimer horses, he totally freaked out, busted out of his fence, went running."

Marion told her the whole story—the horse jumping off the cliff, how she teleported to the snow-covered beach, seeing not-Marion in her mother's arms.

When she finished, Zoey stared at her, expressionless.

Marion deflated. "You don't believe any of this."

"No, I do, actually, and . . ." Zoey's eyes widened. "Wait. 'There is such a thing as a tesseract.'"

"A what?"

"You tessered." Zoey pounded her fist against the chair's arm. "That's what you're describing. You *tessered.* That can't be a coincidence. I wonder . . ."

She swiveled around in the chair, typed carefully into the password box. With a soft chime, the desktop appeared, tiled with neat rows of folders.

Zoey let out a shaky laugh. "*Tesseract.* He left the clue for me."

She opened a file labeled with that day's date. A video appeared—a frozen image of Chief Harlow, sitting where Zoey was sitting now.

"Those are the clothes he was wearing this morning," Zoey said quietly. "He recorded this right after I ran away from him."

Marion wanted to ask what had happened, why Zoey had run, but then the recorded Chief Harlow began to speak: "Zoey, record this video on your phone, and then delete the file from my computer."

He paused, waiting. Zoey pointed her phone's camera at the screen and started recording.

"This message, first and foremost, is an apology," the recorded Chief Harlow began. "I didn't mean to scare you this morning, Zo. I know I did, and that's unforgivable."

Marion glanced at Zoey. She had pressed her lips together in a tight hard line, her eyes bright and unblinking.

"Second," the recording continued, "I must apologize for this: I've been lying to you for a long time, and it's time to come clean. I hope you can understand why I kept this from you, even if you can't forgive me for it. I've screwed up a lot, sweetie, even as recently as just ten minutes ago. I could've handled so many things so much better. And I should have."

He paused and looked away from the camera, his jaw clenching. "I work for an ancient organization called the Hand of Light, along with thousands of other men around the globe. Some of them will arrive on Sawkill shortly. Some are already here."

"Briggs?" Zoey whispered.

"Our mission," Chief Harlow went on, "is to hunt down the creatures that have invaded our world. The world is bigger and older than you think, Zoey. There are many pockets of it, inaccessible to most humans, full of beings both remarkable and terrifying."

Chief Harlow drew in a deep breath. "One of these monsters lives here, on Sawkill. It has been hunting girls for decades. I believe it killed Thora. And Charlotte. And Jane."

Marion felt like she had been punched. She gripped the edge of the desk, leaned heavily against it.

Charlotte.

"The creatures can't be killed by any conventional means," Chief Harlow went on. "We—the Hand of Light—have tried for centuries. Even modern weapons barely slow it down. We have devised a particular method of extermination that has a high rate of success, but not without great cost. Zoey . . ."

Chief Harlow leaned a bit closer. "I let you move to Sawkill because I thought you would be safest near me. Given my knowledge of the monsters, and my connections with fellow soldiers like me who live all around the world, I thought having you here, potentially dangerous as it was, would be better than not knowing where you are, wondering every morning if—somewhere, in some town—you'd been taken by one of them. I was wrong. This is all happening more quickly than I've ever seen it. I think that the rate at which these girls have been disappearing means we're all in immediate danger."

His voice broke. He looked down at his phone, wiped his face. "Zo, why aren't you answering your phone, sweetie? I'm gonna come find you. If you see this message before I find you, then you've got to leave. You need to get off this island. Take our boat, get to shore. I've bought you a ticket from Boston to San Francisco for tomorrow morning. Go stay with your mother, and don't ever come back here. Don't worry about Grayson, or Marion, or anyone. Get as far away from Sawkill as you can. Stay indoors. Don't go out at night. Don't talk to strangers. Run, Zoey."

Marion, rigid, stared at the screen. The world had shrunk to the sounds of Chief Harlow's voice and the ragged push and pull of her own breathing.

Then, from upstairs, came the sound of the front door slamming shut, and a man calling out, "Zoey?"

"Oh my God." Zoey leaped up from the desk. "My dad's home. Shit. *Shit.*"

"Wait!" Marion grabbed her arm. "He left this video for you. He obviously wanted you to find it. Why would he be upset that we're down here?"

The sound of a man's voice drifted down through the ceiling—a voice Marion didn't recognize.

Zoey froze, listening.

"Who is that?" Marion whispered.

"No clue."

The sound of brisk footsteps tapped a countdown across the ceiling.

"I'll go stall them." Zoey ran for the exit. "Delete the file, turn off the computer, then hurry upstairs and move the dresser back."

Marion nodded, deleted the file, emptied the trash, then switched off the computer and turned—

And stopped.

Zoey was standing by the bottom step, gazing up at the secret door with a carefully closed-off expression.

A pair of boots walked down the stairs. They became a pair of legs in blue jeans, then a torso with a holstered pistol at the belt, then a white man with a shaved head and piercing blue eyes. He smiled first at Zoey, then at Marion.

"Excellent," he said. "I was getting tired of your father stalling, Zoey. Come into the kitchen, both of you. I'll make tea. We have much to discuss."

The sight of Zoey speechless lit a fire in Marion's belly. She stepped forward, fists clenched. "Where's Chief Harlow?"

"Right here, Marion," came the voice of Chief Harlow, upstairs in his bedroom. "It's all right. There's nothing to be afraid of."

Nothing to be afraid of. It was almost enough to make Marion laugh. Instead, she clasped Zoey's hand and led the way upstairs.

ZOEY

The Truth

In the kitchen, Zoey filled up four orange cups with water from the tap, brought them one by one to the table, then flung herself into a chair, crossed her arms, and glared back and forth between her father and Agent Briggs, fingernails digging into her flesh.

Marion held her cup between her hands but didn't drink from it.

Zoey's father gulped down his entire glass.

Neither Briggs nor Zoey touched theirs.

Outside the kitchen, in the foyer, the old family cuckoo clock struck one in the afternoon.

"All right," said Zoey's father, setting down his cup. "The situation is this: you know the island tales about the Collector."

Zoey remained very still, watching her father closely. In her father's message, he had seemed panicked, ready to shove her off the island at the next possible opportunity.

But now he was sitting placidly at the kitchen table, like she hadn't just watched that terrifying video, like everything was the same as it had been before she'd run from the house this morning. And as far as he knew, maybe she hadn't watched the video.

Maybe he didn't want Briggs to know he had left it for her?

Maybe, thought Zoey, suddenly queasy, *he doesn't trust Briggs.*

What had he called that organization in his message?

The Hand of Light.

"Zoey told me about the Collector," said Marion. "A local fairy tale. An urban legend."

He nodded. "And one rooted in truth. There is indeed a monster on this island, and—"

"And he eats girls." Marion looked at Briggs, her gaze steady and clear. "Doesn't he?"

Zoey couldn't help it; she glanced over at her father, wishing she could tell him right then and there that they'd watched the video, wishing she could have him to herself for a moment, to ask him what was going on without Briggs nearby. And for a second, their eyes locked, and something about the expression on her father's face—that careful placidity, the steadiness of his gaze, the square wall of his shoulders—told her what she needed to know:

He guessed that she'd watched the video.

And he was glad.

Briggs nodded. "He does eat girls, Marion, yes. And he's not the only one. There are many, all across the world."

"Where do they come from?" Marion asked.

Briggs leaned closer, like a professor excited to lecture on his favorite subject. "Imagine, if you will, a sponge—"

"Animal, cleaning, or Bob?" Zoey interrupted.

Her father gave her a Look. Marion exhaled a soft laugh.

"What?" Zoey returned her father's Look with one of her own. "I assume specificity is important here."

Briggs's small smile did not meet his eyes. "Let's go with cleaning." He retrieved a flat orange sponge from the sink. "Exhibit A: a sponge. If you consider it from a distance, it looks fairly solid." Briggs backed away from them, sponge resting flat in his palm. "Wouldn't you agree?"

Zoey bristled at the overly patient quality of his voice, but Marion simply nodded. "Yes, all right."

"But if you look more closely," said Briggs, returning to them, "you'll see that the sponge is full of holes. This is also true of the world." He set the sponge in the center of the table. "If you looked at it from afar, you would see a solid globe. But if you know what to look for, you'll find that it's full of craters and divots, pockets and tunnels. Some big, some small. We call them obscurae, plural. Obscura, singular. They are old, and they are many. And some of them are full of monsters."

Zoey kept her face a mask of careful disinterest. But her blood raced and roared, and she was beginning to feel dangerously light-headed. The world was expanding too quickly for her to keep up.

"Where did the obscurae come from?" Marion picked up the sponge, turned it over in her hand. "What made them?"

"We're not sure," Briggs replied. "It's possible they're entry points to a multiverse. Other scholars subscribe to a more fantastical theory—that the obscurae are lingering remnants of an old magic we can't possibly understand, which originates in a place completely inaccessible to both us and the monsters. In our lore, we refer to this realm as the Far Place."

"Whose lore is this, exactly?" asked Zoey. "And what scholars?"

Briggs opened his mouth to answer, but Marion cut him off. "The monsters . . . They live in the obscurae?"

Chief Harlow nodded. "And, now, they also live here. Some of them, anyway. We don't know if the invasion is deliberate, or if some of the creatures have accidentally wandered out of their worlds and into our own."

The map. Zoey thumped her clenched fists against her thighs. *The red dots are where the monsters live.*

How much red had dotted the map? Thirty cities? Forty?

Her father glanced her way, then back at Briggs.

"So, if the monsters can travel between our world and theirs," said Marion slowly, "can we travel to the obscurae, too?"

The kitchen, which had already been quiet, seemed to grow an extra layer of silence.

Now Marion's voice was the one to return to Zoey: *I was*

in this other . . . place. I don't know where. I've never seen a place like that.

Teleportation.

Tessering.

Zoey, veins suddenly sizzling, fought to keep her face devoid of expression.

Briggs leaned back in his chair, stretching out his legs until they bumped into Zoey's. "It has been attempted. Not successfully, I'm afraid."

"Well, then . . ." Marion sandwiched the sponge between her hands, then looked at Briggs with wide, innocent eyes. "Can they be killed?"

No. They couldn't. Zoey's father had said as much in his video. But of course Marion wouldn't know that, because Marion hadn't seen the video, because there *was* no video, as far as Briggs was concerned.

Zoey wanted to plant a big sloppy kiss on Marion's cheek.

"I'm afraid not," said Briggs, with a sigh. "We've tried many different methods over the centuries, but the creatures are clever and fast, and they take many forms. They can essentially regenerate faster than we can hurt them. They self-destruct and disappear into hiding to recover, then respawn in a different location, and the process begins again."

Zoey clenched her jaw so hard her teeth hurt.

In her father's video, he'd said there *was* a way to kill the monsters: *We have devised a particular method of extermination that has a high rate of success, but not without great cost.*

So Briggs was lying.

Or else, her father was.

"Who's we?" Marion asked. "You said, 'We've tried many different methods.' We who?"

"The Hand of Light," Briggs answered, his posture straightening. "We are an old organization. We hunt the monsters, and we try to prevent as many deaths as possible."

Zoey's father shifted in his chair, cleared his throat, slumped a little, and clasped his hands on the tabletop.

Was he trying to act like he was ashamed, to have kept this revelation from his daughter for so long?

Or was he praying that she wouldn't spill the beans about his video? Maybe this was information only Briggs was authorized to share?

Marion looked at Zoey's father. "You're one of them, too?"

He gave her a tired smile. "I am."

Zoey planned to make a scene, pretend that this was the first she was hearing about the Hand of Light, that she hadn't been suspecting monsters all along.

But when she opened her mouth, what came out was this: "If you're going to try to catch it or something, or at least track it, I want to help."

"Absolutely not!" Her father's voice exploded, making Zoey jump. He pushed his chair back and stood. "I'm done sitting here. I'm done with this. Every minute we sit here is a minute closer to his next kill."

"Now, Ed, there's no need for shouting," said Briggs. "You're going to frighten the girls."

"Good, they should be frightened—"

"Shut up." Zoey placed her hands flat on the table and stood. "Just shut up, Dad."

Both men fell silent. Marion watched her quietly from her seat.

"For months, I've been wondering what happened to Thora," Zoey said. "I theorized, I asked, I ranted, I cried. I wanted answers and couldn't find any. Nobody could. Except you had them the whole time," she said, pointing at her father, "and never told me."

"I wanted to protect you."

Zoey scoffed. Her hands were shaking, as was her voice, which really pissed her off. A shaking voice made her sound frail, breakable, and she was neither of those things. She was *furious.*

"So you didn't think I could handle what's really going on?" she muttered.

Her father's expression grew bleaker by the moment. "I didn't want you to be afraid—"

She cut him off. "My best friend disappeared. I was already afraid. But if you'd trusted me enough to be straight with me, maybe I would have been less afraid. Or at least I would have known the truth and could have looked my fear in the eye." Zoey's cheeks flushed hot as she glared at her father. His eyes were bright, and his mouth wobbled like he was trying not to cry, but she wouldn't feel sorry for him, she *wouldn't.* "You've made a fool out of me. You treated me like some dumb, fragile kid."

"Zo—" Her father's voice cracked. He held out his hands to her in supplication.

"This thing killed my best friend," said Zoey, ignoring him to look at Briggs instead. "I'm gonna do whatever I can to help you hunt it down."

Briggs smiled gently. "Well, Zoey, that's a really nice offer, but . . ." He scratched the back of his head, wincing a little. "The thing is, sweetie, your dad and I, and our friends . . . We know what we're doing, we know our procedures, and this is really something we'd rather you left to us—"

Zoey spun away before he could finish, before she could fly at him and slap him for talking to her like she deserved nothing more than a pat on the head.

And before the tingle building up her arms and legs detonated into something like whatever it was that threw Val into those snapdragons.

She stormed up the stairs and to her room, opening and slamming the door shut. She crawled under her quilt and lay there, her humming hands clutched against her chest to calm them down.

A few minutes later, Marion entered.

"I told them I wanted to check on you," said Marion. "They're making sandwiches. They said to take our time."

Zoey snorted, which made her eyes sting. "How generous of them."

"What can I do?"

"You know what I'm thinking?" Zoey wiped her face with

the back of her hand. "I'm thinking that these monsters they're hunting . . . They don't work alone."

Marion crossed her arms over her chest, frowning. "What are you saying?"

"You know exactly what I'm saying." Zoey waved at Marion impatiently. "I'm saying the recent discovery of creepy old dude-cults doesn't change the fact that I don't trust Val Mortimer, or her mother, and I never have, and I never will. And the second—the *second*—I have any sort of actual evidence I can give weirdo Briggs down there, I'll do it. I'll sic the whole damn cult on them."

Marion was quiet for a moment. "You think Val and her mother are *helping* this monster?"

"Don't give me that *You're crazy, Zoey* tone of voice, Marion." Zoey glared up at the ceiling. "Not today."

After a long beat of silence, Marion pulled off her boots and hoodie, then slipped under the quilt beside Zoey before pulling the soft patchwork fabric up to their chins.

Zoey shifted away a little, her ceiling-glare deepening and her mind racing. She didn't *think* Marion had sent those texts about Thora, but what did she know? Really, she hardly knew the girl. And apparently, she hardly knew *anything.*

She closed her eyes, trying not to think about her father's wounded expression. *I wanted to protect you.*

The clock on her nightstand ticked through the silence. Marion's breathing came slow and steady.

It took a long time for Zoey to find her voice again, to ask the question that was bothering her more than any other—the question that neither her father nor Briggs had addressed, not in the kitchen and not in the video.

"Why do the monsters eat girls?" she asked at last. Her voice sounded small.

When Marion didn't answer, Zoey turned on her side to face her. "Marion?"

"Because," Marion answered, looking beyond Zoey to the sea, "when a predator hunts, it seeks out the vulnerable. The desperate."

Zoey's laugh was bitter. "Oh, and we poor delicate girls are vulnerable and desperate, is that what you're saying?"

"What I'm saying," Marion said, now looking right at Zoey, her gray eyes bright, "is that girls hunger. And we're taught, from the moment our brains can take it, that there isn't enough food for us all."

MARION

The Crown

Charlotte had been missing for five days, and Marion didn't want to think about it for at least a couple of hours. She didn't want to think about monsters that ate girls, the men who hunted them, and a world pocked with obscurae.

She wanted, simply, to exist for a while in stillness.

She left Zoey's house, picked up her mother from the police station, and drove home with her in silence. Only after Marion parked the car did her mother speak.

"What was all that about earlier?" she said quietly. "What were we running from?"

Marion sat with her hands on the steering wheel, staring up the drive at Kingshead, and feeling so suddenly, utterly tired that she couldn't think of a good lie.

"Can I tell you about it later?" she said. "Can we just . . . have lunch instead?"

After a moment, her mother's soft hand squeezed her own.

"All right, my little mountain," her mother said quietly. "Don't worry alone for too long, though, all right? You can tell me, whatever it is."

Marion considered turning into her mom's arms and burrowing there until the world repaired itself.

But if she hid herself away, who would hide her mother?

Marion blinked away her tears and stepped out into the afternoon light.

That evening, Marion warmed up a bowl of vegetable soup on the stove and made her way slowly into the living room, oven mitts on her hands.

At the sound of steps on the front porch, she froze. A knock rapped, soft and swift.

The creatures are clever and fast, and they take many forms.

Marion glanced at the kitchen, where a set of knives gleamed on the countertop. If she threw the bowl of steaming soup at whatever it was, that might give her time to grab the knives.

"Marion?" called Val, from outside. "I brought movies. I thought maybe you'd want some company?"

A war broke out in Marion's gut.

On one side: Bring Val inside, feed her soup, coax information from her. Keep your head. Keep your wits close. Dance around the subjects of monsters and hidden world-pockets, and watch Val's face for secrets and lies.

On the other side: Bring Val inside, feed her soup, ask her about her mother, ask her about growing up rich and beautiful, ask her about what keeps her up at night, ask her, listen to her, tell her stories, touch her face, find another wall to press her against, ask her of what future she dreams, and what future she dreads.

Another knock, more hesitant: "Marion?"

Marion's mother, tucked under a blanket on the couch with sitcom reruns flickering on the TV, called out, "Is someone at the door?"

"It's Val." Marion set down the bowl on the end table, her head quietly spinning, her cheeks flushed. "Hold on, I'll be right back."

It was, maybe, a little selfish and self-centered, and maybe even a little stupid, but Marion couldn't stop smiling. Despite her grief, despite the monsters lurking in the near-dark, she smiled. She opened the door, and her mind screamed, *What if Zoey's right? What if she's behind it all?*

But still Marion beamed. It felt rebellious, to beam. It felt like sticking up her middle finger at the world and laughing.

"What's wrong with being selfish?" Marion asked. A strange greeting, but oh well. If Val wanted to leave, she could.

But Val didn't leave. She stood on the porch with an armful of movies, wearing sweatpants and a baggy Sawkill Day School T-shirt. Her hair was slung up into a high, messy ponytail. She wore no makeup whatsoever.

Marion hungered at the sight of her. Staring at Val was a revolt against the world, against logic, against Zoey.

Val arched an eyebrow. "'What's wrong with being selfish'?"

It was a test, Marion decided, her heartbeat tapping against her throat. If Val thought Marion was weird for asking such a question, for answering the door unlike other people answered doors, then Marion would turn her away. Claim a headache. Explain that she needed time alone with her mother.

She would, in other words, chicken out and come to her senses.

But Val just laughed, low and throaty. "Not a damn thing wrong with it, in my book."

And Marion's relieved smile welcomed her inside.

"You're really good with her," said Val, two hours later, tucked into a corner of the couch while Marion's mother slept at the other corner and Marion herself tidied the living room.

As she moved toward the kitchen, Marion felt Val's eyes on her back—and maybe, if she wasn't imagining it, also sliding lower.

She applauded herself for choosing the polka-dot pajama shorts. They weren't the sort of garment she'd usually wear in front of people who weren't family; they hardly covered the things shorts were designed to cover.

The dishes put away, Marion returned to the living room, put a finger to her lips, and nodded at the stairs. Val smiled and gathered up the movies they hadn't yet watched, ridiculous romantic comedies full of mush and meet-cutes that made her mother smile.

Once Marion had helped her mother to bed and left her

dozing with a glass of fresh water, Marion and Val headed for the stairs.

With every step, Marion felt *this close* to stumbling. After two hours of sitting beside Val, surreptitiously watching Val watch the movie, watching Val laugh, watching Val pick at her nails and twirl strands of hair around her fingers, Marion's blood raced so hot and fast she feared she might erupt.

"I mean it," said Val, trailing Marion up the stairs. "You're a good daughter. You're so gentle and patient with her."

Marion tried not to wonder if Val was buttering her up for some nefarious purpose.

Marion tried not to think about her own ass, and Val's face, and the proximity of the two.

Marion tried to remember to breathe.

"I do what any daughter would," Marion managed. Miraculous, that she could form words. *Well done, tongue and brain.*

Val's laugh was harsh. "Not really. If my mom ever needed me to take care of her, I'd give her both middle fingers on the way out the damn door."

Marion's bedroom. *Oh, God, oh, God.* She turned the handle and led the way inside.

"Why don't you like her?" Marion switched on her desk lamp. "Your mom, I mean."

"Because she doesn't love me," Val answered at once. She sprawled across Marion's bed, staring at the ceiling, one long leg swinging alongside the mattress like a pendulum.

Marion busied herself with starting one of the movies, for

background noise. Ostensibly for watching, but *right*, like Marion would be able to pay attention even if all she and Val did was sit rigid, side by side, not touching.

Remember, you're here to observe her, question her, lie to her, chided a voice in Marion's head that sounded remarkably like Zoey's.

"Because my mother manipulates people," Val continued, "and taught me how to do the same thing. Because she chased away my father before I could even meet the man. Because she doesn't love me, and yet had a kid anyway. Because she wants that same sorry life for me."

Val paused, cheeks pink and indignant. She glared at the ceiling, and Marion, fists clenched, her inner Zoey-voice telling her to chill out, nevertheless imagined kissing the perfect straight line of Val's nose.

"Because for a long time," Val continued, "that's the kind of life I wanted, too. All because she told me to want it. Because she taught me to be a girl who wants what other people want and ignores my own heart."

Marion searched for something to say and came up with nothing.

"If my mom was the next one to disappear," said Val, her voice tight and toneless, "I wouldn't bother to look for her."

And, without stopping to think, Marion marched over to Val, ready to slap the shit out of her.

Val sat up, looking suddenly mortified, and when Marion swung out her hand, Val caught her wrist and stopped her.

Val, unsurprisingly, was strong. Marion had felt that lean strength last night in the stables, dragging her fingers up and down Val's body.

Now, she could hardly see Val's face for her tears, and she wasn't sure what she was most upset about—what Val had said, or the fact that she couldn't seem to think straight with Val so near.

"That was an asshole thing to say," Marion spat.

"God, I'm sorry." Val tried to touch her cheek, but Marion jerked away.

"You can't just say stuff like that and get away with it." Marion turned, wiping her eyes. "Just because you're rich and beautiful—"

"I know."

Marion couldn't contain a harsh sob. "Do you realize I've lost half my family?"

Marion moved away, stumbling a little, and leaned hard against her dresser. She was the most rotten person in the world. Her Zoey-voice screamed: *Val could have killed Charlotte!* But Marion didn't believe that, did she? Agent Briggs and Chief Harlow, they hunted monsters. A monster had killed Charlotte.

A monster, not Val.

"Marion." Val's voice, very close. "I'm sorry."

Marion glared back at her, not caring that she could already feel her skin splotching, her face swelling. She was such an ugly crier.

Val moved closer, her eyes shimmering. "I'm sorry. I am, I'm the worst."

“Fuck you, Val,” Marion whispered.

Val leaned in, brushed her cheek against Marion’s cheek.

“I’m sorry,” Val breathed across Marion’s skin, making her shiver. “I’m an ass sometimes.”

“Most of the time,” Marion said, letting herself melt into Val’s touch. Her trembling legs wouldn’t hold her up for much longer.

“Most of the time,” Val agreed, laughing a little. When Val wiped a tear from her chin, Marion could no longer resist.

She cupped Val’s face in her hands and kissed her.

Val gasped against her mouth. Her hands flew to Marion’s waist, and then she smiled so broadly that Marion did, too. Their teeth clacked together, bumped lips, bumped tongues, and Val laughed again, tugging Marion back to the bed. With Val’s hands sliding up under her shirt and her own hands impatiently tugging off Val’s pants, Marion forgot that she’d never properly made out with anyone, that she wasn’t gorgeous and lithe like Val or tiny and elfin like Zoey.

As Val’s lips kissed up and down her neck, across her collarbones, and lower, skimming over her breasts, she forgot that she was Marion—the rock, the good, steady girl.

She forgot that her father was dead, and that Charlotte was almost surely dead, and that her mother might live forever in a fog.

She forgot that everyone on Sawkill was out hunting not just for one missing girl but two. That the woods outside her window had witnessed twenty-five girls vanish into the night.

She forgot all about the Hand of Light and monsters, and

Zoey being pissed as *hell* once she found out about this.

Marion forgot everything but Val—her touch, her warmth and softness, the sounds she made when Marion kissed the tender skin behind her ear. Val's hands skimmed down her bare torso, and Marion arched into her touch.

"You make me forget everything I hate," Val murmured against Marion's belly. "And I hate a lot of things. You make me forget," she said, punctuating the words with a kiss to Marion's trembling skin, "who I was born to be."

"Val?" Marion gripped the sheets hard, body twisting. She needed to be closer to Val, needed Val against her breasts, her belly, between her thighs.

"Hmmm?" Val murmured, wrapping her limbs around Marion, pulling her close, twining her legs with hers.

"Shut up for a while?"

And Val laughed again, soft like the drop of starlight. She kissed Marion's mouth right as her fingers slid down Marion's shorts, between her legs, kissing her to muffle her soft, high cries, kissing her until she could hardly breathe. A fall of golden hair draped around Marion, dragging lightly across her skin. Val's ponytail had come loose, surrounding Marion in Val's scent, Val's warmth, Val's voice.

When Val finally broke away, she pressed her panting mouth against Marion's neck, and whispered things to Marion that she honestly couldn't decipher, because Val's fingers were drawing Marion higher and higher, and Marion clamped her thighs around Val's hand, and moved against it, circling, and she couldn't stop moving, not even for a second. If she stopped, she would die.

"Please," Marion begged, clutching Val to her, sliding her hand down Val's bare back, under her shirt and then into her pants, palming her supple skin. "Please, *God.*"

Val smiled against Marion's breasts and acquiesced, pressing her thumb right where Marion wanted her to until she came apart on the tangled damp sheets, her world a pulsing haze of warm red and black and gold.

"Marion?"

Soft lips, brushing against her own.

"Helloo-oo-o, Marion."

Teeth, lightly nibbling on her jawline.

Hours later, years later, still blinking herself back to reality, Marion opened her eyes.

She saw Val smiling down at her, and then, behind Val, a cloud of the tiny black-eyed moths fluttered down from the ceiling. They alighted on exquisite, oblivious Val, coming to rest on her shoulders and at the ends of her hair. They encircled her scalp, a delicate fluttering crown.

"Hey," Marion breathed, a shaky smile on her face. She closed her eyes, blushing, and turned her face into her pillow, and laughed.

Her, whispered the moths, laughing along with her, their joy unfettered. *Her.*

Val.

Val grinned, and flopped down on the mattress beside

Marion, sending thousands of white wings fluttering up around her like tossed snow.

Marion gazed over at her. In that moment, she was not a rock but a girl. Not a fatherless, sisterless daughter, but a living, breathing, selfish creature who wanted. Who *craved.*

The rest? It could wait until tomorrow.

She pressed Val gently into the mattress and whispered, "Your turn."

VAL

The Red Room

The next morning, Val crept home at dawn to find her mother standing in the foyer, already fully dressed, sipping a cup of tea.

Val froze. "Mom! You're up early."

"Good morning, Valerie," said her mother. "I just received an interesting phone call from the police."

As Val watched, a lock of hair slipped loose from her mother's chignon. Val's insides shrank away from her skin. She resisted the urge to run; running would only make things worse.

"They found Charlotte Althouse's severed hand in our woods." Val's mother walked to the hall table, set down her tea. "It was clutching a necklace, a chain with a starfish charm."

"Oh, God," Val whispered. She placed a hand on her stomach, where only a few minutes ago, Marion had pressed a hot, open-mouthed kiss. "They don't know yet. I should go tell Marion—"

"There's no need for that." Her mother's voice shook, barely containing itself. "Chief Harlow assured me he was on his way."

As if on cue, a car door slammed, then another.

Val hurried to one of the windows flanking the door. She watched as Chief Harlow and a white man she didn't recognize walked up the Althouses' front steps and knocked on the door.

Val hurried to the latch. "I should be with her—"

"No, Valerie," said her mother. "You'll stay right here, and you'll explain your negligence to me. You'll explain why you left that girl's hand out for anyone to find."

Val hovered at the window, unable to move. Mrs. Althouse's scream of grief tore through the morning air like the rending of the earth. The woman sank to her knees on the porch, Marion catching her right at the end, while Chief Harlow stood over them with his hat held against his heart.

Val's eyes filled with tears. She stepped away from the glass and pressed her back against the door. She leaned into the unyielding wood and struggled to gather her breathing.

Her mother appeared beside her, gazing out the window. "Hunters have come to our island. They're going to try and sniff us out. They're going to try to kill him."

A wild hope erupted in Val's heart. "Hunters? Who are they?"

"It doesn't matter. They'll fail." Her mother glanced at her. "But they'll know he has hosts. That's what he told me. He told me they know how this works, at least enough to be a danger to us. They'll be looking for us, and could very well discover everything—if, that is, we continue to carelessly leave body parts lying around."

Heat climbed up Val's body, which thrummed with the desire to run, but she didn't dare move.

"We existed for generations on this island," her mother continued, "undisturbed and untroubled. Until you came along, that is. My daughter, the one to bring ruin down upon me. Well." Her mother laughed softly. "Not if I have anything to say about it."

Her blood roaring in her ears, Val watched her mother quietly turn the locks on the front doors.

"If you'll join me in the library, please?" Lucy Mortimer murmured, then glided past Val through the foyer, to the heavy double doors at the other end.

Val considered running. She could sprint down the driveway, throw herself at Chief Harlow, point back at Kingshead and scream, *In there! That's where the killer is!*

But then what?

He would find her. He would make her life even blacker a hell than it already was.

So Val followed her mother. The cold brick floor shocked her bare feet like the jab of tiny swords. Her skin tingled sharply; she was allergic to the very air. Normally, she wouldn't be trembling. Normally, she wouldn't feel a thing. She would bear her punishment in silence, then hide herself away in her room until she felt capable of looking people in the eye and keeping her mouth shut.

But that morning, every breath Val sucked in reminded her of the new lines of her body—awakened by Marion's hands, baptized by Marion's lips. By the time her mother closed the library doors behind her, Val felt completely unstitched.

She heard the turn of the key.

She closed her eyes, hoping it would be over quickly.

It wasn't.

Her mother yanked her around with a fist in her hair, backhanded Val once, twice, then threw her to the floor.

Val couldn't move—head spinning, ears ringing. She tasted blood and swallowed it, because the rug had cost thirty thousand dollars, and her mother might actually kill her if she stained it.

This, though? The beating? It was nothing. It was simply a lesson, and one Val knew she deserved.

"Get up," her mother ordered. "Get up and look at me."

Val obeyed, but she was still grabbed by the throat and shoved against the nearest bookcase. Pinned there, her mother's soft hands around her throat, Val let herself be half strangled. Her face swelled with blood; she lost all sensation in her fingers except for a strange sizzling heat. She choked, gasping, and the heat traveled first up her arms and then dropped down to rest in her stomach like a swallowed star.

When her mother released her, Val slumped to the ground, heaving, and realized too late that she was crying. Crying was not a thing that the women of her family did. He did not abide frailty; he suffered no weak links.

But her mother had seen, and yanked her to her feet, slapping her once more. Val stumbled and caught herself on the back of the chaise longue. She glimpsed her own tear-streaked, bloody-lipped face in the mirror against the far wall, and felt so utterly, blazingly sorry for that poor girl, so desperate to protect her, that her body spasmed, as if she'd stepped out of frigid darkness into a scorching desert at midday.

The world shifted and sharpened against her skin. The ground was hot coals beneath her bare feet.

She whirled on her mother and rasped, "Get the *fuck* away from me." Then she planted her right hand on her mother's chest and electrified her.

The blistering heat detonated from beneath the floor and sliced up through Val's limbs like lightning. It gathered white-hot in her palms and made her glow—every strand of hair, every carefully cultivated muscle, every bead of sweat.

For two seconds, Val was nothing but energy and rage and blood and bone. She gripped her mother and branded her. The front of Lucy Mortimer's blue silk blouse caught fire and turned to ash. She screamed, and Val staggered away a second later—no longer illuminated, a mere girl once more.

A red handprint remained on her mother's chest.

Glistening. Smoking.

Cooked.

Val stared. Her mother stared back.

For a moment, the known order of things flipped upside down.

Twin thoughts exploded in Val's mind:

Like Zoey?

Like Marion.

A girl with incredible strength.

A girl who can vanish.

A girl who burns.

Val hurried to her mother, hands dim and outstretched. "Mom, I'm sorry! I don't know what happened!"

An instant later, Lucy Mortimer returned to herself. "Look what you've done," she said hoarsely, tears shimmering in her eyes, her face tight and pale. "You've made him angry with me."

She grabbed Val by the collar, opened the secret door behind the bookshelves, and dragged her daughter down the stairs.

"No!" Val screamed, raking her fingers across the wood-paneled walls, her nails catching on each groove. Not the red room, *not the red room*, it wasn't her time yet!

But she was too frightened to fight very hard. What had *happened*, up there in the library? Whatever it was, her skin still tingled from it. Her vision swirled with glowing shapes, like she'd stared too hard at the sun. Memories returned to her: Herself, flying back from Zoey, scraping her skin across the ground. Marion, seen from Val's bedroom window, flickering out of existence like someone almighty had switched her off.

Val's palms burned her clenched fingertips. If she opened her fists, what would happen? Would that light return? Would she torch the mansion to ashes?

She kept her fists tightly shut, and closed her eyes, and

gasped out a little sob. She would contain herself. She would swallow, and swallow, until the burning feeling in her chest, in her limbs, in her gut, subsided. Because if she hurt her mother again, and too badly for her to survive, then it would be Val's turn.

Val's turn to lie with him in the red room.

Val's turn to host him, to anchor him in this world that was not his own.

Val's turn to bear the mark that her mother wore low on her belly, where no one else could see but him. And at the thought of that, with the electricity still faintly coursing through her body, Val threw up the toast she'd nibbled on, giddy and not at all hungry, in Marion's kitchen that morning.

Her mother made a disgusted sound, released her, and let her fall. Val landed in a puddle of her own sick beside the bed.

"Get a hold of yourself," her mother ground out, her hair fallen loose now, her cheeks flushed. "When I come back, I expect you to be my daughter again."

Then she turned and left, not looking back even as Val crawled after her, pulling at her skirt.

"Mom, *please*! Don't leave me here!" The door slammed shut in Val's face. She screamed for help, even though she knew the walls of this room were too thick for any sound to escape them. She beat against the walls, in the damp, still dark, until her fists were raw.

Val tucked herself into the corner farthest from the bed and hugged her knees to her chest. She prayed, to any god who hadn't written her off as completely lost, that *he* wouldn't come sniffing around and find her.

When she fell asleep at last, blistering white light hurtled scattershot across her dreams, like the veins of a pitiless universe.

THE BEAST'S HOWLS COULD NOT be heard in this world, not by human ears, but the Rock heard every one.

It heard the furious hunger in the sound, and knew the beast would feed again, and soon.

Before the moon filled in two days' time, fresh blood would once more paint the Rock's woods a bright shivering red.

The Rock sensed all this, as it watched the girl huddled underground. Encased by walls of the Rock's own stone, carved to stand cruel and unfeeling, the girl wept. When each of her tears hit the floor, the Rock felt the impact like the drop of comets from the sky.

The Rock wished, not for the first time, that its hands were solid enough to cradle the lost and lonely.

The Rock wished it had the power to banish the evil and the profane to the farthest, darkest realm, all on its own, without asking such tasks of its young.

Courage, the Rock hummed through its deep roots of sea and silt.

Courage.

Courage, dear heart.

VAL

The Scent

The next day, Val felt him awaken.

She sat in the corner of the red room with her knees drawn to her chest, her stomach tight and empty, her eyes swollen and red. His hunger came on suddenly, as if her veins formed the curve of a fragile egg, and suddenly the shell was splintering. Two minutes later, the door to the red room opened, revealing her mother—hair curled, high-necked blouse shielding her burned décolletage.

Val's gaze fell at once to the spot where her scorching hand had fallen.

Her own chest tightened, remembering.

Was it a thing to fear, that power?

Or a thing to find again?

And, churned her tired thoughts, *is it a power I share with others?*

With Zoey?

With Marion?

"Clean yourself up," Val's mother instructed, watching Val stagger to her feet. "Don't keep him waiting."

Silently Val obeyed, her eyes lowered to the ground but her heart wide-awake and pounding. Her mother flinched away from Val when she passed.

Val said nothing, but as she climbed the stairs to the library, she touched the finger-shaped bruises on her throat. She recovered the memory of her mother's fists and allowed them to strike her again, and again, and again. She walked up the stairs to her bedroom: One step, punch. Two step, *punch.*

With each remembered strike, Val's tired head cleared.

With each phantom burst of pain, the dying fire in Val's heart grew and sparked.

In her room, Val took the time to shower.

If she showed up in the stones smelling of vomit, he'd make her pay before she could even begin to try anything. She examined her reflection in the mirror as she combed the knots from her wet hair, and then, as she bent over with the hair dryer blasting, hoping the noise would confuse his senses, she dared to think, *Are you there?*

She didn't know what she expected to answer her.

But something had happened in the library, and if she could make it happen again, maybe soon her mother wouldn't be the only creature to bear Val's bloody brand.

Keep a morsel for yourself, her grandmother had instructed.

Don't lose yourself to him.

Not all of you.

Val stood in silence, her hair falling frizzy and golden down her back. She glared at her reflection and tried to remember: What had she been feeling, in the library, right before she had hurt her mother?

She closed her eyes, fists clenched, and after a moment of reconstructing the scene in her mind, the feeling returned to her:

Pity, for her own tired self.

Anger, at the life she had been forced to live.

And a desperation to change it, even if the thought terrified her.

Heat gathered beneath Val's feet, then traveled up her shins, her quads, her abdomen, her sternum.

Something stung her palms, and when she dared to look down, uncurling her fingers, she saw, in the center of her hands, two white knots of light, crackling like tiny twin galaxies.

They blinked once, twice, and disappeared—but their heat lingered, warming her.

Trailing her fingers along one of the black Mortimer pasture fences and humming Sylvia Mortimer's lullaby, she found Quinn Tillinghouse walking home from John Lin's house.

Who is the fellow with the bright clean grin?

Do you want, fairy girl, to weave a spell for him?

Val felt him behind her in the woods, following her. She kept her fists closed, tried to measure her breathing so he wouldn't see anything was amiss.

Could he sense it, though?

Could he read the map of her blood and sniff out the scent of her treachery?

Quinn had her phone out, and her keys. She held the long ignition key between two fingers, notches out, like a knife—just in case a child snatcher happened by, Val supposed.

Tears sprang to her eyes, despite how hard she was working to stay calm. Quinn was an unbelievable moron. Sneaking out to grab a quick shag with John while everything on the island was in such a state?

Val wanted to scream at her: *Ever heard of masturbating, Quinn?*

Even more than that, she wanted to scream: *Run! Now!*

She hurried over, looped her arm through Quinn's before she could even try to run. And why would she? They were friends, had been for years.

"Quinn!" Val smiled brightly. "Hey, girl."

"Oh!" Quinn jumped, laughed a little. "Val, Jesus. You scared the crap out of me."

"You really shouldn't be out by yourself, you know."

Quinn rolled her eyes. "John said he was too tired to drive me home."

"Ugh, he's such an ass." Val leaned playfully close but kept her voice low. She glanced down at her own hands—nothing. She swallowed against a swell of panic. "Quinn, listen to me. No matter what I say, you need to not react and stay calm, all right?"

"What?" Quinn's arm tensed around Val's. "What do you mean?"

"When I tell you to run, I need you to run home, straight down this road, as fast as you can."

"What are you talking about?" Quinn's voice turned shrill. She looked back over her shoulder, eyes wide. "Is someone—"

"God, Quinn, you're so paranoid!" Val said loudly, cringing at the manufactured quality of her voice. Then, quieter: "If you don't want to die tonight, then run when I tell you to. Stay out of the woods, stick to the road."

From behind them sounded the snap of a twig, the thud of something falling to the ground. Val nearly recoiled. The sound of him existing in the world was so *solid* now. Once, he had been a shadow only she could see.

Quinn whirled, squirming in Val's grip. "Who's there?" she cried. "Stay away from us! Oh, God." Quinn fumbled for her phone, let out a frantic sob. She started to run while dialing, tripped over a crack in the ground, stumbled.

Val knocked the phone out of Quinn's hands, shoved her down the dark road toward town. "Go! *Now!*"

Quinn ran, screaming for help.

Val turned to search the darkness. She tried to remember the library and recover that hot, invincible feeling, but Quinn was screaming, and Val's palms remained dark and useless, and then it was too late.

A hand smacked into Val's belly. It gripped her dress and threw her to the ground. Her jaw knocked the hard earth. She bit her tongue and tasted blood.

"You faithless bitch," growled a wheezing, alien voice—he must have been too hungry, too exhilarated, to assume a proper human form.

Val tried to push herself up, but her vision spun, and she collapsed. She raised her head in time to see a flickering darkness, bat-shaped and human-size, lunge through the air and tackle Quinn. It latched on to her face, smothering her cry of horror.

Silence. The woods and their creatures had gone still.

Then Val heard the sound of Quinn's body being dragged nearby. He yanked Val to her feet, pushed her forward into the trees. He moved with ease, like ink sliding through water. His grip on Val's wrist was sickeningly solid, his footfalls hitting the velvet forest floor like boulders flung from catapults.

"You're looking well tonight," she forced herself to say, grasping desperately for a handle on the situation. "I've never seen you so strong—"

"Remember that," he rasped, tongues flicking wetly at her ear, "the next time you consider disobeying me."

Val shook her head, tears blinding her. "I wasn't—"

He squeezed her wrist so hard the pain snatched her breath away. His form towered over her; the air, the ground, Val's entire existence bent toward him, sucked in by the singularity of his anger. "*Walk faster.*"

Val fought to stay upright as she led the way home. Her use to him as navigator was the only thing keeping her alive—and she knew that this might be the last time he had need of her for such a thing.

She stole one last look at her unlit palms, and hope crumbled like ash under her feet.

There was a nicely shaped gray stone, just inside the perimeter of white ones. It was low and flat, and it was, her mother had once joked, Val's throne.

"Mine was bigger," Lucy Mortimer had remarked, upon seeing it for the first time. She'd cupped Val's cheek, her eyes flat and cold. "But I'm sure that doesn't mean anything."

That was where Val sat, as he pinned Quinn to the ground in the center of the stones and got to work. He ripped and he clawed, he carved and disemboweled, he slurped and he drank, he flayed and he peeled. By the end of it the stones were red, the ground was red, and Val was reddest of all.

Splashed from head to toe with it, Val sat with charm-school posture, and thought distantly of Jackson Pollock paintings. (Perhaps she would ask her mother to acquire one for her bedroom.)

She wondered if school would start up again in the fall like normal, considering all the tragedies of the summer. (Maybe they'd shut the hellhole down for good.)

She wondered what she would do until the next and last kill, to pass the time. For of course the last kill would happen, probably in a matter of hours, judging by the look of him—already peeling his glutted self off the ground, already looking human again. A new form, one she'd never seen: Like Dr. Wayland, but more overtly masculine, more muscled, his clothes barely containing his sculpted body, his smile toothy and his posture military and his pale hair cropped close to his head. He was the mirror-universe version of Dr. Wayland, one who could kick the last breaths out of anyone he didn't like and would laugh while doing it. His bright white gaze flitted about the clearing, and his fingers twitched at his sides, like he was already scouting the woods for the next meal. Soon he would break free of all need for the Mortimers, and run off into the wild to hunt as he so desired, all because Val had failed to stop him and would doubtless fail again if she tried it.

She stared numbly at the carnage before her, tears filling her eyes.

Marion, I'm sorry.

She closed her eyes, desperate for the memory: Marion's face, smiling up at her, her dark hair tangled and love-mussed.

Marion's sleepy murmurings, drifting up from where she lay tucked beneath Val's chin.

Marion, laughing. Marion, gasping. Tasting Marion, holding Marion, making Marion smile and cry out and gasp for breath—

"Who's Marion?"

Val's stomach shrank into a cold metal knot and plunged beneath the sea of her flaming blood.

The little boy stood before her. It was a relief to see that familiar form, instead of the monstrous, unstoppable Dr. Wayland. Blood stained the boy's mouth and hands and angelic curls. His wide blue eyes looked up at her with a carefully fabricated ingenuousness.

"Tell me?" He sidled closer, placed two pudgy red hands on her leg. Even through her jeans, she felt the wet heat of his grip.

Val, fighting for calm and finding none, attempted subterfuge. Usually, his mind was fuzzy after a meal. Maybe, if she spoke carefully enough, she could dislodge his memory of Marion, alter it. "I— No one. I was just daydreaming—"

"You're lying." The boy's voice was cold. His eyes flicked away, then returned. In his gaze turned a calculation. "The other girl. The second sister." A slow smile spread across his face. "Oh, yes. I remember her now. Marion. Yes. I've been her before. I've played with her mother. Come. Let's get cleaned up and go pay them a visit. It's been too long."

Val couldn't move. Her panic was too complete.

Bringing him to Marion would be bad, but perhaps salvageable.

Refusing him would be disastrous.

Val took his hand and unsteadily led him out of the stones. Behind them, the remains of Quinn's body lay scattered. The air vibrated against Val's skin—the veil he used to keep the stones hidden from outsiders.

Val opened and closed her fists, thinking quickly.

"Marion's nothing much, you know." She kept her voice casual. "Kind of plump. Plain, really." She dared to fiddle with his hair, rearrange a matted red lock. "She's not your type, as I'm sure you've figured out by now."

He smacked her hand away and twisted her arm so hard that blades of pain shot up to her shoulder.

"Wait," she gasped, but it was pointless to plead with him. He didn't stop until she was silent and on her knees before him.

"Oh, Valerie," said the boy, tipping up her chin so she had to look at his baby-faced grin. "It's too late for that. Any girl who could inspire you to betray me is special indeed."

MARION

The Collector

Marion watched Zoey for signs of imminent combustion.

"You slept with Val," Zoey said, lying on the floor beside Marion's bed.

"Yes."

Zoey nodded, her expression grim. "Where?"

Marion pressed her palm against the mattress. "Here."

"In your bed?"

Marion shut her eyes. They were swollen from crying, itchy and raw, and her throat hurt from trying to hold back sobs so she could be strong for her mother. There was a hole in her heart, a Charlotte-shaped hole, that had been ripped cruelly asunder—but only the day before she'd been making Val writhe under her mouth, and Val had held her, after, with trembling hands, and she didn't think it was right or fair for one girl's body to feel so much chaos at one time.

"Yes," she whispered.

"Well," said Zoey flatly. "Jesus H. Christ."

"Are you mad?" A stupid question, Marion supposed, but then another possibility entered her mind. "Are you . . . jealous?"

"Frankly, Marion," Zoey said, sitting up, "I'm really goddamn confused."

"Okay . . ."

"You might even say I'm non-fucking-plussed."

"Zoey—"

"To hear that you slept with my mortal enemy, my nemesis, the daughter of the sex-dungeon-haver—"

"I know—"

"The girl who probably killed Thora, who maybe killed . . ."

Zoey fell silent, looked away.

Marion sat up. "You know that isn't true."

"No. I don't."

"We know what killed Charlotte. It was the monster."

Zoey glared up at her. "We've discussed this. Monsters don't always work alone. *Jesus*, Marion." She wiped a hand over her face. "I can't believe you'd do this."

Now Marion was the one glaring. "We agreed that I should get close to her. You thought it was a good idea!"

"And did you get any information out of her?" Zoey asked. "Any clues about the monster? Any answers as to how the hell some girl-eating creature lives for generations on an island without anyone finding it? Did you find out anything like that, Marion?"

Marion's cheeks grew hot. ". . . No."

"And why not?"

"I was . . ."

"You were maybe a little distracted?"

Marion fumbled for words, her fast-rising anger muddying her thoughts.

"Why'd you do it? Tell me." Zoey wrapped her arms around her legs, mockingly thoughtful. "Really, I want to hear your reasons why you let this happen."

"Because she's beautiful!" Marion couldn't sit still any longer. She climbed out of bed and started pacing. "Because she's nice to me, and it makes me feel special. Like someone sees me. Like *you* see me, the real me, but, you know . . ." Marion waved her hand around. "With, like, sex involved. Because my sister's dead"—Marion's voice choked on the words—"and my dad's dead, and my mom's so sad I'm not sure she'll ever recover and be the person she used to be. Because I wanted to *feel* something." She smacked her palm against her chest three times, and each thud knocked her tears closer to their exit. "Really *feel* like I'm here, and alive, and I wanted not just to feel alive, but to feel *good*, for once. To feel really, really good."

She turned to face Zoey, refusing to blink. "And because I wanted her, and she wanted me. And because I don't think she hurt anyone. I think the monster did—not her, or her mom." She blinked, and tears rolled down her cheeks. "Because she's lonely, and so am I. Okay?"

Zoey considered her for a long moment. "You could have

chosen anyone else, Marion. *Anyone* but her, and it would have been fine."

Marion scoffed, wiping her eyes. "So I need to run my sex partners by you?"

"You know that's not what I'm saying," Zoey replied, her voice breaking. "I'm saying Val stole Thora from me, so I ended up being pissed at my best friend until the day she died. I'm saying *not her.*"

And suddenly the anger rising in Marion's chest caught fire. "I know about you and Grayson," she said. "Charlotte told me. And just because you can't figure out how to have sex like a normal person doesn't mean I can't enjoy it for myself."

As soon as the words had been said, Marion regretted them.

Zoey's body sagged, like some of the air had been let out of her.

"Zoey . . ." Marion shook her head. "Zoey, I'm sorry. I didn't mean that. You know I didn't."

Zoey just looked at her.

"I wasn't thinking. I was mad, and Charlotte—" Marion cut herself off. She would not use her grief as an excuse. "Doesn't matter. I shouldn't have said that. I didn't mean it, and I don't think it. That was the shittiest thing—"

"Yes," Zoey burst out, her eyes vivid with tears. "That was the shittiest possible thing you could have said to me. Do you know how many nights I've lain awake wondering what's wrong with me? Why I can't *enjoy sex* like a *normal person*? Do you know how many cruel things I've heard said about me since

Grayson and I broke up? That he dumped me because I'm black, that he dumped me because he just wanted a quick fuck, that asexual people are fundamentally broken—"

"Of course you're not broken, Zoey," Marion said, desperate to hug her but assuming this was a privilege she was no longer allowed. "No one worth a damn actually thinks that. I don't think that."

Then, downstairs, the doorbell rang.

Val's faint voice called out: "Marion? Are you home?"

Zoey raced out the door and downstairs.

Marion's heart dropped. "Zoey?" She ran after her, but Zoey was fast, and Marion's feet were still tender. Hobbling toward the stairs, she heard the front door opening, and then Val's voice, surprised: "Zoey?"

Zoey's chipper reply, free of tears: "The one and only!"

"What are you doing here?"

"Hanging out with Marion."

"Oh, right. You two are . . . friends."

"Righto, Valerie. Do you want to come in?"

That's when Marion heard the rapid clicking noise moving along the wall, down the front foyer, into the hallway, and deeper into the house, like the skittering of claws across a hard surface.

Marion's eyes refocused. A sharp twang inside her resounded, like a finger had plucked her ribs electric, and a voice had whispered, *Pay attention now.*

The bone cry began, a shrill dissonant grind beneath her

skull. A moth appeared, wiggling out of the dark hallway light fixture and drifting toward the stairs.

Marion followed it slowly down.

Val: "Listen, um . . . Don't take this the wrong way, but I think you need to leave."

Zoey, innocently: "Oh? Why's that, Val?"

"I need to talk to Marion, privately."

"Because you're such good *friends* now?"

Marion reached the bottom of the stairs, and as soon as she turned the corner to face the hallway, she saw it—a patch of darkness, oddly shaped, like a child's angry scribble. It scurried across the ceiling, away from Marion, and gathered in the farthest corner of the living room, above the couch where her mother slept.

Two white eyes appeared in the darkness, wide and unblinking. Then the shadow slid down the wall, behind the arm of the couch. Waiting.

The words of the rhyme crawled up Marion's arms: *Beware of the woods and the dark, dank deep*.

She crossed the hallway to enter the living room, her frantic heartbeat flooding her mouth. Beyond the shriek of the bone cry, the others' voices came faintly.

Val, seeing her: "Marion? Hey—"

Zoey, turning: "Oh, Marion! Just in time. Valerie here thinks I should leave. Maybe I should, so you two can have some alone time?"

Marion moved slowly across the living room, her breathing

high and thin. The television was on low volume, an old black-and-white movie flickering from frame to frame.

She spoke into the shadows. "Hello?"

Her mother shifted in her sleep, smacking her lips.

A little boy's voice replied from the unseen corner: "Hello, Marion."

He'll follow you home and won't let you sleep.

Marion hesitated, hardly able to swallow. "Who are you?"

The lone moth hovered above where the thing hid.

You know the answer, said the little moth voice.

"Some friend you've got," said the boy, and just as Val and Zoey entered the room, a tiny fist thrust out of the corner, grabbed the moth, and disappeared.

The bone cry, abruptly, ceased.

Zoey jumped back. "What was *that*?"

Some friend you've got. Not Zoey, Marion thought, her bile rising, because she could hear the monster's jaws grinding, tearing the moth's body to shreds.

It wasn't talking about Zoey, or Val.

It was talking about the moth.

"They help me, sometimes," said Marion, approaching slowly once more. She had to get him away from her mother. "The moths, I mean."

"How curious," came the little boy's voice.

Zoey grabbed Marion's wrist. "Who *is* that?"

"Marion, don't go over there," said Val, her voice strained. "Please, it's not safe."

Zoey, sharply: "How would you know? Val, who is this?"

"She's right," giggled the little boy. The plump child's fist returned, caressing her mother's pant leg. "I'm not safe."

"Get away from her!" Marion meant to run over, as any girl protecting her mother would, but instead, she vanished from one spot and appeared in the other—right there, in the corner, looming over a tiny blue-eyed boy with white-blond curls.

Val gasped, her voice full of tears. "What the hell?"

Zoey grabbed a poker from the fireplace. "Val, get her mom out of here."

Marion had half a second to notice the scraps of moth wings dotting the boy's lips before he jumped up, latched on to her torso, and climbed up to her shoulders, his pudgy cheeks red with rage. She staggered back and fell, hitting her head on the floor. Her vision blacked out and returned. The boy smacked her across the face and bent to her throat with his teeth bared.

Zoey's poker flew, smashing into his temple. He didn't budge, the skin unbroken. His head snapped up and he snarled at her, the sound issuing from his throat not a sound that any human child could make.

"Val," Marion gasped, searching, the boy's hand tight around her throat. Dimly, she saw Val guiding her mother into the other room. Her mother was still half-asleep; the sleep aid Dr. Wayland had prescribed to her, to help her find rest even in her grief, was damn good. She murmured, "Val? What's going on?"

Zoey's poker flew once more. "Get off of her, you son of a bitch!"

"Jean Grey," Marion croaked, reminding Zoey. She felt

an electric mightiness gather underneath the hardwood floor, pooling beneath her own shuddering spine and Zoey's feet. "Do it again." She clawed at the boy's fingers, dodged his gnashing teeth. "Focus! *Hurry!*"

Zoey dropped the poker. The floor sizzled and snapped at her approach. She grabbed the boy's collar and threw him—twenty yards, across the house, into the kitchen. He crashed into the refrigerator, howling like a kid having a tantrum. At the impact, the boy disappeared and the dark shape returned, a rageful shadow that engulfed the kitchen cabinets in blackness. The childish fury became an unearthly one, and its howl—both guttural and piercing—smashed every piece of glass in the house.

Zoey dropped to her knees between Marion and the kitchen, her trembling arm outstretched, her palm rigid.

"What is it?" she cried. "Marion? You okay?"

Gasping for breath, Marion rolled over to face the kitchen. A creature, earless and head on backward, vaguely lupine, vaguely masculine, composed of shifting shadows and a slippery, scaly hide, scrambled toward them. Bumped into walls, knocked over chairs—a disoriented but determined crab.

Its white eyes stared, unblinking. Leathery wings sprouted, slapped wetly against the walls. When it screamed, Marion thought she heard her name.

That gave her the jolt of fear she needed.

You tessered, Zoey had said.

"Hold on," she instructed Zoey, and Zoey grabbed on to

her hand, right as the creature started dragging itself across the floor, right as the sharp electric force thrumming beneath Marion shot up and consumed her.

She held tight to Zoey with one arm, thought of Zoey's house, planted her other palm flat on the floor—a conductor between her body and the island's rocky guts.

Because she had decided that this strength surging up her body belonged to her, yes, but also to Sawkill Rock—to the moths and to the sea, to the horse that had shattered his bones in the water, and to the black shivering trees where the police had found her sister's hand.

"I hear you," she whispered, wondering what, exactly, was listening—and then shoved hard at the ground.

An inhale. Zoey's terrified sob. The snap and jolt of the world turning inside out.

An instant later, they landed in the Harlows' quiet, warmly lit kitchen—hard, on their hands and knees—and the last thing Marion knew before she passed out was Zoey latched on to her, face buried in her hair, whispering over and over, "Hold on, hold on, hold on," like a rosary prayer, or a spell crafted to ward off the devil.

ZOEY

The Wall

When Zoey came to, the first thing she did was try to call out for Marion, but she only managed a cough.

"Hey, hey, it's okay," came her father's voice. The couch cushion sank under his weight. "I've got you."

Zoey now recognized her surroundings—the brown fabric of the couch, stained but worn smooth and soft. The exposed wood rafters outlining the vaulted ceiling. Gentle yellow lamp-light, orange-and-blue-striped rug on the dark hardwood floor, framed sepia photographs on the marigold yellow walls (her grandparents, her aunts and uncles and father when they were young, and Zoey when she couldn't even crawl).

Across the room on the love seat, Marion slept soundly, a blanket tucked around her.

"Zo?" her father murmured, stroking her cheeks. "Zoey, look at me. You're okay."

"Dad?" Zoey's voice broke. She *was* alive, wasn't she? "Daddy?"

"I'm here." He looked her square in the face, smoothed his hand across her hair. The lines around his eyes and mouth grounded her in the real, in the tragically finite. "I'm right here, sweetie."

"Where's Briggs?"

He frowned at her. "Briggs? He's down at the station—"

"Tell him to get his ass over here." Zoey clutched her father's shirt. "We need to figure out a way to kill this thing. *Fast.*"

Then, as the memories returned to her—how that little boy had screamed, the sensation of the poker slamming into his cranium, the heat shooting up her arm when she flung him away—Zoey's face crumpled. Wrapped in her father's arms, she wept.

Later, near dawn, Zoey awoke to a quiet house.

On the other side of the living room, her father had fallen asleep in his recliner, his mouth hanging open.

Marion was sleeping, too, snug on the love seat.

Not surprising. If Zoey had zapped them both to the other side of the island, she'd probably be exhausted, too.

She considered Marion for a moment—how even in sleep, her mouth seemed tight with worry—and couldn't muster up a single iota of good feeling. Maybe it was ungracious of her, what with all Marion had been through, and how she had possibly just saved their lives, but Zoey didn't feel like making excuses for her behavior, for the hurtful things she'd said, so she didn't.

She imagined folding herself into a suit of unbreakable armor and left the living room, headed upstairs to change out of her jeans, into something more comfortable. But once she entered her bedroom, she froze.

Sitting there, in the center of her bed, was her father's black book.

A slow tingle crawled its way up her body.

Had her father put the book here? Or Briggs?

Or someone else?

Zoey sat on the edge of the bed, cradled the book in her palms, took a deep breath.

Opened it.

She flipped past the pages of text she'd already perused. Drawings of the Collector—dark and grinning, man and beast. The sketched girl with her sword and the words beside her: *SEMPER TRES.*

She'd looked up that phrase online, too: *Always three.*

She turned the page.

Here was another girl, her arms and legs rimmed in fire. Another smaller flame burned where her heart would be.

Zoey's body hummed like bees were gathering along the underside of her skin. She turned the page.

A third girl stood, head thrown back to the stars, arms flung out on either side. The position of this girl's body was open, vulnerable. Zoey wondered: Was she fighting? Or was she submitting?

Zoey turned a few more pages, each lined with neat labeled

boxes of text and more illustrations of girls—a girl flying through the air, a girl with lightning shooting out of her palms, a girl with wings sprouting from her back.

Then, more writing. Diagrams of shapes. Formations that Zoey didn't understand.

Then: Another girl. Different from the others. Not a silhouette, but naked.

She stood framed in darkness that reminded Zoey of the Collector's shadowy form lurching through the Althouses' kitchen. Above the triangle of hair between the girl's legs, a black smile grinned across the pale skin of her pelvis.

Zoey stared. Was it a tattoo? Or a cut?

Beside the naked girl was one word: *REGINA*.

Zoey knew that one, from copious hours spent perusing baby name websites with Thora, finding the perfect name for this or that character.

Regina meant *queen*.

She glanced back at the girl. The queen? The queen of *what*?

Zoey gazed at the drawing with a hand over her belly, then held her breath and turned the page. The illustration that stared back at her made her utter a sharp cry:

A girl straddled another girl, plunging a knife into her belly.

A third girl clung to the stabber, drawing a knife across her throat.

And the first girl, the girl on the ground, lay with her wide mouth unhinged, her tongue long and rigid. A dark misshapen form, a furious cloud of blackness, swooped down from the sky, reaching for the dead girl. Its clawed hand grasped her tongue, and its nebulous inky frame surrounded them all, bearing down on them like a cyclone. Someone had illustrated the scene with so many pen marks, heavy and fat, that the darkened paper was ridged and shimmering, imprinted.

In the center of the reaching black cloud were two round white eyes.

Zoey flung the book across the room. It hit her wall of bookshelves and dropped to the floor.

This was bullshit.

This was bigger than Thora, bigger than Grayson stuck at home translating a million words of nearly illegible Latin, bigger than her father and some random FBI agent.

They needed help.

And Zoey was going to go get it.

She found her backpack, began to pack. Jeans and boots, shirts and jackets, socks and underwear. Clothes for Marion, too—too big for Zoey, or not really her thing anymore—because they couldn't return to the cottage, not ever again, no way. A few hand-me-downs from her mother that Zoey had planned on repurposing someday, into shredded, undefinable, middle-finger clothes that would no doubt make Val's Waspy heart shrivel up and die.

They'd call Marion's mom—oh, *God*, they'd left her with Val.

"Shit," Zoey muttered. She retrieved the black book, shoved it in her bag, zipped it closed. They would have to go find Marion's mother and pick her up, and Grayson, too.

"What happened to you and Marion?"

Zoey whirled. Her father stood at the threshold, arms crossed over his chest.

"I thought I locked the door," Zoey said, blinking.

"What happened?"

Zoey slung her bag over her shoulders. "I'm going to get help, and you're coming with me. You, Marion, her mom, Grayson. I guess Briggs, too, he seems all right."

"You're going to get help?" her father repeated.

"Look, this creature is too much for, like, five people to figure out alone. There are other members of the Hand of Light, right?"

"Zoey—"

"Honestly, maybe we should call in the military, too." Zoey marched past him into the hallway, then looked back over her shoulder. "Have you guys tried that before?"

"Zoey." Her father hadn't moved. He stared out her window. "What happened to you and Marion? I was in the kitchen, and then the next instant, I heard this crash. I went into the living room, and there you both were. On the floor, like you'd dropped down out of the sky."

He turned, his eyes bright and his mouth working like he was trying to keep himself stitched together. "Tell me what happened, Zoey."

Zoey's heart jumped into her throat. "Nothing happened. We just . . . we came in through the front door."

"You're lying."

"Seriously, it's fine—"

"Just tell me!"

"Okay, okay, *chill*, you're freaking me out," Zoey said in a rush. "We were at Marion's, and the Collector attacked her. Marion, I mean." She shook her head, laughing a little. "It looked like a little boy. It made this sound like, I don't even know, like a horror-movie sound. A demonic sound. He tried to bite her."

Her father stood with fists clenched. "And then?"

"I beat the shit out of him," she replied, eyes filling up at the memory. "God. I took a fireplace poker and whacked him upside the head a few times, and it didn't do a thing. He just hissed at me, and then . . ."

She stared out the window, watching the Eye of Sawkill turn.

"Tell me, Zoey," said her father tightly.

"Then I went Jean Grey on him," she answered.

A pause. "What?"

"I punched out my hand, and he flew across the room. Away from me, away from Marion." She inhaled and exhaled. She threaded her hands into her hair with a tiny choked laugh. "Then Marion brought us here. She tessered us across the island, to safety."

"Oh no." Her father moved into her room, unsteady. He sat on the edge of her bed and dropped his face into his hands. "No, no, no . . ."

And suddenly everything became clear to Zoey.

The girls drawn in the book—wings on their backs, lightning in their hands. Flying girls, burning girls.

Girls who could tesser themselves great distances in the blink of an eye?

Girls who could throw a monster across the room.

She and Marion—or girls *like* her and Marion—were in her father's black book. And now her father was slumped on her bed, defeated. Zoey's eyes prickled. An electric hum vibrated through her limbs like the sensation of being watched, only ten times stronger.

She moved across the room and stood before her father. "You know what this means, don't you?" she whispered. "What is it?"

A long beat, as the Eye of Sawkill circled through the brightening morning, and the branches outside her window whispered and clacked. Then her father raised wet eyes to gaze at her, and Zoey took a step back from him, because that look was not a good look.

It was the look of someone whose world was collapsing around him.

"Do you remember in my video," he said, his voice ragged, "when I told you we had devised a method of extermination to kill the monster?"

"Yes," Zoey whispered, heart pounding in her ears.

He dropped his head, squeezed his eyes shut. "I wanted to get you off the island before the others arrived, but it wouldn't have mattered. It had already begun. Oh, God. *Zoey.*" Her father cried out into his hands. "I should never have let you come here. What the hell was I thinking?"

"Dad, calm down and talk to me." Zoey gripped her father's shoulders, trying not to recoil at the anguish on his face. "What's happening? What's the method of extermination?"

"A select few have the power to slay the beast," he replied. "Girls, always. Extraordinary girls. There are always three."

SEMPER TRES.

Zoey started slowly backing away. "You mean . . . we can fight him?"

Her father's shoulders slumped, his face sagging. Slowly, he was deflating. "You can try."

Zoey pressed her hands to her stomach. "Do we have to?"

"You don't have to fight. But you do have to stay."

"Stay where? Sawkill?" A distant buzz hummed along the horizon of Zoey's existence, inching ever closer.

"I don't know why it happens. But it happens every time, every place." Her father closed his eyes. "Once a girl's power has awakened," he said, as if reciting a well-known scripture, "she is bound to the land on which the beast crawls, and there she must remain, until the work is complete—"

Zoey marched back over and slapped him.

"Did you draw them?" She stood over him, palm stinging from the impact, her whole body rigid and her eyes blazing with tears. "Those pictures of the girls killing each other? The naked girl with the cut on her abs?"

"No," her father replied, his voice tired and thin. "That book is the collected observations and teachings of all the knights who have lived on this island, since long before I moved here."

"*Knights?* Christ. Is that what you call yourselves?"

He looked at her helplessly. He held out his hands, beseeching. "I never should have let you come to Sawkill."

"No," she snapped. "You shouldn't have."

"I thought you would be safe near me; I thought that if I kept you close—"

"Well you were really damn wrong, weren't you?"

Zoey stormed out the door. Downstairs, Marion was sitting up, blinking sleepily. Briggs sat beside her on the couch; as Zoey approached, he dropped Marion's hand.

Zoey's stomach curdled at the sight of him.

"Zoey?" Marion's voice was hoarse. Shadows ringed her eyes. "What's going on?"

"We're leaving." Zoey grabbed her arm, pulled her from the couch. "We're getting your mom, and Grayson, and we're going to the mainland to get help."

"Not a good idea, Zoey," said Briggs, vexingly calm.

Marion stumbled after her. "Wait, *Zoey—*"

With every second, Zoey felt more certain that Briggs would jump off the couch and tackle her. *A select few have the power to slay the beast.*

Yeah, well, that sort of thing sounded nice in stories, but Zoey didn't so much like the idea of her and Marion having to face off against some monster by themselves.

Except . . .

SEMPER TRES. Always three.

But who was the third?

Outside, on the porch, Marion pulled Zoey to a halt. "Hey, slow down. Talk to me. What happened?"

"We're getting the hell away from here," said Zoey. "That's what."

Marion stared at her. "I'm not leaving this island until I find justice for my sister."

"This isn't about finding justice, Marion. This is about the island being owned by a *monster* who, a couple of hours ago, almost killed us. Or don't you remember?"

"You're just going to run away? Leave everyone here to fend for themselves?"

"I'm going to get *help*," said Zoey, "so that the people on this island actually stand a chance."

Zoey turned to walk away, only stumbling for a half stride when Marion grabbed her backpack.

"Zoey, wait!"

But Zoey slipped loose of the straps, panic roaring loud and hot in her blood, and ran.

A car was making its way up the road toward her house—three cars, headlights on—and Zoey ignored them. She made it to shore, followed the boardwalk down to the beach, found her father's tethered rowboat. Pushed the boat out to the gray churning sea, jumped inside, grabbed the oars.

How many mornings had she and her father spent in this

boat, navigating the tiny coves on Sawkill's western coast? Dozens. A hundred. He'd taught her how to fish, how to row.

She knew it was ridiculous to row the little dinghy all the way to the mainland, especially with her arms already shaking. Stupid superpowers. Stupid Jean Grey.

But what else was there to do? Sit around and wait for the late-morning ferry to leave? No, thanks. She'd row until she hit kinder soil; she'd row and not look back. She'd find soldiers, missiles, rockets. She'd ride back to the island on a battleship, waving a flag with Thora's face sewn onto it in fiery colors.

She gasped, nearly faint from having fought so hard to hold in her sobs that she'd seriously, literally, forgotten to breathe.

And now the boat wasn't moving.

Looking back, she saw the Rock sitting between the dark sky above and the dark water below, its lumpy back hairy with trees, its Eye standing tall and lonesome.

Zoey turned around and searched for the mainland. She squinted, shivering. There—lights, tiny and fairyesque, blinking through the dawn.

She gripped the oars once more and rowed.

With a jolt, the flat paddles hit a wall. A low thud resounded through the oars, up Zoey's arms and into her shoulders. The boat shuddered, and it didn't move. The waves rocked her, sent her bobbing like a buoy, but her boat stayed put. More accurately, it drifted side to side, it even inched back a little closer to shore—*thanks, Tides, some friends you are*—but the boat wouldn't move forward.

"Nope," Zoey said, refusing to believe it, and rowed.

The boat shuddered once more. And again, and again. Each time Zoey tried to move, the boat disobeyed. Some fool had erected a damn wall in the middle of the ocean.

"Fine, you sick bastard," Zoey muttered to Sawkill.

She slid out of the boat and into the frigid black depths.

I'll swim it if I have to, she thought, her teeth chattering, her body stiff and unwieldy. *I'll swim it, and you can't stop me.*

She swam, clumsy, already spitting up seawater. She was good at swimming, but she couldn't breathe that well and cry at the same time.

"Pull it together," she told herself, and swam until she hit the wall.

It pushed her back, gentle, like she'd bumped not into brick but rather a fleshy membrane.

She tried again and again, and each time the wall blocked her. She swam to the right, shivering, shuddering, and tried again. No good—membrane. Invisible and impermeable. She sucked in a breath and dove, as deep as she could go, so deep that her ears hurt and the weight of the ocean nearly pulled her all the way down.

Eyes stinging, lungs burning, she groped in the darkness—and met only that same warm, supple barrier.

Goddamn it, goddamn it. She screamed underwater, using all the rest of her air. She heard her own muffled voice and panicked. The instinct to survive was a powerful thing. She found strength, somewhere, and kicked herself toward the surface.

A hand grabbed her arm and pulled her the rest of the way up.

"Okay, it's all right," said a voice—a stranger's voice, male and tenor, much thinner than her father's.

Zoey blinked, saw a narrow, light-brown face smiling down at her. He was reaching out of a pontoon boat; Zoey heard the churn of a motor.

"It's okay," he repeated.

But Zoey was *pissed*. The wall had thwarted her escape, and the wall belonged to the Rock, and islands didn't get to tell her what to do. *She* got to tell herself what to do.

She drew in a ragged breath, choking on water, and let out a crackling roar of fury.

The man released Zoey and flew away, flung off into the water. The waves crested and broke, ripples shooting out from Zoey's trembling body. The pontoon boat nearly tipped. Someone inside it yelled: "Jesus!"

Zoey knew she couldn't tread water for much longer, and when the next hand reached down to pull her up, she let it.

"I've got you," said Briggs, reaching down out of the boat. To her sea-clogged eyes, his eyes sat dark and hollow in his pale square face. "Everything's going to be okay now." He squeezed her shoulder. "We're here to help you. You don't have to worry."

Zoey let herself be pulled aboard, her mind scrambling to catch up.

"We?" she rasped, and then saw, huddled in the boat behind Briggs, a few men she didn't recognize—hatted and faceless, coats slick from the sea. Her father sat among them, struggling to get to her.

And Zoey understood at once: the Hand of Light had arrived on Sawkill Rock.

She hocked up mucus and spat it in Briggs's face.

"I don't like cults," she said, and fainted.

THE ROCK COULD NOT ALLOW any of them to leave.

One of the girls quietly, efficiently, took her mother to the police station for safekeeping.

(*Not safe there*, thought the Rock. *Not safe anywhere.*)

One of the girls awoke from a restless night plagued with caged dreams. She shivered and she longed. She thought of knives, of pills, of cliffs. She thought of an ending. But, oh, that wasn't fair, because she wanted to *live*. The Rock felt the girl's desperation like the pull of a building storm.

One of the girls tried to swim to freedom. When that failed, she spat and cursed. She fought and raged.

But the Rock, regretfully, could not allow her to leave.

The Rock could allow none of them to leave.

Not until it was finished.

VAL

The Mark

Val awoke with a terrible feeling in the pit of her stomach. Her tired mind felt ready to spill over, like she'd spent the night reading a dense book written in antiquated language and tiny text.

Then a pain in her belly reached up and punched her. She shot upright, hands clutching her middle, and then, maybe because the idea of pain in such a place reminded her of pregnancy, she craved the sight of her mother.

Val climbed out of bed, grabbed the rose-colored silk robe from her desk chair, and crossed to the wing that contained her mother's rooms. Val raised a fist to knock quietly on her mother's door—but it was already open. She let herself in, bare feet sinking into the plush white rug that covered the floor.

"Mom?" She peeked at the bed, saw a mess of rumpled

white sheets and abandoned pillows. The east-facing wall, painted such a pale blue that it shimmered silver in the moonlight, hugged three windows that stood cracked open. A cool night breeze fluttered the sheer curtains.

Standing there with the wind kissing her bare legs, Val felt a helix of dread unwind in her heart. The pain in her belly returned—a slow grind, now, like a pestle against the mortar of her insides.

She moved swiftly through the silent house, and when she entered her mother's library, she went straight for the bookcase that hid the stone passage to the red room.

One book, two books, three books, four.

Where Val's fingers touched the spines, soft warmth blossomed. She thought she felt the echo of Marion's presence—her hand over her own, their joined fingers pushing the books back into their catches.

Val shook off the half-formed vision as the bookcase swung open. She couldn't enter the red room with thoughts of Marion fogging her mind—not now that Marion had made a fool out of him by escaping him unscathed.

She walked downstairs, keeping her mind cool and open, and then she entered the red room and the pain in her belly exploded. At once she understood why her stomach had been hurting her, why her veins had been aching.

Because now, she was the only one to be anchoring him in this world.

Now, all his hunger and rage, all his desperation to be

free—here at the end, in his last days of dependency—was for Val and Val alone to contain.

Her mother's body, clad in her robe and nightgown, lay in a pool of blood on the floor—chest caved in, limbs torn, body twisted. Eyes open. Mouth gaping.

Val stood and stared, pain grind-grind-grinding in the pit of her torso.

Breathe through the pain, Valerie, her grandmother had instructed, years earlier. *He can't stand it when we beg.*

She straightened her back and squared her shoulders. Her fists clenched and unclenched.

A measured voice drifted toward her from the door on the far wall: "Your turn."

Dr. Wayland. The *new* Dr. Wayland—button-down shirt and tie underneath a sand-colored cashmere sweater. Biceps that could crush boulders, hands big enough to encircle Val's head. Sharp clean jaw and flickering white gaze.

Dry-mouthed, she watched him approach the monstrous red-draped bed and sit on the edge of the mattress and pat it. He seemed insensible to the bloodless corpse at his feet.

"My turn?" she asked, proud of her uncracked voice.

His eyes narrowed. "Don't stall."

But Val would stall if she damn well pleased, because her mother was dead. She'd been torn apart and gutted, and Val figured she deserved a few minutes to process things. She deserved to keep this morsel to herself—this moment, this warped grief.

This body.

She resisted the urge to run her hands over her own arms, torso, face, just to make sure it was all there. It was magnificent, this body—not because it was beautiful and strong, though it was, but because it was *hers*. With a radiant burst of clarity, she decided that she was not going to let him touch her. Not that way. Not tonight.

Not ever.

Val crossed her arms over her chest and cocked her hip to the side, attempting to be playful. Sometimes he liked that. "I guess Mom pissed you off, huh?"

He watched her, unblinking. The lines of his jaw shifted and re-formed. "No. You did."

It required every ounce of the strength that had been beaten into Val to keep her facade from shattering. "Is that so?"

"You let Zoey hurt me while you stood there and watched. You didn't help me when they began attacking me. They got away."

No, Val wouldn't think about Marion. She'd scrape her brain clean until the only thing left was the bright shiny middle—untouched and unspoiled.

"I didn't realize you intended to kill them that night," Val said, trying on her own unblinking, scary-as-shit look, because maybe that would make her feel less like running back up the stairs screaming—never mind that he would catch her, never mind that running would just make things worse. "I thought you simply wanted to observe Marion. See what the 'big deal' was. Not that there is a big deal, there's nothing going on between us. In fact, I think you've grown a bit paranoid."

She paused, and then did lick her lips, *damn it*, because she had started to ramble. Because he wasn't moving, not a muscle, not a hair or a blink, and her courage was fading as quickly as it had come. "Do you even know that word? Do they have it where you come from? It's not a good one. It means you're losing your mind."

He watched her for a long moment, and then he said, "Come here, Valerie."

And Val—Val said, "No."

Another long moment, and then at last he moved, clasping his hands on his lap. A darkness juddered around his body, obscuring his hair, his sleeves, his shoes.

His false form was losing cohesion. Very, very not good.

He was getting hungry again—already, so soon after Quinn.

He would need to consume one more, her mother had estimated. One more kill, one more meal, and he would break free of them.

And now Val was the only one left to stop him.

"I noticed something interesting on your mother's chest," he said, voice pleasant. "A scar in the shape of a handprint. Do you know what caused that?"

Val's palms tingled, remembering.

"I don't know what Mom got up to when I wasn't around," Val said, trying to sound bored, not sure if she was succeeding.

"She was into some weird stuff, I know that. Well." Val gave him a little smile. "And you know that, too."

"You understand, don't you?" he said, ignoring her. "I killed your mother so that I could make you my queen. I'd like to keep you close to me from now on. That seems to be the wisest course of action, to keep all my eyes on you. And she was getting old, anyway. I prefer the way you look. I very much prefer it."

A jolt of something hot and sharp shot up from the ground and smacked Val's kneecaps, her wrists, the hollow of her throat with an indignant electric crackle—as if it had been called to her by her own frantic will.

Burn him, the feeling seemed to say.

Val kept her fists closed, to hide the white-hot pulsars she could now feel simmering in the center of each palm. The ground trembled slightly under her feet, like the Rock was coming awake beneath her soles. It reverberated up through her every bone, left her boiling.

"I'm not going to sleep with you," she declared.

Then he smiled, such a wide, giddy smile that Val took a step back.

"Fine," he said agreeably. "But you will take my mark."

And the next thing Val knew, Dr. Wayland was gone, and she was on the floor. Blackness slammed down on the red room. Something sharp—a scalpel, or a claw—pierced the cotton of her shorts and the skin of her belly and drew a wide grin between her pelvic bones.

Val screamed. Fists still closed, she was too shocked to use them, but she knew she must keep them that way. *Don't let him see don't let him see.* A power surged through her that was not hers, but his. Dark and oily, it wriggled and writhed, coating her innards, burrowing into her bones. He was a ship dropping anchor on her ocean floor, securing himself against her solidness, her humanity.

Val gagged, turned her face away from him. She knew that once he'd finished marking her, she would be his. She would bear the brunt of him—his hunger, his anger, the pain he felt at being stuck in this world half-formed. Until he killed once more and broke free, Val would be the thing that allowed him to survive. She was his host. His alien power crawled into her belly and nestled there like a parasite, just as it had happened with her mother, and her grandmother, and all the Mortimer women before them since Deirdre had made that long-ago deal with the devil and doomed them all.

Val dared send out one desperate thought to the Rock. In that cold room of stone, she was surrounded by earth. Sawkill was her home, and she had given her blood to its soil more than once, and her pain was so complete, so excruciating, that it afforded her a primal sort of understanding: the Rock and the light in her palms were one and the same.

So she thought to the Rock, delirious with agony: *Please, hide. Don't let him find you.*

And the Rock obeyed. The white light hiding in Val's fists faded, seeped back into the ground where it had been born. She was left alone on the floor beside her mother's body—alone, with the light gone from her palms, and a new, slick darkness coating her insides. Alone, with a smoking mark curving across the pale flesh of her belly—a black moon on a trembling white sky.

MARION

The Queen

Marion walked into the empty living room of her family's cottage. Every step she took crunched glass under her feet; the mirrors and windows still stood vacant, shattered by the Collector's roar.

But the monster itself was nowhere to be found.

Marion wasn't sure what she had been expecting, coming back here. If the Collector had been waiting for her, then . . . what? She couldn't have fought him alone. It was foolish for her to have returned, yet here she stood. She searched the shadows for signs that what had happened hadn't *really* happened, but the evidence was everywhere: The kitchen chairs strewn across the floor. The ruined cabinets where the Collector, flung aside by Zoey, had smashed into them. The fragmented windows, framing the world in tidy square mouths lined with uneven teeth.

Marion listened to the quiet.

She had taken her mother to the police station, which was brightly lit and freshly, constantly full of people, now that a third girl had gone missing.

Quinn. Jane.

Charlotte.

Marion clutched the starfish charm around her neck and inhaled. She thought she could still smell Charlotte's scent in the air of the cottage, and if she was wrong, if it was simply her imagination creating Charlotte's scent, then she didn't want to know that. She was appreciative of her imagination, if that was the case.

She didn't ever want to forget—not Charlotte's scent, not her voice, not the texture of her hair.

Her phone beeped. A text from Zoey:

Meet me at Grayson's immediately. 34 Herring Way.

Then, a few seconds later:

He finally finished translating.

The Tighe house was humbler than most on the island—a cheerful blue-and-white farmhouse that Marion thought would look more at home somewhere in the Midwest, surrounded by fields of corn.

Marion arrived before Zoey did. Grayson greeted her at the door, looking a little ruffled and unbalanced. His eyes were bloodshot and puffy, circled by shadows.

Marion knew the feeling.

"Hey, Marion." Grayson beckoned her inside. "Please, come in."

He led her to the living room, and Marion took the opportunity to inspect him. Hands shoved in his pockets, sleeves rolled up to his elbows, brow furrowed as if deep in thought. Long and lanky frame, all knobs and sinews. His eyes, blue and guileless behind the square black frames of his glasses, flicked over to Marion as she settled in an oversize armchair.

"Zoey told me what happened last night," he began, standing awkwardly by the fireplace. "At your house."

Marion nodded. "I figured she would have. It was terrifying—"

"Not only that." Grayson drew in a breath. "About what you said to her. About us."

Marion's chest tightened with shame. She crossed her arms over her middle. "Oh."

"Yeah. Look—"

"I'm sorry, really, I was . . . I'd just found out about Charlotte, I haven't been sleeping—"

Grayson waved her quiet. "It's fine. I mean, it's not fine, but I get it." He sat down in a chair opposite her, rested his elbows on his knees. "I don't know what you've heard people say about us, but whatever it is, none of them know what they're talking about. Zoey can tell you the rest someday; that's not my place, but I'll tell you this much: I love her."

He laughed a little, shrugging. He dragged a hand through his hair. "I love her, and if it were up to me, we'd still be together.

So don't believe whatever bullshit you hear about me, or about her. And for God's sake, Marion." His gaze sharpened. "Don't ever say anything like that to her again."

Marion shook her head. "I won't, I promise. It was . . ." She swallowed her excuses. "It was shitty. I was wrong. I'm really sorry."

Grayson nodded once. "Good. Thank you. And . . . really, Marion." His expression softened. "I'm so sorry about Charlotte."

For a moment Marion couldn't speak. She nodded tightly. "Thank you. I appreciate that."

The front door slammed open and shut. Zoey clomped in, kicked off her sneakers, threw herself down onto the sofa, and tossed the book onto the ottoman. She'd ridden her bike over; her oversize, bright-pink rain jacket smelled of the sea-kissed woods.

"You really should lock your door, Grayson," she admonished, not looking at Marion. "Are your parents here?"

He shook his head. "They're down the street at the Davies' house, trying to convince them not to pack up and leave Sawkill."

Zoey snorted. "They *should* leave. And so should anyone else who can."

Marion tried not to think of the terrible truth that Zoey had shared with her: if her father was right, neither Marion nor Zoey could leave the island. Not while the monster still lived.

Not while their bodies could do the things they could do.

There are always three.

"Where are your dad and Briggs?" Marion asked, somehow managing to speak.

"Dad and Briggs and all the other *knights*," Zoey replied, "are setting up headquarters at the hotel, since our house doesn't have enough room."

"Setting up headquarters? What does that mean? Shouldn't they be out there hunting this thing?"

Zoey glanced at Grayson. "Somehow I don't think it's gonna be that simple."

Marion followed her gaze. "What did the book say?"

Grayson, looking slightly ill, stood up, retrieved a folder of papers from the end table, sat back down, and stood up once more. "How about some water first? Anyone want some water? Good."

Once he'd left, leaving the folder sitting in his place, Marion cleared her throat. "Zoey?"

Zoey glared at the hearth, arms crossed. "Yes?"

"You're still mad at me."

"Yes."

Marion's eyes stung. "I'm sorry I said—"

"I know." Zoey blew out a sharp sigh. "Let's not talk about that right now, okay? We have bigger problems on our hands."

Grayson returned with three glasses of water.

Marion took the offered glass, clinging to it like a lifeline. She wanted to move closer to Zoey but couldn't find the courage for it.

"All right." Grayson opened his folder of papers. "I don't know how to begin, really."

"At the beginning," said Zoey, brooding over her glass of water. "That's usually a good option."

"Yes, but . . ." Grayson scrubbed a hand through his hair, then paused, and looked sheepishly first at Zoey, then Marion, then Zoey again. "I feel sort of weird doing this. Like I'm some asshole professor mansplaining the situation at you."

"Look," said Zoey, "while Marion and I were out fighting literal monsters with our superpowers, you were sitting here with your dictionaries, obsessively translating this stupid book. You've earned your time in the sun. Lecture away, Professor Asshole." Zoey reclined in her chair. "Oh, and I assure you, the minute you start mansplaining anything to me, I'll be the first one to let you know about it."

Grayson smiled softly at her. "I have no doubt about that. All right. So." He looked back at his notes. "I think I'll start at the least terrifying thing and then work my way up from there."

Marion raised an eyebrow. "Grayson, that is so not reassuring."

"Sorry. Okay. We'll start with the queen." Grayson took a deep breath. "The Collector—well, first of all, according to this book, that name is unique to Sawkill's monster. Other monsters around the world, the Hand of Light refers to them by different names, according to the local legends and lore that have built up through the centuries around the monsters' reputed existence—Kula, Le Mangeur—"

"What does this have to do with the queen?" Zoey interrupted.

"Well, according to this text," Grayson replied, beginning to pace, "the monsters all function in this world in the same fashion. They need an anchor to exist here, and to be able to take different forms. Otherwise they wouldn't be able to exist outside the obscurae." Grayson paused. "You know what those are, right?"

Zoey gave him a truly impressive eye roll.

He held up his hands. "I just wasn't sure what you already knew."

Marion butted in gently. "We know what the obscurae are. Keep going."

"Well, according to the book," Grayson continued, "the monsters attach themselves to a particular family, and the connection passes on with the birth of each generation. The family serves as an anchor, stabilizing the monster's power and allowing him to exist in this world."

Zoey tensed, the lines of her body suddenly rigid.

Grayson opened the book, flipped to a page displaying an illustration of a naked girl with a curved mark on her abdomen. "The queen."

Marion took the book from Grayson, ran her fingers over the illustration. "What does she do? And what is this mark?"

"Others in the family may be connected to the monster," Grayson explained, "but the queen is the one most closely bound to him. She obeys him completely. She doesn't have a choice. Her will is consumed by his will. The mark is a scar left behind from when he . . . joins with her."

Zoey looked ill. "When he *joins* with her?"

"Please don't make me elaborate."

Marion shivered. The drawing of the naked queen under her fingers suddenly felt warm and alive. A flash of memory—Val's soft skin under her trembling hands.

"Grayson," Zoey said abruptly, "do you still have that baseball bat?"

Grayson looked surprised. "Yes . . ."

"Can you get it for me, please? I don't want to listen to this stuff without a weapon in my hands."

"What, in case the Collector shows up in the kitchen?" Grayson asked.

Zoey stared him down. "Does that seem out of the freaking realm of possibility?"

"You don't need a weapon," said Marion quietly, still staring at the drawing. "You *are* a weapon, Zoey. We both are."

The room fell silent.

"Yeah, well," Zoey said at last, her voice shaking. "Maybe I want an actual solid blunt object to wave around, just in case."

Once Grayson left to find the bat, Marion sat tense and frowning, the book like a two-ton brick in her lap, until Zoey said, "So what does all this sound like to *you*? Because I sure as hell know what I think."

Marion decided to play dumb, because, yes, she knew exactly what Zoey meant—but she wasn't sure she could bear saying it aloud. "What does what sound like?"

"Come on, Marion." Zoey slapped the sofa cushion. "A family connected to the monster? A connection passed down from generation to generation?"

Perhaps, Marion thought, *if I just shut down my brain and refuse to listen to her, then nothing will change. The world will remain as it is. I will know nothing.*

"I don't understand what you're implying," she lied.

"Yes, you do. It's the *Mortimers*." Zoey grabbed the book from Marion and shook it at her. "Every Sawkill girl who's died or disappeared over the past twelve decades has had a connection to the Mortimer family in some way. Val is freaky, and so is her mom, and Grayson said her grandmother was, too. They're ice queens, a whole family of them. Beautiful and terrifying, and no one on Sawkill can *touch* them? Sounds like a monster family to me."

Grayson returned with his old wooden bat and held it out hopefully. Zoey took it from him, stretched up on her toes to plant a sloppy kiss on his forehead, and then started swinging the bat through the air, face screwed up in concentration.

"Val wouldn't," said Marion, hating the sound of her own voice—how small and fragile it sounded, how her words dropped like stones from her tongue. "She *wouldn't*. It's not possible."

"You didn't see anything like that marking on Val when you slept with her, did you?"

Cheeks flaming, Marion flinched. *Slept with her*. As if it

were as simple and meaningless as that. "That's not something I want to just go around telling everyone, Zoey. And I think you know that."

"Grayson's not 'everyone,'" Zoey reasoned, though she didn't meet Marion's eyes. "If he's going to know what's going on, then he needs to know what's going on. All of it."

The grandfather clock in the living room chimed nine times, and Grayson waited until it had finished to ask the question Marion had fervently hoped no one would ask:

"So . . . you think the queen could be . . . Val?"

Zoey looked evenly at Marion.

"No," said Marion, unable to meet their eyes. "When we . . . When we slept together, I didn't see anything like that on her."

Zoey asked sharply, "Are you sure?"

"Zo," murmured Grayson. "Come on, ease up a bit."

"I think I'd know." Marion blinked away a hot rush of tears. She rose from the armchair, grabbed her jacket and purse, and headed for the door. "I've gotta go. See you later."

Zoey followed her. "Marion—"

"Shut up, Zoey."

She marched outside and down the porch stairs, shoved her hand in her pocket, and pulled out her car keys.

"Let me go with you," Zoey said, trotting alongside her. "Please, you shouldn't go alone."

"No." Marion opened the Volvo's rusted blue door and slipped into the driver's seat. "It's not her. I'm going to prove it to you."

Then she slammed the car door shut and drove away, Zoey diminishing in the rearview mirror from a worried-looking girl in a pink coat to a lonesome column of shadow to darkness.

Marion slipped into Kingshead using her mother's keys and crept upstairs, her sweaty hand clutching the polished banister.

It was as Marion crossed the landing from the east wing to the west that she realized she hadn't seen Ms. Mortimer in a while. Not that she was complaining. The woman wasn't exactly the most welcoming human to have ever lived.

Still. It was odd, wasn't it? For the mistress of Kingshead to have disappeared?

The dark quiet of the house, the niggling feeling of unease that had sat curled on her shoulders since leaving Zoey and Grayson—it was making Marion paranoid. Ms. Mortimer probably hadn't disappeared. She was most likely busy in town helping the volunteers, offering moral support to the community—

Val's bedroom.

Marion pressed her fingers lightly to the dark wood, closing her eyes and biting her lip. Her body, warm and tingling, felt ready to float and drift. Amplified: her breathing, her racing blood. The door itself: cracked open, emitting a thin stream of light.

Marion peeked inside.

And what she saw was Val, clad in cotton underwear pale pink as new petals, golden hair flying wild down her back. She was examining the flat plane of her lower belly—across which stretched a black mark thin as a crescent moon.

A ragged sound Marion couldn't contain burst from her lips.

Val turned, startled. "Who's there?"

Pushing the door open, Marion revealed herself. She watched in silence as Val's eyes widened and her mouth parted in shock. Her hands flew to her belly, but the black grin was too wide for her to cover, and anyway, what did she think? That by hiding it, Marion would forget what she had seen?

"Marion," Val choked out. She took a step, halted, then seemed to realize that, wait, as far as Val was concerned, Marion didn't know anything, she didn't know a damn thing, and let her hands fall. "Let me explain." Watching Val compose herself was like witnessing a maestro write her magnum opus. Her mouth melted into a rueful smile. "I was out riding and had an accident—"

"Shut up, Val."

Val's pale face grew paler. "Marion . . ."

"Did it hurt her?"

"What?" The word escaped her lips in a puff of air.

"When he killed Charlotte, did it hurt? Was she in pain?"

Val's stricken expression told Marion everything she needed to know. Marion nodded, lips tight.

Val said quietly, "Marion, please . . ."

Remembering when Val had said just that—but sweetly, desperately, her fingers tangled in Marion's hair, her hips arching off of Marion's bed—Marion looked at the ceiling and snapped in half. She had to lean against the doorframe to hold herself up, trying and failing to grapple with the realization that the girl she had slept with—the girl she had begun, stupidly, to think she could maybe *love*—had led her sister to her doom.

Zoey was right. Zoey had been right from the beginning.

Val moved toward her, whispering her name, and Marion pinned her with a deadly glare.

"I hope," Marion said, fighting hard to keep her tears from falling, "that whenever you die, it lasts for a long time, and hurts you more than you ever dreamed possible. And I hope that as you lie there in agony, you think of me, and remember that wherever I am, when I hear of your death? I'll rejoice."

Then, pushing herself off the wall before Val could touch her, Marion remade the trembling shards of herself into something like a girl, and fled.

ZOEY

The Extraordinary

Zoey sat on the floor in Grayson's living room, her father's book lying on the carpet in front of her. It wasn't cold enough for a fire, but Grayson had built one for her anyway, in an attempt to stop her shivering. As she watched the flames, her eyes unfocused, she glimpsed in their shifting shapes the illustrated figures in her father's book, now given new meaning.

It was a ritual.

According to Grayson's translation, that was the "method of extermination" the Hand of Light had devised.

A ritual soaked in blood. A ritual centered around sacrifice.

Grayson was bustling about in the kitchen, wiping down the counters and dusting out the cabinets. The compulsion to clean was a trait he'd inherited from his father, and something Zoey had always appreciated because she could not have cared less about whether any kitchen cabinets, anywhere, were clean. But, she had to admit, it was nice when they were.

Zoey had just pulled her legs to her chest and rested her chin on her knees when a quiet knock sounded at the front door.

She shot to her feet and hurried to the foyer, Grayson right on her heels with a dishrag flung over his shoulder. A quick glance out the peephole revealed a Marion-shaped person, but night had fallen, and Zoey had to make sure.

"Marion?" she called out. "Prove it's really you. What's Grayson's professor name?"

"Professor Asshole," Marion said at once, her voice hollow.

Zoey opened the door to reveal Marion standing on the other side, looking dazed and sickly pale, dark hair plastered to her head. It had started, softly, to rain.

"Marion?" Zoey was afraid to touch her.

At the sound of Zoey's voice, Marion's empty expression collapsed, and she staggered forward into Zoey's arms.

And just like that, Zoey knew.

Grayson quietly closed and locked the door, and Marion's sagging weight forced Zoey to lower them both to the floor as gracefully as she could manage. Leaning back against the door, Zoey held Marion close as she wept on her shirt. She stroked Marion's hair, tenderly combing out the wet snarls.

Standing a few feet away, Grayson shot Zoey a sad look and then moved to the kitchen to put a kettle on for tea.

When Marion at last whispered against Zoey's neck, "I

thought I might have started to love her," Zoey felt such a rage building inside her that she could have sworn she felt fire spark from the ends of her hair.

The next time Zoey saw Valerie Mortimer, she would show her not a scrap, not a *crumb*, of mercy.

After Zoey helped Marion back to the armchair, Marion stared at the fire for a while, drifting in and out of sleep. She lay wrapped up in Zoey's favorite of the Tighe family's afghans—an ugly, fluffy thing, orange and white and asparagus green.

The first time Grayson had kissed her, they'd both been tucked under that blanket, watching but not really watching *Alien*. Normally Zoey would have been pissed at anyone coming between her and Ellen Ripley, but this was *Grayson*, and his kisses, although they hadn't exactly set her on fire, had left her so soft and relaxed that she'd hardly noticed when Kane's chest burst open.

The first time she and Grayson had had sex, they'd lain on top of that same blanket, in the bed of his truck, serenaded by crickets and hugged by dusk—soft violet sky above, soft black grass below.

And it hadn't been bad. It hadn't been great, either—at least not for Zoey—and as Grayson held her afterward, catching his breath and drawing circles on her shoulders with his thumb, Zoey had realized she could happily exist for the rest of her life without doing that ever again.

Does that mean I'm broken? she'd wondered, tears pricking

her eyes as she stared at the stars coming out to play, winking down at her like they knew things she didn't.

On the day she split with Grayson, she'd asked him that same question: "Does this mean I'm broken?"

He'd answered immediately: "No. It doesn't. And I don't care about the sex, Zo. I want to be with you."

Zoey, though, had recoiled at the idea. He would grow to resent her. He would break her heart, and she would break his.

She'd backed away from him, shaking her head. "I'm not going to change my mind, Grayson."

"Zo, *please,* I'm not asking you to—"

Zoey had left him then, unable to bear the gentle sound of his voice or the sight of his tears.

And that was that. The end of Zoey and Grayson. Grayzo, she'd told him once, would be their ship name.

RIP Grayzo.

So as Zoey sat across the room from Marion, listening to the sounds of Grayson baking cookies in the kitchen (really, was the boy an actual saint?), she couldn't help staring at that damned ugly blanket and stewing in a state somewhere between regret and not-regret.

"Thanks for letting me cry on you," came Marion's soft voice. Curled up under the afghan, propped up by Mrs. Tighe's ridiculous collection of throw pillows, Marion peeked out from under a wave of black hair and offered Zoey a tired smile.

"Don't thank me," Zoey said darkly, which was probably not the best way to begin the conversation. But if Marion wanted a friend who made a point of saying the right things at the right moments, well, she'd have to look elsewhere.

Zoey stood, the quiet panic she'd tamped down for a half hour now finally emerging. "Grayson?"

He poked his head out of the kitchen, saw that Marion was sitting up, fully awake, and deflated. "Right." He took a breath. "Right." Then he disappeared, replaced by sounds of running water and dishes being stacked.

Marion clutched the afghan at her throat. "What is it?"

"What's what?"

"You're panicking."

Zoey waved her off. "Only slightly."

"Zoey."

Stalking circles around the room, Zoey waited for Grayson to join them. Then she retrieved her father's book from the end table and squeezed herself into the armchair beside Marion, and opened it to the pages Zoey wasn't sure she'd ever be able to stop thinking about, not for the rest of her life.

Marion looked at the pages, aghast. "What *is* all this?"

Zoey glanced up at Grayson.

Grayson took a deep breath and sat on the edge of the coffee table. "It's a ritual the Hand of Light has devised. When completed, they've found it banishes the Collector back to one of the obscurae. Not forever. Their notes say that the monsters end up returning, maybe not always to the same place, but the banishment doesn't kill them or anything. They always return. They go into hiding, regenerate, and return. Sometimes it takes years, though. Even decades."

Zoey watched Marion's gaze drop to the illustration lying open in her lap—three girls. One stabbing. One slicing. One being consumed by a black cloud with white eyes.

"All right, so . . ." Marion shook her head a little. "What is the ritual, exactly?"

"*Semper tres.*" Grayson flipped back to the page with one of the sketched superhuman girls—the girl brandishing a sword. He pointed to the words scrawled beneath the girls' feet. "It means 'Always three.' That's the key, it seems. They need three girls for the ritual. And not just any three girls."

Grayson glanced at Marion, and then at Zoey, his gaze worried.

"Three extraordinary girls," Zoey said for him, remembering her father's words. She drew her limbs into a knot at Marion's side. Even with the fire, even with Marion's body squished against hers, Zoey couldn't stay warm. "We're supposed to fight each other, using our power. We beat the shit out of each other, and the Collector can't resist the call of our blood. The call of our *fury*."

She rolled her eyes, scrambling desperately for levity. "It's so dramatic."

"He follows the call to the site the Hand of Light has chosen for the ritual," Grayson continued. "A controlled location. The Hand of Light has weapons. Guns, swords, knives. They make sure the girls can't escape. They turn them against one another. The girls fight, the Collector comes, and he begins to . . ."

Grayson's voice dropped off.

"He eats them," Marion whispered, her eyes glittering. "Doesn't he? Just like Charlotte."

Zoey swallowed hard. *Just like Thora.*

Grayson nodded miserably. "The consumption of each girl weakens the monster, but he'll be unable to resist. He gorges himself, and the Hand of Light ensures that until that's done, neither he nor the girls can run away. Once all the girls are consumed—"

"Blam-o." Zoey slapped her hands together. Grayson and Marion both jumped. "The girls' power zaps the monster back to the hellhole from whence he came. And what's worse? Apparently once girls start dying really quickly like they've been doing around here? It means the monster's close to breaking free."

Marion looked up at her, eyes wide. "Breaking free of what?"

Zoey drew in a deep breath, let it out slowly. Steadily she met Marion's gaze. "The queen. And once he's free, he'll kill anyone. Not just girls. *Anyone*. And he won't need help to do it."

"And once he's free," Grayson added, hands clenched in his lap, "it's much more difficult for the Hand of Light to track him down. He can still be tempted by the ritual, by the combination of the three girls, but once he's no longer contained to a specific area, it's like the hunting equivalent of searching for a needle in a haystack." He exhaled, rubbed his hands over his face. "At least, so the book says."

"Which makes me wonder if the Hand of Light would even

care about hunting down these monsters," Zoey muttered, "if no one else but girls were ever in danger. How much do you want to bet the Hand of Light formed because some old rich men figured out these monsters could develop a taste for man-flesh and wanted to protect their own asses?"

"Can I once again apologize on behalf of men everywhere?" Grayson offered. "Because we can really fucking suck sometimes."

Zoey arched an eyebrow. "Sometimes?"

"Most of the time."

"There it is."

Marion had sat quietly during their exchange, and continued to for two straight minutes. Zoey counted the seconds to keep from screaming.

Finally, Marion looked up at her, clear-eyed and calm. "If we do what Grayson described, if we go through the ritual, then the Collector will go away, before he manages to break free of . . . of the queen? No one else will die?"

This was so far removed from the words Zoey had expected to hear that she actually squawked.

"What?" She scrambled away from Marion as if she had been burned. "*If* we do this? No. *Hell. No.*" She stood, fuming. "We are not letting some dickhead man-cult use us like this. There has to be another way."

"Okay," said Marion. "And what would that be? This way has worked. The book says so."

Zoey spluttered, words failing her. "It doesn't matter

anyway," she blurted at last. "Three extraordinary girls." She pointed at herself, then at Marion. "One, two. We don't have a third."

"So we find her. And then we begin the ritual, like the book says."

Zoey laughed, just shy of hysterical. "Nope. Nuh-uh. Not gonna happen."

Marion watched her patiently. "Then what do you suggest? We try to banish him all by ourselves? Unguided? Uncontrolled? I don't know about you, but I don't exactly feel like a pro with my power or anything. What if I can't make it work? What if *you* can't? What if we die trying, and then he's still here, and he breaks free and starts killing everyone we've left behind?"

Silence stretched between them, tacky and dense. The grandfather clock burst in with twelve brassy chimes, and Zoey growled through the din, "Grayson, permission to smash your clock with my baseball bat so it never bothers me again."

Grayson, head in his hands, said flatly, "Permission denied."

"So?" Marion watched Zoey, her eyes still swollen from crying, her lips pale and chapped. "What's your *other way*, Zoey?"

Standing in the middle of the room with her fists clenched, Zoey had not even a whisper of an answer.

THE ROCK WISHED IT HAD the ability to stop the world from spinning.

If only there was a way to keep its daughters safe from harm, even for only a little while longer!

But this was a futile wish, and a waste of time. Ordinarily, to the Rock, time was a mammoth entity, boundless and malleable.

But not tonight. Tonight, time was a cruel taskmaster. Tonight, the Rock was on human time.

Tonight, the beast was on the move.

The Rock was, too.

Through its crown of trees, along its ridges knobbed like bones, the Rock sent whispers crashing like the endless envious waves.

Find one another, instructed the Rock—white wings fluttering, black grasses rustling, forest creatures scrabbling with a panic they could not name.

Find one another, and hold on tight.

The Arrival

On the bench behind Kingshead, overlooking a sea full of abandoned bones, Val sat barefoot in a soft gray nightgown, staring at her hands.

Inside her, the waxy blackness of his presence was squeezing each of her organs, sucking hard on the underside of her skin, anchoring him to this world. He shivered and gnawed at her veins, impatient to be free of her. It wouldn't be long now. The weight of him inside her cells gave her a new sensitivity, like she'd sprouted tiny antennae of her own, coating her body like a velvet sleeve. She could read the state of him so much more clearly than she ever had before.

And it was true: he needed only one more kill, one more meal, before he would be able to stand on his own.

A tingle distracted Val—twin itches, burrowing into the

hollows of her palms. She glanced down.

Her hands . . . they *glowed*.

Val closed her eyes and turned her thoughts outward—to the black windblown trees surrounding her family's home, to the horse farms and their glossy dark hills, to the pebbled paths weaving through the five woods like veins.

To the Rock itself.

Why are you doing this? she thought, just as she'd done in the red room, when she'd asked the Rock to hide her light. She'd asked it, and it had listened.

It had obeyed her.

And now . . . would it answer?

Out here, on her bench, hidden from the trees and facing the endless expanse of the sea, Val felt . . . well, not safe, she never felt that, but at least, for the moment, she felt unseen.

What are you? she asked. She planted her bare feet on the sand-strewn black rock. She imagined that the blood coursing through her body would extend like a raging river, down into the island. It would gather information there and come back as a gentle rain, cooling her forehead.

What are you?

A pause. A beat of waiting silence. Val held her breath.

Then she felt a blazing heat gather itself, as it had done in the library—right before she'd burned her mother—and in the red room, when he'd marked her as his queen.

She smiled, faintly.

That day, she had pleaded with this energy to hide.

Now, she welcomed its return. It punched up through the rock beneath her like an electric fist.

Hello, Rock, she thought.

Then Val rose, only slightly unsteady, and the brilliant fist thrust up through the soles of her feet and into her torso, collecting around her chest and in the center of her clenched palms like white-hot stars pulled down from the heavens.

Distantly, she recognized that she hadn't thought this through very well. Experimentation was . . . not a good idea. He would sense the intrusion, the crackle of the white foreign heat against the blackness with which he'd slickly coated her insides.

He would not be pleased. He would want to find the root of this foreign power and tear it out.

But she heard nothing. She felt nothing. No displeasure, no punishment. He could, very easily, if he wanted to. He could cause her pain even from the other side of the island. She'd seen it happen to her mother a thousand times, seen her collapse and clutch her belly, soundless agony carving terrible shapes across her face.

Val waited. She cupped his mark with glowing hands.

Nothing. Only the waves; only the wind.

She opened her fingers and then clenched them again, the sensation like submerging herself into a fizzing hot bath.

Then, a flash of white, fluttering down from the gray sky: A moth, hovering a few inches in front of her face—tiny and pale, black spots like eyes on its wings. It whispered gibberish as it flew, its tiny moth voice childlike and clear. With a contented sigh, the moth alighted on Val's wrist, just beyond the reach of the brilliant light resting in her palm.

So said the moth: *This power is the Rock's, and it is yours, too. Use it.*

They are coming.

Val stared at the moth. "Who's coming?"

The moth fluttered up the trail back to Kingshead. Val raced past it, heart suddenly pounding. The back of her neck tingled, like ghost fingers were tapping out a sonata on her skin.

She burst into Kingshead—such a tomb it was, with her mother gone, and she wouldn't be able to deflect the questions for much longer: *Where's your mother, Val? Is she sick? Tell her we hope she feels better soon!*

Val hurried to the front parlor, used her buzzing fingers to part the gauzy curtains. Four cars, headlights off, moved slow and silent up the drive to the Althouse cottage. They parked, surrounding the house like points of a compass. People climbed out—men, Val thought, in dark coats and hats. They held guns. Some entered the cottage. Others stayed at the cars. A few of them moved down toward the trees, the edge of Kingshead Woods. Twenty men, maybe. They were moving too swiftly, too darkly, to count.

Marion?

Val didn't grab her boots. She wanted to feel the Rock between her toes.

She slipped out the front doors, and ran.

ZOEY

The Rock Speaks

Zoey should not have fallen asleep.

Pumping her legs, pedaling her bike faster than she'd ever dared pedal it before, she raced across the island from Grayson's house to Marion's. Her phone vibrated in her pocket. Grayson, probably. He'd no doubt woken up by now and found her gone.

He would have to wait.

Zoey had awakened twenty minutes ago, having fallen asleep on the couch in Grayson's living room, to find Marion's chair empty, her purse and jacket left behind.

She'd *gone*—but where?

Home, Zoey assumed, or Kingshead. Back to Val?

Later, she would yell at Marion. Later, once she'd found Marion safe and alive, and not ripped to pieces or fed to a monster as Val watched, cackling.

Zoey tightened her grip on the handlebars, Grayson's bat wedged under her arm like a rocket launcher. The air vibrated around her, buzzed against the back of her neck, snaked between each of her fingers and toes. When she focused her eyes on the road before her, the edges of her vision shimmered like a mirage on a sun-drenched plain. If she decided to jump off her bike and then turn and blast it into the sea with her bare hands, she thought, maybe, she could do it. If not into the sea, then pretty damn far.

Despite everything, Zoey smiled.

You are *a weapon, Zoey.* Marion had said it, and now Zoey said it, a tiny chill skipping up her sides: "I am my own weapon."

It was like something out of one of the wild fantasy stories she and Thora had written—several binders' worth of original epics that they had both sworn to each other would never again see the light of day.

The pain of Thora was like a splinter in Zoey's heart. If she picked at it too much, it would dig in deeper, so she only ever looked at it sideways. Look at it dead on, and the pain might just sear her alive.

But tonight, with dawn still two hours away and the wet world glittering black like an evil queen's wood, Zoey faced Thora unflinching. She opened up her chest cavity and welcomed in the raw night air. It plucked at her splinter, shoved against it, and shifted it. Her heart ached, and she relished the bite of pain.

She relived Marion's words—*Just because you can't figure out how to have sex like a normal person*—and let the memory slap her up and down her ribs.

Over and over, she pictured the heartbroken expression on Grayson's face as she'd told him she could no longer be with him.

Zoey turned her bike sharply left and plunged into the edge of the Kingshead Woods, plowing through a cluster of bushes. A cloud of tiny white wings erupted, thumped lightly against her face and arms.

Moths, whispering: *Faster, Zoey.*

Faster.

Zoey pedaled past the Mortimers' pastures, dimly noticed horses running alongside her. They matched her pace on their side of the fence, tossed their heads, snorted into the night air. The tires of Zoey's bike carved a blazing path through the mud. Branches whipped against her, and she didn't mind their sting. They encouraged her; they pushed her on. They were ancient mothers, wise and tired. They had witnessed unfathomable joy and unbearable pain.

A moth alighted between Zoey's knuckles, clung to her with furry feet. Its tired wings quivered—two unblinking black eyes.

Be ready, it warned her.

Ahead, the dark peaks of Kingshead emerged from the trees.

Then Zoey heard a scream.

MARION

The Martyr

Marion followed the bone cry's path through the Kingshead Woods, her palms bleeding, preparing herself to die.

It seemed to her the most logical decision to make. There was no need for anyone else to die but her.

She had cut open her palms with a knife she'd stolen from Grayson's kitchen, and now she wandered through the woods, smearing her hands across the trees. The Collector, she hoped, would catch her scent. She would be irresistible to him. An extraordinary girl, right? He'd hunt her, and then, ignoring the bone cry rattling in her ears, urging her to run, Marion would let the beast grab her. Once in his clutches, she would tesser. She would think of the snow-covered beach, the strange lavender sky, and bring them both to that obscura, hidden somewhere in the deep of the world.

And if he killed her there—which, of course, he would—then, well, she would die.

But no one else would. And then he would be trapped there, banished, hopefully for years.

It was the most logical decision to make.

As she trudged through the trees, the dissonant metallic whine ringing in her ears, Marion told herself that this decision was not only logical; it was the fate she deserved, for failing to keep Charlotte safe, for not suggesting other places for them to live, for not immediately sensing the horrible truth about Valerie Mortimer. It was also, maybe, a little bit brave.

She did not feel brave.

She closed her eyes, shutting out the sights and sounds of the woods so that the only thing she knew was her own body—blood roaring, heart pounding so fast she feared she might scare herself to death before she even found what she was looking for, and the call of the bone cry.

She almost started to run. It would be easy, to run, to hide in some dark hollow until someone else took care of the situation. Someone mightier.

Marion opened her eyes and returned to herself—feet planted in the mud, wind-bitten trees bowing over her like naked hags foraging in the weeds for hidden dark treasures.

"Go out a hero," she muttered, limbs shaking as she started climbing up a ridge woven through with roots and crested with scratchy brush. "Isn't that what people always do in the movies?"

She wiped her sleeve across her face, stumbled over a knot of weeds. It would certainly feel more heroic if she could stop crying.

God, how long had she been searching these woods? Dawn was still a ways off, she thought. The world inside the woods was dark and muted, painted in shades of graveyard gray and rot brown. Every tree looked the same, and the bone cry was a loud, uninterrupted drone banging against the sides of her skull, a persistent warning.

Where was he, then?

Marion stopped in a small clearing, not fifteen feet across, and threw up her hands. "Where are you? Huh?" she shouted to the trees. "Come get me, you sick bastard!"

As if in answer, a scream pierced the night.

Marion whirled, searching through the dark woods.

It came again, and this time it said a word, and this time Marion recognized the voice:

"*Marion!*"

Her mother.

MARION

The Circle

Marion didn't stop to think beyond the simple fact of her mother in danger.

She ran, keeping the looming bulk of Kingshead in front of her, like the north star gone haunted and dim. She heard branches crack behind her and wondered if the Collector was in pursuit, but she couldn't bring herself to look.

One lonely thought drummed through her body, riding the roar of her blood and the high whine of the bone cry: *Not Mom. Not her, too.*

But when Marion burst out of the woods, and then ran up the sloping ridge to the perimeter of shrubs and grasses that ringed the cottage's backyard, she realized her prayer had been uttered in vain.

For there stood the Hand of Light—twenty men, black and

brown and white, wearing dark coats and hats. Marion hadn't yet met all of them, but she knew at once who they must be. They stood in a circle within the cluster of oak trees in the back corner of the yard, which was thick enough to hide them from any prying eyes up at Kingshead or down on the road to town. Silent and still, they looked like the tall stones of ancient England, arranged pleasingly for the gods.

One of them had a gun pressed to Chief Harlow's temple.

And another had Pamela Althouse's arms bound behind her, and a small blade pressed into the skin of her throat.

"Marion?" Her mother's lips trembled. "What's going on? Who are these people?"

Marion's throat was so choked with fear that she could hardly speak. "It's gonna be okay, Mom."

"Hello, Marion," said Briggs, stepping forward. "I'm so glad you came. I figured you would." Then Briggs peered past Marion into the woods. His smile widened. "Ah, Zoey! Welcome."

Marion turned to see Zoey emerging from the woods, her arm raised in the kill position—straight out in front of her body, palm flat and rigid. Her other hand gripped a baseball bat.

Marion rushed for her. "Zoey, get out of here, *run*!"

Zoey ignored her, instead taking a defensive stance right in front of her. "Let him go, Briggs. And Mrs. Althouse, too. Or I start fucking up all your shit in a major way."

"Once I finish speaking," said Briggs, "you'll have five seconds to surrender yourself to me, without any trouble, or I'll tell Peters to kill your father." Briggs tilted his head slightly to the left. "Don't think I won't do it, Zo. I don't need him. But I need you."

"What, for your little ritual?" Zoey's voice trembled.

Briggs smiled. "Exactly. Five."

Chief Harlow choked out, "Zoey, I'm sorry—"

"Four."

"I tried to stop them—"

Zoey's hand shook in the air. "It's okay, Dad. I promise you everything's gonna be fine."

"Three."

Mrs. Althouse let out a gasping sob.

"I didn't want this for you," said Chief Harlow, tears tracking down his stubbled cheeks. "I'm sorry I let you come here."

"Two."

Then, beside Marion, Zoey went so tense the air started snapping around her like ice over glass.

"You *bitch*," Zoey ground out.

Marion turned, following Zoey's glare.

There was Val, flying down the hill toward them in a nightgown and bare feet, her hair streaming like a golden banner. And even now, knowing what she knew, Marion could hardly bear to look at Val; her moonlit beauty was astounding.

Then, before anyone could stop her, before Briggs could finish his countdown, Zoey dropped the bat and ran, flinging out her hands like she was slamming shut a door.

With a cry of shock, Val flew away from her, landed hard in the grass some twenty feet away.

"Zoey, no!" Marion cried, but Val was already jumping to

her feet, running back toward Zoey with her hands—oh, her hands. They were on *fire.*

Marion watched, dumbstruck, as Val sped toward them like a constellation knocked out of the sky—three stars, one in each palm, and one in her chest, burning bright like someone had stuffed Sirius into her rib cage.

Zoey backed away, eyes wide. "Holy shit."

The third girl. *Three extraordinary girls.*

SEMPER TRES.

Val lunged at Zoey, knocking her to the ground. Zoey's head smacked against the earth. Val pinned her to the mud and punched her jaw once, twice. When her fists hit Zoey's face, they sizzled like meat against a grill.

Chief Harlow cried out, struggling to free himself.

Zoey screamed and thrust her hands up at Val's chest. Val flew back into the circle of men. They caught her, trapping her in a nest of arms. Marion saw one of them bury his face in Val's hair and inhale. Then they shoved Val back into the circle, back at Zoey.

But Zoey was ready. She crouched, hands out and lip bleeding. Val flew at her, lighting up with every step. With twin furious screams, they collided. Val's hands struck Zoey's stomach like the crash of fireworks. Zoey spun, flinging Val to the ground. Val lay there, gasping. The light in her chest flickered out, and then flared back to life. Zoey straddled her and punched Val again and again.

As for the men surrounding them, they did nothing. They tightened the circle, huddling closer and closer with eager eyes.

They waved their guns like flags. They were *laughing.*

"Wonderful!" Briggs crowed. "We hardly had to do anything at all. Do you see, my friends?" He raised his hands, addressing the surrounding men. "Even these extraordinary girls are susceptible to the same weaknesses that plague their entire sex. They want this. In their heart of hearts, they *want* to destroy each other."

Marion had been in a daze, watching the impossible unfurl at lightning speed before her eyes. At Briggs's words she snapped.

"Stop it!" She ran at Zoey, pulled her off a gasping, bleeding Val. "Zoey, *stop*!"

She staggered away, Zoey in her arms. Zoey pushed free, spun on her heel, eyes bright and wild, and slammed her palm into Marion's chest. The impact was like someone had thrown a brick at her. Marion flew back, hit the ground. Dazed, breathless, she allowed herself to be helped to her feet by two men with clumsy gloved hands. She felt a hand at her breast, another at her hip, and then they shoved her toward Zoey.

"Stop!" Marion held her head, unsteady on her feet. She forced herself through the pain, grabbed Val's arm, and tessered them both a few feet away.

One of the men let out an appreciative sigh.

Without Val's body beneath her, Zoey fell to her hands and knees.

At Marion's side, Val panted, her face splattered with blood, "Thank you."

Suddenly, Marion's eyes were full and hot. Even now, the sensation of Val's skin under her hands was lovely enough to crack open her heart all over again.

"Marion," Val began, reaching for her. "I'm so sorry—"

Marion shoved her roughly away. "I should let her kill you."

Briggs withdrew a long knife from a sheath at his hip—a wicked, ancient-looking blade with a dark, elaborately carved hilt and a curved tip. He held it to the sky, flat on his palms.

"God understands," Briggs called out, "that these beasts are not supposed to be here. He has, in his wisdom, sent these girls to us. These girls whose power is contentious and self-defeating—except for in the hands of those strong enough to wield it. Our hands, my brothers. In *our hands*, these girls will be lifted up. Their sacrifice tonight will help us trap the beast while he is still bound to his queen. Their sacrifice tonight will ensure the safety of the world that depends on us to protect it."

Then he intoned a phrase in Latin, and the other men repeated him—a chorus of voices, low and masculine, uttering words Marion couldn't understand but knew were meant to precede her death.

Val turned away from Marion, launching herself at Zoey.

A crack from the woods, a rustling of trees.

Marion whirled, squinted past the swaying, chanting circle of men at the trees beyond.

Was that a flicker of stars?

Or a flash of white eyes?

The bone cry escalated, climbing frantically up the walls of her skull.

Marion turned, her mind scrambling to get a hold of itself over the baying howl of her panic. She locked eyes with her mother, who was straining away from the blade at her throat. Veins dissected her white neck into sections like countries on a bleached map.

Val and Zoey wrestled in a tangled, snarling knot on the ground. One of Val's nightgown straps had fallen off her shoulder. She had ripped off Zoey's jacket and was now wrapping it around Zoey's throat, trying to choke her. Zoey elbowed Val in the stomach, sending her flying back.

The men, leering, rapturous, caught Val.

Marion ran for the baseball bat, placed it in Zoey's scorching, outstretched palms.

"Zoey! Listen to me." She caught Zoey's face in her hands, forcing eye contact. "This is *exactly* what they want. You're bleeding, and so is Val, and so am I. He's *coming*." Marion shook the bat in Zoey's hands. "Remember Grayson. Remember the book."

Zoey blinked, then blinked again. Some of the fury faded from her eyes.

"Oh, God," she whispered.

Marion turned and found Val in Briggs's arms. He swiped his own hand across her bleeding lips, then smeared her blood across his face.

Marion heard Zoey cry out from behind her, "What the *fuck* is wrong with you?"

The trees beyond the circle moved, like black curtains parting to announce the next act. Darkness flitted across the world, climbing from tree to tree.

The bone cry humming electric up her legs, Marion ran for

Val and tore her from Briggs's arms. She slapped her, to make the men think all was as it should be.

"Val," Marion gasped, pulling Val into the center of the circle, toward Zoey. She threw Val to the ground. "He's here. The Collector. We have to leave. *Now.*"

The bone cry was so loud Marion could hardly hear even the hoarse groaning cries of the men calling for her blood.

Val nodded, wide-eyed. Her body jerked, yanked by forces Marion couldn't see. Val's jaw clenched; her muscles strained, as if she were pulling against the tide.

She obeys him completely. As Marion remembered Grayson's description of the queen, her veins flooded with ice. *Her will is consumed by his will.*

"Stay down," Val whispered harshly. "*Hurry.*"

There was no time for second guesses. Marion grabbed Zoey and pulled her to the ground. Val crouched between them, bowed her head, and positioned her arms, ready to spring up off the ground and run.

Then Val detonated.

The ground shook under their feet, like it was a dead engine someone had jumped angrily back to life. The lights at Val's palms and chest burst into an incandescent field, consuming Marion and everything around her. She faintly heard Briggs's cry of dismay, the circled men falling to the ground like zapped bugs.

An inhuman shriek rang out—bestial and rasping, a glottal flap of wet skin.

Marion shielded her eyes. A hand slick with blood clasped her own—Zoey, her expression taut and afraid.

"Take us somewhere safe." Zoey's eyes flicked over to Val, her jaw jutting out sharply. "All of us."

With one hand in Zoey's and the other gripped tightly in Val's, unharmed by Val's dimming light, Marion felt as if something incomplete had been, abruptly and utterly, made whole.

She didn't hesitate, or think of her mother or of Chief Harlow, or what had happened to Briggs and his men, or if the Collector was pouncing for them.

She closed her eyes and pushed all the energy she contained out and down—into the black mud, into the stone beneath her feet, into the Rock itself. And the island—blazing, furious, trembling—rose up to meet her.

God understands, Briggs had whispered, *that the beasts are not supposed to be here.*

Marion couldn't imagine a God like the one she'd grown up hearing about—some man sitting in the clouds, maneuvering the pieces of the world to suit his whims because he, of course, knows best.

But she could imagine a God in the shape of an island crowned with trees, brooding in the middle of a black sea.

Somewhere safe, she thought to the Rock, her grip tightening on Zoey and Val. She knew the Rock heard. She felt its ears prick and its great beastly heart awaken and its rage solidify, matching her own.

She disappeared.

ZOEY

The Purge

When Zoey opened her eyes, she was flat on her back in a bed of moss, and the night sky above her rested in the narrow palms of many-fingered tree branches.

Her hands tingled painfully; her head fizzed and rocked like she'd tumbled off a storming sea onto solid ground.

"Marion?" Zoey found her bat lying in the brush and felt a fierce rush of gladness that Marion had retrieved it. "Val?"

She found them, Marion to her right and Val to her left, each of them slowly coming back to themselves. Marion's tesser had dropped them in a thicket choked with brambly undergrowth, and small bent trees coated in brittle, sea-crusted bark.

Marion held her head, eyes gazing blearily at nothing in particular. Val crouched on her hands and knees, her arms and chest still rimmed in light. She glared at the ground and breathed evenly through her nose, her lips clamped shut. Then she pressed one of her glowing hands to her stomach. A few seconds later, she turned away to vomit.

"Tessering's no joke, is it?" Zoey tossed in Val's general direction. She kicked herself free of the thorny bracken's grip and made her way to Marion, ripped the turquoise paisley scarf from her hair, and dabbed her bleeding lip. "Where are we?"

"I'm not sure," Marion answered, her voice thin. "I took us somewhere safe, and that's all I know. I didn't think to tell it where to go."

"Hey." Zoey ducked to look Marion in the eyes. "It's okay. You did good."

Marion's smile trembled. "I'm so tired, I . . . I don't think I can get us home."

"We're on one of the Smalls," Val croaked, her voice rattling and sounding not entirely normal. She pointed through the trees toward a thin string of distant lights that Zoey now recognized as downtown Sawkill. They shimmered across the water, a line of mystics making their pilgrimage to the shore. "On Hare's Tail, I think."

"Why are you here?" Marion asked, not looking up as she tended to Zoey's hand. Her movements were gentle, but her voice was not. "Why did you come tonight?"

Val, coughing, said weakly, "I wanted to help you."

Marion's jaw clenched. "Like you helped my sister?"

"If you try anything funny," Zoey added, glaring at Val, "I swear to God I'll blast you to the bottom of the sea."

"She saved our lives," Marion muttered, staring at the ground. Her eyes held a bright sheen.

"I don't care." Zoey pointed at Val. "Don't think you'll get any mercy from me, not even for a second."

Then, from Val's spot in the weeds, came a low gurgle of laughter.

"Mercy," growled Val, but not really Val, for that voice was not hers, and vibrated with a malevolence that sent a shiver of fear sliding down Zoey's arms. "Mercy is not a concept in which I believe."

Then Val's head whipped around to stare at them, her eyes gone entirely white. Still on her hands and knees, she lurched toward them in an awful, unsteady crawl.

"Shit," breathed Zoey, grabbing her bat and jumping to her feet. "Marion, get behind me!"

Marion scrambled to obey.

"Marion, get behind me!" Val mocked.

Zoey put up her hand, concentrated on the solidity of her feet planted in the mud, imagined hot electric rods spanning from her calves down into the earth and the rock and the sea.

Her hand surged to life, every finger buzzing with a current of power.

Val hesitated, cocked her head violently to the side like a rabid dog.

Zoey beckoned. "Just try it, you piece of shit."

"What did you do with Val?" Marion demanded.

"Val has made me angrier than I ever believed possible,"

said Val, and then sprang up from the mud, teeth bared. Her lovely face elongated and darkened, like ink was collecting beneath her skin. Her eyes blazed white.

Zoey let out a battle cry and thrust her palm at Val's leaping form. The air rippled, slammed into Val's abdomen.

A sound emerged from her throat—part monster, part girl. Her body jerked at the navel. She flew back into the trees and out of sight.

Zoey thrust the bat into Marion's hands, and together they plunged past the nearest line of trees into darkness.

"If I end up having to kill her," Zoey muttered, "just know that I'm sorry. Not for her. For you."

Marion said nothing.

They found Val writhing at the base of a squat black tree, her body twisting in a cradle of roots. Her ragged screams cut the air into pieces; her illuminated palms flickered in and out, like light bulbs in a gale.

She turned at their approach, her eyes shifting from storm white to ink black, to an ordinary, pleading blue.

"Please," she gasped. "Help me."

Her back arched and then flattened, slamming her first into the air and then back down onto the roots. Her hands, ribboned with blood, tore at the bark as though she were fighting toward the surface for oxygen.

Zoey froze. She didn't want to grant Val mercy, but her stomach turned at the sight of Val convulsing, her body being used and flung and ravaged like a doll's.

She remembered Grayson's voice uttering the translated words from her father's book:

She obeys him completely.

She doesn't have a choice.

Her will is consumed by his will.

Beside Zoey, Marion let out a choked sob. "Oh my God . . ."

"Oh my God, oh my *God*." Val heaved herself into a sitting position, her bloodied fingers still digging into the roots. She fixed Marion with a flickering, scornful stare, her shoulders and legs jerking. "You know, Val only liked you because you were an easy target."

"Don't listen to him, Marion," said Zoey. "He's a liar and a murderer."

"She needed a quick screw to take the edge off," taunted Val, her voice caught somewhere between the Collector's and her own. "And she knew you were desperate for it."

Marion's reply rang out steady and clear. "That's not true."

Val pressed her glowing hands to her nightgown. They burned holes through the thin fabric, then met her skin and sizzled. Val screamed in pain. Her eyes flickered to blue. She gagged, gasping for breath.

She looked at Zoey, pleading. "Help me! Please . . . Hold down my hands."

Val slammed her palms onto her stomach. At the impact, fresh black bile oozed from Val's lips and nose, down the shuddering front of her gown.

Marion let out a soft, anguished cry.

Zoey realized what was happening with such a sharp stab of disgust that her stomach turned over.

Then, with a rasping roar, Val sprang up from the roots and leaped at them.

Zoey sucked in a breath and flung out her fists.

Val flew back from them, slamming into the fat black tree. She dropped to the roots and didn't move.

Zoey and Marion ran to her. Zoey kept her hands out, her arms rigid. She imagined sending all the energy contained in her body to rest against Val's glowing hands, keeping them flat against Val's belly.

"Please, I'm trying . . ." Val gazed up at them with a film over her pale blue eyes. Her body seized with a violent cough. More black liquid bubbled out of her lips. Her eyelids fluttered; her palms flickered, dimming. "I'm trying to . . ."

Marion knelt at her side. "You're fighting him." Marion covered Val's hands with her own. At her touch, Val's hands swelled softly back to brightness. Her body twisted in pain. Tears leaked from her eyes.

"Marion," came her true voice, hoarse and desperate. "I'm so sorry. I should have jumped." She gasped, blinking. "I should have ended it . . ."

"No." Marion shook her head, mouth in a tight line. "No, you shouldn't have. Don't say that."

A crack, a snarl, and then Val's body jerked away from them.

"Hold her down!" Marion cried.

Zoey muttered, "Damn it," and obeyed, because the

alternative was to blast Val, and keep blasting her, until there was no life left in her body. If Val had truly been owned by this beast for God knows how long, then . . .

A tight hot lump formed in Zoey's throat, pushing tears to her eyes.

Then Val doesn't deserve to die like this.

Not by his hand.

And not by mine.

Zoey cursed every curse she knew and straddled Val's hips, her knees digging uncomfortably into the roots. Her buzzing hands hovered over Val's chest, defibrillator-like, and her legs clamped down on Val's body like a set of tiny human prongs. No matter how hard Val bucked, no matter what horrible things she shouted at her, Zoey kept her pinned in place beneath the tree, her sizzling hands glued to her belly. Blood seeped out from between Val's flaming white fingers.

Beads of sweat rolled down Zoey's back. Her stomach rebelled against the smell of cooking flesh.

Courage, dear heart, murmured a tiny white moth, fluttering down out of the trees to land between Zoey's knuckles.

Val shrieked, her body bowing up off the roots with such force that she looked like she might split in two. She spat a mouthful of steaming black liquid at Zoey's face.

Zoey gagged, spitting and heaving. Every bone in her body screamed at her to run. She pressed down harder against Val's torso. The thrum of the stone and mud and water beneath her trembling legs kept her vital, kept her upright and thrumming.

Marion wiped Zoey's face with her free hand, her fingers cool.

"Listen to me, Val," said Marion, her voice calm. "I'm going to talk to you until this is over. Okay?"

Val growled, her head snapping from side to side, "When this is over, I will tear you apart!"

"No. When this is over, we're gonna have a nice long talk. Just you and me."

"You are filth," shouted Val. "You are carrion—"

"Remember when I kissed you, in the stables?" Marion cupped Val's sweating cheek. "I'd never kissed anyone like that before. I'll never forget it, Val."

The brilliance in Val's chest flickered, sending fingers of light shooting all down her body. She sobbed once. "Marion, help me!"

"I'm right here." Marion gazed at Val, steady and unflinching. "We both are. Me, and Zoey. We're not leaving you."

Zoey's hands were going numb, and her shoulders ached like they'd been pierced by hot irons. "I won't be able to do this for much longer."

Her vision dimmed, then brightened. She gritted her teeth, imagining the sketch of the girl in her father's book—a sword in one hand, the other held out like its own shield.

"Come on, Val," Zoey muttered. "*Come on.*"

"You're doing great," soothed Marion. "I'm so proud of you, Val."

Val drew a great, ragged breath and roared up at Marion, "I

will devour you for decades, and you'll feel every moment of it!"

But Marion didn't let go of her hand. "I'm right here," she murmured. "I'm right here, Val."

She didn't let go even when Val's furious shouts dissolved into awful, bubbling breaths, and racking coughs that made Zoey's chest hurt to hear them. When Val's eyes fell shut and she began to silently convulse, Marion sprang into action. Releasing Val's hand, she ripped off her jacket and said to Zoey, "We have to turn her!"

Zoey released Val's limp, shuddering body, bearing down against the urge to collapse out of sheer relief. Then, together, she and Marion turned Val onto her side, used their own hands to keep her glowing ones pressed to her stomach. They wedged Marion's balled-up jacket between the back of Val's head and the root behind it, and then they each held her by the shoulders—Zoey behind Val's body, Marion's in front—as she threw up fountains of tar. And with each mouthful spewed, Val's hands and chest grew brighter, until she subsided, wheezing, and opened her eyes.

They were watering, bloodshot—and the same crystalline Mortimer blue that Zoey had always so passionately cursed.

Marion let out a shaky burst of laughter. "Val, you did it."

"Wait just a second." Zoey gathered her last shreds of strength and readied her hands, just in case. Her shoulders flared with pain in protest. The moth remained between her knuckles, wings slowly beating. "Is he gone?"

And Val, tears rolling down her flushed cheeks, pulled up

the torn scraps of her gown to reveal her abdomen. Two smoking, bloody handprints flanked her navel like the wings of a bird coming to rest. Below them stretched a pale pink smile of scar tissue—an echo of what had once been.

VAL

The Pledge

By the time Val could once again open her eyes, she realized she had been moved away from the tree against which she'd been thrashing. She now lay close to the sea, on a gentle rise of land coated with downy tufts of grass and pockets of rough gray sand. From very near came the rhythmic lapping of waves. The sea breeze kissed the bits of her skin bared to the night.

She lifted herself up on shaky arms, wincing from the pain of her belly. Someone had pressed a sweater to her stomach to stanch the bleeding, tied it around her waist with a belt.

Marion's sweater.

"Marion?" Wildly, she looked around, her mouth sticky and sour, only to be caught by two steady hands on her arms.

She blinked, her vision clearing, and then she saw

her—Marion, sitting in front of her, shivering a little in her camisole, her hair dark and tangled, her pale skin luminescent in the moonlight. Despite everything, Val felt overwhelmed with the urge to kiss her.

For a moment she actually considered it.

Marion, though, must have seen the thought show on her face. Her concerned expression slipped behind a door.

"Don't," she said quietly.

"I'm sorry," Val replied, and then realized there were far too many things she could be apologizing for, which made her feel faintly sick.

Without thinking, she folded her arms around her middle and drew her knees to her chest. The resulting pain nearly knocked her flat, and she cried out, unfolding herself. Carefully breathing in and out, she mapped the path of bruises and cuts along her thighs, up her back, dotting her belly and arms.

Marion moved toward her, then abruptly stopped. She looked away, biting her lip.

Val blinked a few times to keep her tears under control and turned her gaze to the sea—the titanic churning flatness of it, the cresting waves blinking in and out of moonlit existence like fireflies, the stars looking down coldly upon the mutable chaos of Earth and deciding, perhaps, that it was better to exist up in the quiet void of space, after all.

A circling light drew her eye. On Sawkill's western shore, the lighthouse stood tall and lonesome.

"Zoey calls it the Eye of Sawkill," said Marion at last.

Val turned, pulse leaping in her throat at the sight of Marion looking out to sea, the wind whipping her hair across her cheeks. "The what?"

"You know." Marion gestured across the water. "Like the Eye of Sauron. In Mordor."

Val shook her head. "The Eye of . . . what?"

Marion smiled a little. "Yeah, I know. *Lord of the Rings.* Zoey's been trying to get me into it."

"Never seen it. Or read the books."

"Yeah." Marion's face was unreadable. "Me neither."

Without warning, Val's ravaged nerves gave way. She managed to hide her mouth behind her sleeve and turn away, but swallowing down her sobs made her burning throat ache so badly that she just cried harder.

Soft fingers pressed her own. Marion's voice came quietly: "Val . . ."

"Good *God.*" Zoey stalked over, announcing her presence with an aggravated huff. "My phone service blows chunks out here. Er." She stopped just within Val's line of sight. "No offense, Val. I meant normal, human chunks. Not, like, gross monster chunks. But, whatever, I saved your ass, so I can say what I want."

Val looked up at Zoey through tear-heavy lashes.

Zoey remained unmoved. She crossed her arms over her chest. "Do you have something to say to me?"

Val nodded miserably. "I . . . The things I said while he was in me," she began, the words so dreadful that she nearly lost her courage. "The things I did. I'm so sorry." Without thinking, Val clutched her stomach, then hissed when her hands touched her wounds. Fresh tears stung her eyes, but she couldn't muster the energy to wipe them away. "That's not enough. I know it's not enough. I . . ." She looked helplessly up at Zoey. "I don't expect you to forgive me."

"I don't expect me to, either," Zoey said at once.

Marion kept her eyes on the water. "Zoey's father has a book full of information about you," she said, "and the Collector, too."

Val nodded. "The Hand of Light. He mentioned them. He knew they were watching him."

"He?" said Zoey.

It felt strange, to call him by a fairy-tale name, when to her he had been more than that. Not a story, not a legend; a reality.

"The Collector," Val answered quietly. "I was born with him inside me."

Zoey stood still as a sentinel. "The book says you didn't have a choice but to obey him. That his will consumed your own."

"I had a choice." Val kept her voice flat and plain. "I could have ended things, if I'd had the guts for it. I could have killed my mother. I could have killed both of us. Then . . ." Val drew in a shuddering breath. "That might have done it, forced him out of our world for a while. But I couldn't. I didn't. And now . . ."

At the thought of her mother's ruined body, Val squeezed

her eyes shut. "Now she's dead, and he's not, and I'm . . . I'm still here."

Zoey's voice cut cleanly. "Your mom's dead?"

"Yes," Val replied. "Lucky her."

"Don't say that," Zoey snapped. "Not when people we love are dead and gone, not when we'd do anything to get them back."

Val shrank into the throbbing bend of her body. "You're right. Of course, I'm . . . I'm sorry."

"You could say that for the rest of your life," said Zoey, her voice thick, "and it wouldn't be enough."

"Then I'll say it for the rest of my life," Val replied, opening her eyes to return Zoey's steely gaze with one of her own.

"What can you tell us about him?" Marion placed her hand on Val's. Immediately Val's fingers, tensely curled into the sand, relaxed. "Anything to help us fight him."

"He can exist outside the stones, but only in an unstable form," Val said. "His vision, his movement—they're not dependable. He needs help to reliably get around, though not nearly as much as he used to. He's so much stronger now. And he can take different forms—"

Zoey cut her off. "That we know. What else?"

"We were running out of time." Val stared at her hands. "He's been feeding, evolving, ever since he first arrived here. Each kill requires less and less time for him to digest. Each kill grants him more power. Soon, he'll be free. He won't need me. He won't need anyone." Her stomach seized; a wave of pain pulsed through her. "Mom thought he would only need one more."

"And then he'll be able to go wherever he wants," Zoey, said, her voice unsteady. "*Kill* whoever he wants. Not just girls. *Anyone*."

Val nodded miserably.

"Oh my God. He could be stalking that last person, whoever it is, *right now*."

"But he probably can't leave the stones," said Marion. "Right? He's trapped there? Now that you've . . ." She gestured at Val's belly.

A tremor of fear shook Val as she imagined him there—waiting, raging. "I suppose he is. Wait." She glanced over at Marion. "How did you find the stones? I remember . . ." She flushed a little. "I overheard your conversation with Zoey that night."

"What does it matter how we found them?" asked Zoey.

"The stones are where he entered our world," Val replied, "through a tear in the woods. My grandmother called it a gate. It's hidden really well. No one can find it except for those of my family's line."

"And Marion," Zoey said, lightly thumping Marion's leg. "We found it, the first night we met. I tried to go back afterward, by myself. Couldn't find them." She looked curiously at Marion. "Maybe it has to do with your tessering. If it's a tear between worlds, it makes sense that you would be sensitive to it."

Marion drew in a sharp breath. "Oh, God. Tessering." She faced Sawkill, hand over her mouth. "My mom. Your *dad*, Zoey. We just left them there with Briggs, and I'm too weak now; I don't think I can get us back. Shit. *Shit*."

"Hey." Zoey knelt in front of Marion, gathered her hands in her own. "It's okay. Those assholes won't hurt them. They need them to get to us, remember?"

Val's throat tightened as she watched the two of them—the ease with which they touched each other, how comfortable they appeared existing in the same space.

Val supposed, a sick fall of resignation settling in her hollowed belly, that she would never again enjoy that sort of rapport with Marion, or with anyone. She'd forfeited all rights to such comfort from the moment she'd emerged from her mother's womb, born to a world full of monsters.

She planted her palms in the sand, forced herself to speak. Maybe speaking would keep her from unspooling altogether. "So what do we do now?"

Zoey considered Val. "Grayson has his mom's boat," she said slowly, "and her old shotgun, Lord help us. He should be here in a few minutes. If my text got through, that is. Beyond that . . ." Zoey hugged her middle.

"Whatever we do," Val said, "we'll have to do it fast. Normally I'd say he wouldn't leave the stones on his own, not for long enough to do any damage and not with me so far away from him—but he's probably never been this desperate before. There's no predicting what he'll do."

Marion moved away from both of them and stood. She faced Sawkill, arms rigid at her sides.

"You'll hold off the Hand of Light for as long as you can," she said. "The two of you and Grayson. Maybe your dad, Zoey, if he can get free. And while you fight, I'll go to the stones. I'll tesser myself and the Collector into an obscura. I don't want . . ." She paused, cleared her throat. "When he comes for me, I don't want anyone else to have to see."

When she turned, her eyes held a sheen that shredded what remained of Val's heart.

"Just promise me," said Marion quietly, "that when I'm gone, you'll take care of my mom. I'm worried she'll try to hurt herself."

"Absolutely not." Val rose, gritting her teeth against the echoing pain. "You're not going to some other realm alone. If you go, we go with you. We'll help you fight him—safely, where no one else can get hurt—and once he's dead, you'll bring us all back home. No one's dying tonight but him."

She glanced down at Zoey and extended her hand. "We'll hunt the fucker down. Together."

Zoey clasped Val's hand and rose to her feet. "I wasn't kidding, about not forgiving you."

"I didn't think you were," Val replied. "But for now . . . ?"

Zoey nodded tightly. "For now, we have an alliance."

Marion watched them, uncertain. "I don't know what will happen to us once we get to the obscura. The book says he can't be killed—"

"Screw that book," said Val. "It was written by men." She held out her free hand to Marion. "We're rewriting it."

After a moment's hesitation, Marion placed her hand gently in Val's. At her touch, Val's skin warmed all the way through—from her fingertips to her sore belly to the battered lines of her legs.

"Together," Marion said quietly, with a small, cautious smile.

The rattle of an approaching boat motor cut the moment in two. Zoey gave a whoop and raced down the shore to the water, waving her arms at a long, sleek speedboat. It pulled as close to shore as possible. Then Val saw Grayson Tighe leap out of the boat, run awkwardly through the shallow water, and sweep a cheering Zoey up into his arms.

She watched them embrace, Grayson's hand cradling the back of Zoey's head, her legs latched around his hips, and felt as though she might drift in that spot forever, unmoored and unmatched, trapped on this span of empty beach by the excruciating force of her own longing.

Then Marion's quiet voice pierced her: "Even knowing what I know, and knowing what you've suffered, I'm not sure I'll ever be able to forgive you for what you did. Or that I should."

Val couldn't bear to look at her. She half blinked, afraid to set loose her sudden rush of tears, and stared stubbornly at Grayson lowering Zoey to the ground.

A cool hand touched her face, turning her gently. Val met the blazing expression on Marion's face with hope blooming in her heart.

"But I really want to try," Marion whispered, and when she gently leaned her forehead against Val's cheek, Val let out a small sob of relief.

It was then that the air around them exploded with gunfire.

ZOEY

The Pursuit

The first two bullets pierced the water not three feet from where Zoey and Grayson stood.

The third hit Grayson's leg.

He cried out and collapsed, reaching for his calf. His hand came away wet and black in the darkness, and when Zoey crouched beside him, propping up his body with her own, she realized, with a lurch of unmitigated horror, that two other speedboats were racing toward them from Sawkill—and that the gunfire had ceased.

Because she was essentially now wrapped around Grayson, a human shield.

Because the Hand of Light had no qualms about hurting him—but they would not hurt her, or Val, or Marion. Not until they had them right where they wanted them.

"They're after Grayson," she cried, looking back to find the others, but they were already there—Val and Marion, charging through the water toward the boat. Val's hands sparked like white embers flaring back to life. She reached the boat, Marion's sweater still strapped to her waist, and climbed swiftly aboard before heading to the captain's seat. Marion positioned herself between Grayson and the approaching men, threw Zoey's bat into the boat, then ripped off her shoes and socks and tied one sock around Grayson's wound, her movements steady and sure.

Grayson leaned hard against Zoey's side, tears brightening his eyes.

"Zo," he said breathlessly, "you didn't tell me there'd be men with guns chasing us."

She scoffed, trying to avoid looking at his leg and not think about what would have happened if the bullet had hit higher, in his stomach or chest or head. "Except I'm absolutely certain that I did."

"Oh, that's right. And I decided to come anyway."

"Because you're an idiot."

Grayson's face was tight with pain. "Because I love you."

"Like I said." Zoey dropped a kiss on his forehead, a hot lump wedged in her throat. She and Marion helped Grayson up into the boat, onto a low bench on the starboard side.

He clung to her arm, his breathing strained. "I'm pretty scared here, Zo. Don't tell the others."

"Your secret's safe with me."

"It's just that I've never gotten shot before."

Zoey sat beside him, cradling his head against her chest and glaring out at the water. "If they try to hurt you again, I will personally slam their sorry asses into those cliffs."

"Can I just say it's really hot that you're not hyperbolizing?"

Zoey's mouth quirked into a watery smile. "Yes, you may indeed say that, and frequently. You know I love it when you use those five-dollar words."

Marion stood at the port side railing, her back to everyone and her black hair streaming out behind her—a dark queen, surveying the battlefield.

"Can you drive this thing?" she called back to Zoey.

"On it," came Val's voice, right before the boat's engine roared to life.

As they sped across the water toward Sawkill, Zoey kept her eye on the two boats in pursuit—small and determined, their lights out and their engines furiously churning the water. She imagined each of them heavy with the weight of angry, thwarted men denied their moment of glory. Adrenaline pulled tight across her limbs, heat slithering from the dip between her collarbones to the ten points of her fingers.

She glanced up at the captain's seat, where Val stood with rigid posture, glowing hands gripping the rudder, possibly melting it. Bruises and blood mottled the back of her neck.

Not long ago, the sight of Val had turned Zoey just shy of homicidal.

Now . . .

"So Val's one of us now, huh?" asked Grayson quietly.

"Hell no," Zoey replied. "She's just . . . useful."

Then, Marion, still facing away from them, began to laugh.

Val looked over her shoulder. "What's she laughing about?"

"Uh, Marion?" Zoey called out. "Honey? The laughing is a little freaky, FYI."

Marion turned, her face lit up with what Zoey thought might just be mischief. "Don't be freaked out. It's just that I've had a really, really great idea."

"It had better be spectacular," Grayson said, looking up from Zoey's shoulder. "They're gaining on us, fast."

Zoey looked out at the water and confirmed it. "Shit. They'll be on us as soon as we dock."

"Almost there!" Val pointed ahead of them at the Tighe family's pier—a weather-grayed boardwalk that rambled down the grassy hill from the Tighe house before jutting out over piles of stone slick with brown moss.

At the pier's edge, pistol in hand and hat perched on his head, stood a man. Zoey squinted through the night, her pulse a thin buzz in her ears.

"Someone's there already," Val warned. "What should I do?"

Zoey's fingers curled around Grayson's hands. "It's my dad."

"Can we trust him?" Val glanced over. "He's one of them, isn't he?"

"He is," Zoey said grimly, "and I don't know."

"We don't have time to try and dock somewhere else," Marion added.

Zoey stood, one hand still clutching Grayson's, the other clenched in a fist. "If he makes one wrong move, you have my permission to attack him."

"Didn't you, like, *just* figure out how to use this power?" Grayson whispered urgently. "Zo, you could really hurt him."

"Then I guess he'd better not try to hurt *us*," Zoey replied. She raised her voice as Val maneuvered the boat into the dock slip. "One wrong move, Dad, and we'll blast this dock to pieces."

"I understand," he called back. He crouched at the pier's edge and held out his hands. His lip was bloodied, his right eye swollen, but he gave the girls a reassuring nod. Behind him, previously cloaked by the darkness of the night and the rocky climb of the hill that led to the Tighe house, stood a gaping Sergeant Montgomery and two other Sawkill police officers.

Marion positioned herself between Zoey and her father. "Some friends you have, Chief."

"Those men aren't my friends," he replied, his voice made of iron. "Not anymore."

Marion considered him for a long moment.

Val approached cautiously. "They're right behind us, Marion."

"We'll take care of them," Zoey's father replied, extending his hand.

At last Marion relented and climbed out. He helped Val out next, and when his gaze fell upon her black-stained nightgown, the sweater tied around her belly, his mouth turned down at the corners. He shrugged off his jacket, draped it around Val's shoulders, and squeezed her arm. When Zoey caught the wobbly look of gratitude Val cast upon her father, the answering burst of warmth in Zoey's heart made her feel like the carpet had been ripped out from under her feet.

She stumbled right into her father's arms, squeezed her eyes shut, and allowed him to hold her to his broad chest for the space of two inhales.

"Grayson's hurt," she said, pulling away, her voice coming out small and shaky. "Not bad, I don't think, but they shot him in the leg."

"Who the hell *are* these people, Chief?" asked Sergeant Montgomery.

The look Ed Harlow cast out to the water turned Zoey's blood hot-cold. She had never seen such an expression on his face.

"They're fanatics," he replied softly. "And until recently, I was one of them."

He glanced at Marion. "What do you need us to do?"

Marion didn't hesitate, her eyes afire. "Hold them off. We need to get to the stones."

"Rosco," her father barked. "Get Grayson up to his house, and stay there with his parents. Your mother's up there with them, Marion. She's fine, and she's not alone."

Marion gave him a curt nod, her face unreadable. "Thank you." She turned to Zoey and Val. "Are you still with me?"

And though Zoey's legs shook, she said, "Hell yes," at the same time as Val replied, "Ready."

Marion nodded, gave them each a small smile. "Then let's go."

She and Val ran up the pier toward the boardwalk, each of them limping slightly. Hiding her face from her father, afraid that he would know from one look what they planned to do—if he didn't already—Zoey leaned off the pier to capture Grayson's face in her hands and plant a ferocious kiss on his mouth.

"I love you," she breathed, her forehead touching his, and then before he could reply, she grabbed her bat and raced up the pier to follow her friends, tears in her eyes and an inferno raging in her heart.

ZOEY

The Call

But when they reached the Kingshead Woods, something changed.

Their feet hit the soil, and suddenly running through the woods felt like running through one of those terrible dreams in which the air looks like air but it isn't. Instead it's something invisible and viscous, and running is impossible, a sluggish and desperate crawl.

Marion touched Val's shoulder, then flung out her other hand to stop Zoey in her tracks. Zoey leaned against a nearby tree to catch her breath, clutching the stitch in her side. Then she saw Marion's expression and tensed.

"What is it?" Val asked. Despite being freshly exorcised, she only had a slight shimmer of sweat on her brow. Zoey was too tired to feel annoyed.

Marion's gaze was distant, her cheeks flushed. "I hear it."

Zoey straightened. "The bone cry?"

"Yes." Marion's solemn gaze lifted to Val's. "He's close. And he's not alone."

Just as the words left her lips, a man leaped out from the trees, bloody hands reaching.

Val shoved Marion out of the way and whirled on their attacker. Her hands lit up like the novas of distant twin suns. Scrambling to his feet, the man threw up his arms to shield his eyes. Another man burst out of the brush, the blood of fresh burns painting his pale skin.

Briggs.

Zoey raced toward him, her bat gripped in one hand. A surge of movement rippled through the ground beneath her, like the bristling of an angry wolf's fur.

She reached Briggs and thrust her hand at him.

He ducked. He'd been expecting this.

She lunged into empty space, flailing to keep her balance, and turned just in time for his fist to hit her jaw. She landed in a heap on the ground.

"Not this time, you little bitch," spat Briggs. His voice came to Zoey through a muddle of pain. She tried to stand and fell once more. A callused hand gripped her arm and yanked her to her feet.

"Stop," Briggs called out, his voice frayed as if someone had taken a razor to it. "Or I swear to *Christ* I'll bash her brains in."

Oh, God. Oh, *God*.

He had her bat.

Zoey felt a surge of unreasonable fury. That was Grayson's bat, and he'd loaned it to her. It may not have been as impressive-looking as a sword, but still—there was no way in *hell* that this psychopath had the right to touch her and Grayson's *freaking awesome bat-sword.*

She tasted blood and spat it, aiming roughly for Briggs's face. But it was dark, there were way too many trees in this forest, and her head was spiraling like a top.

"You can't kill her," came Marion's voice, which sounded steadier than Zoey imagined hers would be, if she ever managed to speak again. What kind of bastard slapped a teenage girl like that? Oh, right—the kind of bastard who deserved to have his junk eaten by cockroaches.

"And why is that?" Briggs asked.

"Because you need her for your ritual."

A chorus of laughter rippled through the woods. Jesus, how many of them *were* there?

And then Zoey realized that those boats that had been following them must not have held more men than two drivers, and maybe one shooter.

Her heart turned to lead.

The Hand of Light had been waiting for them, this whole time, here in the Mortimers' woods.

"She doesn't need to be unharmed for the feeding," Briggs replied. "Her body, whatever state it's in, as long she's breathing, will suffice."

"What's wrong with you?" Zoey had never heard Valerie Mortimer's voice sound so unfinished. "None of this is necessary—"

"*I* will decide what is necessary!" howled Briggs, his grip tightening painfully around Zoey's arm. "This is the way it is done. This is the way our fathers taught us."

"Your fathers," Val replied, "were full of shit."

A sharp crack rang through the trees, followed by a muted cry from Val.

Finally, Zoey's vision began to settle. She could now see the situation they were in—a tight circle of men. Marion to her right, Val to her left, both of them held by two men, one at each arm. Zoey herself was held by Briggs. Three other men hovered nearby, gloved hands holding knives, firearms slung over their shoulders. One of them moved away from Val, a grim sneer on his face.

Val straightened in the arms of her captors. She breathed tightly through her nose, a red handprint blooming on her cheek.

"You're going to regret hurting her," said Marion. She had the look, Zoey thought, of a parent waiting patiently for a child to realize his mistake. "You're going to regret a lot of things."

Briggs, passing Zoey off to one of his lackeys, ignored her. He withdrew his dagger from the sheath at his hip. "The Collector must feed. He must be banished from our world. So it has been done, and so it is done, and so it shall always be done."

"And so it shall always be done," repeated the men,

reminding Zoey of the way Borg drones proclaimed they were going to assimilate you, that resistance was futile, that you were screwed and there was no way out, sorry about that. At the thought of never again having *Star Trek* marathons at Grayson's house, while his dad popped in every few minutes to remark upon the breathtaking badassery of Kathryn Janeway, Zoey clenched her aching jaw to keep from either sobbing or screaming in rage, she wasn't sure which.

For the second time that night, she watched Briggs approach. With an exhausted sort of acceptance she thought to Sawkill, *Well, sorry. We tried.*

But then Marion spoke.

"And so," she said, her voice low and serene, "it shall never be done again."

Silence followed her proclamation. Zoey had just enough time to observe that Briggs had frozen, and that the other men were shifting uneasily, before the Kingshead Woods erupted into hoofbeats.

The men holding Zoey released her. Briggs whirled to the east and dropped the bat, his face falling slack with terror.

Zoey tried to look, too, but couldn't. Val grabbed her hand before she had the chance, dropped to the ground at Marion's feet, and pulled Zoey with her. The men around them screamed and ran—but resistance, in this case, was indeed futile.

Zoey felt the island thrumming under their feet, heard the thunderclap rhythm of what must have been dozens of hooves, and understood: Marion had asked the Rock for help, and it had answered by summoning all the horses from Kingshead.

Zoey huddled on the ground, Marion's legs a solid wall against her back, Marion's hand a gentle reassurance on her head. Zoey pressed her face into Val's neck and breathed in her scent—the sea, her faint gardenia perfume, the bitter black bile still crusting her arms. Zoey listened to the men's screams abruptly silenced as they were trampled, heard them run away and beg the woods for mercy, flinched as they were kicked into trees and flattened against boulders.

When all was silent at last, Zoey dared to raise her head, her hands clutching Val's close to her heart.

A dozen Mortimer Morgans stood a few yards away, scattered throughout the trees. Their velvet-dark sides heaved; their nostrils flared. Two pawed the ground with their front hooves.

But they came no closer, now that their work was finished. They were, Zoey suspected, frightened of the girls they had saved. Especially the one who stood tall and unbroken, staring back at them like she was one of their own—a wild, dangerous creature, somehow sewn up into the form of a girl.

Val let out a shaky breath against Zoey's shoulder. "Jesus."

Marion helped them both to their feet. They stood amid this ruination of men, hands joined and gazes locked. Then they turned, as one, and walked deeper into the forest.

VAL

The Gate

The moment Val saw the stones appear ahead of them in the woods, white and unassuming, she jerked to a halt. Lightheaded, she clutched the rough bark of a nearby tree, turned her face into a clutch of wet leaves.

"What is it?" Marion's voice came to her as if through a dream. Val realized the steadiness she felt at her elbow was in fact Zoey, holding her up.

"Sorry, I—" Val took a few deep breaths to calm her roiling stomach. She was no longer content to give him her tears.

Marion cupped her face and directed her gaze up from the ground. "I'm here," she said, her thumb caressing Val's cheek. "We're both right here. You don't have to do this alone anymore."

Zoey squeezed her hand, and the simple gesture gave Val

enough strength to look up at Marion with clear eyes and say, "Let's go slay this son of a bitch."

Her words were flint against steel; three pairs of eyes flashed in the night. They turned and ran.

Zoey took the lead without being asked, and as Val watched her leap into the stones, she felt a surge of affection so ferocious that, when she pushed off the ground to take that final step, euphoria swept through her body.

She landed within the stones on two solid feet, heard the furious snarl of the monster who'd owned her body since she took her first screaming breaths between her mother's legs, and turned with blazing hands to face him.

He huddled in a corner of the stone circle, a patch of scribbled ink against the softer darkness of the woods. When Val's gaze landed upon him, he flew. He roared and ricocheted. He careened through the space allowed him by the stones; he clawed for freedom and was denied it.

Val stood, knees loose and ready, light swelling in her hands. As they'd discussed, Marion stood behind her, with Zoey on her other side. They flanked Marion—one girl with fire at her fingertips, the other vibrating with raw electric power.

They'd decided that it might be impossible for Marion to find the original gate the Collector had crawled through. And, considering that it had been made by a monster not of their world, it might not even be possible for them to pass through it.

So Marion had decided she would have to make a gate of her own.

The Collector fell silent, gathering himself between two far stones. Dark jagged cords stretched from where he lay to the low-hanging branches of an oak tree. The tree shivered and creaked; a branch snapped in half. Two white, round eyes opened in the darkness. Val was reminded of a child playing hide-and-seek, waiting for just the right moment to jump out and scare the seeker. It wasn't the point of the game, but that savage animal heart could not resist.

Laughter, slick and congested, bubbled up from the ground where he waited.

"Oh, I see," came the little boy's voice, though he had not taken that form. Val suspected that, without a host, he had only enough strength to create fragments of his false selves. The air around him crawled, infested. "You've come to play with me. How kind."

Val's skin erupted in goose bumps.

"Wrong," came Zoey's tense voice. "We've come to destroy you."

"Wrong." Now the little boy's voice held no trace of amusement. "You've come to feed me."

His white round gaze flicked to Marion. "I see you, little traveler."

His voice spat every word like a mockery. Val blinked, sweat stinging her eyes. In the space of that blink, he lunged at them.

Val dug her heels into the black mud and thought of the long reaches of stone beneath her feet. The Rock that had been her home, and her mother's home, and her grandmother's. It had witnessed their suffering; its children had been stolen from it by a beast that did not belong. And now it had had enough.

So had Val.

Half crouched between Marion and the Collector, Val thrust out her hands and watched her light fly.

He shrieked and recoiled, springing across the stones to dodge Val and attack Zoey instead. Val heard Zoey's distant shout, felt the ground vibrate as though something deep below had jerked awake. The Collector screamed once more, a wildcat yowling for its kill, and launched himself above them. His misshapen form blocked what little Val could see of the dimming moon. A righteous rage spiked in her breast.

That moon was not his to smother.

She twisted around, feet firmly in place, reached down into the ripe soil with every thought she possessed—every ounce of energy, every feeling—and let herself effloresce. Fire scorched her chest, her lungs, her palms. The heat ripped tears from her eyes, but she did not waver.

Then, like a door slamming shut on a room flooded with warmth, Val's light vanished. Every ounce of strength she'd felt coursing through her body disappeared.

Bereft, she asked the Rock: *Where did you go?*

The answer became clear in an instant.

The earth directly underneath Marion's feet shook, ready to ignite.

Marion drew a shaky breath.

"Now," she whispered, and her eyes locked with Val's—triumphant and a little sad.

For one vicious instant, Val considered aborting their plan. She would wrap Marion in her arms and shield her from the necessity of what was about to happen. She would burn around her, an unwavering human flame, until the Collector scorched himself to ash trying to get to them.

But instead, she tore her gaze from Marion and dropped to the ground. She wrapped her arms around Marion's left leg and saw Zoey, inches from her, eyes wide and teary, do the same to Marion's right. In the space between Marion's calves, their knuckles knocked together like a clumsy kiss.

Above them, the Collector shrieked and dove at Marion, his fall erratic but inevitable. Zoey's fingers clamped tight over hers. Val pressed her cheek against Marion's thigh, squeezed her eyes shut. A tidal wave crashed through Marion's body, surging up from the wet rocky ground beneath them. Val's hands stung as if they were being molded to the surface of the sun. Marion shuddered violently, Val's and Zoey's firm grips clearly the only thing holding her up.

Beneath them, the Rock opened. The sea surged up to meet them and swallowed.

QUICKLY, NOW.

Quickly, the Rock explained in whispers, in the flutter of a thousand wings, in the shifting of the known universe against the unknown:

Please.
Please understand.
I am a small rock.
I am a great Earth.

This is only one monster.
This is one of many monsters.

You are a small girl.
And you are a small girl.
And you are a small girl.
You are mighty.
You are one, and one, and one.
You are fragile.
You can move mountains.
You are breakable.
You will never break.

This power is mine.
And now is it yours, too.

You must keep fighting.
You must never stop fighting.
You must light the path for others to find their footing.
You must—

MARION

The Obscura

Marion had expected this tesser to be a violent affair. She'd anticipated being knocked against unseen walls as though traversing a wormhole from a sci-fi movie, ripped across the universe from one existence to another.

But instead, she slipped easily through a cool narrow space, not so slim as to feel claustrophobic, thin enough to press against her skin like an embrace. The twin sensations of Val and Zoey clinging to her legs anchored her. The air around her was smooth and supple. For a moment Marion imagined herself floating luxuriously through a pool of pure mountain water, as yet untouched by mankind.

She wondered if she would see Charlotte, and she cried out, desperate, into a seam of sky. The knotted air caught her voice and warped it.

Then her feet slammed to ground; the illusion of ease fell away.

At first her disorientation was so complete that she couldn't lift her head, much less stand. She lay on something flat and hard. She moved her fingers and felt a rough surface—packed sand, covered in a fine film of grit. A strange scent filled her nose, sour and sharp and full-bodied. Gasoline mixed with the bracing bite of snow.

Opening her eyes, she exhaled; her breath turned to clouds in the frigid air. She heard a slow, uneven crackling sound somewhere to her left, reminding her of a frozen lake ready to shatter. A flutter of fear stirred in her chest.

"Get up, Marion," she whispered, mostly to reassure herself that she seemed to still be alive.

She pushed herself into a sitting position, wobbled for a moment, and stood. Her legs felt rubbery and abused, freshly born. Taking in her surroundings, her mind seemed to separate from her body, refusing to accept that what her eyes told her was not, in fact, a remarkable lie.

Beside her, Val and Zoey shook themselves awake and rose to their feet. The three of them stood in the center of a vast salt flat, gleaming white and unending. The black sky overhead was frightening for its brilliance, painted in glittering waves of galaxies so near that Marion felt certain she could stretch out her arm and scoop the stars into her palm like fresh powdered snow. Fat white trees dotted the flat. They were bulbous, sick-looking, the land around their roots sitting in piles like slabs of cracked sugar.

Marion's skin hummed with recognition. Those trees—she'd seen them before, in the first obscura she'd visited. The snow-covered beach, the amber sea.

She examined the nearest tree. It stood straight for a couple of feet and then jutted to the side. Branches sprouted from its swollen trunk, haphazard and agitated.

And that's when Marion realized that the bone cry was gone. She could neither hear it nor feel it nearby, silent but waiting. The twanging taut cord that had lived in her chest since Nightingale threw her had gone utterly silent.

Without its familiar hum to keep her company, the absence of Charlotte felt like a physical lack, raw and roaring.

Steam escaped from the bark of the alien trees, unfurling in thin spools. Marion didn't like them. They weren't Sawkill's trees—craggy but good-natured, spooky in the right light but ultimately well-meaning, their rough bark crusted with the sea. These trees were ill, unnatural. They were facsimiles of trees crafted by cruel hands that knew nothing of warmth.

Marion approached the nearest one. She reached for its lowest branch, hesitated, then convinced herself to touch it.

The surface stung her hand with cold. Marion peered more closely. The trees were covered in a lustrous gauze of ice that caught the starlight and winked at her when she moved. That was the crackling sound—these trees growing and breathing beneath their wintry coating.

She rubbed her palms together, suddenly desperate for warmth. She couldn't decide if the sight of the trapped trees was exquisite or terribly sad.

"What is this place?" breathed Val, coming to stand beside Marion.

Zoey paced nearby, her skin a glimmering soft brown in the eerie starlight. She'd managed to hold on to her bat through everything, and Marion felt comforted by the earthly sight of it.

"It's an obscura," Zoey whispered. "I guess." Another pause, and now her voice wavered slightly. "If the Hand of Light knew what they were talking about, that is."

"I knew he was from a place like this. A hidden part of the world. He bragged about it, like that made him special." Val dragged her fingers along a branch. Her fingers came away dusted with minuscule ice flakes. "But it's not what I expected, and I don't know what it means."

Zoey's reply came quietly. "Neither do I."

Marion thought of the black book, its binding stuffed with illustrations and scrawled instructions. An idea had been forming in her mind, ever since Chief Harlow and Briggs had told her about the Far Place, that night in Zoey's lamplit kitchen. She hadn't told anyone about her idea. She had hoped, perhaps stupidly, that she would never have to. But now, it seemed, the moment had arrived.

Zoey turned her free hand over in the air at her waist. Around her fingers, the air shifted, like she'd dragged her hand through water. "I still feel Sawkill. How is that possible?"

Val glanced down at her own palm, where a tiny flame sprang to life. "The moth told me that Sawkill gave this to us. It's the Rock's power—"

"And now it's ours, too," Zoey finished, eyes wide. "I heard that just now, before we landed here. Or, I *felt* it, I guess."

Marion stared at Val in wonder. "You saw one of the moths?"

A shy smile tugged at Val's lips. "Yeah."

Zoey hugged the bat close. "Okay, so what now? What do we do?"

Marion opened her mouth to reply, and then caught Val's expression—so full of an awful sadness that Marion felt the weight of it solidify in her chest like a stone.

"Please don't," Val whispered. "You don't know what will happen to you there."

Marion hadn't had the chance to tell Val what Briggs had told them—that beyond the obscurae existed a Far Place unreachable by human and monster alike. She assumed Zoey hadn't had the chance, either. And yet . . . that look on Val's face.

Val had guessed Marion's plan. Val *knew*.

"How do you know about that?" Marion asked, attempting to act calm.

"Sometimes," Val replied, after a pause, "after feeding, he would tell me things. Like a drunk man spilling secrets. A few times, he mentioned something called the Far Place. A realm beyond his home. He was afraid of it, Marion. More afraid of it than anywhere else."

"Why?" Zoey asked.

"Because he didn't understand it." Val's brow furrowed. "He told me that place was a trick, a deceit. He told me it was an ending, and it terrified him."

And so that's where I have to go, Marion knew. Her heart kicked against her rib cage in protest. *That's the only way to truly kill him.*

She hoped.

Soft light peeked through the cracks between Val's fingers. Her eyes glinted brighter than the impossible stars above. "You don't have to do this. I'll burn him. Zoey will smash him to pieces."

"And if that doesn't work, and we all die trying?" Marion kissed Val's faintly glowing palm. The minuscule white flame resting on Val's life line warmed Marion's lips. She realized she would never again make Val come apart under her mouth—that she would never make *anyone* feel such pleasure, ever again, that she would never be hugged, that she would never feel cold, that she would never wake up in sunlight on lazy mornings— and swallowed against the bitter tightness of her throat. "He'll go back to Sawkill, or somewhere else, and more people will die. I can't let that happen."

"Wait, *what*?" Zoey hurried over, bat held loosely at her side. She looked from Marion to Val and back again, shaking her head. "Tell me I heard you wrong just now. Marion, there are *tons* of monsters, all over the world. Dad and Briggs said so, and they may have lied about some things, but I don't think they lied about that. Even if we get rid of this asshole, more will still be out there!" Her tears spilled over. Impatiently she dried her face. "It's not our job to save the world. It can't be. That's not fair."

"If it's not our job," Marion asked quietly, "whose is it?"

Then the tree Marion and Val had been standing beside exploded.

Branches went spinning, shedding thin spirals of ice flakes as they flew. Marion ducked, stumbling over a crack in the ground.

Val and Zoey lunged in front of her, crouched defensively—Val's hands raised and flashing, Zoey with her bat ready to strike in one hand and her other hand flat like a shield.

Then Zoey moaned, "*Shit.*"

The tree had been decapitated, its branches flung across the flat like the perimeter of debris surrounding a detonation site. Out of its swollen trunk oozed bubbling black liquid and thick globs of sick yellow pus. Tiny mouths within the pus opened and closed, letting out small agonized screams.

Crawling out of the tree, dragging himself up from inside the ruined trunk, was a pale, flesh-colored beast with long limbs and cratered skin. Lidless black eyes—like holes drilled into soft clay—gazed unblinking from beneath a severe, jutting brow framed by batlike ears. Long flaps of skin trailed between his shoulders and elbows, and long two-clawed hands shaped like hooked scythes. From the skin flaps hung clusters of bloodied feathers; between his joints stretched ropy strings of flesh that bunched together and pulled apart with his every movement. Slippery knobs of skin floated up and down his arms like melting wax, merging with the elastic joint-skin to knit new hands that punched out of his arms—thick and bludgeon-like, with long bent fingers. His back legs ended in long, clawed feet with toes thick as tree branches. Glistening with slime, they curved under the narrow soles of his feet and seemed to bear all his weight.

He blinked, drew in a rattling breath. His lipless jaw, so wide it hinged just below his ears, dropped open with an ear-splitting roar. Inside his gaping mouth writhed a dozen smaller ones, bursting out like tentacles and lined with tiny chomping teeth.

Watching him emerge from the tree as if in slow motion, Marion at first was full of a desperate, screaming doubt.

Surely this wasn't right.

She was imagining things. She was dreaming. This was a friendly beast who suffered from unfortunate genetics. He would guide them home, share with them the secret of destroying all the world's monsters. They would return to Earth bearing instructions for lasting peace.

Then the creature roared. Zoey dropped her bat, clapping her hands over her ears. Val did the same, turning to shove Marion back. "Run!" she shouted, though Marion could hardly hear her over the din. "Run, Marion!"

The monster lunged, his fleshy wings opening wide. He shrieked with what Marion knew in her bones was pure, vicious appetite.

The next few seconds passed with excruciating slowness:

Val was the first to act. She screamed and met him halfway—part girl, part dazzling incandescence. The monster slammed into her; his wing clipped her chest and swiped her easily aside.

She let out a pained cry, hit the ground hard, and rolled.

The monster landed, shaking the world. His left wing sizzled, charred. For the first time Marion realized how large he was—tall as a grizzly on his hind legs, longer than a giant squid.

She knew Sawkill probably couldn't hear her—or if it could, that it might not be able to help her any more than it already had—but still she thought of the Rock and prayed for help.

I need to take us to the Far Place, she thought. *Me, and the beast.*

Zoey rushed at the Collector with a furious battle cry. She dodged his first blow, one of his sword-size claws swiping through the air mere inches from her back. She ducked and wheeled back around, slammed her bat down on his tail—fleshy and ringed, like a rat's, and thick as Zoey's torso. Then Zoey jerked up her hand and aimed.

Marion's skin jolted, electrified. Energy crashed into the Collector's chest like a battering ram, but it didn't fell him. He shook his head, saliva flying from his mouth, and swung around to knock Zoey clean off her feet with one of his back legs.

I need to send them home, Marion thought desperately—to the Rock, to herself. Zoey moaned, clutching her side. Val shakily tried to push herself back to her feet; her bloodied nightgown hung in shreds.

At the sight of them reeling and wounded, something inside Marion responded—a coiling, a gathering.

I need to do both at once.

And soon.

The Collector's bulging head whipped around to look at her. He roared, and terrible pain shot through her skull, ear to ear, and the question from her childhood returned to her: *What do you think it feels like to be electrocuted?*

This. It felt like this.

Charlotte had always laughed at her for being scared of storms. *Love, the chances of that are one in a million. Don't be afraid. I've got you.*

In the cloud of pain clogging her vision, Marion saw Charlotte's smiling face.

Sisters two and sisters true, whispered Charlotte's ghost.

Marion clutched the starfish charm at her neck. *You love me, and I love you.*

Then she laughed. Inside her, the Rock wound tighter and tighter—a spring ready to launch.

This power is mine, and it is yours, too.

"Val!" she called out. "Zoey!"

Her voice, all things considered, sounded pretty commanding to her own ears, and she applauded herself for being not just a good, steady girl—not just Marion the rock, Marion the plainer sister, Marion the grave little mountain—but a woman who would be remembered by the people who mattered.

The Collector leaped—his many mouths gaping open to taste her, his hairless wings spread, the layers of his scream cutting the air like claws on glass.

Beyond him, Val raced to her side. She was shouting

something, but Marion couldn't make out the words. Zoey was there, too, reaching for Marion with one hand.

The spring of power inside Marion uncoiled.

Heat blasted through her body. At her pulse points—temples, wrists, throat—her skin pinched and puckered. Beneath her, the world opened—not just the ground, but the entire fabric of where she stood. Layers of earth and energy and stardust peeled back to reveal the yawning chasm beneath.

She looked down, once, and thought she saw the familiar glimmer of moonlight on black waves, and a swirling dark miasma that called to mind lessons from last year's physics class—dark matter, black holes, event horizons.

Then she reached up, grabbed the Collector's scaly, wet hide. A claw sliced her arm open from wrist to elbow, but she held fast.

Then the Far Place sucked her away from the world she knew, and she dragged the monster down with her.

THE FIRST TIME MARION TRAVELED to one of the hidden, hollow places of her world, it had been brief, and a surprise. A peek down a secret pocket. A glimpse of an alien burrow and a glittering golden sea.

The second time she traveled, it was gentle. A slide through a river and a slip behind a veil.

The third time, when she dared to reach beyond the places known to both man and beast, it was far from gentle.

It was an eruption.

It was a breaking.

It left her unmade.

VAL

The Dawn

Val landed flat on her back. The cool ground beneath her was riddled with rocks.

She blinked, feeling frozen between *here* and *elsewhere*. Above her rambled a familiar treescape. Then her breathing returned in an abrupt, choking gasp.

She rolled over, pressed her hands into the mud, and looked up to search the woods. They weren't as dark as they had been when she'd left them; the sky beyond the stern black branches had lightened to a newborn gray.

"Marion?" Her voice came out in shambles. When she tried to stand, she fell back to the ground.

She suspected that final tesser had been a difficult one for Marion to accomplish—what with the monster latching around her body and all, and the fact that the place she'd been going had been . . . Except Val didn't know or understand or *want* to understand the place Marion had been going.

But somehow, Marion had managed it—Marion, *Marion*—and now Val was home.

Zoey sat hunched beside Val on her hands and knees in the dirt. She coughed, wiped her mouth across the back of one shaking hand.

The other hand still tightly held Grayson Tighe's baseball bat. The sight of it tore Val in half and sent her spinning away atop the sea winds.

She must have made a sound; Zoey turned, her face crumpling with grief and pity.

"Val, come here." She reached for her, half crawling.

Val slapped her hand away. She didn't deserve comfort. She could repent for the rest of her life and it would hardly make a dent. "Don't touch me!" she sobbed.

She decided, staggering away from Zoey, that she didn't have the capacity to fathom what had happened—to her, to Marion, to all of them. The men who had hunted them, the corpse of her mother, the wide, flat space of the hidden realm where the Collector had revealed his true form. An infestation of monsters, old and inimitable, that prowled the world hunting girls.

Words circled her brain: miracle, phenomenon, abomination, plague.

Faintly, she heard Zoey speaking to her: Val, you're shaking. Val, you're gonna pass out.

But Val's mind wouldn't stop racing.

Maybe the Hand of Light wasn't once made of men who wouldn't listen to reason, who would lead girls to slaughter if it meant their rituals were validated and their truth absolute.

Maybe, Val thought, somewhere in the world was a Hand of Light chapter composed of women, or kindhearted men. Maybe there were other ways to slay these beasts—many other ways—and none of them would require the world to give up its bravest girls in sacrifice.

But none of that mattered at the moment. Nothing mattered but the loss of too many lives at Val's hands, and the loss of one in particular.

"Val," Zoey whispered, "please say something."

Val collected herself as her mother had taught her. She raised her chin, squared her jaw, and proceeded west through the woods.

"Where are you going?" Zoey called after her. Val heard her footsteps, slight and hurried. "Val!"

"I'm going to wait for her."

"Wait for who?"

"For Marion."

Zoey was beside her now, tearful. "Val, stop."

But if Val stopped, she'd collapse. If she stopped, she might never start again.

"Val," Zoey whispered. "Marion's gone."

Val did not reply. She walked. She walked across Sawkill, from the eastern Kingshead Woods to the western Spinney. Zoey, beside her, said not another word. They stayed clear of the roads and kept instead to whatever trees they could find, because in the trees' whispers sat half-formed words that reminded them of Marion, of the Rock, of the obscura. They passed by the Von Neumanns' farm, and the Hawthornes'. At every fence stood a horse with pricked ears and curious bright eyes, watching them pass.

Val was grateful. The sight of the still, silent horses reminded her, oddly, of the frigid glacial plain of the obscura, the icy trees swollen with blight and monsters. She allowed herself to imagine that she would soon pass a shrub, turn a fence corner, look past the flanks of a curious yearling, and see Marion walking toward her through the misting jade fields.

It was the sort of cruelly intoxicating vision that Val should not have allowed herself, the sort of imagining she did not deserve.

And yet she couldn't resist, didn't *want* to resist.

Don't ever hope, Valerie, her grandmother had told her once. *Don't hope for things to get better. Don't hope for a different world.*

Hope, Sylvia Mortimer had said, *is a lie that only weak-minded people believe.*

Val settled on a flat jutting rock beneath the lighthouse and turned her face to the sea. A moment later, Zoey sat down beside her—not near enough to touch, but near enough that Val felt comforted.

She decided her grandmother had been wrong.

Hope, she thought, breathing with the tide, was a choice that only those with resolute hearts dared to make.

ZOEY

The Reformer

When they retreated to the Tighe house, a group of people waited for them—Mr. and Mrs. Tighe. Zoey's father. Grayson, leg bandaged and some of the color returned to his face. Both his hair and his glasses sat endearingly askew.

And then there was Mrs. Althouse. She rose from the armchair draped with Zoey's favorite afghan and turned to face them.

Though the twin prospects of her father's embrace and Grayson's kiss in her hair were so comforting that Zoey nearly ran to them, she instead inhaled long and slow, and focused her attention on Pamela Althouse alone.

She didn't really know the woman, had hardly spent any time with her except for a few fleeting moments. But her pale, drawn face held so much of Marion in it—dark hair, sad gray eyes, a gentle expressiveness to her mouth—that Zoey's gut twisted painfully.

Val squeezed her hand. Zoey had volunteered to begin the tale, but she knew Val's signal for what it was: *Do you need me to go first?*

Zoey drew a breath and steeled herself for a task she'd never thought she'd have to undertake: *Ma'am, I'm sorry, but your daughter is dead.*

Honestly, she wasn't sure if this woman would survive it.

But Mrs. Althouse spoke first. "It's okay," she said, her voice firm at its center and shivering at the edges. "I know you tried."

Astonished, Zoey's mouth dropped open. Beside her, Val jerked as if struck.

Then Zoey glanced past Mrs. Althouse to Grayson. He sat on the couch with his leg propped up on the tufted leather ottoman. Her father stood behind him, his hand on Grayson's shoulder, and gave her one slow nod, his dark eyes bright with love.

And Zoey knew that the gratitude she felt toward them in that moment could not ever be properly described.

"It's okay," Mrs. Althouse said once more, her mouth trembling, and opened her arms to them. It was a gesture of welcome and an offer of solace—but also, Zoey thought, a plea for help.

Zoey hesitated approximately .47 seconds before running awkwardly into Mrs. Althouse's arms. She shared some qualities of Marion's—her soothing solidness, the scent of vanilla lotion, fine black hair lumpy with tangles.

Zoey felt Val hesitate beside them, and Zoey wondered just how much her father and Grayson had revealed.

She also wondered, a reluctant ache in her chest, how many genuine hugs a girl like Valerie Mortimer had received in her strange, solitary life of servitude and lies.

She set her jaw and glanced back at Val. "Come on," she whispered. "Come here."

Val shook her head. "I don't— I *can't*—" She stepped back, sank unsteadily onto a nearby chair. The look on her face reminded Zoey of a lost child. "Not yet."

Zoey turned back into Mrs. Althouse's arms, hiding her face in that Marion-esque hair. If Val wasn't ready, that was fine. That was, maybe, as it should be.

In the meantime, Zoey would relish any and all hugs she could get for herself.

"It's all right," breathed Mrs. Althouse, with such tenderness that, suddenly, Zoey could hardly stand to exist inside her own skin. "It's all right now. I think we'll be all right."

Zoey squeezed her eyes shut and wished fiercely that this would turn out to be true.

No one particularly wanted to go home, so they didn't.

Mr. Tighe made up the guest room for Mrs. Althouse, and then, on the couch in Mrs. Tighe's study, set up a pallet of what looked like every blanket in the house for Val. But after five minutes of being in there alone, Val came to find Zoey, dragging her quilt behind her.

Zoey was in Grayson's bed, waiting for him to come upstairs. He had insisted on cleaning up the kitchen before turning in, otherwise the crusty layers of casserole on their late-night dinner plates would fester and haunt him, snickering in the kitchen while he lay awake staring at the ceiling.

The adorable little freak.

"Come here," Zoey told Val, patting the mattress and scooting over to make room. "Don't worry about cooties. Grayson washes his sheets like twice a week."

Val slipped under the covers and lay there, unmoving, like the human-size lightning rod that she was. "Seems wasteful."

"But also extremely sanitary." Zoey propped her head up on her elbow to watch Val. "You can unclench and lie in the bed like a normal person, you know."

Val's mouth worked, like she was either trying to decide what to say or attempting to hold back tears. "Do you think he'll come back? Do you think he'll get us?"

The questions didn't surprise Zoey. She'd been wondering the same things, too frightened to say them aloud.

She inspected Val's stoic face—the perfect straight line of her nose, the sharp curve of her jaw. Mrs. Althouse had convinced her to bathe, to wash her hair and scrub the black stains off her skin, and then she'd helped Val bandage the handprint scars on her belly and gathered her damp golden hair into a loose braid.

The expression on Val's face as Mrs. Althouse so gently cared for her, like an abused pet that could hardly believe its luck, had lodged in Zoey's ribs like a thorn.

Finally, Mrs. Althouse had instructed Chief Harlow to take Val's ruined nightgown and, on his way to the police station to check on the apprehended Hand of Light survivors, please burn the damn thing so Val never had to look at it again.

Zoey had also bathed, also at Mrs. Althouse's insistence, and at Grayson's tender behest.

"Don't get me wrong," he'd told her, gathering a stack of clean towels from the linen closet, "you look completely badass. Total warrior queen. But even warriors take care of themselves when they have the time." Then he'd handed her the towels and kissed her nose.

So Zoey had obeyed, scrubbing herself raw under scalding hot water. She'd picked obsessively at the grime beneath her nails until the water had run cold, and then she'd sat on the side of the tub and sobbed, only coming out when Mrs. Althouse knocked on the door and announced quietly that Grayson had just pulled a casserole out of the oven.

As she'd dressed in a set of Grayson's old pinstriped pajamas, it had occurred to Zoey that Mrs. Althouse was hovering over them, making sure they ate and bathed, because she had no one left to mother. After that she'd had to sit on the toilet and hug herself for a good five minutes before finding the strength to head downstairs.

"Maybe he'll come back," she told Val, not sure what to think or for how long bad dreams would vex her sleep. "Maybe he won't. Maybe it'll be years, or decades. But I don't think so.

At least not here, not near us."

Val still stared at the ceiling. "Why don't you think so?"

Zoey felt suddenly so tired that the only option left to her was the familiar slip into humor. "Because I think we probably scared the ever-living shit out of him."

She was rewarded with a soft laugh from Val, and a slight relaxing of her own shoulders.

Then Val said, after a moment, "I don't know how to do this."

"Do what?"

Taking a shaky breath, Val turned to face her. "I need to be close to someone. I need to be held." She paused, blinking rapidly. "But I don't think I deserve it. I'm not sure that I—" She closed her eyes, her hands clutching the hem of her quilt. "I feel like I'm going to float away if I don't touch someone. But I can't stand the thought of asking you."

Zoey watched Val struggle in silence, waiting for her pocket-Thora to protest: *You feel sorry for my killer? Really, Zo?!*

But instead, her pocket-Thora whispered, sad and ghostly: *She's suffered enough, and she will continue to.*

So Zoey nestled close to Val, slipping her arms around her. "We fought a monster together," she said quietly. "I haven't forgiven you yet, and I don't know that I will. But I can hold you for a while. You deserve that much. And so do I, frankly." She inhaled, exhaled. "I deserve to move on."

At first Val lay stiff and startled, hardly breathing.

Then, with a soft, wounded sound, she melted into Zoey's

embrace. She touched their foreheads together—a salute. A promise.

A thank-you.

Zoey awoke again, later, when Grayson tiptoed inside the room.

She opened her eyes and saw him holding a finger to his lips. "Pillow," he mouthed, gingerly selecting one from the bed.

Zoey slid out from Val's arms and followed him downstairs. They didn't speak until they'd curled up on the sofa, beneath the afghan that had christened their first and only lovemaking.

"I don't want to leave her alone for too long," Zoey announced, once she'd had just about enough of the grandfather clock's incessant ticking. Her fingers itched for her bat, which lay beside Grayson's bed upstairs.

Just in case.

"You could have stayed up there," Grayson said reasonably.

"Yes, but I needed a cuddle."

"Val was cuddling you."

"A boy cuddle."

Grayson nodded. "I am an excellent cuddler."

Tucking her legs beneath her, Zoey snuggled against his lanky frame. "Did you bake more cookies?"

"Not yet." He shifted to look at her, his expression eager. "Do you want me to?"

"Oh my God. No. I mean, yes, but later."

He subsided, reluctantly, and then blew out a slow breath.

Five minutes passed. Ten. Grayson's breathing came slow and even.

Then Zoey thumped her fist lightly against her thigh, making him jump.

"I want to figure out better ways to hunt monsters," she declared. "There has to be a way that doesn't kill off more girls like Marion."

"You'd be an excellent teacher."

Zoey glanced at him. "If I opened a school would you be the housekeeper to my headmaster?"

"What kind of school, exactly?"

"One that teaches extraordinary girls how to use power like we did, and root out evil, and destroy the shit out of it."

"That sounds incredible," Grayson said.

"Wonderful. You're hired."

"But wait. As housekeeper, could I wear an apron of my choosing?"

"No," said Zoey, grinning. "One of mine. On occasion I might let Val choose."

He let out a beleaguered sigh. "So will you open this school here, or far away?"

"Kingshead, maybe."

"Ah."

"Val's going to stay there, look after the farm. It's way too big a house for one girl to live in. Or even, like, fifty girls."

Grayson appeared to be deep in thought. "Would your students be required to wear uniforms?"

Zoey answered at once: "Yes. Wizard robes."

She thought that would elicit a laugh, but instead Grayson smiled wistfully at her. "We would be working pretty closely together, as housekeeper and headmaster. I'm not sure I could . . ." He looked away, his eyes suddenly bright, and laughed ruefully. "I'm sorry, Zo. I swore I wouldn't . . . Jesus."

Zoey's heartbeat thundered in her ears. She eyed the Tighe family's movie collection and spotted a familiar cover. "I'm sorry to tell you," she began, reaching desperately for a subject change, "that I don't think I'll be able to watch *Alien* again for a really, really long time."

"Zoey—"

"Much to my dismay, my love for Ellen Ripley has its limits. No more xenomorphs for me. I declare a xenomorph moratorium. A xenotorium."

"Zo." Grayson gathered her hands in his own, kissed them tenderly. "I don't know if my heart could take being near you like that and not being *with* you."

Zoey looked at him—his clean, square jaw, the fall of dark hair over his forehead. She tried to think of something to say, but all her words seemed inadequate.

He swallowed, hard, his gaze flitting across her face, and then he looked away. "You know, right after you broke up with me, I was mad at you."

Her stomach dropped. "Mad at me?"

"I couldn't understand why you didn't want to have sex. Everyone wants to have sex."

The words knocked Zoey's breath out of her lungs. "Not everyone," she managed.

"I know." He pressed her hands gently with his fingers. "I know that now. Anyway, I was angry, and confused, jealous. Basically I was an ass. I thought maybe there was someone else. I thought I'd done something wrong, or that it hadn't been good for you—"

She released a frustrated breath. "I told you before, that has nothing to do with it."

"I even thought for a while that maybe I should just stop seeing you. Completely. Even as friends."

Zoey closed her eyes. "God."

"But I couldn't stand that, Zo. I tried for, I think, a day, and that was that. And then, over the past few weeks, with all of this going on . . . And then you left me on that boat, with no idea where you were going or what was about to happen . . ." A piece of his voice broke off and shattered. "*Fuck*, Zoey." He dragged a hand over his face. "I thought I'd never see you again."

Zoey stared up at him, rapt. "Language," she chided.

His smile was soft upon her face. "I realized on that boat that I'd rather live a lifetime without sex if it meant spending even one more day with you."

Zoey couldn't help it; she burst out laughing.

Grayson pulled slightly away, frowning. "Well. That's not the reaction I was expecting."

"I'm sorry, it's just—" Zoey was doing that slightly alarming thing where she was laughing and basically crying at the same time. She wiped her eyes. "That was such a *declaration*. And so, like, *final*. A lifetime without sex, Grayson? There's no need to punish yourself for me."

"I don't even know if I *want* sex."

Now Zoey was the one to pull back. "Okay, but you told me you *did* want sex."

"I mean . . ." Grayson blew out a sharp breath. "I haven't slept with anyone since you." He paused, eyes dancing. Gently, he added, "I could have, mind you—"

Zoey rolled her eyes. "Oh, of course, naturally."

"But I didn't want to. Not if it wasn't you."

"Grayson." Zoey shook her head, recentering herself. "I don't want you to become someone you're not, even for me."

"And I don't want you to become someone you're not for *me*."

"Okay, so . . . Where does that leave us?"

"Maybe it leaves us here: we're seventeen."

Zoey raised an eyebrow. "An astute observation."

"Maybe we just . . . try it. If you want," he added hastily. "If you're not interested, then tell me to shut up and get over myself, and I will."

"Try it?"

"A relationship. You and me." He looked hesitantly up at her. "If you want."

A light, fizzy feeling bubbled up from Zoey's toes to her cheeks. "Grayson, I'm serious when I tell you that I may never want to have sex again."

"And I may never want it again! Who knows? But you."

Now he cupped her face in his palms, reverent. "You, I want. However I can have you, Harlow."

Tears welled in her eyes. *You, I want.* "And if I never want to have sex again? And you decide that you do?"

"Then maybe it won't work out. But, God, Zoey, don't you want to try?"

His earnestness tore at her, and then remade her into a whole, shining creature that dared to embrace this moment—and not laugh, or run away, or spike it with barbs.

"Maybe," she said slowly, "I'll find out that I want to have sex with you. On occasion."

"Maybe," he agreed. "Or maybe you won't. And that's okay."

"Maybe I'll transform overnight into a sex fiend."

"Maybe I'll decide to take a vow of abstinence."

Zoey's laugh came out faint and shuddering. She blinked, and tears fell onto Grayson's stroking fingers. "Maybe you'll go off to college and forget about me."

"Maybe we'll just be a plain old slayer-school housekeeper-and-headmaster," he said, his eyes so soft that Zoey had to close her own. "Best friends and colleagues. Nothing more."

She nuzzled her nose against his chin, whispering, "Maybe this is a stupid high school fling."

"Maybe," said Grayson, brushing his lips across her cheeks, "we'll grow old together."

Maybe, Zoey thought, as she opened her mouth to Grayson's kiss, *has lots of potential.*

MANY HAD OBSERVED, IN THE last few blessedly quiet weeks on Sawkill, that a new beacon had appeared near the top of the old lighthouse.

It was different than the familiar, cycling light that the island's residents had watched for years.

This light was smaller. It sat for hours, unmoving—sometimes at night, sometimes during the day. Sometimes on the east side; sometimes on the south, or the north. On occasion it glowed so dimly that the casual observer might mistake it for an optical illusion.

Other times it flashed so brilliantly that anyone happening to glance out their window might think a meteorite had fallen to ground.

Those were the people who went searching. If someone was fooling around on the lighthouse, then they really ought to find out. They would call the police chief, tell him what they'd seen. He'd listen patiently to their claims, tell them he'd been up to the lighthouse just that afternoon while out on patrol, and had seen nothing out of the ordinary.

Everyone took the chief at his word. He'd arrested and jailed the awful men who'd killed those poor girls, after all.

A cult of kidnappers and killers, preying on girls for decades?

The residents couldn't stop thinking about it. It was not an easy tragedy to shake. How could they have never noticed? How could they have missed the signs? The revelation made them stop and reassess themselves, made them take second looks at their mirrors and hold their breaths when the house settled at night.

But still, a small curious few were not altogether satisfied with Chief Harlow's reassurance about the strange light, and when they struck out on the lighthouse road, determined and square-shouldered, none of them knew that the Rock was watching their approach.

Once they got too close, the Rock made sure every one of them was gently turned away—a washed-out path, a dead-end road, a soft sweep of wind scented like salt and fresh bread and home, which distracted the seekers and caused them to turn back. They gave up cheerfully, writing off their fleeting curiosity as a sign that they ought to pull out one of their old children's books and give it a reread, for the sake of nostalgia.

The Rock watched them go, venerable and untamed. It was protective of the old, tired lighthouse, and of the children waiting inside.

Watching the sky and the water for their lost sister.

Waiting, and searching, and hoping.

The Rock hugged the lighthouse like a mother warms her young.

VAL

The Lighthouse

It had been six weeks and four days since Marion left them.

Not *died*. Val refused to think of Marion that way, though when Mrs. Althouse told the rest of the island what had happened—that Marion had been chosen by the cult as their next victim, that she had fought her fate until the last moment, that Mrs. Althouse had faith Marion would reappear, somehow, someday—the people of Sawkill gave the woman who had lost her husband and both her daughters looks of actual, genuine pity. Not manufactured, not fleeting. They invited her over to their houses for dinner; they included her in family movie nights. It was an unspoken decision reached by the island's entire population: Mrs. Althouse should never have to feel alone again.

Especially not until she accepted the fact that her daughter, whose body had never been found, was not coming home.

A fresh wind slapped its way up the lighthouse and whipped strands of Val's hair around her face.

Beside her, curled up on a sea-bitten bench, Zoey shifted in her sleep.

Val adjusted the quilt around Zoey's chin, then brought her own steaming thermos of tea to her lips. The tea slipped down her throat and heated her cold limbs. It was only mid-September, but up on the lighthouse observation deck, one needed a quilt, a hot thermos, a scarf.

Setting down her tea on the old plank floor, Val decided it was time to turn on her light. She'd eaten her sandwich, she'd drunk her tea. Now it was time to get to work.

She left Zoey on the bench and walked around to the deck's western curve. She leaned against the metal railing with its chipped black paint—probably lead based, probably carcinogenic, but honestly, when you'd fought a monster, when you'd been enslaved to one, when you'd watched your first real love disappear into a void you couldn't understand, environmentally unsound paint was the least of your worries.

First, she said hello to the Rock. She had decided over the past few weeks that it deserved politeness and most likely seldom received it.

"Good evening," she whispered to the wind, like the proper lady she was, and then she breathed in deep and unclenched her fists.

Two delicate white flames flared to life in her palms. A

third unfurled within her ribs; its warmth bled down her spine and pooled in her belly.

Thus illuminated, Val waited.

She sometimes waited alone. Sometimes she preferred and requested it. Sometimes Mrs. Althouse waited with her. Sometimes Zoey and Grayson brought up a picnic basket, a pile of coats, playing cards, and flashlights. They would sit on the floor and play Go Fish by the light of Val's fire.

They would coax her home, hours later, bleary-eyed and hoarse-voiced.

"Marion wouldn't want you to drain yourself dry for her," was Zoey's common refrain.

Val gazed out over the water. Twilight dressed both sky and sea in fairy-tale shades. Amber honey and queen's violet, the orange fire of a priestess's flame, the effulgent blue of water lit from below by spirits.

She withdrew the thin silver necklace from her pocket. Wearing Charlotte's starfish was not a thing she would ever do; that line was etched in stone, and Val refused to cross it.

But, since Mrs. Althouse had gifted it to her, Val had kept it always on her person. It was stupid, maybe, but considering everything that had happened, Val thought that if any physical thing in the world might show some sign of Marion's return, this necklace and its tiny sea creature would be the first one to do so.

She dangled the necklace from two glowing fingers and watched the starfish spin before her eyes, turning amethyst in the iridescent light. Then her eyes slipped across the sea—one more survey before settling back onto her bench for the long wait—and she saw, carving the pearled water in two, a long narrow band of ripples.

Her breath caught in her throat. She glanced at the starfish—nothing—and then back at the water. The ripples did not disband, as normal ripples would have. They remained, shivering in place as if pinned there by a tremendous tug of gravity, somewhere deep on the seabed.

Zoey awoke with a yawn, sitting up bleary-eyed. "Val? Do you feel that?"

Val figured she would hate herself for this, more than she already, quietly, permanently, hated herself. She might even hate Sawkill for it.

Playing tricks, old girl? she thought to the Rock. *Is this how it's going to be?*

Unable to move, unwilling to believe or deny what she saw, Val stood frozen in place—until she saw the moth.

It floated down to her like a piece of shaved sky, catching the twilight on its wings. Only when it perched on her trembling hand did Val see its true colors—eyes black like the sea at midnight, white like the flame of her own heart.

So said the moth, its feelers kissing her fingers: *Go to her.*

MARION

The Starfish

Marion figured she was dying.

She was not.

First there was a nothingness. She was not a girl, or even a human being.

Then she was stardust, examined by the cosmos.

Distantly she heard terrible noises of punishment. A drop of memory: She had pulled a beast down with her. It had wrapped its tail and raging wet claws around her. It had strangled her. The word *scream* floated up through the dormant huddle of her consciousness, but even half-alive as she was, she knew that word was not enough to describe what she was hearing.

But she let the screams pass her by and continued on her

way, whatever that way was.

Stardust cares not for the agony of demons.

Her time in this Far Place lasted an age.

She saw things: A planet blue like a child's marble. A house vast and sad, ringed by horses who tossed their heads uncaring. Deserts plagued by phantoms that stole girls from their tents. Jungles haunted by monsters that no one could see. Cities full of lonely people so desperately unhappy that they sought out rumored beasts and exchanged freedom for power.

Marion saw herself, a floating girl, wrapped in a galactic cocoon. Fetal, as she had been at the beginning, except her hair was long and her breasts were full. At her pulse points—temples, wrists, throat—shimmered a faint crystalline web of scars, pulsing faintly with pain.

Not even souls who fought to protect the defenseless could emerge from the Far Place without cost.

But Marion didn't mind these tithes, nor did she mind the fathomless void surrounding her. She was not entirely alone, here.

She felt a presence neither kind nor cruel. It observed her. It allowed her to pass.

For a second age, she walked a lightless path.

There was a ground beneath her feet. At first it felt dry. Sand? That was a word she had once known. Then her feet moved through water—an inch at first, and then a few. It rose to her knees, her thighs, her belly.

She was frightened, but she tried not to be. The path was hers, and she trusted it. Whatever watched her in this place, she sensed it would be pleased if she kept on—and aggravated if she did not.

She walked until the water rippled just beneath her eyes.

Then she glimpsed a light. Tiny but untiring, it rested on a faint white line, some distance away.

A horizon?

She took a breath and plunged deeper. The water consumed her.

She walked until the soles of her feet tore open. She swam until her lungs burst, until her burning limbs snapped off from the force of her desperation, until her belly swelled with water and deep-sea silt formed a dark crust over her eyes.

But then her lungs re-formed. Arms and legs, new and uncertain, clawed clumsily along the ocean floor. Her feet—size eight! she remembered now—repaired themselves, paddled left right left right. Her eyes saw gaping luminescent creatures, the carcasses of ships, and deeper, more secret things in the black depths below her that she didn't understand.

She realized that she was being remade.

The light was growing larger, and her new lungs scorched her insides. She needed to breathe. Stars don't breathe, but girls do. This was obvious to her now.

She followed the shining white light ahead of her and cried out for it, voice muffled by the churning salt waves. She hoped that it wouldn't burn out before she could reach it.

The path ended. Before her was an indistinct expanse, sloping up into a world that frightened her for a reason she could not explain.

Her feet sank into wet sand, and she gasped, inhaling water. She stumbled; her knees crashed against a cluster of shells. Coughing, she scrambled to regain her balance. Her hand landed on something hard and prickly.

Her stinging eyes opened just enough to glimpse a familiar five-pointed shape at her fingertips, half-buried in shifting dark sand.

Something essential returned to her—the final piece.

She burst up into the world that the light called home.

Her first breath hurt.

Her second felt divine.

She touched a beach—she knew this, the word returning gently to her—and the beach felt familiar.

Pebbles as big as quarters and as small as needle eyes.

Coarse dark sand.

Tiny shells that wriggled back underground once the waves had returned to their maker.

The second thing she touched was a hand, reaching for her.

And the third? A tiny silver starfish, dangling from a white flame. Marion touched her own neck, felt a slender silver chain around it.

My little starfish.

Sisters two and sisters true.

"Marion," called a voice, so loud that it hurt her tender ears. Yet she turned toward it, blindly seeking.

"Marion, we're here, we're right here."

"Marion, oh my God . . ."

She knew those voices.

"Can you breathe?" asked one. "Shit, is she breathing?"

"Don't leave me again, Marion," said the other voice. "Please, God."

The voice started sobbing, and if Marion's squinting vision wasn't telling her lies, then this second voice belonged to the light that had guided her home.

A name floated to the surface of her mind.

Val.

"Val," she croaked. Her first word.

"Yes, yes." Marion's finer senses returned to her: Val's fingers stroking Marion's hair out of her eyes, lips hot and frantic against her brow. The light Marion had followed home burned in Val's chest, quiet and matter-of-factly warm. Of course this light had guided her home.

Of course this light belonged to Val.

Which meant . . .

Marion glanced left: Zoey's black-and-orange curls, her

bright brown eyes, her wide smile. She hooked her arm through Marion's, pressed her forehead against Marion's shoulder. She was laughing; her tears warmed Marion's chilled skin.

"Zoey," Marion whispered, with a shaky smile.

Val touched her cheek to Marion's own. "Don't leave us again," she pleaded.

And Marion looked up at Val, to show her unequivocally that this was no joke, no dream, that she had come home, and replied, "I'm not going anywhere."

ACKNOWLEDGMENTS

The idea for this book developed in a slow and somewhat ungainly fashion over the course of a few years, and crystallized when Diana Fox said to me over lunch, "You should write something creepy involving horses." I'm paraphrasing, but that was the sentiment, and it helped me tie together the disparate pieces of the book that would someday become *Sawkill Girls*. So, Diana, I must thank you.

Many thanks to my agent, Victoria Marini, who provided me with exuberant live updates as she read the first draft, and whose boundless enthusiasm for this project, and for all my work, keeps my confidence afloat and my heart hopeful.

Warm thanks to my editor, Claudia Gabel, whose keen eye and sharp mind helped me shape this book into something fiercer and smarter than it once was.

Thanks to Stephanie Guerdan, Katherine Tegen, and the entire Harper team for believing in this book, and for working so hard to make it pretty and get it into readers' hands.

To the Bearsville coven of 2016—Alison Cherry, Michelle

Schusterman, Lindsay Ribar, Mackenzi Lee, Lissa Harris, Jenna Scherer, Jen Malone, and Melissa Sarno—thank you for listening to me read the scary stuff from this book, particularly since we were living in a haunted house surrounded by Builders at the time.

To my early readers—Karen Strong, Renee Harleston, Nita Tyndall, and Nicole Brinkley—thank you for your insight, your wisdom, and your patience.

As always, to my family and to my girls—particularly my Slytherin queens Lindsay Eagar and Diya Mishra—thank you for your hearts and your claws, your light and your love.